The Reappearance of Rachel Price

Also by Holly Jackson

A Good Girl's Guide to Murder series
A Good Girl's Guide to Murder
Good Girl, Bad Blood
As Good as Dead

Kill Joy
Five Survive

The
Reappearance
of
Rachel Price

HOLLY JACKSON

Delacorte Press

Text copyright © 2024 by Holly Jackson
Jacket photography copyright © 2024 by Christine Blackburne

All rights reserved. Published in the United States by Delacorte Press, an imprint of Random House Children's Books, a division of Penguin Random House LLC, New York.

Delacorte Press is a registered trademark and the colophon is a trademark of Penguin Random House LLC.

Visit us on the Web! GetUnderlined.com

Educators and librarians, for a variety of teaching tools, visit us at RHTeachersLibrarians.com

Library of Congress Cataloging-in-Publication Data is available upon request.
ISBN 978-0-593-37420-7 (hardcover) — ISBN 978-0-593-37421-4 (lib. bdg.) —
ISBN 978-0-593-37422-1 (ebook) — ISBN 978-0-593-81046-0 (int'l ed.)

The text of this book is set in 11-point Utopia.
Interior design by Ken Crossland

Printed in the United States of America
10 9 8 7 6 5 4 3 2 1
First American Edition

For my little sister

My Family Tree

| Maria Price | Patrick Price | | Edward Boden | Susan Boden |

| Sherry Price | Jefferson Price | Charlie Price | | Rachel Price |

Carter Price

Me

Key

☐ Deceased

▨ Not sure

MDBo ☰ Menu   All   Search MDBo

The Disappearance of Rachel Price

[Documentary] [Crime]

Filming 2024   ☆ Rate

Crew:

Ramsey Lee ... producer, director

James Myers ... camera operator

Saba Iqbal ... sound department

Ash Maddox ... camera assistant

ONE

"What do you think happened to your mother?"

The word sounded wrong to Bel when he said it. *Mother.* Unnatural. Not quite as bad as *Mom.* That one pushed between her lips, misshapen and mad, like a bloated slug finally breaking free, splatting there on the floor for everyone to stare at. Because everyone *would,* everyone always did. The word didn't belong in her mouth, so Bel didn't say it, not if she could help it. At least there was a coldness to *mother,* a sense of distance.

"It's OK, please take your time," Ramsey said, the vowels clipped and exposed.

Bel looked across at him, avoiding the camera. Lines of concern crisscrossed his black skin, pulling around his eyes as they fixed on Bel's, because she was already taking her time, too much, more than she had in the pre-interviews the past few days. He reached up to scratch his temple, right where his dark coiled hair faded out above his ears. Ramsey Lee: filmmaker, director, from South London— a whole world away, and yet here he was in Gorham, New Hampshire, sitting across from her.

Ramsey cleared his throat.

"Um . . . ," Bel began, choking on that slug. "I don't know."

Ramsey sat back, his chair creaking, and Bel knew from the flicker of disappointment in his face that she was doing a bad job. Worse. It

1

must have been the camera. The camera changed things, the permanence of it. One day thousands of people would watch this, separated from her only by the glass of their television screens. They would analyze every word she said, every pause she took, and have something to say about it. They'd study her face: her warm white skin and the flush of her cheeks, her sharp chin that sharpened more when she spoke and especially when she smiled, her short honey-blond hair, her round gray-blue eyes. *Doesn't she look just like Rachel did,* they'd say, those people beyond the television screen. Bel thought she looked more like her dad, actually. Thanks, though.

"Sorry," Bel added, pressing her eyelids together, bright orange patches where the three softbox lights glared at her. She just had to get through this documentary, pretend to not be hating every second, talk about Rachel, then life could go back to normal, back to not talking about Rachel.

Ramsey shook his head, a smile breaking through.

"Don't worry," he said. "It's a difficult question."

It wasn't, though, not really. And the answer wasn't difficult either. Bel really didn't know what had happened to her. No one did. That was the point of all this.

"I think she was—"

Someone stumbled behind the camera, tripping on a cable that ripped out of the wall. One of the lights flickered and died, swaying on its rickety leg. A hand reached out to grab it before it fell, righting it.

"Oh shit. Sorry, Rams," the tripper said, chasing the loose wire back to the outlet. Now that the light was out, Bel could see him properly for the first time. She couldn't say she'd noticed him before, when Ramsey had introduced the crew, too dazzled by the lights and the camera. He must have been the youngest of the four documentary crew members, couldn't be much older than her. And he was, just maybe, the most ridiculous person Bel had ever seen. He had shoulder-length brown hair that fell in thick curls, pushed off to one side of his pale face, full of angles and shadows. He wore flared tartan pants and a bright purple sweater with little green-and-yellow dinosaurs marching across his chest.

2

"Sorry," he said again, the *o* giving him away; must be from London too. He grunted as he pushed the plug in and the light sparked back to life, hiding him from Bel. Thank God, that ugly sweater was distracting.

"I told you to gaffer all the wires down, Ash," Ramsey said, shifting to glance behind the box light.

"I did . . . ," came Ash's voice from behind the light, somehow angular, just like his face. "Until the tape ran out."

"Mate, we have like fifty thousand rolls upstairs," Ramsey replied.

"Fifty thousand and one," said the woman standing behind the microphone: a long pole balanced on a tripod, with a fluffy gray head hovering over Bel and Ramsey, just above the shot. Saba, that was what Ramsey had called her, introducing her as *the Sound Person*. She was wearing a huge pair of headphones that dwarfed her face, pushing the brown skin of her cheeks into unnatural folds.

"Sorry," came Ash's voice. "I'll fix it later."

"It's OK," Ramsey said, his face softening for a second. Then, to the man behind the huge camera: "James, why are you panning to Ash?"

"Thought we were aiming for a cinéma vérité style for the doc, that you might want this in," the camera operator replied.

"No, I don't want this in. Let's reset the shot and go for another take. And everyone watch where you're stepping this time."

Ramsey flashed an apologetic smile at Bel, sitting here on a plush couch across from them all, the cushions artfully arranged and rearranged behind her.

"Ash is my brother-in-law," he said, as though in explanation. "Known him since he was eleven. It's his first job, isn't it, Ash? Camera assistant."

Ash: camera assistant. Saba: sound person. James: camera operator. And Ramsey: filmmaker, producer, director. Must have been nice, to have words like that follow your name, words you'd chosen. Bel's were different: *This is Annabel. The daughter of Rachel Price.* That last part said in a knowing whisper. Because even though Rachel was gone, everything existed only in relation to her. Gorham wasn't its own place anymore; it was the town where Rachel Price had lived.

Number 33 Milton Street wasn't Bel's home, it was the house Rachel Price had lived in. Bel's dad, Charlie Price, well, he was *Rachel Price's husband,* even though the Price part had come from him.

"Ash, the clapper," Ramsey reminded him.

"Oh." Ash emerged from behind the light, a black-and-white clapper board clasped between his hands. Printed on it were the words: *The Disappearance of Rachel Price.* The name of the documentary. Below that, a handwritten: *Interview with Bel.* And she was surprised, really, that it didn't just say *Rachel Price's daughter.*

Ash walked in front of the camera, the hems of his pants swishing loudly together.

"Take six," he said, bringing the clapper stick down to the slate with a sharp bang, hurrying out of the shot.

"Let's start again." Ramsey let out a long breath. They'd been here for hours already, and it was starting to show on his face. "Your mum has now been missing for more than sixteen years. In all that time, there has been no sign of her. No activity on her bank accounts, no communication with family, no body found despite extensive searches. Of course there have been *sightings,*" he said, leaning on the word too hard so it came out sideways. "People on the internet who claim to have seen Rachel in Paris. Brazil. Even one a few months ago nearby in North Conway. But of course, these are unsubstantiated claims. Your mum vanished without a trace on February thirteenth, 2008. What do you think happened to her?"

Bel couldn't say *I don't know* again, otherwise she'd never be allowed to leave.

"It's as much a mystery for me as the rest of the world," she said, and from the flash in Ramsey's eyes, she knew that was a better answer. OK, keep going. "I know all the theories people have about what happened. And if I had to pick the one . . ."

Ramsey nodded, urging her on.

"I think she was trying to leave. She left. Then maybe she was killed by an opportunistic killer—that's the term the media uses. Or maybe she got lost in the White Mountains and died in the snow, and an animal got to her remains. That's why we never found her."

Ramsey leaned forward, finger cupping his chin thoughtfully.

"So, Bel, you're saying you think the most likely scenario is that your mother is dead?"

Bel half nodded, staring down at the coffee table in front of her. The full glass bottle of water that was a prop only, she wasn't allowed to drink it. The marble chessboard laid out with all the pieces prepared for battle, her knees pointed down the center in no-man's-land. This repurposed conference room in the Royalty Inn hotel on Main Street was the stage. The water bottle, the chessboard and the cushions were the props. None of this was real to anyone else, it was all for show.

"Yes. I think she's dead. I think she died that day or not long after."

Did she think that? Did it really matter? Gone was gone.

Ramsey was looking at the chessboard too now.

"You say you think your mum was trying to leave," he said, bringing his eyes back. "Do you mean that she was running away?"

Bel shrugged. "I guess."

"But there is compelling evidence that opposes the *ran away* theory. Rachel didn't withdraw any money from her bank account in the days and weeks leading up to her disappearance. If she was planning to run away and start a new life, she would have needed money to do that. Not only that, but she didn't take her wallet containing her ID with her, and she'd left her bank cards at home. Nor did she take her phone. She didn't pack any clothes or belongings. None at all. She didn't even take her coat with her on that freezing day, it was left in the car too, with her phone and wallet."

And me, Bel thought.

"What do you say to that?" Ramsey asked her.

What did he want her to say?

"I don't know." Bel went back to those three words, hid behind them.

Ramsey seemed to sense the barricade, backing off and straightening up.

"You're eighteen now, Bel. You weren't even two years old when Rachel went missing. Twenty-two months old, in fact. And of course, one of the most notable things about this case that sets it apart from all others, was that you were with her. You were with your mum when she disappeared."

"Yes," Bel said, knowing what question was coming next. It didn't matter how many times it was asked; the answer was the same. And it was worse for Bel, trust her.

"And you don't remember anything at all that day? Being in the mall? Being in the car?"

"I don't remember anything," she said flatly. "I was too young to remember. Or to tell anyone what I saw that day."

"And here's the craziest thing." Ramsey leaned forward, words spiking in the middle as he attempted to keep his voice even. "You were a toddler, too young to communicate properly with anyone, with the police. *But* if someone did take Rachel, abduct her from the car where it was found abandoned with you inside, that means you must have seen exactly who it was. You saw them. At one point in time, you must have known, however briefly, the answer to the mystery."

"I know."

Crazy, wasn't it? The craziest thing, in fact.

Bel closed her eyes, three blazing sunspots invading the dark world inside her head. Those lights were just too bright. Were they giving off heat too, or was that just her imagination? Explain why her face was so hot, then.

"Are you OK to continue?" Ramsey asked her.

"Yeah." She didn't have a choice, really. Contracts had been agreed to, waivers and releases signed. And, most importantly, she had promised her dad. She could pretend to be nice, for his sake. Say *yes* and *no* and *sorry* in the right places.

"You really have no memories from that day at all?"

"No." And she wouldn't the next time he asked too. Or the one after that. She had no memory of what happened, no idea. Just what she knew later, when she was old enough to know things: that she had been left behind. Abandoned there in the backseat of the car, however it happened.

"This case is one of the most discussed and studied on true-crime podcasts and social media, enduring in the public consciousness even sixteen years later," Ramsey said, eyes glittering. "The name Rachel Price is almost synonymous with mystery. Because her disappearance was like a puzzle, and it's human nature to want to solve a puzzle, don't you think?"

Was Bel supposed to answer that? Too late.

"And that's because," Ramsey continued, "Rachel seemed to disappear twice that day. Can you tell us what happened that afternoon, at two p.m.? Where your mum and you went?"

"Again?"

"Yes, please. For the camera," Ramsey said, taking the blame off Bel and putting it on the camera instead. Cameras didn't have feelings. Ramsey seemed nice like that. But then, of course, he wanted her to think he was nice, didn't he?

Bel cleared her throat. "That afternoon, I was in the car with Rachel. She drove us to the White Mountains Mall, which is in Berlin. Not far from Gorham, about ten minutes away. Security cameras recorded both of us walking into the mall. Rachel was carrying me."

"And why were you at the mall?"

"She often took me there on her days off, I've been told," Bel said. "Rachel used to work at a coffeehouse there. Went back for the coffee, to see her old friends. That wasn't out of the ordinary. It was called the Moose Mouse Coffeehouse."

Of course, Bel didn't remember that, but she'd seen the security camera footage since, the last images of Rachel Price alive. Sitting at the coffeehouse, baby Bel in a bright blue padded coat with marshmallow arms, wriggling in Rachel's lap. Surrounded by empty tables. Blurry but happy, those tiny figures seemed. Not knowing that they were both about to disappear, one for good.

"But what *was* out of the ordinary," Ramsey countered, "is that after you finished your drinks, Rachel got up to leave, still carrying you. You walked away from the Moose Mouse Coffeehouse at two-forty-nine, the cameras show us this, we can follow you on the footage. But then you turn a corner, a blind spot between the mall security cameras, and . . . ?"

He seemed to be waiting for something.

"We disappeared," Bel said, filling in the blanks.

"Vanished into thin air," Ramsey added. "You don't appear on the camera you should have if Rachel had kept walking. You don't appear on any of the cameras after that, none of the ones by the exits. Nowhere. Which means you couldn't have left. And yet you did. You both disappeared inside that mall, and there is no explanation. Any idea how?"

"I don't know, I don't remember." Bit of a running theme.

"Police analyzed that footage after Rachel's disappearance. They studied and counted everyone into the mall, and counted everyone back out again. The numbers matched except for two. You and Rachel. The only two who entered and never left. The police even considered whether you'd left in disguise for some reason, changed your appearances, but that didn't work with the numbers. You'd simply vanished."

Bel shrugged, unsure what Ramsey wanted her to say. She was un-vanished now.

"The next thing we know, you've reappeared. You were found alone in Rachel's car, abandoned on the side of a road, close to Moose Brook State Park. The car was pulled up on the shoulder, in the snow, headlights on, engine still running. A man"—Ramsey checked his notes—"Julian Tripp, was driving past and found you just after six o'clock. He called the police immediately—"

"He's actually my homeroom teacher now. Mr. Tripp."

Ramsey smiled, didn't mind the interruption. "Small world."

"Well, small town," Bel corrected him.

"I think it's clear why true-crime fanatics have focused on this case. There have been no answers since the trial ended. It can't be solved and it will never make sense. It must be so much harder for you because you were there for all of it." Ramsey paused. "What has it been like, Bel? Growing up in the shadow of this impossible mystery?"

No one had ever put it quite like that before. It did feel like a shadow, most days, a dark, unpleasant thing that you looked away from if you knew what was good for you. And Bel did. She rubbed her nose, hard enough to click the cartilage inside. Then remembered she was on camera, the microphone hovering above her. Damn. Hopefully Ramsey would edit that out.

"It's been OK," she said eventually. "I accepted a long time ago that we would never have answers. It's not my fault I can't remember any of it; I was just too young. And because I don't have those memories, we will never solve the Rachel Price mystery, but I'm OK with that. Honestly. I have my dad." Bel paused, a small smile stretching her mouth, pulling her chin into a point. "He tried his hardest to give me as normal a childhood possible, under the circumstances. He's the best dad I could ask for. That's why I don't want people to feel sorry for me," she said, meaning it. She hoped the camera could tell that. "I'm lucky, actually—"

"Um, Ramsey," Ash's voice floated in beyond the light.

"We're filming, Ash." Ramsey turned to glare at him.

"Oh, I know." He sidestepped closer and Bel could finally see him again, blinking him into existence. "It's just that we've gone over schedule, and I think . . ."

He gestured at the door, leading into the lobby of the hotel. Encased in the window panel was a face, pushed up against the glass, watching them. Bel shaded her eyes with a cupped hand, but the lights were still too bright to see who it was.

"She's here already," Ash said, checking the time on his phone. "She's early."

"Who's *she*?" Bel asked. She knew that Carter and Aunt Sherry weren't filming their interviews until next week.

"Shit," Ramsey hissed, checking his own watch. He glanced quickly at Bel, eyes wide, losing their kind lines.

Bel leaned forward, losing hers too. She hardened her voice. "Who's here, Ramsey? Who's *she*?"

TWO

The door pushed open, shushing on its hinges.

"Hello?" A woman's voice sailed into the room. "The girl at the front desk said you were filming in here."

Did Bel know that voice? There was a flicker of recognition, but she couldn't place it, not without a face. She tried to see, her stomach clenched, slug waiting in her mouth.

Clicking heels on polished wood as the woman approached them.

Ramsey pushed up from his chair, nodding at James behind the camera as he did.

"Hello," he said in a bright voice. "Thank you so much for arriving *so* early, I hope your journey was OK. We were just finishing up here, Susan."

Bel swallowed, jaw unclenching. For a second there, she'd thought he was about to say R—

"Nice to finally meet you in person," the woman said, walking over to Ramsey, taking his outstretched hand, bracelets tinkling at her wrist as she shook it up and down.

Susan? Why couldn't Bel think of any Susans?

"Likewise," Ramsey replied.

She stepped into the light, well-dressed in a dark skirt suit and a frilly emerald scarf, and Bel could finally see who she was. Of course. Because she wasn't Susan to Bel. She was Grandma. Rachel's mom.

"Rams, should I—" Ash began, still floating there awkwardly, an unclear hand gesture, thumb pointed at Bel.

"Oh, well now," Grandma said to Ash, looking him up and down. "Aren't you quite something?"

Bel stood, cushions falling out of their neat arrangement behind her.

"Hi, Grandma."

The camera stood up with her, James removing it from the stand and placing it on his shoulder in one swift movement, stepping back to widen the shot.

Grandma blinked back at her.

"That isn't my Annabel, is it?" she said, voice rising at the end. "Oh my goodness, just look at you."

In the next moment, Bel's face was pushed into that frilly emerald scarf, as Grandma folded her into a tight hug, a cloying smell of perfume filling the back of her throat.

"I can't believe it, you look so grown-up."

"Well," Bel said, her rib cage too tight. "That's because I *did* grow up. I've looked like this for a few years now."

Grandma stood back to study Bel, bony fingers hooking onto her shoulders.

"God, you look so much like Rachel."

No she fucking didn't.

Grandma's eyes misted over, a tremble in her bottom lip as she bit down on it.

"Grandaddy would have been so proud to see you all grown up. I'm sad he missed it. If only your father hadn't kept us away from you so much. Cruel, really. My only grandchild."

She let go of Bel and reached into her pocket for a wrinkled tissue, blowing her nose loudly, a bird-caw filling the room.

"Didn't even let you come to the funeral." Grandma sniffed.

Bel wouldn't let that slide.

11

"That's because you told him you didn't want him there," she replied, sharpening her tongue, locking her jaw. Was Bel allowed to swear at the woman—how old was she? Early seventies? That was acceptable, right?

"But I wanted *you* there, Grandaddy would have too. But the only thing he really wanted, before he died, was to finally see his daughter's killer behind bars. Where he belongs," she said pointedly, wiping her nose again for effect. And then: "Cancer. Four years ago," speaking the words in Ramsey's direction.

"Very sorry," he said, almost a whisper, like he didn't want to intrude on the scene, disappearing into the background. Were they supposed to be filming this?

Grandma smiled sweetly at her, but all Bel could think of was Dad calling Susan a *Masshole*. Because she was from Massachusetts, and she was an—

"Oh, I've just had a perfect idea," she continued, oblivious. "You could come stay with me this summer. It would be so lovely; you can help me out with the horses. Spend some time in the house your mom grew up in, get away from *that* man. What do you think, Annabel?"

What did Bel think? That it was an empty offer, and if Grandma really cared, she would have visited, or called. But she didn't. And when these cameras were gone, she'd fly off and disappear again. People did that.

"Sounds too good to be true," Bel said. See, she could be an asshole too. "And *that* man is my dad."

Grandma's teeth snapped together. "That man is—"

"He did not kill Rachel."

Bel's eyes filled with fire, just the two of them in the room . . . and a British film crew, hiding in the dark. "You got what you wanted, Grandma. He was charged with first-degree murder. He did his time in jail, waiting for the trial. And guess what? They found him innocent."

"*Not guilty* is not the same as innocent. And juries can get it wrong," Grandma said, lips moving too much around the words. "I'm not the only one who thinks so. Everyone knows he did it."

"He had an alibi," Bel spat back, throwing in an angry smile. "You seem to conveniently forget this."

"He still had time," Grandma scoffed, turning to find Ramsey.

No, Bel would not let her have the last word; not when the cameras were watching, not about Dad.

"He was at work that day. At around two o'clock, he cut his hand. Badly."

"Injuries sustained when he killed her."

Bel laughed. "There were witnesses. Multiple people in the auto repair shop who saw him cut his hand, Grandma. He bandaged it up and drove to the nearest emergency room."

"In Berlin, where you and Rachel were." Grandma's eyes lightened, like she'd scored a point. Just wait: Bel was going to bury her.

"That's a coincidence." She locked her jaw and took aim. "He's captured by security cameras the entire time he's waiting for a nurse to get his stitches. The entire time he's in the hospital. He leaves at five-thirty-eight exactly and drives home. That takes around sixteen minutes, by the way, like his defense attorney said. Which brings us to five-fifty-four p.m. when Dad gets home. I'm found by Mr. Tripp a couple minutes after six p.m. The police arrive and call Dad at six-twenty-five, once they identify me from Rachel's ID. Dad was home for that call. Plus an earlier call to Rachel's phone at six-oh-four, when he's wondering where we are, which also pinged the cell tower proving he was at home. If you're saying he drove straight to the abduction site, nineteen minutes away from the hospital, that means he had only eight minutes to abduct Rachel, kill her, dispose of her, and get home in time for that phone call. The drive home itself is six minutes. It's impossible. He didn't do it." Bel caught her breath. She'd learned it all by heart long ago; wasn't the first time she'd had to use it. "You think that's enough time to kill someone and hide the body forever?"

Grandma looked pale, skin hanging in creases around her mouth; a life spent frowning. "That's your mother you're talking about."

That word again. Just as unnatural in Grandma's voice.

"What's going on here?" A new voice entered the room, one Bel would know anywhere.

13

"Dad?" she said, searching for him beyond the glare.

Charlie's silhouette crossed the room toward the film set, boots heavy against the floorboards, shoulders heavy inside his grease-stained shirt.

"You told me you'd be done with Bel at two," he said, eyes on Ramsey, one dirty hand skirting over his short hair, dark creamy brown like he had his coffee, a touch of gray at the temples. "It's almost three-thirty. I got worried, her phone's off."

"Sorry." Ramsey bowed his head. "Time got away from us."

"Charlie Price," Grandma said, holding on too long to the hiss at the end of his name.

Charlie's eyes finally found her, widened in recognition.

Bel caught movement over her dad's shoulder, watching as Ramsey turned to James. *Keep rolling,* he mouthed silently, spinning his fingers. The camera obeyed.

"What is she doing here?" Charlie asked the room.

"They're making a documentary about my daughter, why wouldn't I be here?" Grandma retorted, puffing up beneath her bright green scarf. She glanced down and wrinkled her nose. "I see you still haven't learned to wash your hands."

"I was at work, Susan," Charlie said evenly. "Some of us work for a living."

"Urgh, there he goes again," she sniffed. "So combative all the time, Charlie. Must be awful for you to be around that every day, Annabel sweetie."

"I—" Bel began.

"It's OK, Bel, you don't need to answer that." Her dad blinked slowly at her, his pale-blue wide-set eyes telling her everything he needed to. Angry people look guilty, he had always said.

"Does he not let you speak, sweetie?"

"Susan, please," Charlie said through gritted teeth, taking a bite out of the stale air.

"Such a temper," Grandma replied, but she was the only one with a raised voice.

The knot was there again, in Bel's gut, tightening and tightening, chasing its own tail.

"Why are you still filming?" Charlie switched his attention to the boom microphone floating above his head, positioned in Saba's steady hands. "Stop recording, please."

"Why, Charlie?" Grandma said. "You don't want the world to see who you really are?"

The air in the room thickened, clotted and gummy as Bel forced it down, feeding that knot in her stomach.

"And who am I really, Susan?" Charlie turned back to her.

"You want me to say it again?"

Charlie backed off, lips pressed into a stiff smile, fingers skimming the stubble on his chin. "No, that's OK. You've said enough over the years. Surprised you aren't bored of talking to the cameras by now."

"I'll stop when everyone knows the truth," Grandma bit back.

"This is pointless," Charlie sighed. "You lost your daughter that day, Susan. I lost my wife, life as I knew it. Come on, Bel, grab your things and let's go. You must be hungry."

She must be, but she couldn't feel it around the terrible knot in her stomach.

"I worry about Annabel," Grandma said then, grasping for her arm again, but Bel stepped out of her reach. "I worry about her in that house, alone with you."

"Don't be ridiculous," Charlie said. "Bel, come on."

"Coming." But she didn't move; she was blocked in between them and the table with the chessboard, stuck in no-man's-land.

"Ridiculous, is it?" Grandma said, closer to a shriek, the edges of her words crashing together. "Ridiculous how the women close to you all seem to end up dead."

The room dropped into silence, sickly as it closed in.

Charlie narrowed his eyes, the movement creasing his face the same way as a laugh. "What do you mean by that?"

Grandma's neck stretched out of her green scarf, like she thought she was winning the war.

"Your mother, she died when you were sixteen, didn't she?"

Bel tried not to gasp. Grandma couldn't be implying that . . .

"That was a tragic accident," Charlie said, voice low, a muscle ticking in one cheek. "She fell down the stairs and hit her head. I was asleep at the time."

"Of course you were," Grandma said, a mocking coo in her voice, like she was soothing a child. "But here's the thing, two tragic deaths starts to look like a pattern, Charlie."

Charlie laughed, a hollow sound to hide the hurt, shaking his head. "Great," he said. "So I'm a wife-killer and a mother-killer now too. Awesome."

Fuck. He shouldn't have said that. It was obviously sarcasm, anyone could see that, anyone with sense, but the camera was rolling and in the wrong hands someone could make that look very bad. Why had Dad agreed to this documentary anyway? Nothing good could come of it. Bel needed to do something bigger, something worse, to help him now.

"Fuck you, Susan. Fuck off back to your fucking horses, you horse-fucker," she said.

Now someone in the room did gasp.

Grandma retracted her neck, staring at Bel open-mouthed. Winning shot. Battle over.

"Come on, kiddo," Charlie said, suppressing a smile as they caught each other's eyes. "Let's go." His face hardened. "Ramsey, I need a word with you, outside. Leave the camera."

"Yes, sure," Ramsey replied, emerging once more from the background. "Ash, see if Susan would like a drink. Cup of tea? Coffee?"

"It's far too late for caffeine," Grandma sniffed, dropping down on a corner of the couch, defeated.

"Oh, right," Ash said, shuffling in awkwardly. "Um . . . beer?"

"No, Ash," Ramsey hissed, following Charlie to the door. "Get her water or something."

"Water or something, coming right up." Ash pointed an assured finger to the ceiling, spinning on his tartan legs to follow Ramsey out.

Grandma wasn't looking at Bel, avoiding her—no change there,

16

then—digging around for something in her purse. In fact, no one was currently looking at her, Saba and James turning their attention to their respective devices, fiddling with buttons and switches, the camera pointed away. Now was Bel's chance.

She reached down, fingers outstretched, and swiped the black queen from the chessboard, tucking it up her sleeve before anyone looked. Hers now. The knot came undone in her gut, the pressure easing, a new lightness in her head as she felt the cool marble against her skin. A strong feeling, but it never lasted. At least the thing itself was permanent.

Bel walked away without a backward glance at the queen-less board, or the woman she hardly knew sitting behind it.

"Bye, Grandma," she called over her shoulder, cheery and bright. "So good to see you! Come visit again sometime."

Outside in the parking lot, the cool April breeze tickled Bel's face, the relief already on its way out, a new baby knot of tension ready in her belly, biding its time. Main Street was loud; the noisy whisper of cars, the seismic rumble of a passing eighteen-wheeler, and some kids squawking across the road, playing with the plastic moose outside Scoggins General Store.

Bel spotted her dad and Ramsey, halfway down the lot, close to Dad's gray four-by-four, dusty and mud-flecked.

"I swear to you," Ramsey was saying, hands clasped together in front of his chest. "It was not intentional. We went overtime with Bel, it took a little while for her to loosen up. And Susan arrived an hour earlier than we told her. They were not meant to overlap, I promise."

Bel knew he was telling the truth, but Ramsey hadn't helped her out back there, so he was on his own.

"That didn't stop you taking advantage of the situation, keeping the camera rolling," Charlie said, wiping at the stain on his shirt. "Look at me: I didn't know I was being filmed today."

"I'm sorry, but we are making a documentary. That's literally our job, to keep the cameras rolling. You agreed to all this, you signed a contract."

"Not like that, and you know it."

"Come on, Charlie, it's not like you're being unfairly compensated here. And I emailed you to let you know about Susan's interview."

Charlie scratched his head in frustration.

"Look." Ramsey leveled his gaze at him. "This film is about you and your family, the first time you've ever spoken publicly, a glimpse into your lives, and how they've been affected by Rachel's disappearance. What Susan thinks of you—that's all part of it. The world has heard from her before. But it's up to you to shape the narrative you want to tell. And, for what it's worth, I thought you handled yourself very well in there."

Whatever Ramsey was doing, it was working. Charlie sighed, blew out his top lip.

"Fine," he said. "Just no more *overlaps*. No more surprises."

Ramsey held up his hands in surrender. "No more surprises, you got it. So we'll see you and the rest of the family at your house tomorrow? We'll start setting up at eleven, if that's still OK?"

"Yes, fine," Charlie said, ready to go; Bel could read it in the shift of his shoulders.

"You were great today, Bel," Ramsey said, sharing his smile with her. "Really great. Thank you."

Had he already forgotten all the times she'd answered *I don't know*? Maybe the Grandma stuff made up for it. Shame, Bel had probably appeared nice and sweet up until that point. Oh well. *She* was allowed to look bad.

They were almost at the car when Dad finally turned to look at her, locking eyes.

"Horsefucker," he laughed. "Who raised you?"

"Oh, some terrible person."

Dad laughed harder. Good, she wanted to make him laugh, after that. Then, shaking it off, he asked: "Was it OK, the interview? Nothing too difficult, too upsetting?"

"Nah, it was fine. Just long. And I wasn't allowed to touch the fake water."

She reached for the door handle.

"Oh wait." Dad stopped her. "I've got a bunch of tools and stuff on the front seat. Why don't you hop in the back instead, kiddo?"

Bel stared at the backseat, through the grimy glass of the window. She swallowed, eyes pulling away.

"No, I'll sit in the front," she said quickly, opening the passenger-side door.

"Bel, there's crap all over it. Just go in the back."

"No, no, no, it's fine. See." She climbed in, over the bulky toolbox and piles of papers, food packets and bottles of Mountain Dew—because Dad was a child who still drank Mountain Dew. She lifted the toolbox and settled into the seat, placing it on her lap. It was heavy and uncomfortable, no space in the footwell between the junk and her backpack. "See, plenty of room."

Dad shook his head, started the engine. "Bacon sandwiches for lunch?" he said, not looking for the answer, because he didn't need to.

"You know me too well."

THREE

Bel found her in their favorite place: the far end of the cemetery, beneath the red maple tree that bled its leaves for miles. They were morbid like that. Heels kicking against the stone of the raised wall.

Bel walked toward her, past mottled headstones and eyeless angels, old bouquets of flowers just starting to smell. She stopped twenty feet away, hand cupped over her eyes.

"Well, I'll be," Bel called. "Is that Carter Price, ballerina extraordinaire and soon-to-be documentary star?"

Carter stirred, cheekbones sharp up to her blue eyes, a diluted blue, like unsettled water. Nicer than Bel's eyes. Price eyes. Carter tilted her head, her waist-length coppery-brown hair slipping over her shoulders, catching the bright sun, keeping it.

"Shut up, you." Carter glanced down at her hand, something tucked between her fingers.

"You smoking?" Bel asked, climbing up to sit beside her.

"What gave you that idea?" Carter raised the cigarette to her lips. "Since when?"

"Since yesterday," Carter coughed. "Don't tell my mom. Took it from her purse."

"I don't tell anybody anything," Bel said, sliding over until their knees touched. "Give it here a sec."

Carter balanced the cigarette between two skinny fingers, passed it over.

"Thanks." Bel pushed the end between her lips for one deep drag. Then she stubbed it out on the wall, dropped it to the grass below.

"Hey." Carter turned to her, annoyed. "I've seen you smoke plenty of times."

"Well, you're better than I am. And you're fifteen." Bel patted her on the back, not not-patronizing her. It was her job, after all: older cousin.

"Fuck sake," Carter hissed.

Bel withdrew her hand. "How are your feet today?"

Carter glanced down at them, black Converse pivoting on the end of bare legs, flexing the lines of muscle along her calves.

"Fucked up. But fine, you know."

"Aren't we all," Bel said, with a grin, ready to poke Carter in her armpit, the place she was most ticklish. Carter saw it coming, swatting her hand away, hitting it harder than she needed to, the slap of flesh on flesh, bone on bone.

"Ouch," Bel cackled, cradling the hand. "We are in a cemetery, you shouldn't hit. Disrespects the dead."

"Fuck off." Carter smiled.

"So does fucking swearing."

"Well, you taught me that," Carter countered.

Strangers sometimes mistook them for sisters. They didn't look that much alike; Carter certainly got all the good genes on her side of the family. But they'd grown up together, almost as close as sisters. Bel and her dad lived at 33 Milton Street, and his brother Jeff lived with Aunt Sherry and Carter in number 19. Quite literally a stone's throw away, well, a couple throws; Carter and Bel had tried it before. Got in big trouble, of course; Ms. Nosy next door told on them.

"Is that them?" Carter said, pointing with the sharp arrow-tip of her nose. Bel followed her eyeline. From here, you could just about see the road in front of Bel's house, the minuscule LEGO-shape of a white van pulled up outside, tiny stick people emerging, moving arms and legs.

"They'll be setting up the lights and stuff. Should probably head back soon."

"How did the interview go?" Carter picked her nails for something to do now the cigarette was gone. She was always moving somehow, never still. Drumming fingers and jangling legs.

"Fucked up but fine, you know," Bel echoed her. "Then Rachel's mom turned up."

"The *Masshole*?" Carter stared at her.

"Mmhmm."

Carter clicked her tongue, understanding all the spaces between Bel's words, a language of their own.

"Don't know why they want me in the documentary," she said. "I was born after Aunt Rachel disappeared. I never even knew her."

"I never really knew her either," Bel added, like it was a competition. "Oh, I should warn you. One of the documentary crew, the camera assistant, he's the strangest person you'll ever meet. Literally the love child of a washed-up rock star and a clown. And he's useless; Ramsey clearly only gave him the job because he's his brother-in-law. If we get bored today, we can just make fun of him."

"Bel, be nice."

Bel hissed, hiding from the sun. "I can't, it burns."

Carter shook her head. A small laugh, weighed down by something.

"You're not nervous, are you?" Bel asked. "You'll be fine. Better get used to it, right? Soon you'll be way too famous to remember your poor old cousin."

"Sorry, what's your name again?" Carter said.

Bel poked her, getting through this time. "I thought you'd at least wait until you got into Juilliard and fucked off to New York forever to forget about me."

Everyone left, eventually. Wasn't just Rachel Price. People were temporary. It was the one thing you could count on: people always left, even Carter.

"I might not get in," Carter said, voice smaller still.

"Of course you will, if you want it enough." Bel nudged her, feeling the hard rail of her ribs. "Come on, we should head back. Your audience awaits!" She shouted that last bit, to embarrass Carter in front of all the dead people, laughing at them from their graves.

Thirty-three Milton Street was already buzzing with people and equipment. Large metallic trunks clicked open, belching camera parts and long poles, softbox lights lying unassembled on the living room carpet, Charlie lava-stepping around it all as he delivered the crew mugs of coffee that they absolutely didn't have enough hands for.

Uncle Jeff and Aunt Sherry were already here. As soon as Bel and Carter walked through the open front door, Sherry pulled Carter to the side.

"I laid out an outfit for you, honey," she said. "It was on your bed."

Sherry must have spent hours getting ready: her hair was styled in neat brown curls, her pale skin closer to powdery orange now, clumping in the lines around her eyes, thick mascara, and bronzer to give her the cheekbones that Carter had naturally.

Jeff was doing what he did best: getting in the way.

"So, Ramsey," he said, following the man around while he attempted to set up. "Would I have seen any of your work before?"

"I've made a few documentaries," Ramsey said, picking up a yarn-ball of cables. "Did one a few years ago, about an Alaskan husky who worked pulling sleds. It was called Snow Dog. Disney bought it."

"Oh yes," Jeff said, scratching his salt-and-pepper hair. "My friend Bob, from Vermont, he used to have a husky. I think I've heard of that film."

No, he hadn't.

"The dog dies, real tearjerker." Ramsey sidestepped him to get to one of the recently erected lights.

"Was that the last thing you worked on?" Jeff said.

Ramsey glanced toward the front door: the only escape route. "No, I shot another doc last year. About a high school principal in Millinocket, Maine."

"I think I've heard of that too!"

Ramsey smiled. "You must be thinking of something else, mate. It didn't get picked up by a broadcaster. No one will ever see it."

"Why's that, then?" Jeff asked, not reading the room. To be fair, there was *a lot* going on in the room.

"Um . . . ," Ramsey said, the word trailing off awkwardly, gaze circling, searching for help. His eyes caught Bel's. No help here, *mate*.

"Yeah, Ramsey," she said, doubling down on him. "Why is that?"

He scrunched his eyes at her, like he knew she was trying to make him uncomfortable but he found it amusing instead. Guess you come to know someone pretty well when you're trapped in a room with them for hours, repeating the same conversations. Maybe Bel liked Ramsey after all.

He gave in. "Some of the networks said it lacked a *human element*. Don't know how they worked that out—it was all about humans. So plotty and twisty—you couldn't write it, honestly." He shook his head. "But clearly they thought it was missing something."

"Right." Jeff was still in the conversation. "That's a shame. Do you have a broadcaster yet for *The Disappearance of Rachel Price*?"

"Not yet." Ramsey smiled. "But we will. It's an incredible story."

"Plotty, twisty," Bel remarked.

He saluted her with the camera lens in his hand.

Jeff wasn't done with Ramsey yet, but Bel tuned him out as her dad approached, offering her a coffee now. In his favorite mug, shaped into Santa's bulbous face.

"Ms. Nosy's watching from the street, by the way," she said, taking the mug, the surface of the paint cracking slightly, Santa wearing those thousand Christmases all over his porcelain skin.

"Ms. Nelson, Bel," Charlie corrected her, knocking his finger under her chin. "While I remember, you didn't seal the trash can properly this morning. You've got to tie it with the cord, remember, it's bl—"

"Black bear season, I know," she finished for him. She thought she remembered doing it, hooking the bungee cord over. Must be thinking of another time. "Sorry."

"Lucky your daddy's here to fight off any bears."

"Hey, I'm the mean one," she sniffed. "I'll do the fighting."

Charlie grinned at her, then turned to slap Jeff on the back. They were both, by chance, wearing dark green sweaters and jeans.

"Jefferson, stop chewing Ramsey's ear off. Let him get back to work."

Jeff, despite being three years older, listened to his brother, backing off to find someone else to bother.

"When's your dad arriving?" Ramsey asked Charlie, more wires in his hands.

Charlie glanced at his watch. "The caregiver should be here with him any minute. Had a bit of a difficult morning."

"Great. We're almost ready to go here. James—where's that HDMI cable gone?"

"I'm ready to start miking up," Saba said, appearing out of the chaos. "Ash, you take Charlie and Bel, I'll do the others."

Ash straightened up from behind the largest metal trunk. He was wearing a white tee covered in cartoon strawberries, under a blue denim shirt tucked into slightly darker blue jeans. Of course, flared at the bottom, if you were asking.

"Just going to change my sweater," Charlie said, disappearing into the hallway.

"No stripes, please," Ramsey called after him.

"Hello again." Ash shuffled to Bel, unraveling a microphone pack. "Can I?"

"Can you?" Bel said, arms out scarecrow-wide, like he was about to frisk her.

"I just clip this on here first."

Ash stepped forward, his face far too close to hers, breath warm and minty. His eyes were green, she hadn't noticed that before; an unclean green, like football-field grass. He clipped the tiny microphone onto the collar of her baseball shirt and spooled up the wire.

"Now, this has to hide down here," he said, nodding awkwardly at the front of her shirt. He pulled gently at the material of her collar, averting his eyes as he fed the mike pack under, holding on to the wire as it rappelled down her chest.

"So," he said, "do you prefer apples or bananas?"

"Huh?" Bel said.

"Well, it's a bit awkward, me just fiddling with you, so I thought I'd do a conversation," he said, the body pack finally emerging from the bottom of her shirt.

"You'd *do* a conversation, huh?" she said, skin tingling where the cold wire pressed into it.

"Well, it worked. We are conversing." He held up the pack. "Now this clips on behind you. Have you got a pocket on your trousers, or . . . ?"

Bel turned around for him.

"Don't we need to do more conversation if you're about to touch my ass?"

"Oh, I saw a moose this morning," Ash said, fiddling with her back pocket. "It was massive."

"Well, you are in New Hampshire now."

"OK, you're all wired up."

Bel turned to face Ash, looked him up and down, moving her eyes but not her head.

"Double denim," she said.

"Oh, thank you," he replied, patting his clothes.

"Wasn't a compliment."

"Where's the HDMI cable?" came Ramsey's voice, more desperate now.

"I left it over there," Ash called, pointing over Bel's shoulder. "By the tripe."

"Aha," Ramsey said, somehow locating it with those instructions.

"Tripe?" Bel asked Ash.

"Tripod," he said. "I decided to shorten it. You gain a second every time you abbreviate. Those seconds all add up in the end. Time is money, my friend."

"Yet you just wasted nine more explaining yourself."

"Oh yeah," he said, looking intently at his fingers, like he was counting them.

Bel narrowed her eyes. "You aren't a real person, are you?"

He shrugged, deadpan gaze and an unbothered smile. Not the reaction she was looking for.

"I'm gonna . . . go over there," she said, leaving if he wouldn't.

"Oh wait, let me turn you on!" Ash said, loudly, the chatter in the room dimming around them.

Bel felt a warm and uninvited flush creeping up her face.

"Huh?" Voice breathy and awkward.

"Your microphone," Ash said, with an almost-knowing smile, moving to fiddle again with Bel's back pocket. Damn, did he know the game she was playing? He might even be better at it than her. Bel had underestimated him: she'd have to be even more unpleasant to win.

"Done, you're good to go." Ash straightened up, that same grin still on his face. Urgh, he was annoying.

Bel walked away without another word. If you don't have anything not-nice to say, don't say anything at all.

Her dad came down the stairs then, dressed in a navy sweater instead, just as a knock came from the side door, where he'd installed the ramp.

"That'll be Yordan with Grandpa." He hurried off to greet them.

"OK, Price family, can you head to the sofa?" Ramsey called. "We are ready to begin."

"Does the camera really add ten pounds?" Aunt Sherry asked Ramsey, sitting between Charlie and Jeff on the forest-green sofa, eyeballing the camera.

"You look great, Sherry," Ramsey said from behind it, glancing down at the monitor. "Now can we get the girls to sit in front of the sofa. Yes, like that, in the spaces between. Perfect."

Someone squeezed Bel's shoulder; it was Dad.

"Carter," Sherry whispered, "tuck your legs over to the side, honey. No, yes, like that. Good girl."

"Dad, don't touch that, that's your microphone," Charlie said. Grandpa's wheelchair was pushed up against the side of the sofa, extending it.

Yordan, the caregiver, was standing awkwardly at the back of the room, behind the crew. His dark hair was shaved close to his head, his dark beard not so much. Grandpa always complained that Yordan didn't shave, on the days he remembered who he was.

"All good?" Ramsey checked in with Charlie.

"For now." Charlie nodded. "I'll get Yordan to take my dad home if I think it's getting too much for him."

"Of course. Thank you so much for joining us, Patrick," Ramsey said, voice loud, clean gaps between each word.

Grandpa pointed a shaky finger at him. "You're the filmmaker from L-L-London."

"Yes, that's me." Ramsey smiled. You wouldn't know they'd already had this conversation just minutes ago. "Nice to meet you."

"Never been to London," Grandpa said. "Have I?" He looked at Charlie.

"We can all go together, Pat." Sherry leaned forward. "See Carter perform with the Royal Ballet someday."

Oh, so it was London now? Even farther than New York.

"Mom, you're confusing Paw-Paw," Carter said quietly.

Paw-Paw had been Bel's name for their grandpa first, when she was a toddler and two different syllables had been too much work. Bel didn't know if that had been pre-Rachel or post-Rachel, Grandpa probably wouldn't remember now either.

"So I've hooked up to your TV there," Ramsey said, overenunciating for Grandpa's sake. "We're going to play three clips from your old home videos, thank you very much, Charlie and Jeff, for sending those over a few weeks ago. I want you to watch them together, as a family, and just react. Organically. Tell me how it makes you feel, any memories of Rachel you want to share. I'll dip in and out with questions. Sound good?"

"Sounds good," Charlie replied for the family. Which was lucky, because it didn't sound good at all to Bel. She wasn't sure she'd ever seen these home videos before, and she wasn't sure she wanted to, not with a camera pointed in her face. Carter poked her in the ribs and she stopped slouching.

"Camera?" Ramsey said, stepping back, out of the way.

"Rolling," James answered.

"Ash?"

He moved forward with the black-and-white slate. Today, the scene was labeled: *A trip down memory lane.*

Ash snapped down the clapper board.

Grandpa flinched at the sound.

"This first clip is from Christmas 2007," Ramsey said, crouching by the laptop plugged into the TV, the screen mirrored. "Seven weeks before Rachel disappeared."

He pressed play and the TV sparked to life.

And there she was: Rachel Price.

The same as she looked in the photo they'd used on the missing posters. Wide smile that pulled her chin down into a point, dark gray-blue eyes, long golden-blond hair, almost as long as Carter's in this snapshot of time. She was wearing a bobble hat here, so you couldn't see the small birthmark high on the right side of her forehead, a flattened circle of freckle brown. An *identifying mark* if they ever found a body, which they hadn't.

Rachel looked young, now Bel thought about it; she never got much older than this. Rachel Price un-disappeared. Pre-disappeared. Standing in the snow, wearing a long gray coat, the same one she'd left behind.

Rachel narrowed her eyes, stared right through at Bel, into Bel.

She shivered, hairs standing up on her arms, but she wouldn't let it show.

Not to the camera.

Not to Rachel.

FOUR

Rachel Price alive again, brought back through time, lips grazing her bared teeth as she smiled through the cold.

"Jeff," she said in a voice that almost sounded real. "Are you recording?"

"What gave you that idea?" came Jeff's voice, distorted and crackly, too close to the microphone. "The camera in my hand?"

Jeff-from-now laughed at his own joke.

The angle shifted as past-Jeff stepped forward, and now Bel could see a well-padded baby in the cradle of Rachel's arm, body in line with hers, fast asleep. Not just a baby, it was Bel, she knew that, yet she felt detached from the small sleeping child; they were from two different worlds.

"Look at you," Sherry-from-now said, just as the past version of her spoke too:

"I'm giving up if no one's helping me with this snowman!"

Younger Sherry walked on-screen, prints following her in the snow, Charlie too. They were bundled up in thick coats and gloves, hats that swallowed half their frost-pinked faces.

A snowball exploded against Sherry's chest, spattering white dust on her chin.

"Jeff, I'll kill you," she growled at the camera. "You could have hit the baby."

"Anna's fine." Rachel smiled down at the baby, eyes glittering. "She can sleep through anything."

Bel forgot, for a moment, that that was her; the first part of her name that she'd amputated years ago. She didn't know Rachel had called her Anna; no one had ever told her.

"Come on, Charlie, Jeff. One of you hop on!" came Grandpa's old voice—older but younger. He still sounded like himself; Bel missed that. The camera panned to find him, squatting on a blue sled that was far too small for him, let alone another grown man.

A grin split her dad's face, this younger version of him in the snow. He squeezed Rachel's shoulder as he passed, giggling when he dropped onto the front of the sled, tucked between Grandpa's legs.

"Go on, Dad!" Jeff called.

Grandpa kicked off against the snow and the sled started to move. Jeff chased after them, feet crunching. The camera swerved and Bel finally knew where they all were. She could tell by the junk pile of rusted cars and dead equipment in the distance behind them. She recognized the old red truck in the middle of the pileup, and the tall framework she always thought looked like a mechanical giraffe. Called it Larry. They were at Price & Sons Logging Yard, owned by Grandpa, and his dad and grandpa before him. It had gone out of business maybe thirty years ago, before her dad or Jeff had really had a chance to become *those* sons, but it had a good slope down toward the river and was the perfect place to sled when the snow was right. As long as you didn't go anywhere near all the old trucks and saws and dangerous equipment, otherwise Grandpa got mad.

He wasn't mad now, though, laughing as he and Charlie sped down the hill.

The sled tipped over, Charlie did it on purpose, a cascade of snow glittering down on him and Grandpa. They laughed and laughed in the way that hurts if you do it too long, half buried there.

Rachel's voice floated in from behind the camera, detached from her body. "Oh no, they're gone, Anna. We lost them in the snow forever."

The clip ended, and the television screen went dark.

"Wow." Sherry was the first to speak. "You forget just how young she was when it happened."

"So young," Jeff agreed. "I mean, there's only nine years now, Bel, between you and your mom there."

It felt much greater than that.

"There was quite an age difference between you all, wasn't there?" Ramsey said. "Nine years, Charlie, between you and Rachel."

"Yes," Charlie said, speaking around the lump in his throat; no one else would hear it but Bel. He fiddled with his left hand.

"How is that for you, to see those happy family memories?"

"It's hard," Charlie sniffed. "When I see Rachel smiling like that, it makes me want to smile too, with her, like it's instinct. She was infectious like that. I know it's a thing people say, and maybe she didn't light up *every* room, but she lit up every room for me." He paused. Bel glanced back and saw that his eyes had gone glassy, the silent threat of silent tears. "But I know I'll never see her again, and it takes my body a few seconds to catch up. It's hard," he summed up again. "Sometimes it's easier, not to see her face."

"I can't help but notice you're still wearing your wedding ring," Ramsey said. Bel couldn't help but notice either now because her dad was fiddling with it, spinning it around the pudge of his finger, backward and forward.

Charlie looked down at it, like he was seeing it for the first time. "Yes, I still wear my wedding ring." A small, pained smile. "If I'm being honest, I'm not sure I could take it off anymore if I wanted to." He attempted it, pulling at the metal band. "No, stuck on there pretty good. Guess my fingers are a little fatter than they used to be. It's engraved on the inside, the date of our wedding: July twenty-third, 2005. Best day of my life . . ." An empty laugh, to push away the tears. "I like wearing the ring. It's a little reminder of Rachel, of the life we had together, however short it was. Means she's still here in some small way."

"That's really sweet, Charlie," Sherry commented, leaning across to pat him on the knee. "Going to make me cry over here."

Ramsey looked almost annoyed at the intrusion, the moment gone, Dad's face straightened out.

"Now, Carter," Ramsey said, and she almost jumped, so surprised at the sound of her own name. "You never knew your aunt Rachel; you were born four months after she went missing. What has that been like, growing up with Rachel having such a presence in your life, when you never actually met her?"

Carter cleared her throat, shifting her legs. "I mean, I think it's that word you said. Presence. She might have disappeared, but she's always been a part of my family, one of the Prices, even though we had no overlap. It's like with older relatives you never meet, like Grandma Price." She gestured at Grandpa, who stared ahead at nothing. "You feel like you knew them, because of the memories and stories people share. And without Rachel, I wouldn't have Bel, so . . ."

Carter trailed off, smiling at Bel instead, and somehow that said enough, that said more. But it wouldn't last forever, people didn't, and Carter would be gone in two-and-a-bit years.

"Great answer, honey," Sherry said, dabbing her eyes. Carter shifted her legs back.

"Yes, it was," Ramsey agreed. "And in some small way, you did overlap with Rachel in that clip. Because, Sherry, you would have been pregnant with Carter that Christmas, wouldn't you?"

Sherry's eyes calculated, flicking back and forth. "Yes," she said, "you're right. It would have been early on; I wasn't yet showing."

"Thank God, otherwise we would have had to cart you around on that sled." Charlie leaned forward to tease her, his breath in Bel's hair. "She just ballooned up like a whale at what, six, seven months. And then . . ." Charlie stopped to rub his nose. "Well, then I was arrested in June, in custody, so I never got to see you at your biggest, didn't actually get to meet Carter until she was six months old."

"It's a great feeling when your brother-in-law refers to you as a whale," Sherry laughed, stretching her powdered-sugar skin. "But he's right, I did just pop out of nowhere. I remember, we hadn't really told anyone yet. Jeff and I struggled for a long time to have a baby." She took Jeff's hand out of his lap. "We'd been trying almost ten years, so we'd learned to keep things to ourselves, to not get too excited in those early stages. I was thirty-eight when we had Carter, our miracle baby. But then, you know, it was everything going on with Rachel's disappearance, and we didn't want to add to any of that stress and upheaval. So we kept it to ourselves, until we couldn't keep it to ourselves anymore."

"Because of the whale-belly," Charlie added.

"Well, she doesn't look like a whale anymore." Sherry bent forward to tickle the sides of Carter's long neck. Carter tried to pull away and Sherry dropped the smile, but her dimples stayed, an afterlife preserved in makeup. She withdrew and looked up at Ramsey. "Sorry, I know that's not what this documentary is about. Us. You can cut the useless parts out, right?"

"No, no," Ramsey corrected her. "This *is* what the documentary is about. All this life stuff, family stuff, and how Rachel's disappearance affected other aspects of everyday life people wouldn't think of. You keeping your pregnancy under wraps, Charlie not meeting his niece until she was six months old because of the trial. That's the story I'm interested in telling. The Rachel in everything. It's all good stuff."

"All good stuff, Carter." Sherry glowed, running her fingers through her daughter's copper hair. "We must have known she was going to be tall and beautiful, huh? Named her after Carter Dome, it's a mountain close by. That's where me and Jeff—"

Charlie coughed, cutting her off, choking on nothing.

"What?" Sherry turned to him. Bel did too.

Charlie laughed awkwardly through his nose. "I know Ramsey asked for honesty, but you don't have to say *everything* on camera."

"What are you talking about?" Sherry rounded on him. "It's where me and Jeff got engaged."

"Oh," Charlie said, lips puckered out, holding on to the shape. Then a louder "Oh," before he cracked up, a loud, wheezing laugh that came from the ribs. "I thought you were going to say it was where Carter was, y'know, *conceived*."

"What, no!" Sherry screeched, hands raised in defense. "Did you really think that was the reason we named her that?"

"Dad!" Bel did her duty, telling him off, splitting the word into two disapproving syllables.

Jeff and Sherry were hooting now too.

"Urgh, Uncle Charlie." Carter pulled a face, looking out at Ramsey and the rest of the crew. "I guess you can't choose your family, can you?" she said with a sniff.

"This is perfect, guys." Ramsey grinned down at the monitor. "Really great. The next clip is from January 2009."

He pressed a button and the television static-crackled back into life, taking them to a different living room: the one in Grandpa's house.

The shot settled on the chair in the corner of the room. Bel was sitting on Grandpa's lap while he read to her from a green hardcover book. She was much bigger than they'd last seen her, but still tiny, the book almost as big as she was.

". . . the memory thief studied the back of her pretty red head," Grandpa was reading out in his deep storybook voice. "The knife still clutched in his hand."

"Pat," Sherry's voice chimed in behind the camera, "pretty sure that book is far too old for her. Doesn't even have pictures."

"Don't be silly, Sherry," Grandpa shot her down, returning his eyes to the book. "She doesn't know what it's about, just likes the sounds, don't you, Annabel?"

"Ye, Paw-Paw," little Annabel said, well on her way to three years old, fingers tracing the page.

"She loves it. It's a special book, isn't it, little one?"

The camera shuffled over to a car seat positioned by the sofa. There was a new sleeping baby there, a pink-faced Carter.

"They should be back soon, shouldn't they?" Sherry said, a quiver in her voice.

"Any minute," Grandpa replied, one in his too.

"Wait." Sherry's breath rattled, windstorm hard, behind the camera. "I hear a car. I think that's them. Annabel, come with me, honey!"

Sherry hurried out of the room, blurring the shot. She pulled the front door open, the chirping sounds of a small girl behind her. "Annabel, it's your daddy, look!"

A small black truck had pulled up outside the house. The driver's-side door opened and Charlie stepped out, wearing a smart suit, the tie undone into two loose snakes flapping over his shoulders.

"Where is she?" he called to Sherry, grinning. "Where's Annabel?"

The angle shuddered as a small blond head pushed through Sherry's legs.

"There she is!" Charlie crouched down with his arms outstretched, voice thick with tears already. Uncle Jeff stepped out of the truck behind him, but Charlie only had eyes for her. "Come here, baby girl."

"My daddy!" small Annabel screeched as her little legs raced beneath her, unsteady and unbalanced, jumping toward him headfirst. Her dad caught her before she hit the ground. He straightened up, holding her tightly in his arms, her face buried next to his, coming up wet with his kisses and his tears.

"Daddy's home," he said into her ruffled hair. "Not leaving again. Never leaving you again, I promise, Annabel."

The small child nodded, snatching his promise from the air, pressing her hand to his mouth. Charlie blew a loud raspberry against it.

"Daddy, 'top it. Come see my baby." She pointed a stubby finger back toward the camera. Back toward her eighteen-year-old self, sitting on the living room floor, watching.

The screen went dark.

A sniff behind Bel; her dad was crying in this timeline too, dabbing at his eyes with his darkening sleeves.

"Sorry," he coughed, embarrassed. Bel wrapped her arm around one of his legs.

"No, don't be sorry at all," Ramsey said gently. "Can you tell us what was happening in that clip?"

"Not sure I can," Charlie said, a shuddering huff. He hid his face.

Sherry was crying too, in a prettier way, face intact.

And Grandpa wouldn't remember. That left only Jeff.

"That was the day of the verdict," he said, finally getting a word in edgewise. "The jury reached their decision after two days of deliberation. Sherry stayed home to watch the kids. Dad couldn't bear to come to the courthouse; he was sick with nerves, terrified it would be a guilty verdict, so I went alone. The jury returned a verdict of *Not guilty*. Which meant that Charlie was finally free, that he could finally come home. It was an emotional day."

"You spent a total of seven months in custody, Charlie, awaiting trial," Ramsey tried with him again. "That must have felt like a very long time."

Charlie nodded. "Too long. To be away from Bel when she was so young. But that was a good day. Bittersweet, because we still didn't have Rachel and no answers on what really happened to her. But it was the end of such an awful period of my life. I was just so happy to be back with my family."

"We were happy to have you back," Jeff added.

"Yes," Sherry sniffed. "Not that we didn't love having Bel. She came to live with us when Charlie was arrested, and we had a new baby on the way imminently. Went from having no children in the house to two in quick succession. It was . . ." Sherry paused, chewing on the thought. "Eventful. A little overwhelming. But Bel was a very sweet little girl. She used to ask us: *Where's Mommy? Where's Daddy?* Didn't she, Jeff? But eventually, she stopped asking. And once Carter arrived, Bel was obsessed with her. Used to call her *my baby,* like you saw there."

Bel turned to Carter, mouthed *my baby* at her, more demonically than Sherry had described it.

Carter snorted.

"And Patrick helped us out a lot, didn't you?" Sherry directed the words toward Grandpa. "We had a home birth, when Carter arrived— I'm not into hospitals or needles and all of that crap."

All of that crap. Don't get her started on homeopathic teas.

". . . So Pat took Bel for a few days when Carter was born. He helped us a lot with the girls, loves his granddaughters. You loved reading to Bel, didn't you, Pat? We were all figuring everything out together, as a family unit. I think we did a pretty good job."

"Yes, you did," Charlie said softly. "And I'm so grateful you were all there for Bel when I couldn't be. I'll never be able to thank you enough. Don't think I've said it as much as I should."

"You don't need to." Jeff looked across Sherry at him, brother to brother. "That's what family is for. I had no doubt they were going to find you innocent that day. That's why I took Charlie's truck to the courthouse; I knew he would want to drive it home, a free man."

"That's right," Charlie said, wiping his eyes. "My Ford F-Series. I loved that truck. I'd only bought it a few weeks before I was arrested and I—"

"Gotta go to the bathroom," Jeff muttered quickly, standing up and walking away from the sofa before anyone could say anything.

Ramsey's eyes widened. The rest of the crew exchanged looks.

"Jeff, you can't just—"

But Jeff could, because he was already gone, out into the hallway, closing the bathroom door behind him. Not good at reading rooms, Uncle Jeff.

A moment later, Ash pulled a pained face, lifting the headphones off his ears, holding them over his head like a crown.

"He's still got his mike on," he said.

"You can hear him peeing?" Bel asked.

"Oh yeah. Really going for it."

Carter smacked her forehead. "Kill me now, honestly."

"I thought he just didn't want anyone to see him cry," Charlie said, finally drying his eyes. "But on the topic of peeing and my favorite truck . . . ," he began.

"Don't you dare." Bel spun around to shoot him a look.

Charlie giggled, ruffling her hair.

"Go on," he said. "It's cute."

No, it was not cute, the very opposite. And there was an entire British film crew here. Not to mention the camera.

Her dad poked her in the back. "I've already started now."

Bel sighed, turned away. Well, fine, if it cheered him up. But she wasn't going to help him tell it.

"I loved that truck," Charlie said to Ramsey, throwing himself right into the story, permission granted. "Would have kept it forever. But . . . Bel and I were in North Conway, can't remember the reason now."

Bel did. "We went to Story Land for my twelfth birthday."

"Right," Charlie said. "We stopped at Taco Bell on the drive home. I leave Bel in the truck while I go in to grab the food. And when I come back out, she'd wet herself *all* over the backseat." He chuckled, telling the story with his hands too. "I mean *everywhere*. So much pee."

"Uncle Charlie," Carter said, voice chiding, dipping deeper with his name.

"You left me there for, like, three hours," Bel protested, a heat in her cheeks that was worse than the story itself.

Charlie laughed harder. "It was ten minutes. Fifteen tops. Too many milkshakes at Story Land, I think, kiddo." He leaned all the way forward, wrapping her in a bear hug from behind, an annoying number of kisses to the top of her head. "But we could never get the pee smell out. So that was the end of my beautiful truck, my first drive as a free man."

"RIP," Bel grumbled.

"Rest in pee?" he added.

Bel wouldn't dignify that with an answer.

The sound of a toilet flushing, Jeff whistling as he walked back in. Definitely didn't wash his hands, then. Carter sank even farther into the floor.

"Jeff." Ramsey stood up, voice as light and breezy as he could make it. "No big deal, but next time, could you wait until we aren't in the middle of a segment to go to the toilet?"

"I really had to pee," Jeff said, retaking his place on the sofa.

"Oh, we know," Ash muttered, replacing the headphones over his ears.

"I wanted to return to something Jeff said about that clip," Ramsey said. Then, somehow softening and raising his voice at the same time, he asked: "Patrick, do you remember why you didn't want to go to the courthouse the day the verdict was read? Patrick?"

"What?" Grandpa croaked at his name.

"Were you nervous the verdict was going to be guilty?"

"Who's that?"

Charlie shifted on the sofa, moving closer to Grandpa. "Dad?" he said softly. "He's asking you about the trial. Remember? About Rachel?"

"Rachel," Grandpa said, choking over the sharp word, a cobweb of dried spit at the corner of his mouth. "Rachel. Charlie's girlfriend."

"Wife," Charlie corrected him with a gentle smile. "It's OK, take your time, Dad." Charlie brought himself even closer, arm around Grandpa's shoulders.

"Rachel," he tried again. "Sh-she was, wasn't she . . . stop it," Grandpa spat suddenly, picking one hand up from his lap and flinging it toward Charlie's face. The slap made contact, just, a soft burst of violence before Charlie caught Grandpa's hand, cupping it gently between his much bigger hands. Safe hands.

"It's OK, Dad," he whispered to him. "I'm here. You have nothing to worry about."

"Jeff?" Grandpa asked him.

"No, it's Charlie. I'm here."

Yordan stood to attention at the back of the room.

"It's OK," Charlie said to him, glancing at Bel to tell her as well. And it was OK, if her dad said it was.

He turned his gaze to Ramsey. "Dad lost a lot of his memory when he had his first stroke, last summer. It was a bad one. Been in a wheelchair since the second. He has vascular dementia, so he's losing more of his working memory, his speech, old memories. He can get aggressive without meaning to."

Ramsey probably knew all of this; her dad must have explained it already. Maybe he was saying it now for the camera, so people didn't think Grandpa was just mean.

"I think he's lost most of the time that Rachel was with us. I'm not sure he even remembers the girls," Charlie said sadly, refusing to look down at them.

Not remembering was a little like leaving.

"He doesn't have those memories anymore. I'm not sure it's fair of us to ask him about Rachel, it will only distress him."

And maybe Bel was the only one who could truly understand that.

"Of course, I'm sorry," Ramsey said. "I shouldn't have. I thought I saw him smiling during the video. I'm sorry."

"It's OK."

"Are we OK to carry on?"

And they were, because Dad said it, a small red mark growing on his cheek.

"This final clip is an important one," Ramsey said, zeroing in on Bel instead.

Great, her turn in the spotlight? She'd been trying to go unnoticed, which was not the same as disappeared. Sherry and Dad were easy shields.

"The reason this one is special," Ramsey continued, "is because it might be the last-ever video of Rachel Price, other than the security footage from the White Mountains Mall. This video was taken, by Rachel, on February eleventh, 2008, two days before she disappeared."

He let that hang in the air for a moment.

"Here we go."

He pressed play.

A close-up of a child in a yellow onesie, lying on the carpet, a gummy baby-tooth smile at the camera above. Bare chubby feet pressed together like thoughtful hands, waiting for something.

"Who's the best girl in the world?" the voice behind the camera asked, soft and breathy and sure, like it already knew the answer. Familiar somehow too. One oversized hand reached down, coming from the sky to tickle the young child. She giggled, balling her little baby fists, spitting bubbles as her happy tongue poked through. Freezing when the hand withdrew, like she only came alive at the touch. Tickled again.

"Are you a mommy's girl?" the voice asked. The child squealed in response. "You are, aren't you? You're a mommy's girl, Anna-Belly-Boo."

"Ma-ma," the child answered, stilted and bright.

41

"Yes, Anna. You love your mama, huh?"

"Thess," said the kid, confident it was a word. "Thess ah mama blong-itf." Confident that that was a sentence.

"Yeah, good girl," Rachel said, pretending to understand. "And Mommy loves you more than anything in the whole wide world. Doesn't she?"

There was a sound, the soft crash of the front door closing, somewhere off camera.

"You're here already," Charlie's voice, muffled in the background. "How did you get home?"

"Jules gave me a ride," Rachel replied.

"I would have come get you," he said. "Rachel, honey." Closer now. "You didn't shut the front door again. You really need to check, it's freezing out. Aren't you cold?"

"Not really," she answered. "We're not cold, are we, baby girl?"

Young Annabel hitched up her feet, blowing another happy bubble.

The clip ended.

Black screen.

Bel swallowed, a wad of thick saliva sticking in her throat. The room was silent, everyone waiting for her to say something.

"Yeah," she said, which might as well have been nothing. "I hadn't seen that before." Saying something without saying anything. Bel turned back to the camera, catching Ash's eyes on the way over. He gave her a small double thumbs-up, held tightly to his strawberry-covered chest. Urgh, he could shove those thumbs up his—

"What are you thinking, Bel?" Ramsey asked. "How does it make you feel, seeing that clip? Just two days before everything changed, forever."

How did it make her feel? Uncomfortable, throat-swollen, sweaty-palmed.

"It's nice," she lied. "To see a normal moment like that. I don't remember any with her. But I seemed happy there."

"Yes, you did." An encouraging smile on Ramsey's face. "As did Rachel, I think. Very happy, no hint of the impending disaster. I got emotional when I first saw it, I'll admit," he said, "because it's just so clear how much your mum loved you."

Did she? More than anything in the whole wide world? Well then, why did she leave Bel behind in the backseat of her car just forty-eight hours later? Disappeared forever. Explain that one.

"Another thing I couldn't help but notice," Ramsey continued. He couldn't help noticing a lot, huh? Should see a doctor about that. "There's the physical resemblance between you and Rachel, but the thing that gets me here, is how similar the two of you sound. Your voices when you speak are almost exactly the same."

"Yeah, I noticed that," Jeff chimed in. "Really similar, now you're all grown up. We'd probably get you two mixed up all the time on the phone if . . ."

Yeah, if . . .

Bel knew they were right. It was the reason Rachel's voice felt familiar, because she definitely wasn't recalling it from memories. She had none. Ramsey was waiting for her to answer, but she didn't want to speak in Rachel's voice again.

"Something else we saw in that clip." Ramsey turned his attention to her dad instead. "Charlie, at your trial in December 2008, you gave evidence that in the months and weeks leading up to Rachel's disappearance, you noticed a change in her behavior. That she was becoming forgetful, seemed preoccupied, distracted. Those were the words you used. Could you tell us about that?"

Charlie sat up straighter, the old sofa creaking beneath him. "It was nothing major. Just like you saw there with the front door. Rachel was forgetting things she didn't used to. Leaving the oven on, burning food. Forgetting that Bel was in the bathtub. Stove, faucets, windows, baby monitor. Things like that. I thought it was a case of the—what do they call it again—yeah, baby brain. Maybe going back to work, even part-time, it was too soon or something. I'm sure that's all it was."

Bel shifted, the floor suddenly too hard beneath her. Because she wasn't so sure that was all it was. Leaving the front door open when she didn't mean to, water still running after she'd gotten out of the shower, not sealing the trash can even though it was black bear season and she knew she had to do that and thought she had. Her dad was never mad, if anything he was too nice about it. Had he noticed the similarities? He'd never mentioned it. Which was good, because Bel didn't want to be anything like Rachel Price. If she lit up rooms, Bel would darken them. If she was forgetful, Bel had to try that much harder not to be.

"And Bel," Ramsey said, "I know it's been sixteen years, and you think your mum is most likely dead. But if she did, somehow, come back after all this time, what would you want to say to her?"

Bel didn't even know how to begin to answer that. And that was fine, she didn't owe Ramsey everything in her head. She could keep some back for herself. "I don't know, I didn't really know her."

"*I* know," Charlie said, stepping in, saving her. "I've thought about it a lot, have dreams about it, even. I would just want to hold her. Wrap my arms around her and just tell her how much I love her. How much I've missed her. Before any questions, those can come later."

Sherry blew her nose, loudly.

"You OK, honey?" Jeff asked her. She waved him off.

"It won't ever happen, I know that," Charlie said, voice splitting in two, catching the tears before they fell. "But that's what I'd do."

FIVE

Nightstands were made for secrets. And Bel had more than most, so many that she'd had to clear a shelf inside her wardrobe for the overspill, hidden behind her balled-up socks. And under the bed.

She opened the nightstand drawer, contents rattling as she did. Lip balms and hand sanitizers, a little saltshaker from Rosa's Pizza, bookmarks, pens, one AirPod—that one she felt real bad about—nail polish, a glove with the tag still on, a little figurine that might have been a Happy Meal toy, a tiny screwdriver and the black marble queen from the chessboard at Royalty Inn. Bel added one more secret to the pile: the scrunchie she'd taken today off a freshman's desk in the science lab. The tug of shame as Bel welcomed it home, skin alive with the feeling, itchy and warm. Looking down at her menagerie of stolen things, each one small enough to hide in one hand.

Bel closed the drawer, hiding them away. Hidden but not gone. Things couldn't get up and leave like that. Unless she was in a Pixar movie, and Bel was pretty sure she wasn't.

She got into bed, making eye contact with the book waiting for her on top of the nightstand. The plot hadn't really got going yet—a lot of backstory—but something exciting was going to happen soon. It had to: the title promised it.

She checked her phone—not for any messages, there wouldn't be any—but to make sure she'd set her alarm for school tomorrow.

Now that she'd stopped rustling, she could hear the faint murmur of voices downstairs. It wasn't the TV; Dad's program had finished at ten. Someone must be here. Who was at their house this late?

Bel kicked the comforter off, crossed her room with light, barefoot steps and cracked the door. The voices growing clearer the farther she pushed it, standing half in and half out of her room, eyes on the glowing stairs.

Her dad was speaking now, in the living room below.

". . . way too late, I don't know why you're saying this now. What happened? Did it not go well today, the interview?"

"No, it was fine."

It was Uncle Jeff, she recognized his voice, but there was an edge to it that she didn't often hear, an uneasiness.

"Fine, I think. I answered everything. But I was nervous about accidentally saying something that made you look bad, so I thought about my answers carefully before I gave them, and Ramsey commented that I was taking my time. So maybe it looked like I was trying to hide something, I don't know."

"But you aren't hiding anything," Charlie said, his voice soothing. "None of us are hiding anything, so you have nothing to worry about. It's all fine."

"Maybe. I don't know, Charlie. I don't know if this documentary was such a good idea. Things have been normal for a long time. Good, even. You remember what it was like, back when she first disappeared, or after the trial. All that attention, the media, people in town having *opinions,* the broken windows, that psycho obsessed with the case. You have no idea what kind of spin this documentary might have; they could be trying to make you look guilty. They can do that, you know. Editing. The soundtrack, the perspective. Easy to make someone look like a villain. I don't know why we're doing this, why we're risking bringing all that negative attention back into our lives."

"We're doing it because we have to, Jeff," her dad answered, still nice, still calm, but Bel could hear a rare hint of impatience. "You think I wanted to do it? You think I wanted the cameras around, intruding in our lives, bringing up these old, painful memories? But we have to and it will all be fine, I promise. They can't make me look guilty because I'm not guilty, we all know that. They'll be done in a few weeks and then we can all move on with our lives. Hey, it might even be a positive thing, this documentary. People will finally get to see the real us, our family, how much we all loved Rachel. It might be the thing that finally clears my name for good."

"But maybe it's not too late to—"

"Not too late to *what*?" Charlie cut him off. "I signed a contract; the family's participation was part of that deal. I sold them my life rights, Jefferson. They paid me forty thousand dollars. It is too late to go back and this discussion is pointless."

Bel shifted her position, knees cracking in the silence, holding her breath to listen harder.

"I'm just trying to help you," Jeff said. "I don't think you've thought this all through."

"I have thought it through hundreds of times," Charlie said, and now he was angry. Bel never heard him angry. "I don't see you volunteering to pay for Dad's care, Jefferson. Do you know how expensive it is to have a full-time caregiver? Have you even given it one thought? No, because it's my job yet again to take care of everything. We needed the money, Jeff. More money than you or I have. The documentary is paying to take care of Dad. You might not want to do it, *I* don't want to do it, but we had no other choice."

Bel was listening, learning, but Jeff clearly wasn't.

"There must be another way to help Dad and—"

"You're right, Jeff." Charlie's voice grated. "We did have two options to get that kind of money. One was to take part in this documentary. And the other was to finally apply for Rachel's death certificate so I could cash in on her life insurance policy. That was the bigger payout, for sure. But which of those options makes me look worse, do you think? Which one of those makes me look guilty?"

He was right, of course. Dad was always right. They would fall apart without him, the whole family. He did the worrying and the thinking and the planning, so they didn't have to. Bel knew he must have had a good reason for finally agreeing to talk to the cameras after all these years.

"I'm sorry," Jeff said, backing off, giving up the edge in his voice. "I wasn't thinking . . . about Dad, about the money. I didn't realize that's why you agreed to the documentary. I'm sorry. Thank you for taking care of Dad, for putting him first."

"I don't need thanks," Charlie said, back to normal. "It's Dad. I'd do anything for him. Do anything for any of you."

"I know you would," Jeff said.

Bel hadn't really heard Dad and Uncle Jeff argue before. Playful ones, sure, brotherly teasing and overreacting, but never something where real *sorry*s had to change hands like that. Because Dad didn't argue; he wasn't built that way. He and Bel had never had a real fight, not raised voices, or heated words they'd regret later. Bel had tried, of course, many, many times, when she needed somewhere to put her anger. But at the first sign, Dad would simply tell her he was going to leave the house, so they could calm down in their own space and time, find kinder words to work it out. Mostly he didn't actually have to leave at all. It worked every time, unlit whatever fuse there was, untangled whatever misunderstanding. He was good like that; the only one who would never leave her. And Bel found other places to put her anger.

"Sorry," Jeff was still saying downstairs. "I'll do the rest of the filming. Whatever they want me to do. I'll even try to enjoy it."

Bel promised the same.

"Oh, fuck off," Bel said when she spotted Ramsey and the rest of the crew outside the entrance of Gorham Middle & High School the next morning.

Carter jostled her shoulder as they crossed the street together. "Did you know they were filming here today?" she asked under her breath, hiding it with a smile.

"No." Bel tightened her grip on the straps of her backpack, knuckles bursting through the skin like armor. "But it's nothing to do with us."

"If it's nothing to do with us, why is Ash waving at you?"

Ash was wearing black check pants—bottom half almost normal— but he'd paired those with a mustard-color sweater vest over a shirt with a large, ruffled collar, hair tied in a small bun on top of his head. Jesus, he was at an American high school, they were going to eat him alive. People were already pointing and staring, though it might have been the camera they were looking at.

Bel and Carter approached. They had no choice; the crew was blocking the entrance.

The principal was there too, talking eagerly to Ramsey, eyebrows and teeth dancing around his face. Most exciting thing to happen to him all year, probably; hadn't looked this perky since the game against Pittsburgh High, where Joe Evans puked red Gatorade all over the basketball court. People screamed because it looked like blood. *Go Huskies!*

"Hello, Bel, Carter!" Ramsey spotted them, using them as an excuse to maneuver away from Principal Wheeler. Ramsey might be able to read people, but she could read him too.

Bel considered pretending she hadn't heard him.

"Hello," Carter said cheerfully, ruining the game.

"Carter!" a voice called across the semicircle of grass. Carter's friends were waiting for her back there, beckoning her over, backpacks knocking together as the girls huddled closer.

Carter glanced at Bel, like she was waiting to be released.

Bel wanted to say no, but what was the point? "See you later," she said, letting Carter go, because she was going anyway, always would be.

Carter darted off without a second glance back. Her friends rebuilt their huddle around her, chattering excitedly.

"Bel," Ramsey said, bringing her attention back to him. A crowd was starting to form around them, a bottleneck to reach the doors.

"I know we're not scheduled to film with you until Saturday, for the reenactment." His eyes lit up. "Very exciting."

"Fantastic. Can't wait."

"But today we're filming around the school, seeing the place your mum used to work, what it was like to be a high school English teacher here, her life outside of home. We'll be interviewing a few of the teachers who worked alongside her: Principal Wheeler, Mrs. Torres and, of course, Mr. Tripp."

Mr. Tripp—math—but he was Bel's homeroom teacher, and the man who found her in that car sixteen years ago. Why had his name stung a little when Ramsey said it, though? Bel hadn't realized that he taught here the same time as Rachel. Maybe that was the reason he was always nice to her. Rachel took everything.

"But now I've caught you—" Ramsey said.

"Literally—" Bel muttered.

He continued: "—I thought it would be nice to film you, walking the same halls your mum used to teach in. There's a nice parallel there. And it would be great to talk to some of your friends at lunchtime, if they can sign the release forms."

Bel took a breath, straightened out her face.

"Yeah, sure. Lunch. I'll find my friends." Her tongue too fat around that last word, saying it wrong, another slug in her mouth.

"Perfect." Ramsey flashed his teeth.

Bel turned to go through the double doors, disappearing into the crowd, passing Ash. He caught her eye and she caught his. A muscle twitch in his mouth, not a smile, sad somehow. Like he knew the thing she hadn't said and was sorry about it. Well, he would be sorry, if he ever looked at her like that again.

Bel's sneakers screeched against the polished tile of the hallway. More polished than normal. A group of girls were standing by the lockers—juniors—watching Ash through the doors, giggling and falling into each other.

"And the man-bun!" one of them snorted, setting them all off again.

Bel let the strap of her backpack slip from her shoulder as she passed the group, her heavy bag swinging down and knocking into that girl, hard.

"Hey!" the girl shouted, spoiling for a fight, or spoiling for an apology.

Can't hear you, Bel mouthed back at her, pointing at the nonexistent wireless earphones either side of her head.

She continued down the corridor, past the English classrooms. Every day she had to walk right by *The Rachel Shrine,* as she thought of it: a collection of photos and certificates on the wall, old letters and poems written to and about *the best English teacher ever.* The trick was to not look at it, pretend it wasn't there. No doubt Ramsey would want to film in front of it today.

"Bel, hey!" A voice caught up to her, a patter of feet.

Bel stopped, narrowed her eyes before she turned.

It was Sam Blake; her long black hair pooling like liquid over her shoulder, just as it always did.

"I heard what he said back there, about speaking to your friends. I don't mind . . . doing that, I mean."

A stone dropped into Bel's gut, growing into that hard knot of tension.

She sharpened her tongue.

"I don't know, Sammie. Do you still think my dad's a murderer and it makes you uncomfortable when he picks me up from sleepovers?"

"I . . . I . . ." Sam's mouth opened and closed, useless, speechless.

Bel shot her a deadly smile, and Sam withered away, gone again.

It was easy to push people away when you knew how. Bel had a clean record; she was very, very good at it. Making people leave her before they chose to go anyway. Same result in the end, because everybody left eventually, but it hurt less. That was what life was, choosing the way that hurt less.

That was what she would do now.

She shoved open the door to her homeroom and it slammed into the wall, startling Mr. Tripp behind his desk.

"God, Bel," he said, clutching his hand to his chest, hiding what was in it.

But Bel had seen; he'd been checking out his auburn hair in a small handheld mirror.

Camera ready.

His skin was still sallow, though, those same dark rings under his eyes. Hadn't fixed those.

"Mr. Tripp, I just got my period and it's a bad one, blood everywhere."

He stared at her through his tortoiseshell glasses, eyes darting, open-mouthed.

"I'm not feeling well either." Bel coughed a fake, hacking cough, spraying it around the room.

Mr. Tripp stared harder, backing away in his wheeled chair.

Bel coughed again. Groaned. Hands pressed to her stomach.

"Don't feel good at all. Might be Covid. I should probably be sent home."

SIX

Snow on a warm April morning that tasted like early summer, the road sun-dappled, trees in full, green bloom. Fake snow. Made of shredded paper, Ramsey told her. Not everywhere, that would have been far too expensive and they didn't have that kind of budget. But enough to *set the scene,* to cover the ground around the car.

"It's the exact same car," Ramsey said, too pleased with himself. "A 2007 Honda Accord in royal blue."

Bel pretended to be impressed. Well, it couldn't be the exact same car; that one must be in police storage somewhere, but the same in all the ways that mattered. Parked roughly up on the shoulder there in the exact spot it had been found, matched up to the crime scene photos. In the middle of a small, nameless road that led out onto US Route 2, toward Moose Brook State Park at the other end. It was blocked off for filming, vans and trucks parked sideways across the entrance and exit, a morning chorus of angry horns.

Bel's eyes were stuck, tracing the outline of the car. The same car Rachel was driving that day, the one she disappeared from, the one she left Bel behind in.

Ramsey was watching her.

"Let me know if this is too weird for you," he said.

"This is too weird for me."

But Ramsey had already been called away by someone. There

were four more crew members milling around today, another camera rig, more microphones, more metal trunks, more voices. One right in her ear now.

"Hey, Bel," Ash said, the sound of him so out of place in this road that was out of season, out of time.

Bel turned from the snowy scene to face him.

A small camera was mounted on his shoulder, the fluffy pad of an external microphone attached on top. The red recording light blinking. Bel blinked back at it.

"Rams wanted me to film some behind-the-scenes," he explained.

"Fake snow," Bel said.

"Yeah, that stuff is a nightmare. Been here since five. Just got to get through the filming and life can go back to normal."

"Amen."

Hey, maybe they weren't so different after all. Actually, forget that: Ash was wearing a white-and-black candy-striped shirt tucked into green flared pants with bright pink clip-on suspenders. His sleeves were rolled up, revealing one tattooed forearm.

"See you came dressed for the winter weather," she said.

"Always."

"Least you'll scare the bears away," she said, trying to be as quick as he was.

"Wait, there's bears in New Hampshire?" He swallowed, looking nervously at the trees.

Bel laughed, but so did Ash. It was a joke. That was annoying, now he'd think he was funny. Which he wasn't, by the way.

Ash shuffled. "Ramsey said you were ill on Thursday. I hope you're feeling better."

"What are those?" She pointed at him.

"Tattoos. Do they not have those in New Hampshire?"

"Yeah, but what *are* they?" Bel said, studying the designs tracking up just one arm, pale flesh running like tributaries around the gray pictures.

"They're memories. Family stuff, you know."

"No, I don't know," she said, pushing him.

He held out the arm, camera still rolling. "That rose, that's for my sister, Rosie. Took the thorns out because she's nice all the time. The lily next to it, that's for my sister—you guessed it—Lily."

"The leaf?"

"A fig leaf, for my oldest sister, Eve. She's married to Ramsey. I'm the youngest, the baby. That's me, the old campfire. I'm Ash, by the way. Never properly introduced myself. Ash Maddox. That bird above my elbow is my mum, Bridget, but everyone calls her Birdie." Ash twisted his arm, showing her the bare, exposed patch by his wrist. "Gonna get one for Ramsey too. He doesn't like the idea of being an old horned sheep."

"The campfire's the worst one," Bel said, taking a shot, getting him back for the bears.

"Tell me about it." An amused sniff that meant something more. "They're all amazing people, my mum, my sisters, Rams. I'm the only fuckup."

"Have you considered, maybe, just trying to be normal?"

A car pulled into the road then, saving Ash from her. They must have moved the truck to let it through.

"Ramsey, she's here!" Ash called, using it as an excuse to walk away from Bel. He hadn't lasted long. "She's here."

Who was *she*? Not the horsefucker again, surely. Bel was the only one in the family scheduled to film today, the only one they needed, because she'd been the only one there when Rachel disappeared.

The car rolled to a stop thirty feet away, sunlight glaring against the windshield.

The passenger-side door opened.

Rachel Price stepped out.

Bel froze.

A cold winter wind that only she could feel, inside and out, as she came undone.

It couldn't be.

Rachel covered her eyes against the sun. Dressed in the same clothes she was wearing when she disappeared. Black jeans and a red long-sleeved top, under a large gray quilted coat. The coat she'd left behind in the car. The same age she'd been that final day.

"Hi, hello," she said to nobody in particular, in the crisp voice of a New Yorker.

"Hi, Jenn, welcome back," Ramsey said, jogging over. "Bel, let me introduce you."

He caught Bel's elbow, unsticking her, and walked her over to Rachel.

Not Rachel.

A fake Rachel.

Bel could see that now, her mind thawing out, dripping cold down the back of her neck.

"Thanks for the fucking heads-up," she hissed, taking her elbow back from Ramsey, Ash following them with the camera.

Ramsey glanced down, eyes kind and concerned. Yeah, right.

"I told you it was a reenactment," he said. "Thought you assumed."

They stopped.

"Bel, this is Jenn, the actress who'll be playing the role of your mum today. Jenn, this is Bel, Rachel Price's daughter."

"Good to meet you," Jenn said, gum popping in her mouth, sticking out her hand.

Bel didn't take it. She was busy studying the stranger in front of her. The differences were clear, now she was this close: the color of the eyes, the shape of the chin, no birthmark on the forehead. But for a moment there . . .

"You look like her," Bel said, instead of a greeting.

"So do you," Jenn replied.

As if she didn't dislike this woman enough already.

"Not as pretty, though," Bel added as a quick jab.

"Aw, well, your mom was beautiful. I'm sorry about what happened to her," she said, fiddling with a strand of her yellow-blond hair. "I'm obsessed with this case, oh my gosh. I listened to a podcast about it last fall, called *Wine and Murder* or something, and I'm

56

obsessed. Ob-sessed." She split up the word, holding on to it like a snake.

"Yes, you said. Three times."

Bel's eyes flicked over to Ramsey. A blink, slow enough for him to read. Fake snow and fake Rachels. This gum-popping idiot? He blinked back, like he almost agreed with her.

He clapped his hands. "Long day ahead of us. Sooner we get started, the sooner we can wrap up."

"Not soon enough."

"That's the spirit, Bel."

Everyone was waiting. Ash stood there beside the car, headphones cushioned around his neck, beckoning Bel into the backseat.

Fake Rachel was behind the wheel. "You guys don't actually want me to drive today, right? I don't have a license."

Ramsey shook his head, from the passenger seat.

"OK," Ash said, a little louder this time, gesturing at the backseat again.

The window on the other side was rolled down, a camera rig mounted half inside the car, to point directly into Bel's face. Another camera set up on a tripod in front of the car, shooting through the windshield. Battery-powered light boxes hemming them in.

"Let's get started," Ramsey said out of his open window. "Hop in, Bel."

Hop in. Like it was that fucking simple. Oh, she'll just *hop in,* all right.

Bel took a step toward the backseat, the knot growing in her gut, a fake ball of ice, sharp where it melted. She ducked her head, held her breath and climbed inside, Ash hovering too close like he could somehow speed the process along. Bel sat back, hands balled together in her lap, pressing against her stomach, kneading the knot.

"You OK?" Ash said, like he was a fucking mind reader now.

Bel lashed out at him. He was the closest, in range.

"Just shut the door," she snapped, flinching when he did.

Done, OK. She was in the backseat. This wasn't so bad now, was it? No different from the front. Not really.

"We shot the full reenactment yesterday." Ramsey turned around to bring Bel into the conversation. "Louise from the crew, her two-year-old was playing young you, Bel. Very cute. But while we have the *real* you today, this is more the interview part of the sequence. I'll ask Bel questions, and Jenn, today I don't want you to speak or react in any way, almost like you're not here."

Fake Rachel was just a prop, like the paper snow and the undrinkable water.

"Why *is* she here, then?" Bel asked.

"We're going to interpose the interview with shots from the reenactment, so you go from young Bel to you, sitting in that same seat, talking us through what might be happening, what you're feeling. It's hard shooting a reenactment when you don't actually know what happened, but I thought it was important for Rachel to have a presence in both time zones. Here, even though she's not."

Bel had something smart to say to that, but it was too late, Ash was in front of the car, holding the clapper board in front of the camera.

Someone else shouted, "Action!" loud enough that birds scattered.

"How does it feel, Bel?" Ramsey turned to her. "Sitting here, in the same car, on the same road where your mum disappeared? To be reliving this moment?"

Did it count as reliving when you couldn't remember the first time?

"Fine," she said. "Bit strange."

"Why is it strange?"

Because there was a woman cosplaying as her dead mom, sitting in front of her.

"That I'm here, in the same way it happened sixteen years ago. I don't remember being here, but I know that I was. Right here, in a little blue coat."

She was wearing a blue sweater today, like Ramsey asked, the same color, to match. Look how Louise-from-the-crew's cute two-year-old grows up into this haunted young woman, you can tell by the bright blue.

"I wonder, does being here in these exact same conditions, does it spark anything in your memory? Any images, feelings?"

"Shit, yes, now you mention it, I've just suddenly remembered everything and solved the entire case, can you believe it? What a plot twist."

She didn't mean to do that. Just that Ramsey was now the closest, in range. And it was uncomfortable here, on the backseat. But memory didn't work like that. If it was gone, it was gone, or it had never existed in the first place. If Ramsey needed her to have some big revelation for his film to work, she was going to have to disappoint him.

"Sorry."

"Never apologize," Ramsey said. "I like the real stuff, the unguarded moments."

Unguarded? She was as guarded as they came, *mate*. Layers of iron and steel between her skin.

"Maybe it's better to start with the little that we *do* know," Ramsey said, defusing. "Tell us how you were found. I know you don't remember, but what you've learned since."

"This is all I know, from Julian Tripp's testimony. I was found here, in the backseat," she said, so tense that she wasn't truly sitting against it, stopping herself from sinking in, a hot ache in her lower back. "It was freezing outside. Snowing. The real stuff, not paper. But the car engine had been left on, so the heaters were still running, and the headlights were on. Mr. Tripp was driving the other way from Route Two. He spotted the lights, saw that the car had veered off onto the shoulder, half on the road. So he pulled up to investigate, see if anybody needed help." Bel glanced out the window, as she might have done sixteen years ago, through smaller eyes. Had she been scared at the time, sitting here in the dark, all alone? Did she even know what scared was? "He came up to this window. It was dark inside, but he had a flashlight, saw me here in the backseat. He told police that he called out a few times: *Hello? Is anybody here?* When he got no answer, he opened the door to see if I was OK."

"And were you?" Ramsey asked, even though he already had all the answers.

"I was fine, he told police. I didn't seem distressed, like maybe I hadn't been left that long. The heaters were on, so I wasn't cold at all. I was fine, not crying. He said I was babbling words and sounds, nonsensical, trying to talk to him. He'd met me before, but he didn't recognize me right away. After he checked that I was OK, Mr. Tripp called the police. This was all just after six o'clock that evening. He sat with me, to keep us warm while we waited for the police to turn up. He gave me a juice box that he found in the footwell. He saw Rachel's coat and purse there on the passenger seat, where you are now."

Ramsey was quiet, a reverential silence for the front passenger seat. Which was stupid, because this wasn't even the same car. Rachel had never been here.

"It was cold that evening. Freezing, even." Ramsey studied his phone screen. "Twenty-three degrees Fahrenheit, or minus five Celsius already at six o'clock."

"That's cold," Bel agreed.

"Not easy for someone to survive out there in just a thin red top, without their coat," Ramsey said, running his hands over said coat. Not the real one; the police had that too.

"No, it wouldn't be easy," Bel said. Unless you'd planned it.

"But she might not have been out in the elements for long," Ramsey continued. "Police brought in a K-9 unit the following morning. Sniffer dogs who followed Rachel's scent from the abandoned car. They tracked her scent thirty yards up the road that way"—he pointed out the windshield—"where they lost the trail, in the middle of the road. That might have been down to the snowy, windy conditions, and it doesn't mean that Rachel didn't walk into the trees, but police initially thought this indicated that Rachel got into another vehicle there, that's why the trail suddenly ends. Whether by her own will or not."

"Wouldn't need your coat if you're getting into another car," Bel said, putting an end to that thread of discussion, cutting it off like Rachel's trail, vanished in the wind.

"You've touched on something that many online theorists obsess over. The fact that the engine was left on, and the heaters too. If someone did abduct Rachel from the car, people theorize that they left the engine on and shut all the doors on purpose, to keep you safe, Bel, so you wouldn't freeze to death. People think this possible abductor could have been someone known to you, someone who cared about you and didn't want harm to come to you."

That had been one of the prosecution's theoretical arguments against her dad. Scrabbling at straws for their weak case.

Bel shrugged. "I don't think so," she said. "If someone did take Rachel from the car, the engine was probably already running, and if they shut the doors, maybe it's because killing a two-year-old would have gone against their moral code. Or they thought the crime scene would be more inconspicuous with the doors shut. Or maybe it was Rachel herself who did that, who left me here. Whether it was meant to be for a few minutes or . . . longer."

All more plausible. Rachel walking away from the car, walking away from her life, leaving Bel behind, but she didn't want her daughter to actually die in the process. Mother of the year right there.

"On the topic of public opinion, of the enduring obsession with this mysterious, unsolvable case . . ."

He should talk to Fake Rachel there. She'd listened to one podcast and she was Ob-sessed.

"Do you mind if I ask you about Phillip Alves?"

Well, he'd already asked, permission or not.

"That's fine." Bel cleared her throat.

"Phillip Alves, a plumber from Boston, who was thirty-seven at the time of Rachel's disappearance, became fixated on this case when it first hit the news cycle. An obsession that only grew as time passed without answers. He traveled to Gorham, convinced he was the one destined to solve this case, to find Rachel Price. Police suspect he'd been watching your house, going through your trash, taking photos.

Can you tell us what he did to your uncle Jeff and aunt Sherry back then?"

"It was in the early days," she said, "before my dad's arrest. The police were around a lot, as you can imagine, wanting to talk to everybody. Phillip Alves dressed up as a police officer and went to *interview* Jeff and Sherry, asking questions about Rachel and our family. They didn't realize he was an imposter, only found out when they told Police Chief Dave Winter about this interview, but police couldn't find him."

"It's believed that Phillip made regular trips to Gorham," Ramsey said, "over the following months and years, to stalk your family, to search for Rachel, growing more unstable. His wife left him, lost his job because he spent all day researching, reading the message boards. His obsession reached another boiling point in October 2014. Can you tell us about that incident?"

Bel actually could this time, from her own memories, from her statements to police.

"Uh, I was eight years old, in elementary school. It was a Thursday, and I was waiting for my dad to pick me up from school. But this police officer turns up instead, tells my teacher he's supposed to collect me. She believes him, because of the uniform and the badge. So I go with him, he takes me to his car, tells me to climb into the backseat and put my seat belt on. I did. But he wasn't a police officer. It was Phillip Alves."

"He *kidnapped* you," Ramsey said, voice breathy, in the shape of a gasp, like he didn't know exactly how the story ended. Besides, Bel didn't like using that word. So dramatic.

"He didn't really take me anywhere, and I didn't *disappear* for long. He drove a couple blocks away, parked, then turned around to talk to me. Kind of like you are now."

Ramsey didn't like that comparison, she could tell. And Bel didn't like being here, in the backseat again.

"What did he want to talk about?"

"He wanted to ask me questions. Well, he was kind of screaming from the start. Sweating, angry. *Tell me what you saw that day,*" Bel

62

whisper-yelled in the voice of Phillip Alves. *"You saw who took Rachel, tell me who it was. You have to remember something, you were right there. I need to know what you saw."* She stopped; it was hurting her throat.

"Was that terrifying for you?" Ramsey asked. "Eight years old in a stranger's car and he's screaming in your face, demanding answers you didn't have?"

Bel had been old enough to know fear then. But she was even older now, and knew it was better to keep that to herself.

"I just kept saying *I don't know.* That teacher called the police right after letting me go, realizing her mistake. Dave Winter, chief of police, he's the one who found me, got me out of the car. I was only *gone* about seven, eight minutes. Phillip was arrested, and they realized he was the same man who'd interviewed Jeff and Sherry. That he'd been stalking us for years."

"Police of course looked into Phillip, in connection with Rachel's disappearance, but found no evidence of his involvement," Ramsey said, rounding off the story for her. "Phillip pled guilty to charges of stalking, kidnapping and impersonating a police officer, and served three years in state prison. He was released six years ago, but upon his release, your whole family filed a restraining order against him, is that right?"

"Yep. He's not allowed anywhere near us."

Ramsey cleared his throat. "We've actually been trying to contact Phillip, to see if he'll talk to us for the documentary. If we find him and he agrees to an interview, is there any message you would want to pass along?"

Bel thought about that for a moment, now she was ten years older and ten years meaner. "Fuck you, I guess. Why do you think you deserve the truth more than anybody else?"

Ramsey looked pleased with that answer.

"Good," he said. "That's really good, Bel. OK, I think we should stop for lunch."

*　*　*

Lunch was a sad, wilted sandwich and a bag of chips. Bel ate hers silently, watching Ash and James fiddle with the camera rig in the car window, Ash being pointed around here and there, go get this, go get that.

Fake Rachel was standing close by, facing the other way. She hadn't eaten because she was off carbs, apparently, had an audition next week. Made sure everyone knew that.

"I've not done a documentary before," Jenn said to one of the crew. Louise, Bel gathered, the mother of the little Fake Bel.

"No? What do you think of this case? Mind-boggling, huh?" Louise asked her, checking quickly side to side, making sure they weren't being overheard.

Surprise, Bel was standing right here, twenty feet behind them. Should have checked harder.

"Isn't it?!" Jenn said. "Like, how did they disappear in the mall, just vanish into thin air, and then the kid turns up here, alone?"

The kid didn't know either.

"Just crazy," Louise agreed. "What do you think happened?"

"Honestly," Jenn said, her abrasive voice dipping into whispers, not any quieter. "I think it's pretty obvious what happened."

Obvious, huh? Please, do share.

"It was the husband."

The knot outgrew Bel's gut all at once. Winding up her spine, python-strong.

"He must have killed Rachel. That makes the most sense."

"I guess it's always the husband," Louise said, half committed to it.

"I feel bad for the daughter, honestly," Jenn continued. "What a sad, messed-up life."

Bel's fist closed around the chip packet, squeezing it to death. How fucking dare she? Give Bel two minutes alone with her, then she'd have a sad, messed-up face. Best of luck with the audition.

Bel threw the balled-up packet toward Fake Rachel's head.

"Hey!"

It made contact.

Ten points.

But Bel was already moving past them, shoes angry and fast against the rough dirt road. She didn't look back.

Was that what they all thought, the crew? The extra ones today and the original four, the ones Bel was starting to trust. Ash? Ramsey? Maybe Bel had never been in control of the story, just a prop, repositioned where they wanted her.

The knot grew inside, pulling harder, so Bel walked faster, almost a run.

Beyond the replica car, footprints in the fake snow, toward the thick canvas of trees.

They swallowed her whole, welcoming her into their shadows, vanishing her.

"Bel?"

Well, not quite.

"Oi!" A voice followed her into the trees. Ash.

"Oi," Bel repeated, picking up her pace. "Don't *oi* me, what even is that?"

"Where are you going?" He struggled to keep up, the hem of his pants snagging on the forest floor.

"I'm storming off," she spat.

"Oh, right," he said. "C-could you do that a bit later? We've got a few more scenes to shoot."

Bel turned back, wildfire in her eyes, a growl in her throat.

"Fuck off, Harry Styles."

So he did.

SEVEN

Bel ran.

The trees kept her secret, beckoning her through, small pathways opening up, closing once she pushed through. Had they once done the same for Rachel Price, snow-heavy and winter-dark?

The highway was close, cars shushing as they rushed past, keeping Bel quiet. Heart thudding against her ribs, giving life to the knot in her gut.

Stupid. They should never have signed up for this documentary. Never let strangers in with cameras to poke around in her sad, messed-up life. It didn't feel sad and messed-up, but that was all anyone would see.

The trees parted eventually, giving way to a small residential road that looped around to rejoin the highway. Bel could call her dad and get him to pick her up here. He was at work, but he wouldn't mind.

But the knot was still too strong, and she didn't want to have that phone call now, didn't want to explain why she'd walked away from filming. Dad didn't deserve that, and Bel wanted to find the right words first, kinder words, like he'd taught her, because nothing inside her felt kind right now.

She could walk home from here. Did it still count as storming off when it would take the best part of an hour to get where she was going? Walk home, calm down, call Dad. A three-step plan that Bel could follow, just one foot in front of the other.

She walked alongside the highway, nerves spiking when a dirty-minded trucker honked at her, rattling the world beneath her. She was trying to calm down, fuck you very much, sir.

Stepping along the midday shadows of the power lines above, like a grounded tightrope walker. An ATV grumbling by too close, a star-spangled banner snapping in the wind. By the time Bel turned past the Circle K on Main Street, there was a warm patch on the back of one heel, the beginnings of a blister. Still a ways to go.

Counting cars and losing track.

Counting clouds but they outpaced her, leaving her behind.

When McDonald's appeared ahead, she knew she was almost home. Those golden arches, guiding the way.

She turned right after the dollar store, down Church Street. Toward the railway tracks, where she and Carter used to play dares. They got in trouble for that too.

Bel pressed her toe against the metal lip of the track as she crossed over. She could never just walk between, always had to touch them. An unspoken rule.

She glanced up, the cemetery right ahead, then home.

She wasn't alone. A woman had just crossed over the tracks in front of her, on the other side of the road. Walking slowly.

Not even walking, really, shuffling. Feet dragging against the con-crete in shoes too big, soles falling apart, flapping like fish mouths out of water. A horrible grating sound as she stepped, a heavy limp on one side like she'd been walking a lot longer than Bel had.

Then Bel registered her clothes.

A long-sleeved red top. Black jeans.

Golden-blond hair hacked short.

Fucking Fake Rachel. How had she gotten here before Bel?

"Taking your role a little serious, aren't you?" Bel called to her. "It's not like you're going to win an Oscar or anything."

Bel drew closer, the road still between them, which was lucky for

Fake Rachel because Bel's anger hadn't cooled all the way yet. Closer still, and Bel noticed something strange. The bright red top wasn't bright anymore: faded, dirty, patches of brown and dusted white. It was pocked with holes, tiny islands of flesh in a red sea, ripped at the bottom, one sleeve half torn away. The black jeans looked faded too, murky gray, a slit down the back of one thigh, threads clinging across the rift.

Bel narrowed her eyes.

"What happened? Did you fall in a sewer on the way here?"

But how had her hair changed too, in the last hour? Slightly darker, cut roughly by the neck, matted and thick with grime.

"What . . ."

But there wasn't an end to Bel's question. She drew alongside the woman, watching her, matching her slow, shambling steps.

"Who are you?" Bel called across the road.

The woman stopped, turned slowly toward Bel, blinking away the sun.

She didn't need to answer.

Bel knew who she was. Knew bone-deep, innate somehow, something that couldn't be learned, only known, only felt. Her heart dancing itself off a cliff edge, into the roiling acid of her gut.

The gray-blue eyes that matched her own. Delicate, pointed chin. Ashen skin that was paler than she'd known it, more lined, sixteen more years of wear. The small tan birthmark on the top of her forehead.

The woman stared back at her, like she knew something too.

She was Rachel Price.

Reappeared.

EIGHT

Bel couldn't breathe, but Rachel did, raggedy and hard, wincing from the daylight, from the pressure on her feet, holding her body at a strange, twisted angle. It must have hurt, coming back from the dead.

Rachel held one pale hand up to shield herself from the sun, her fingers giving her away, shaking and weak. She studied Bel across the road, swaying reed-soft in the breeze, like she might just blow away, disappear again. Real, definitely real, but impermanent somehow.

Her eyes narrowed, then widened, a hard blink like she was taking a picture with her gaze, recognizing something within Bel.

She stepped forward into the road.

A croak as she tried to talk, raw and inhuman. A voice from another world, where the lost things went. They weren't meant to come back.

The sound shook Bel, brought air back to her in a panicked gasp. Brought her heart back, fight-or-flight fast against her ribs, drowning out her ears. Her feet moved before she could tell them to, terror taking over. Protecting her.

Bel ran.

She ran away.

Shoes slapping the concrete, racing her unchained heart, leaving Rachel behind.

Past the cemetery.

Turn left.

She looked over her shoulder, searching, like you weren't supposed to, in nightmares or in hell.

Rachel Price wasn't following her.

Gone again.

But Bel didn't slow down, flying up the sidewalk. Fumbling for the keys in the front pocket of her jeans, a slick of sweat across her lip.

She veered off, jumping clean over her dad's flower bed and up the stairs to the front door. She missed the lock, gouging a scratch in the green-painted wood. Got it the second time, twisting the key and falling through the open doorway.

Bel grabbed the door and slammed it shut, checking, double-checking, separating herself from the new world out there.

She dropped to the floor, sitting back against the door.

Holding it in place.

Hiding.

Hugging her knees.

This couldn't be happening. Couldn't be. And yet it was. That was Rachel Price on the road, there was no doubt. None. If Bel tried hard enough, could she find some? She'd give anything for some doubt. Was she seeing things, the idea of Rachel implanted in her head by the reenactment? Could this be a scene Ramsey forgot to tell her about? No, don't be stupid, there were no cameras. And how could an actress have stolen Rachel's exact face, a nose that crinkled in just the same way as Bel's?

The truth didn't make sense. But it was the only thing that did.

Rachel Price was back and Bel had lost her mind.

She'd have to find it again, soon, because she had to do something, right? She couldn't just sit here against the door and wish this all away, could she? She damn well could if she wanted to. Rachel had gone away once before, for Bel's whole life, maybe she'd go away again if Bel stayed right here, didn't move, hardly breathed. Allowed mystery to step in again and take Rachel back.

Do something or do nothing. That was the choice. And which was the way that would hurt less? Nothing. That was what Bel wanted. Sit here and wish life back to the way it was five minutes ago. Bel and her dad, and a universe that spun around them. People might think it was sad and messed-up, but it was hers, it was what she knew and she was happy, she was.

But then she thought of her dad. Really thought of him. That was what all her choices came down to in the end: how to make him happy. He deserved it, after everything. He did the same for her, their forever-team of two. Which way would Dad choose?

Bel pictured him, fiddling his wedding ring, back and forth, an endless loop. Unshed tears in his eyes. His words when Ramsey asked, hypothetically, what he would do if Rachel ever came back. Not hypothetical anymore.

I would just want to hold her, her dad had said. Bel remembered that. *Wrap my arms around her and just tell her how much I love her. How much I've missed her. Before any questions, those can come later.* He'd had dreams about it: dreams, not nightmares. And he must have had plenty of the latter. A hard life, haunted by the terrible knowledge that people still thought him a killer. And yet there it was, the proof of his innocence, stumbling around outside. Indisputable proof at last: Dad did not kill Rachel.

Rachel made Dad happy. She lit up rooms for him. Rachel would make him happy again, make life better for him. Bel wanted that.

So she chose.

She was going to do something.

Go back outside. Find Rachel. Bring her home.

Bel got to her feet, knees cracking, and a knock sounded against the front door.

Three taps, knuckle to door, bone on wood. Bel's heart spiking with each one.

A blurry phantom through the frosted glass, mirroring her.

Bel knew.

She wasn't ready, but it was time to pretend anyway. She reached forward, fingers wrapping around the lock, cold metal, warm skin.

She pulled the door open halfway and finally came face to face with her mother, long dead but undead.

Rachel Price.

Right there, across the threshold, separated by just inches now, not sixteen years, not life and death. Breathing hard and blinking harder. A metallic smell of sweat and something sharper. Rachel shuddered, holding on to the frame to keep her upright, leaving a grimy handprint behind.

A door creak in the back of Rachel's throat, quiet and unsettling.

"You live here?" she asked, guttural and raw, a voice that had been used too little or too much.

Bel had lost her own, hiding against the back of her teeth.

She nodded.

"Are y-you . . . ?" Rachel asked, breaking off, eyes heavy and wet, studying Bel from her hair down to her hands. It was a full question, if you knew.

"Y-yes," Bel said, her words cracking too, like she'd forgotten how. "I am."

"Annabel," she said in a scratching whisper, and it wasn't a question this time. Like Rachel just needed to say it, to pair the two together. Face and name. Unlearning and relearning.

Rachel's hand moved from the doorframe, floating in the air toward Bel, reaching for her, to touch, maybe to make sure she was real. Imagining each other and getting it wrong. The hand didn't make it and Bel stepped back. She let the door open all the way, inviting Rachel in because she couldn't find the words to.

"Dad's not here," Bel said, backing off. Rachel limped over the threshold, into the house. Her house. *Their* house. She looked around, eyes watering.

"Looks exactly the same," she said, quietly, touching walls and leaving marks.

Bel skirted around her, keeping her eyes locked on, to shut the front door. Closing them in, together.

A dark trail from the entrance. Not just mud. Rachel was bleeding through her shoes, onto the wooden floorboards.

"New lamp," Rachel said, at the entrance to the living room.

"Should I—"

Rachel started coughing, a deep-down, wicked sound that bent her double.

"You should sit," Bel said, avoiding her as she passed. "I'll get you some water."

Bel ran to the kitchen, hands shaking and clumsy as she pulled a glass down from the cupboard. She filled it and carried it back out, remembering to shut off the faucet.

Fresh blood and mud tracks on the rug, over to Rachel, now sitting slumped on the sofa.

"Here."

Bel offered the glass.

Rachel reached for it, fingers touching Bel's as she wrapped them around. Sharp overgrown nails. Bel shivered and let go, water slopping over the rim.

"Thank you, Anna." Rachel raised the glass to her cracked lips, drinking greedily, like a child who'd played too hard, too long. She drained the glass and put it down on the table, the thunk making Bel flinch, echoing in her chest.

Rachel looked up at her, waiting, like she expected Bel to speak first. Or she was giving her a chance to. Bel didn't know what to say to her, hardly remembered how to talk at all. How was this possible? How was Rachel Price sitting here, in front of her?

Ears ringing, heart hummingbird fast, a strange numbness sliding down Bel's back. Was this what shock felt like?

"We should probably call someone," Bel said eventually, wondering if that was the right thing. "I can call Dad; he'd be here in minutes."

A flicker in Rachel's eyes. Bel didn't know what that meant. This woman was a stranger to her.

"I think we're supposed to call the police first," Rachel croaked, not sure what to do either, both of them lost.

That made sense, of course. Call the police.

Bel nodded. "I can do that. You stay here. You need more water?"

"I'm fine," Rachel said, hissing as she pried off the oversized shoes that were stuck to her, falling apart in her hands. Her feet were a mess; swollen, bruised, dirty, bloody. One toenail hanging off to the side. Where had she appeared from? How long had it taken her to get home? Why had she come straight here, and not found help first?

Rachel saw her looking. "It's not so bad." She gave her a smile that was more like a grimace. "Don't worry."

"I'll get help." Bel backed up into the kitchen, pulling her phone from her pocket. Help for Rachel or help for herself? Wasn't it the same thing? Bel couldn't do this on her own, it was too much. So far beyond too much that her mind was shutting down around her, only able to think two seconds ahead and two seconds back.

She unlocked her phone. Five missed calls from Ramsey, oh fuck, was he in for a surprise. He and the rest of the world who—at this exact moment—still thought Rachel Price was gone forever, as disappeared as anyone could be. Only Bel and Rachel knew the truth. But not for long.

Rachel wanted her to call the police, and it sounded like the right thing, but it didn't feel like it. What had the Gorham Police Department ever done to help? They'd had sixteen years and they never found Rachel. The police did nothing, spinning the blame on Dad as an easy out. But Dad, he'd know what to do, he was the one who did the worrying, the thinking, the planning, the helping. And if Bel called the police, then Dad would never get his moment with Rachel, the one he had dreamed about. Bel couldn't take that away from him.

She deleted *911* from the keypad and dialed her dad's number instead.

He picked up on the fourth ring.

"Hey, just with a customer," he said, his voice like a warm blanket: safe, familiar. The inverse of Rachel. "I'll call you back in—"

Panic rose up, snatching away the warm blanket.

"No, Dad. You need to get home now. Right now. It's an emergency." Bel whispered, so Rachel couldn't hear.

"What's going on?" He was worried now, good thing he was the best at it.

"I can't tell you on the phone." She couldn't, she didn't want

Rachel to overhear, and she didn't want to ruin Dad's moment. He'd waited sixteen years for it. "Just please, come home right now."

"Bel, what is—"

"Dad, please!"

"I'm coming," he said, and she could already hear the sound of his boots pounding the ground, the slam of a car door. Of course he was coming; she'd asked him to. "Can you stay on the phone?"

"No, I can't. Hurry."

"Are you in danger?" he asked.

"No," Bel answered, though she wasn't entirely sure that was true. Her body didn't believe it, heart hammering down her ribs. "It's not like that. Just come, as fast as you can."

"On my way, kiddo."

"Anna?"

Bel spun on her heels, hanging up the phone. Rachel was standing there, a dark silhouette in the doorway, eyes glowing, red footprints on the black-and-white tiles.

"I just called the police," Bel said. "They're on their way."

One small lie. But Rachel didn't know her, she couldn't read Bel like a mom should have.

"Thank you," Rachel croaked, shuffling forward, pulling out a chair at the kitchen table, falling into it.

Bel stepped back, against the counter.

"You don't have to be scared, Annabel," Rachel said, clean tear trails through her dirty face. "Everything's going to be OK now, I promise."

How could Bel tell her that everything was already OK?

"I can't believe I'm home." Rachel blinked in the room, taking it in, Bel with it. "New refrigerator."

Bel swallowed.

"I know you must have a lot of questions for me, Anna," Rachel said, steepling her hands together.

"It's Bel," she said quickly, before she lost the nerve.

"Sorry?"

"Bel. My name. It's Bel now, not Anna. Hasn't been Anna for a long time."

"Oh." Rachel stared ahead, far into the middle distance, seeing something Bel couldn't. Maybe only those who had disappeared could. "I called you Anna. I've been thinking of you this whole time as Anna."

"Sorry."

"Wondering what you look like at each age. What you were doing for your birthdays. What you were good at and bad at. Whether you'd like the same foods as me. What made you happy. I had this whole picture of you in my head, that's what kept me going." Rachel shook off that other place, wherever it was, looked at Bel instead. "You're better than I ever could have imagined. I've missed you so much, Anna. Sorry. Bel."

"That's OK," Bel said, which was good, because she didn't have to respond to that other part. If Rachel had truly missed Bel, did that mean she wasn't able to come back until now? Such a mountain of hard questions, Bel didn't know where to begin: at the start, on that snowy day in February when Rachel disappeared not once but twice, filling in where Bel's memory could not, or today, sixteen years later, and those torn-up feet? "Where . . ." She took a breath, steeled herself, locked her jaw. "Where were you?"

Rachel nodded, glanced down at her grimy hands. Voice just a rasp when she spoke again.

"I don't know."

NINE

I don't know.

Those three little words Bel knew better than most. Both the truth and a blockade, to hide behind when you needed it. But now that she was on the other side of those words, she finally saw why it drove people mad, mad enough to kidnap a small, scared girl and scream at her in the backseat of your car.

"What do you mean you don't know?" Bel stared at Rachel, doubling down, kicking at the blockade.

"I don't know where I was." Rachel sniffed, repeating herself, like Bel always had to. "I don't know where he kept me."

Bel's mind stalled, picking over her words, searching for scraps.

"He? Who's he?"

"I don't know," Rachel said again.

A flash of frustration, warm, pushing against the cold drip of shock. "You don't know?" Bel asked, unable to hide it from her voice.

Rachel shrank. "The man who took me. I never knew his name. Couldn't see much of him."

"How—"

"Kept me in the dark." Rachel cut across her. "Think it was a basement. Can't be sure."

Bel paused, thinking that over. The questions peeled off her tongue, dropping to her gut like a dime down a well. No wishes to be found here. All she could find instead was:

"All this time?"

Rachel nodded. Like a nod was answer enough for all that horror. And it was all she would give.

"H-how long was it?" Rachel asked a question of her own now. "I tried to keep track of time, but it wasn't always easy. I know roughly, I think, but . . ." Bel didn't move and Rachel studied her, picking over her face for clues. "How long?" she repeated.

"Sixteen years, two months."

Rachel's breath shuddered, wiping a new tear before it formed. "You're eighteen now," she said, like that was the saddest part. She'd missed much more than just Bel's eighteenth birthday.

"Yeah."

"I'm sorry," Rachel said.

Sorry for what? For being taken, for being kept? For everything else? They weren't at *sorry* yet, there were still too many questions. They hadn't even scratched the surface of each other, claws out and hungry. But there was one answer that meant the most to her, peeking through their scratches. If a man had taken Rachel, kept her in a dark basement all that time, did that mean she'd never really left Bel behind at all? Did it? Didn't it?

That would change everything.

Bel took one step closer, sliding along the counter.

"How did you escape?" she asked next, wanting to savor that most important question; she wasn't ready for everything to change just yet. Too much had already.

"I didn't." Rachel sniffed. "Never could. I tried so many times, so many ways."

"Then how are you here?"

"He let me go," she said.

"Why?"

"I don't know."

Those words again. But Bel wasn't angry this time; you couldn't know what you didn't know, no matter how many times people asked. She'd lived it, time and again.

"What happened?" Bel said, shifting to what Rachel could know.

Rachel shook her head. "You don't have to hear all this, Anna. You don't have to know, I don't want you to know, that's not fair . . ."

"Please?" Bel circled, hardening her gaze.

Rachel met her eyes.

"OK. He—he came downstairs. I thought it was to bring food. But he didn't have any. He put a bag over my head, a fa—like a fabric bag, a tote bag, so I couldn't see but I could breathe. Then he unbound me."

Rachel glanced down one leg to her left ankle. Bel followed her gaze: red blistered skin in a band of raw flesh.

"Tape?" Bel said, urging her on.

"No, it was a chain. A cuff."

Bel nodded.

"He'd never taken me out before. I hadn't left since I first got there. But he walked me upstairs. Through a house, maybe, I couldn't see anything. He put me into the back of a car. I asked what was happening, but he wouldn't speak. He never spoke much."

"And?" Bel drew closer.

"We drove for a couple of hours. I tried to count the time, but I was distracted. I was scared. Thought he was taking me somewhere to finally kill me. But it was also a relief, somehow. An ending. I said my goodbyes in my head."

One of those goodbyes was for Bel, wasn't it? Maybe the most important one.

Bel stepped forward, and then all the way, taking the chair opposite Rachel.

"But then we stopped," Rachel continued, telling her story, eye to eye across the table. "He didn't even turn off the engine. He got out, opened my door and pulled me out. It was grass, I could feel it, my feet were bare, I remembered how grass used to feel. I thought he would tell me to get on my knees. I thought that was it. But . . . I heard the door slam, and the car drove away. He left me there. I waited a few minutes, listening, making sure, because I thought I could still hear the engine. Then I took the bag off my head. He was gone. I was alone on a road, in the trees. Been so long since I saw trees. It was dark. I was by a river, that's what I could hear."

Bel nodded her on, wondering what it was like to forget the sight of trees, the sound of a river, the feel of grass. She couldn't imagine it.

"I followed the river until I found a street. Then I followed that. No one was around. There were houses, but it must have been so late, or so early. I didn't want to wake anyone, to scare them. I kept going until I found a road sign. Lancaster. I was on Route Two already. I knew if I just followed the highway east, it would take me home. I just wanted to get home. I'm so glad you hadn't moved." She laughed a small, wet laugh, without a smile, without showing teeth.

"You walked?" Bel asked. "All the way from Lancaster? That must have taken . . ." She thought about it. "Like eight hours."

Rachel glanced down at her fucked-up feet in answer. "I found those shoes in someone's trash. Too big for me. Better than nothing."

"Did people see you?" Bel said.

"People saw me. After the sun came up."

"Did anyone try to help?"

"One person did," Rachel said. "But I wasn't getting in the car of someone I didn't know. I knew the way home, and I got myself here."

"Fuck." Bel exhaled. It wasn't the end of the earth, it wasn't even out of state, but—fuck—that was a long way to go. A slow, painful re-appearance. Not the blink of an eye, like the way she'd disappeared.

Bel watched the stranger across from her, less a stranger than five minutes ago, swaying in her chair, the effort of a blink almost knocking her sideways.

She must have been so tired, so hungry.

"Are you hungry?" Bel asked her, and it felt strange to ask something so ridiculously normal. Normal didn't belong here, between the two of them, one a fully grown person from the face of a toddler, the other back from the dead. "I—I could make you a sandwich or—"

The front door slammed, beyond the living room.

Rachel flinched, eyes wide, growing black with adrenaline. Her arms locked against the back of the chair, pushing herself up.

"It's OK, it's just Dad." Bel got to her feet too.

Rachel flicked those otherworldly eyes back at her, standing tall in a way that must have hurt. She hissed through her teeth, clutching her side.

"Bel?" Charlie called through the house, worried. "Bel, where are you?!"

"Kitchen!" she shouted back, and Rachel winced at her voice too.

"What's going on? What are you—"

Charlie appeared in the doorway, eyes catching on the bloody, muddy footprints on the tiles. "What did—"

"Dad," Bel said, making him look up.

He did, first at Bel, eyes narrowed, face lined around them. Then he spotted the new person standing there, gaze following the footprints over to her.

"Wha—" The word died in his throat, eyes snapping open, like they might just keep stretching and stretching, taking his whole face with them.

He stared at Rachel, unmoving.

His keys dropped to the floor, a loud clatter.

No one moved, marble chess pieces pointed at each other, standing in their own squares of the black-and-white tile.

Charlie's bottom lip unstuck, falling open. Bel wondered what was going through his head. Had this been the way he'd dreamed it?

"No," he said, barely a whisper, backing up against the wall, gasping when it stopped him. "This can't be possible."

Bel watched her parents watching each other, though she could only see her dad's face, and something wasn't right.

His jaw hung open. Blinking hard at Rachel, like she might disappear between the flicker of his eyelids. Taken aback each time she wasn't.

This was wrong.

He was supposed to be happy. Wrap Rachel in his arms and tell her he loved her. His wife, his vindication, standing right there in front of him, after all this time.

Was he in shock? Because he didn't look happy. He looked scared.

"How is this possible?" Words found him again. But the questions were supposed to come later. He was supposed to hug her first, say he loved her and missed her. This was the wrong order.

"Hello, Charlie," Rachel said then, and he backed away at the sound of her gravelly voice, flattening against the wall, knocking the clock off.

It smashed.

The sound echoed down in Bel's gut, where it found the knot, growing and turning, spinning into thorns. This didn't feel right at all.

"How is this possible?" Charlie repeated, more certain now, like he'd stepped out of the dream, even though none of it had followed the plan. "How are you here?"

"I came back."

"How?" Charlie said, louder.

"He let me go," Rachel said, quieter.

"Who's *he*?" Charlie asked, eyes straining at their edges, voice too.

"The man who took me."

"Who?"

"I don't know," Rachel said.

Charlie's chest rose with his held breath. "Who?" he said again.

"She doesn't know who he is," Bel interjected, but Dad didn't even look her way, like only one of them could exist at one time and his eyes were on Rachel.

"Took you how?" Charlie asked. Because there were questions and questions, and they were coming first, the mystery pulling hardest. Maybe the *I love you* and the *I missed you* would come after.

"Out of the car." Rachel shifted on her feet, hissing as she did. "He followed me—us—from the mall. I didn't know who he was, but I knew he was following me. I went down those small back roads, trying to lose him. He overtook, cut me off, made me swerve off the road. Next thing I knew, he'd pulled me out of the car. I managed to shut the door, hoping he wouldn't notice Annabel." Rachel glanced back at Bel, her eyes full with something. Maybe the memory of the last time she'd seen Bel's face, that baby, strapped into that backseat alone while Rachel disappeared in front of her. "He dragged me through the snow to his car. Slammed my head against the trunk before he pushed me inside. I couldn't get out. He drove away. No one could hear me screaming."

Bel hung her head, picturing it, re-creating the memory that never was, what she must have seen and forgotten, because she was too young to have the words for it. The truth of what happened, and the answer that mattered most to her, out of all of them. Rachel hadn't left her. She'd been taken away. This should feel good, so why didn't it? Why was the room so stale, and the knot in her gut pulling tighter and tighter?

It wasn't the most important answer to her dad, clearly. There was still too much to know. "What about the mall?" he asked, peeling away from the wall now. Rachel looked confused. "You disappeared twice, Rachel. The cameras saw you go in but never leave. Explain that. Why did you and Bel vanish inside the mall before that? How?"

"Did you call the police?" Rachel asked Bel.

"Yeah," she lied again, looking at her dad, wondering if it was time to actually call them. Maybe after her dad's questions, and the part that came after, the part he'd waited all this time for.

"Rachel?" he said, splitting her name into halves. Still scared, still in shock. Was Bel through hers yet? "What happened?"

Rachel staggered, turning to face him. "The man was there too. That's when I first noticed him, following us, staring at me. It was the first time I noticed him, but I don't think it was the first time he noticed me. I'd been feeling watched for a couple of days, like I was being followed. Something felt wrong, really wrong, and I knew it would be bad if he followed us out to the car. So after we left the coffeehouse, I made us disappear for a while. We hid."

"Hid where?" Charlie pressed, not soft like the way Ramsey did it.

"I used to work in that mall," Rachel said, answering hard too. "The food court was round the corner from the coffeehouse. When they emptied the trash cans, they always took the bags through this

Staff Only door. We went that way, it was unlocked. Just a small corridor with trash and large recycling bins. I was scared the man had seen us, and I thought the door to outside would be alarmed, so we hid. Inside a recycling bin. The one for glass. Paper was too full."

"You hid in a bin with our daughter?" Charlie said, like he almost couldn't believe it. At least that was better than scared, closer to normal.

Rachel nodded. "I wanted to wait long enough, make sure the man didn't find us, that he was really gone. Maybe an hour and a half. Annabel was sleepy. But then I heard voices, and the bin started to move. Someone was wheeling us out, some employees. They didn't know we were in there. I made sure Anna stayed real quiet. They pushed us out the door, round a corner, complaining about how much glass there was. I guess the recycling was being collected soon."

"That's how we left the mall?" Bel asked. "Inside the bin?" The answer to the impossible mystery, that it could never live up to.

"We were inside the bin," Rachel confirmed. "After the employees were gone, I opened the lid and we climbed out. We were in the back section, behind the parking lot. I guess there weren't any cameras there, if they never saw us leave, if no one knew that happened. I never thought about that," she said to Charlie. And Rachel had had a long time to think about everything. "We walked back to the car, a few streets away, and I started to drive home. But the man must have been waiting for us to return. Maybe he'd spotted my car, knew it was mine from another time he'd followed me, I don't know. But I knew it was him behind us. That's why I didn't go straight home, I diverted up toward Moose Brook, to lose him. But he caught up to us."

Rachel seemed lighter, somehow, in the shoulders, now that her story was almost through, the horror almost done. Then maybe Dad could live his dream after all. But Bel wasn't sure it was going to happen anymore.

There was something she didn't understand here, between them. Something thick in the air. Maybe sixteen years was just too much time. Could you still love someone across that vast universe of time and space and mystery? Maybe it was too strange now, but they'd regrow into it. Slow and painful, not the blink of an eye. That was the difference between real life and dreams.

"That's where you've been?" Charlie asked, a dark cloud passing through his eyes. "For sixteen years?"

"In his basement," Rachel answered.

"Who is he?" Charlie tried again, clenching one fist. Focused on the *who*, now that he had the *how*. Who had done all this to Rachel? To him? Who deserved his anger? The man who took his wife and then gave her back.

Now Bel focused on the *who* too, because she hadn't thought it through before, not all the way: that same nameless man from Rachel's story was a real person, still out there now. Bel checked the window into the backyard. He'd been watching then, could he be watching now?

"I don't know his name, never found out. I could describe what he looks like, but he mostly kept me in the dark."

Charlie moved forward a half step, boots crunching the broken glass of the clock.

"And he let you go? Today? How? How did you get here?"

Rachel swayed, catching herself on the chair, holding on to it like a crutch. "He came down to the basement, unchained my ankle, put a bag over my head. A tote bag. Didn't say anything. Just led me upstairs, through a house I guess, into the back of a car."

"How long did you drive for?"

"I don't know, I lost count. Maybe a couple of hours."

"Did you see any landmarks, anything you recognized?"

"No." Rachel coughed into her closed fist. "There was a bag over my head."

"But your hands were free? You could have pulled it up?" Charlie stepped forward again, glass cracking.

"I didn't want to do anything that would make him kill me," Rachel countered. "He parked up somewhere, cut the engine. Pulled me out and left me there. It was Lancaster. I found the highway and walked all the way home. Annabel found me."

She'd left out the part about Bel running away from her, hiding. Retelling it kinder. Wait a second . . . Something else was different too. Something had changed between the story she'd told Bel and the one she just told Charlie. Before, Rachel said that the man had left the engine running when he pulled her out of the car, left her on that road, remember? But she'd just told Charlie that the man had turned the engine off first.

Yes, the car had definitely changed between versions, shifting through time, Bel was sure of it. She was old enough to remember things like that now.

A mistake?

Bel narrowed her eyes, studying the back of Rachel's head.

Only one version could be true. Rachel must have misspoken, either now or with Bel. Yes, it must have been a mistake, because the only other option was a lie, and why would Rachel lie about something like that, such a small detail in such a big story?

A mistake.

Yes, it was just a tiny mistake. But Bel's body didn't believe it, not all the way. Something felt wrong, something in the air, in the buzz in her ears. Could Dad feel it too? Was that why he was backed into the corner again, where the clock used to hang, fear in the lines of his face, even though he'd waited sixteen years for this moment?

Bel and her dad at the outer edges of the kitchen, Rachel in the middle, keeping their eyes on her. Like a thing with teeth that you shouldn't turn your back on.

It was just a mistake, right?

Or maybe Bel was the problem, she could have misheard?

But the thought ended there with a knock at the front door. Loud and hard. Not a knuckle, but a fist.

Charlie jumped hardest, his head thudding against the wall.

"Who's that?" he said, scrabbling along the wall to leave the kitchen, hurrying through the living room.

Rachel glanced back at her, clean grooves through her filthy face, more tears, though Bel hadn't seen them fall. Bel nodded, gesturing her ahead: Rachel should go first.

Rachel shuffled through the living room, her feet drier now, flaking off instead of bleeding.

Bel's eyes drew to the front windows, red-and-blue lights spinning through the glass with the afternoon sun. But . . . she never called 911.

The sound of the front door pulled open.

"Sorry to disturb you, Charlie," a voice boomed through the house, splintering the buzzy, dreamlike quiet that had taken over it. Real life had come knocking.

Bel followed Rachel into the hall, keeping just enough space between them.

Her dad blocked most of the door, but Bel could see the face of Dave Winter, Chief of Police, hovering in the space above his shoulder. Gray face and grayer hair to match, tucked beneath the shiny peaked cap of his uniform. So many times before had the two of them stood like this. The one who knocked and the one who answered.

"We've had a couple of weird calls in. One from your neighbor, Ms. Nelson. She says she saw Ra—"

Dave's dark eyes sorted through the background, flicking from Bel before falling to Rachel. Staying there.

His mouth went slack, moustache hanging over his teeth.

"Holy shit," he said.

He took off his cap, clutched it to the badge pinned over his heart.

"It's true."

TEN

A piece of paper on the table in front of her, a pen resting diagonally across. Bel's typed-up statement.

"If you've read it all through and you're happy you got everything, you can sign there on the bottom," Dave Winter said, across the interview room from her, his peaked cap on the table. He ran his hands through his thinning hair too much to wear it, a nervous habit. If he was nervous, how did he think Bel felt?

"Where is she now?" Bel's eyes trailed down the page, the story of Rachel Price's return as she'd witnessed it, moment by moment, hours and a whole lifetime ago.

"Your mom?" Dave said, sitting down again. "She's in with the feds now. Working out if she was kept out of state, whether this is a federal case or not. Attorney general's office will want to speak to her next."

Bel nodded.

"Sign when you're ready."

Should she bring it up now? The moment might be slipping away from her. But this man wasn't a friend, he was the one who went after her dad, took him away from her. Bel couldn't trust him, shouldn't. But they were all in a different world now, tremors and shakes. Rachel was back, alive, every detail in a changed light, alliances shifting, new sides drawn across the board. Maybe it had pushed her and the chief of police onto the same one, after hating him all these years.

Maybe she didn't need to mention it; maybe there was another way.

"She really walked all the way from Lancaster?" Bel asked, keeping her voice flat, like it didn't really matter. "That would take like eight hours, right?"

Dave whistled. "Long way to walk. She's a brave woman. I understand why she wouldn't want to get in anybody else's car after what she lived through."

"Is there proof?" Bel pushed a little harder.

"Proof of what?"

"That she walked all the way from Lancaster, like she said?"

Dave studied her. Bel blinked, putting up the walls behind her eyes.

"We haven't had a chance to check for footage yet, to verify. But a couple of police departments had calls in this morning, concerned about a dirty woman walking along the highway. So yeah. She really walked all that way to get home to you."

"Have you sent someone to the road where she was left?" Bel sat forward. "You must be able to find the one. Is there a tote bag there? The bag she had over her head? Rachel says she took it off. It should still be there." If it was, it meant that Rachel must be telling the truth, that the thing with the engine was just that: a mistake. Bel only needed proof, for her and the knot in her gut. "Did you find the tote bag?"

"Not yet," Dave said. "All the evidence will be processed, though, don't worry. Her clothes, the crime scene where she was dropped off—when we locate it—tire tracks. We'll get security footage, traffic cameras, anything we can get our hands on, to track the man who took her. Bring him to justice. We'll find him, that's my job. Don't you worry."

That wasn't what Bel was worried about. Not yet. She just wanted proof that Rachel was telling the truth, so it would stop nagging at her, feeding the knot.

Bel glanced down at her statement, ran her finger across the dried ink, coming away clean.

"There's something I should tell you," she said, studying the finger.

"What's that?"

"It's small, probably doesn't mean anything."

Dave's chair creaked as he shifted his weight.

"There was something," Bel continued, "a slight discrepancy I guess, in the story Rachel told me, and the one she told my dad. It's in my statement, I don't know if you noticed."

Dave Winter couldn't be relied on for his noticing; he'd never cared to notice that Charlie Price was innocent all along.

"What was it?" he asked, sharpening his tired, dried-out eyes.

"The engine," she said. "Rachel told me that the man left the engine running when he left her on that road. But she later told my dad that he'd turned the car off first. Just a small thing, really." She feigned a shrug. "Just a mistake, right?"

"Yes, of course." Dave shifted back, like it wasn't worth his notice. "Your mom has been through hell. Hell. The worst a person can live through. Think how exhausted she was, the heightened emotion of seeing her husband and her daughter again after all this time. Trying to give an explanation in that delirious state. That's not the time for giving accurate statements, of course she'd make mistakes, get something wrong. We have the full, complete story from her, now she's had time to rest and process, don't worry."

See? She could believe it, now someone else had said it. Just a mistake, it didn't mean anything more.

"I know this is a huge readjustment for you," Dave said, trying to be kind, thinking her silence meant something else. "None of us saw this coming. No one. It doesn't feel real yet. But soon this will feel like your new normal. Your family back together, a happy ending. And I know it must be scary, knowing that the man who took your mom, who did this to your family, is still out there. But we will catch him, I promise. He will come to justice."

Was that Dave's motto—*come to justice*? Did he use it in bed with his wife?

"A huge readjustment for you too," Bel said, about to bite, chewing the head off his kindness. "God, you must feel just terrible, knowing

90

you were so wrong about my dad. You thought he was a killer, tried to put him behind bars. But he didn't kill Rachel, because no one did. It's almost the worst part, wouldn't you agree?"

Dave sighed and his head fell, hanging between his shoulders. "I'm sorry, Annabel. Truly. A woman was missing, and I was only trying to do my job, to find the truth. I've already spoken to your dad today, after our interview, apologized for my part."

"Oh, you said sorry?" Bel said, a cheap, plastic smile, sharp enough to cut. "Well, that totally makes up for the sixteen years of hell. Thank you for your service, Officer." She bowed.

"Right, OK," he said, pulling his head back up. "Ready to sign?"

Bel picked up the pen. Pressed it to the bottom of the page in a looping scribble, signing her name away. Which was fine, because it was just a tiny mistake, she could stop thinking about it.

"So . . . what happens now?" she asked, handing the signed statement over. She hesitated as his fingers closed around it, the paper pulling taut before she gave it up and released her grip.

"Now I take you through to the tech team, who are going to do a cheek swab. With your permission, of course."

Bel stared at him, the question clear in her eyes.

"DNA test," he explained. "We've taken one from Rachel too. To prove who she is."

"She . . . might not be Rachel Price?" Bel said. And maybe that was it, the thing that felt wrong. Because if it was really her mom, wouldn't Bel feel—

"No, no, of course she is." Dave almost laughed, getting to his feet. "That woman is definitely your mom, there's no doubt. No doubt at all. This is just procedure, you know."

He headed toward the door.

As soon as his back was turned, Bel cradled her hands over the pen, swiping it up her sleeve and standing in one fluid movement.

"And then?" she asked.

Dave turned, his hand ready on the doorknob.

"Well, there will be lots going on with our investigative teams. Jurisdiction to figure out. And we'll need to start prepping for the press conference. Monday morning is looking most likely for that. Everything changes when the media gets hold of this, so we want to be on top of that."

"No, I mean what happens right now. Like tonight. Later."

Dave narrowed his eyes.

"Where does she go?" Bel asked. "Wh-where does Rachel go?"

"Your mom?" he said, eyes softening, a quiet smile in them, crinkling at the edges. "Annabel, she gets to come home with you."

"Oh."

ELEVEN

They stood around in the living room—Bel, Dad and Rachel—not knowing what to say to each other, what to do, how to be, the room fizzing with the absence of living.

Bel was very interested in her fingernails suddenly, picking at them.

Dad cracked first, saving them all.

"Um, do you want a shower?" he asked Rachel.

A question that didn't really need an answer. She was dressed in oversized gray sweats and slippers the police had given her, after taking her clothes into evidence. But she was filthy still, a stuffy smell clinging to the air around her, stale and sharp. Blood, sweat, piss and everything in between.

Only her hands were close to normal; must have washed them after the police finished taking their photos and swabs. The medical team had cleaned up her feet too, disinfecting the wounds and blisters, and the raw, rubbed skin of her ankle. She didn't need a hospital, they said, just needed rest—lots of it—and to rehydrate. Sent her off with a bottle of painkillers.

Rachel looked at him a long moment. "Yes," she said, her voice dark and gravelly, like it belonged to the night. "I really would like a shower."

"You know where it is," Charlie said, awkwardly, his bones locked the same way Bel's did, all angles and lines. "It's a new shower, actually. Redone years ago. Fresh towels in the linen closet."

Rachel nodded, but she didn't move.

Why wouldn't she go?

"There's nice shampoo up there," Bel said, pushing gently. "I make Dad buy the good stuff."

Rachel smiled at her. Her teeth were still good; she must have been able to brush them, wherever she was. Dad must have been thinking the same thing.

"There's new toothbrushes, under the sink," he added. "Help yourself."

"I will." She still hadn't moved. "Clothes? Or did you throw all of mine out? I guess you thought I was dead, so . . ."

Charlie scratched his head. "There might be a few things in the closet still. I'll have a look for you."

Rachel didn't say anything.

"I'll set up the spare bedroom for you while you shower," he continued. "Put any of your stuff I find in the dresser in there. Give you triple pillows; I know you used to like it that way."

Rachel shrugged. "Any pillows would be good." A roundabout way of accepting the arrangement. You were supposed to be sad about that, huh? Finding out your parents slept in separate bedrooms. But Bel didn't have space to feel anything about that, because there was that other thing, ticking over in her gut, like the engine that was either switched off or it wasn't. She needed to talk to Dad, alone.

"OK," Rachel said eventually, hands hidden up her too-long sleeves. "I'll be down soon."

"Take as much time as you need." Charlie dipped his head as Rachel walked past him, like he was avoiding her eyes.

They heard her gentle feet, pattering up the stairs, fading to nothing. The click of the bathroom door, the turn of the lock.

"I'll go fix up her room," Dad said, bones unlocking now, squeezing Bel's shoulder. "Sit down, kiddo. You've had a long day."

But Bel couldn't sit down, not for long, following her dad upstairs a few minutes later. Past the rainforest sounds of the bathroom, steam leaking out the gap under the door. The spatter of a body, moving under the water. And another sound beneath it: was Rachel humming in there? The tune, gentle and unhinged, made the hairs stand up along Bel's arms. She hurried past the door like something might reach under and catch her.

"Dad?" Bel whispered, finding him in the spare room, next to hers. He was fitting fresh white pillowcases over two new pillows. A pile of clothes folded at the end of the bed: one pair of light blue jeans, a couple of T-shirts and sweaters, one pair of striped pajamas. Bel didn't know he'd kept any of Rachel's clothes.

"Dad?" she hissed again, louder, over the noise of the shower.

"Huh? You OK, kiddo?"

No, not at all, what a stupid question. But maybe it was one you were supposed to ask, pretending things were normal when they never would be again.

"Are *you* OK?" she asked him.

He stared down at the bed, running his hands across the patterned comforter, flattening out the lines.

"I'm OK," he said, not confirming it with his eyes, keeping them to himself. "It's just . . . still in shock, is all. Doesn't feel real. Like I might wake up soon and this . . ."

Bel finished the thought for him: *this will all go away.* Rachel would go away.

"Will take some getting used to," he said, carrying the folded clothes, placing them in the top drawer of the empty dresser. "Do you have any underwear, Bel, that you could lend your mom?"

Bel's lip pulled up in a sneer, exposing her teeth.

"Sorry," he said.

"Dad." She hardened her voice, bringing his attention back to her. She didn't know how much time they had. Rachel was out of sight, out of earshot, but even down the hall felt too close. Back to a whisper. "Dad. Do you . . . do you think she's telling the truth?"

His eyes narrowed, flicking side to side, across Bel's face and beyond. "What do you mean?"

"About what happened to her? How she disappeared, reappeared."

His face rearranged, mouth moving around unspoken words. But then he did speak them: "Why would she lie about it?"

And that wasn't a stupid question.

"I don't know," she said.

"Look, Bel." He took hold of her shoulders, gentle but firm. "I think she's been through something horrible, something unbelievable, which makes it hard to believe." A muscle twitched in his cheek, the sad ghost of a smile. "But she has no reason to lie, Bel, and you have no reason not to believe her."

That one hurt. Bel stepped back to steady herself. She thought her dad might be with her on this. He was always with her. And if he said Rachel was telling the truth, then Bel had to believe it. So why was it so hard to make herself believe? That one discrepancy, tightening its hands around her throat, something to push against.

Dad moved to the nightstand, opening the drawer to check it was empty, swiping a layer of dust from the surface with his sleeve. He switched on the little yellow lamp, shaped like a metallic mushroom.

"You're not happy she's back, are you?" Bel could tell. She could tell instantly the moment he'd walked in the kitchen and saw Rachel there, recognized her.

"I am happy she's back," he said, no, he insisted. "I'm happy she's alive, of course I am. She's my wife, the woman I loved most in the world. It's just, it doesn't feel the way you think it will, after all that time. We're in shock, all of us. Things will be strange for a while, kiddo, and I'm sorry about that. But that doesn't mean I'm unhappy. OK?" He knocked his finger under her chin as he passed. "Got my two girls. My family." He glanced at his watch. "It's nine. I know it's late, but I should make dinner, shouldn't I? None of us have eaten properly." He gestured with his head down the hall, toward the steaming bathroom. "What do you think she'd want to eat?"

"I don't know, I don't know her," she said, still stinging. Was it possible Bel was the one who'd made a mistake, not Rachel? Maybe she hadn't been listening properly. She could be forgetful like that. Dad said things would be strange for a while, and that meant Bel too. She definitely felt strange.

"Pizza," Dad said, nodding, agreeing with himself. "I'll order pizza. If there was ever an excuse for takeout . . ."

He left it there, and he left Bel there too, walking out into the hallway, just as the shower screeched off.

They sat in the living room. Dad took the armchair early—it was his spot—so Bel and Rachel were on the sofa, at opposite ends, Bel's legs straight out in front. Hyperaware every time she felt movement in the cushions, a shift in the corner of her eye.

It was even stranger, now Rachel was clean, looking closer to her old self. To the Rachel Price of the family videos and missing posters and news bulletins. The face of the unsolvable mystery, now solved, the forty-three-year-old version of that twenty-seven-year-old missing woman. She was wearing her old navy-striped pajamas. Cheeks still flushed from her hot shower, skin white and clean, grooves of pink where she'd scrubbed too hard. Feet bare: cracked and blistered, tucked up on the sofa. Hair wet, brushed back from her face so her birthmark showed. Now she smelled like coconut and aloe vera, and that was stranger still, because those usually belonged to Bel.

Rachel leaned forward for another slice of pizza from the box, dropping it onto her plate. She didn't eat it right away, the flickering images of the television playing across the glass of her eyes.

She caught Bel looking. A smile stretched across her face, new lines you couldn't see before, the smile duplicating through the skin of her cheeks. Chin pointed just the way Bel's did, stolen from her. She looked happy to be home. Bel tried to smile back.

"I borrowed your hairbrush, Anna," Rachel said. "Sorry, Annabel, Bel. Hope you don't mind."

Bel did mind. More about the name, though.

"That's OK," she said, forcing herself to eat another slice so she didn't have to talk.

"Wow." Rachel stared at the TV. "Look at those graphics. Almost looks like a real dragon. Well, you know."

But no one did know, and no one spoke until Charlie cleared his throat.

"Did you have a TV, in the basement?" he asked, watching the dragon, not her.

Rachel shook her head, making him look at her anyway. "No TV." She took a bite, kept speaking with her mouth full. "No books. He gave me paper and pens. I would draw. Got pretty good at it. Something to keep me busy. And I used to write stories. Lots of them. About you, actually." Rachel looked at Bel. "Both of you. What you were up to. Imagining new chapters in your lives. Imagining our lives if I'd never been taken. I'd write them out and save them to read back to myself, months or years later. I'm no Jane Austen." She laughed a small, controlled laugh. Who could laugh about that, talking about their prison cell? "But it gave me something to do. Kept me sane."

No one said anything for a while, and the silence was too much, itchy as it climbed up Bel's back.

"There's one more slice of pizza," she said to the room, shaking the box.

"No thanks, Rachel," Charlie said without looking. "You help yourself."

Bel's jaw locked. "Dad, that was me," she said quietly.

"Oh, sorry, Bel." He flushed. "No, you have it, I'm full."

Rachel didn't react, but she must have been thinking something, hiding it from her face.

On the television, the dragon was gone. Now there was a man who was supposed to be a prince, pushing a woman up against a dank dungeon wall. Lifting her dress. She begged him not to.

Charlie grabbed the remote, flicking to a different channel. "Something lighter," he said under his breath, stopping on a cartoon where they swore more than Bel.

Rachel was watching him too, something new in her expression, only half readable.

"He didn't touch me," she said to the room as well. "Never like that. Police asked that too. Just used to sit on the stairs and watch me sometimes. Only came close to bring food, and paper. I think he liked keeping me, is all."

"OK," Charlie said, after a moment, because what were you supposed to say to something like that?

"So you can put your dragons back on, if you want," she said. "I'm OK."

"I think it's time for bed, anyway." Charlie switched the TV off, standing with an awkward stretch. "Would be good to get a nice, long sleep. We've all had . . . a day. Bel, can you take the plates to the kitchen?"

Rachel chewed her cheek.

Bel reached over to take the plate in front of her, stacking it with her own, and then Dad's. She carried them into the kitchen, loaded them into the dishwasher, not focusing on what her hands were doing, ears pricked and listening.

By the time she got back to the living room, Charlie was explaining where they now kept the glasses in the kitchen. Bel didn't know they'd ever lived anywhere else. "The cupboard above the microwave. Seemed a better place for them. If you want to take water up to bed or something."

Rachel was standing now too.

"Do you have everything you need?" Charlie asked her. "For bed?"

"Yes, I have everything I need," she said. But the way she'd said it sounded almost like a threat.

"Good." Charlie smiled one small, desperate smile, fighting to keep it on his face. "Well, good night, I guess. S-see you in the morning."

"Yes," she said, rubbing her eyes with a navy-striped sleeve. "Good night. Good night, Annabel."

"Night," Bel said, almost cracking at the strangeness of it all, of playing families. Of how un-normal all these normal things felt.

Bel couldn't sleep. A runner's heart in her chest, beating in her ears. Wondering if the air coming in through the cracks in the door was the same air Rachel Price had already breathed.

It had been three a.m., last time she'd checked her phone. The light was off now, but that didn't help, sleep dancing around in front of her, always one step out of reach. She had to sleep, had to. Because maybe she'd wake up and find out none of this was real after all. That she'd just fallen on the train tracks and cracked her head, inventing everything from that point on. Rachel Price would disappear again, like she was supposed to.

But wishing wouldn't make it true. Rachel was really here, and she was real, but that didn't mean her story was. Dave Winter said it was a mistake. And Dad believed Rachel, or he said he did. But maybe he was doing that for Bel's sake. He always put her first. Maybe he thought she needed a mom.

She didn't. She didn't need anyone.

Bel was about to check the time again, but as she reached out, she heard a click in the dark. The shush of her door, pushing open against the thick carpet. Bel lowered her arm and held her breath. There was a dark figure in the doorway, silvery outline picked out by the moonlight.

Not Dad.

It was Rachel.

Bel forced her eyes shut, pretending to be asleep. Heart faster now, panicked couplets beating a word that sounded like *dan-ger, dan-ger, dan-ger.* Gut knotting up beneath the blankets.

Bel heard Rachel take one step inside the room. The gentle windstorm of her breath, in and out of her nose.

Rachel was watching her sleep.

Except she wasn't asleep.

Go away, Bel thought, squeezing her eyes tighter. *Please go away.* Fighting the battle with her mind. Pushing Rachel away.

It must have worked. A few moments later, the door shushed again, clicked shut.

Bel opened one eye to check, searching for a specter in the dark. But Rachel was gone.

TWELVE

Morning came, eventually, a yellow promise pawing at the sky and her window. Bel hid in her room. Her fortress, badly defended, surrounded on all sides by the possibility of Rachel Price. She could be anywhere, a figure in the shape of her mother, creeping around, laying claim to the house, even though Bel had lived in it longer.

Bel waited, ear to the door, listening. She heard the pad of footsteps downstairs, a clatter in the kitchen, but she couldn't tell whether it was Dad or Rachel. It sounded like one person, no voices.

The front door slammed, and Bel jumped. New footsteps, heavier, and the swish of plastic bags. That must have been Dad, but where had he been? Did that mean he'd left Bel all alone in the house with Rachel? Thank God she hadn't left her room.

Now there were voices, muffled and low.

Bel straightened up, stomach rumbling.

It was safe, now Dad was down there too. Well, safer.

She opened the door and went downstairs.

Charlie was half inside the refrigerator, unloading a grocery bag.

Rachel was by the counter, and she caught Bel first, like she'd been waiting to do just that, eyes trained on the doorway.

"Oh, good morning," she said, a smile on her face as bright as the sun. "I was about to bring you this. I made you a coffee, Anna." She stepped forward, brandishing a mug. "Sorry. Bel. Can't get used to that."

Bel didn't move to take it.

"D-do you like coffee?" Rachel hesitated too, losing the smile. "Sorry. I don't know the things you like. Yet. I want to learn. Everything."

Dad looked over, a nudge with his eyes. Things were supposed to feel strange, remember?

Bel shuffled one foot forward, offering Rachel an inch. "I like coffee," she said.

The smile reappeared. "With milk, right?" She handed it over, their fingers colliding again, a cold afterglow where Rachel's skin had touched hers. At least the sharp, overgrown nails were gone. Bel looked down at the coffee. "Is it too much milk? Not enough? I want to learn," Rachel said again, not stepping back like she should, taking up too much space.

"It looks perfect." Bel took a tiny sip, using it as an excuse to move away, into a seat at the kitchen table.

Rachel beamed down at her. "Do you want anything else? Orange juice? You like juice?"

"I'm fine," Bel said, the words echoing inside the mug.

"Gonna do eggs and bacon for breakfast," Charlie said, coming back out of the refrigerator, crushing the empty plastic bag in one hand.

So that was where he'd been; out getting groceries. Not just leaving to leave Bel here.

He clattered away with pans and pots, busying himself at the stove. Removing two plates from the drawer, forgetting, and going back for a third, laying them out on the counter. Rachel took the chair one away from Bel, nursing her own coffee. In the Santa mug; Dad's favorite.

"Bel," Charlie said, breaking the eggs into a jug. "You cracked a plate last night, when you loaded the dishwasher."

Did she? She didn't remember, but she'd had no awareness of her hands at the time, all attention diverted into her ears, listening out for her parents in the other room. One must have slipped.

"Sorry. I didn't realize."

"No problem, kiddo. Just letting you know." He smiled at her, laying the bacon out on the pan in regimented lines.

"So, Anna-bel," Rachel said loudly, catching herself just in time, cracking Bel's name into self-conscious halves. "You must be in senior year, not long to go. Are you at Gorham High? How's your GPA? Did you apply to college?"

Her eyes seared into Bel's.

Bel blinked them away, looking down at her coffee. "Yes, I'm at Gorham High. GPA is fine." Because fine was easier to say than *distinctly average*, as Principal Wheeler had put it. "I'm starting the liberal arts program at White Mountains Community College in the fall." A good choice, so she could stay at home with Dad, an unspoken promise between them, to never leave the other behind. Except now there would be a stranger in her home too.

"Great," Rachel said, smile hidden behind Santa's on the mug. "Do you know what you want to do yet? I didn't know when I was your age, and I always hated being asked. Sorry."

Was there still a question in there?

"I don't know," Bel answered. Clinging to those safe, dependable words.

"That's fine, you have all the time in the world to figure it out. What about hobbies? Sports—you play any?"

"Not really."

Rachel blinked, a strain in her smile. "So what do you like to do for fun?"

Bel shrugged. "Just, kind of, stay home, I guess."

"Friends over?"

Why was Rachel asking her so many goddamn questions? She hadn't asked Charlie even one. Interrogating Bel, pushing her into corners. And when Bel got pushed into a corner, she normally came out fighting. She bit it down this time, really trying, because she wasn't ready for war; she didn't know yet, whether she and Rachel belonged on the same side.

"Carter comes over a lot," she said.

103

Rachel nodded, a grateful flash in her eyes. "A-and who's Carter?"

Bel forgot: there was no overlap. Carter knew of Rachel, but not the other way around.

"She's my cousin," said Bel. "Jeff and Sherry's daughter. Born a few months after you left."

Her eyes widened. Maybe they'd both picked up on the word Bel had used there. *Left.*

Rachel pressed a hand to her chest, the one with her rings: wedding and engagement. She'd kept them on all this time too. "That's nice. I'm so happy for them; they always wanted a baby."

"Not a baby anymore," said Bel. "She's almost sixteen."

"Do they still live in number nineteen?" Rachel asked. "Jeff and Sherry."

"Yes," Charlie answered this time.

"What about Pat, Charlie?" Rachel said suddenly, narrowing her eyes. "Is he still . . . ?"

"He's alive, yeah," Charlie sniffed, stirring the eggs. "Went to see him this morning, actually. He had a couple of strokes, the first one last summer. Has vascular dementia now, doesn't remember a lot. Not doing so great. We have a full-time caregiver with him."

"Oh, I'm sorry." Rachel put her mug down with a thunk, a splash of coffee over the rim, Santa crying dark brown tears. "That must be tough. What about my parents? Oh, I should call them." She rose up from her chair, almost like she meant to do it right now.

"Rachel," Charlie said in a small voice. He didn't turn back to say it. "Your dad passed away four years ago. It was cancer. I'm sorry too."

She dropped back into her chair, smile peeling away, retreating muscle by muscle.

"I'm sorry," Charlie said again, even though Grandaddy dying wasn't his fault.

Rachel went to *wash her hands for breakfast.* She didn't come back for six minutes, eyes rubbed red when she did. The eggs and bacon and toast were ready and waiting.

"Dave Winter called," Charlie said, snapping a piece of bacon in half. "Chief of police," he explained, reading the confusion on Rachel's face. Maybe she wasn't unreadable to him. "They'll be around this afternoon sometime, to go over details for the press conference tomorrow morning. And see how you're doing, of course. They want to get you booked in with the psychiatrist."

Rachel nodded absently.

Another mouthful before she asked: "Do you know him well, the police chief?"

"We've had our dealings," Charlie replied, a cough to help the bacon go down. "He's the one who arrested me for your murder, Rachel." His eyes were shy, dropping to his plate.

"Right," she said, just as shy, spooling her fork through the pile of fluffy eggs. There would be more questions on that later, Bel thought, once Rachel worked up the courage. There were land mines everywhere here, open your mouth and they blew up. Dead dads and wrongful arrests, and nieces she never knew about.

Charlie's phone rang then, a welcome break in the tension, buzzing angrily against the table. He looked at the screen and ended the call, his face giving nothing away.

Bel's went off too, vibrating in her lap. She glanced down at the name on-screen—*Ramsey Lee*—and let it ring out.

"You should call them," Rachel said, eyes tripping over the sharp lines of the rectangular device in front of Charlie, like this was her first time seeing a smartphone, understanding what it did. "Your brother and Sherry. Invite them over. I'd like to see them, meet their daughter. They should know before the world does, at the press conference tomorrow. You should call Jeff."

"OK."

Rachel couldn't have meant right this second, he hadn't even finished his breakfast, but Charlie picked up his phone and wandered out of the kitchen, disappearing upstairs, like he'd been waiting for any excuse to escape. Like it was unbearable to sit here, being a family of three. Bel got up to clear the table, so she could escape too, clinging to the low hum of Dad's voice through the ceiling.

* * *

A knock on the door. An uneasy knock, at once too serious and too silly, five taps clumped together in a tune. That would be Uncle Jeff, bad at reading rooms, even when he wasn't in them.

Dad had just told him on the phone, repeated it until Jeff believed it. So they knew what to expect, the three of them. But you wouldn't have known it by their faces, when Bel pulled open the door, Rachel standing behind her, still in those striped pajamas.

"Oh my God!" Sherry gasped, somewhere between a whisper and a shriek, flickering between the two. "Oh my God!" More a shriek now, as she barged past Bel, folding Rachel into a tight hug. Rachel returned it, just as tight. "Oh my God!" Sherry held Rachel back to look at her, running her fingers through her short-hacked hair. There was a matching smile on Rachel's face, eyes looming and wet. "Rachel, honey. I can't believe you're alive," Sherry cried. "We all thought you were gone forever. I can't believe you're really here, sweetie. This can't be real."

Sherry squeezed Rachel again, breaking into sobs that shook both of them, locked in an earthquake together.

"We missed you so much," Sherry continued. "God, it's a miracle!"

"Move over, Sher," Jeff said, stepping into the house. "Let me look at her."

Rachel sidestepped back into view, tears falling into her open smile. "Hello, Jeff," she croaked, but her eyes strayed behind him, to Carter, who was now shoulder to shoulder with Bel.

Carter squeezed Bel's hand and Bel squeezed hers back. They didn't always need to speak, that said enough, a language of their own.

"Come here," Jeff said, arms open pincer-wide, catching Rachel. "I can't believe you're really back. It's been such a long time. We always hoped, but I never thought . . ." He pulled away. "So good to have you back, Rach."

"Good to be back," she said, gaze flicking to the front door, to Bel and Carter standing here against the sun.

Jeff followed her eyes. "Oh, Rachel, this is our daughter, Car—"

"Carter," Rachel completed it for him, a nod of her head, almost a bow. "Bel already told me about you."

"Hi, Aunt Rachel." Carter stepped forward, waving one awkward hand. "It's nice to meet you."

Rachel moved too, meeting her halfway. They leaned into a hug, arms slotting in. "It's good to meet you too, sweetie," Rachel said, eyes glittering as she pulled away.

Sweetie. She hadn't called Bel that yet, couldn't even get her name right. Come to think of it, Rachel hadn't tried to hug Bel either. Or Charlie, for that matter, her own husband. The people she should love most. But Sherry and Jeff and Carter walked through the door and they got hugs and smiles and *sweeties*.

"Very good to meet you," Rachel said, another smile for Carter, another stab in Bel's gut. It wasn't jealousy, don't be stupid. It was something else, a side effect of the wrongness of it all, of Rachel, and everything she said and did. Something wasn't right, whatever Dad wanted to believe.

"When's your birthday, Carter?"

"July tenth," Carter answered, still too close to Rachel. Something in Bel wanted to pull her cousin away, protect her from Rachel's gaze.

Rachel nodded. "So you must have been pregnant, Sherry, when I was taken?"

"I was. Not yet showing."

"I'm sure we all have lots to catch up on, sixteen years' worth. Can't do it all here in the hallway," Rachel said, the tears gone but a near-unnoticeable shake in her bottom lip, threatening to bring them back. Maybe she was just realizing; people had had entire lives in the time she was gone. "Please, let's sit down."

Jeff and Sherry walked into the living room, greeting Charlie with more *Oh my gods* and *I can't believe its*. Rachel glanced at Bel, a look in her eyes that was still unreadable. Then she gestured Carter ahead with a kind "After you," following behind her.

No one mind Bel, then. She shut the front door, harder than she had to.

Dad put on another pot of coffee. And Sherry had brought cupcakes; they were just sitting around the house, she thought she might as well bring them. Didn't feel right, though, happy blue-and-yellow frosting with sprinkles, turned this all into a celebration somehow. Bel was full from breakfast: none for her, thanks.

No one asked anything about Rachel's missing time, speaking around those sixteen years in wide, awkward circles. Dad must have asked them not to. Rachel seemed happy with that, focusing on every-one else. She must have been sick of the story of her disappearance and reappearance too, the number of times she'd had to repeat it in the last twenty-four hours: to Bel, Charlie, the Gorham Police Depart-ment, State Police, feds, attorney general's office. Must have been ex-hausting, especially trying to remember all those little details. She'd already messed it up once. Bel needed to stop thinking about it, maybe she should have a cake.

"So, Carter, tell me about yourself," Rachel said, studying her niece, wedged on the sofa between her parents. "What subjects do you like at school? What do you do for fun?"

This question again. Had Rachel forgotten what *fun* meant; was that what sixteen years being disappeared did to you?

"I like English lit most." Carter fiddled with her sleeve.

"Really?" Rachel beamed. "Do you go to Gorham High with Bel? I used to teach English lit there."

Carter nodded politely. She already knew that; she had to walk past The Rachel Shrine every day too. Rachel must not know yet, that she was this town's most popular mystery.

"What's your favorite book?" Rachel asked her.

She hadn't asked Bel that yet. Bel liked to read too.

"Um, I like—"

"Carter's actually a dancer, Rachel," Sherry cut in, a dramatic sip of her coffee. "A ballerina. She has the potential to go all the way."

"Wow, really?" Rachel said, eyes lighting up. "That's amazing. I'd love to see you dance sometime."

Carter swallowed her mouthful of cake. "There's a show, at my dance school, in a few weeks," she said. Was that an invite? Carter never asked Bel to come and watch her.

"That must be quite a commitment, on top of your schoolwork," Rachel said. "Do you enjoy all the dancing, Carter?"

"She loves it," Sherry spoke for her, a proud squeeze of Carter's bony knee. "Lives for it."

Carter nodded, agreeing. She'd told Bel sometimes it was easier to let her mom speak for her; Sherry loved to speak, and Carter didn't always. They worked well together like that, how a mother and daughter should.

"So, Rachel," Sherry turned attention back to her. "Charlie said there's going to be a press conference tomorrow morning. Are you ready for the world to know you're back? It's going to be a media shitstorm, pardon my French."

Rachel looked unsure what to say.

Charlie spoke instead; he'd been quiet for a while, hovering close to Bel's chair. "We've dealt with media shitstorms in the past, we can do it again. As a family."

"Happier news this time," Jeff added. "Finally a chance to clear your name for good, Charlie. No one can think you killed your wife now."

"I don't have anything to wear," Rachel said in a small voice, a flash of shame as she looked down at her pajamas, everyone else dressed for the day.

"Honey," Sherry said, sticking her bottom lip out in sympathy, a flap of her hand. "Don't you worry about that; I can lend you something. Or maybe Bel has something you can borrow." Sherry nudged Bel with her eyes. "You two are the same size. Bel, you must have something your mom can wear. A black dress, something nice?"

Everyone waited for her answer.

"Um, yeah," Bel said. "I'll find something."

"Thanks, Anna," Rachel said, a small smile to match her small voice.

It was Bel, for fuck's sake. She hoped someone else in the room would correct Rachel for her, but a knock at the door saved them.

Charlie stiffened. "Did you order anything, Bel?"

She shook her head and followed him out of the room, to get away from Rachel's eyes, too much like her own.

109

Charlie pulled the door open with an intake of breath.

Ramsey was standing on the doorstep. James next to him, a camera perched on his shoulder. Saba and Ash arranged behind on the steps, a yellow backward cap over Ash's curly hair, the boom microphone hanging above them all.

"Sorry to come by unannounced," Ramsey said, a grating sound as he ran his hand over his stubble. "Been trying to call you, both of you, since you left set yesterday, Bel." He looked sorry about that, like he'd worked out why that happened, solved a mini-mystery in the shadow of the main one. He didn't know that was solved now too. Although Bel bet he was going to find out in *three* . . . "We've rescheduled the reenactment, but that's not why we're here." . . . *two* . . . "Listen, don't really know how to say this, but there's a weird rumor going round. Kosa—who owns the hotel—says she heard from someone that Rachel has re—"

. . . one . . .

The life drained from Ramsey's face all at once, teeth gritted in the shape of his broken word. Eyes wide. Horror or awe or both.

There she was, hanging in the hallway behind, like she'd been summoned by the mention of her name. Hadn't worked for sixteen years, but it worked every time now.

". . . appeared," Ramsey whispered the rest.

Ash rose up on his tiptoes behind, eyes searching for what Ramsey had seen, starting with Bel, trailing to the woman behind.

Fuck, he mouthed silently, leaving his lips open around it.

"Hello," Rachel said, narrowing her eyes, surprised to see a British film crew standing at her front door, staring in shock.

"R-Rachel?" Ramsey staggered. "Rachel Price?"

Rachel stepped forward, glancing at Bel, then Charlie, like she was checking with them first. Neither of them said anything to stop her.

"That's me." She dipped her head. "Who are you?"

"Jesus Christ." He whistled. "No, that's not my name. I'm Ramsey Lee, filmmaker." He offered his hand for her to shake, a visible shiver passing through him when she did. Was he scared, or was this the best thing to ever happen to him? He probably wouldn't struggle to find a broadcaster for his documentary now.

"Sorry, this is very surreal." Ramsey sniffed. "We've been making a documentary about you. I can't believe you're alive. After all this time."

"It was a surprise for all of us," Charlie said.

Well, not Rachel. She knew she was alive.

"Sorry, didn't get a chance to tell you about this yet," Charlie said to Rachel, gesturing at the crew.

"God, it's so strange, meeting you," Ramsey continued. "I've done so much research about you the last few months, it almost feels like we've already met."

"Whoa, hey, wait," Charlie said suddenly, a trace of rare anger in his voice that made everyone stand back, Rachel and Bel too. "Are you rolling?" He eyeballed the camera on James's shoulder.

Ramsey slinked back over the threshold, Prices inside, crew out, redrawing the lines between them. "Well, yes," he said, not meeting Charlie's eye. "I wanted to see your reaction to this crazy rumor. I never in a million years thought that Rachel would actually—"

"Stop recording." Charlie put his hands up to block the camera's view. "She hasn't even had her first full day back yet. We are still processing. The investigation is ongoing. The police won't want us talking to you until they've worked out what information they want released publicly." Charlie ushered them all back, stepping down the stairs in their same formation, not breaking ranks. Ash was on the path, looking at Bel, like he was trying to catch her attention. She gave it to him for one second.

You OK? he mouthed.

Bel took her attention back.

"There's a press conference tomorrow morning in Town Hall," Charlie said, shooing them farther. "After that, I will talk to the police and see where that leaves us with the doc."

"OK," Ramsey said, bowing his head quickly, one finger raised, "but I—"

"What's it called?" Rachel cut in, hovering in the doorway, eyes screwed against the sun. "The documentary?"

Ramsey swallowed, staring up at her. "*The Disappearance of Rachel Price*. Except, I guess we'll have to change the name now."

"To what?"

THIRTEEN

The world knew before midday on Monday.

Rachel Price, reappeared, a tabletop microphone pointed at her face, wearing Bel's long black knitted dress. Sitting between Charlie and Bel, Police Chief Dave Winter on one side of the wide table, someone from the FBI on the other.

It was playing again on the news now, the third time this channel had run it already. Bel watching herself on TV, betrayed by her own face, by how much the camera made her look like Rachel, sitting side by side.

"The suspect remains at large," Dave said again, with a vague description of him that Rachel had provided, a composite sketch on-screen. It could have been anyone. "Please call the following number if you have any information that could assist in our inquiries."

Charlie and Bel never spoke, even though they'd been given microphones. They were just props, the picture of a reunited family. Happy, but not too much, Dave had told them. It wasn't a true happy ending until the man was caught.

They passed to Rachel for one small comment at the end.

"I'm so grateful to be safe and back home with my daughter and husband. I would appreciate if everyone respected our privacy at this time as we readjust to normal life."

Normal was a strange choice of word; life *had* been normal, before she came back. She was the one who'd taken that away.

They weren't taking questions at this time, thank you and goodbye. Sidling out of the room while the journalists murmured hungrily and the cameras flashed, throwing lightning in their eyes.

"Here." Rachel loomed over her now, surprising her, handing over a plate with a sandwich. Bel was careful as she took it, making sure not to touch Rachel's hand. "Cheese, ham and pickle, cut into triangles." Rachel sat on the sofa beside her, dressed in the old jeans and T-shirt Dad had found for her, both too big. "You said that was your favorite, didn't you, Anna?"

She had, yesterday. But she hadn't realized it would be used against her like this. Did Rachel think this was how she became Bel's mom again? Trying to be too normal too soon—it didn't feel right. More than that; it felt wrong.

"Thanks." Bel looked down at the sandwich, still not very hungry. Taking a bite felt like defeat somehow, but she had to; Rachel was right here, watching her, waiting.

Bel bit off a corner, chewed. "Good, thank you," she said.

Rachel gave her a winning smile.

Charlie walked into the living room then, eyes catching on Bel's plate. Rachel hadn't made him a sandwich. He had his work jacket on, keys to his truck dangling from a finger. Oh no.

"Are you leaving?" Bel asked him. She always said that, whenever he picked up his keys, it was one of their routines, their rituals. But it mattered more now.

"Gotta get back to work, kiddo. Told Gabe I would."

He couldn't take the rest of the day off? Bel wasn't going into school; there was no point now. And she knew it would be awful; everyone staring at her now the news was out.

"Do you have to?" Bel asked, panic seizing the knot in her gut, giving him a chance to change his mind, to stay with her.

"I'll be back for dinner."

Bel looked at her phone. It was two o'clock, at least five hours between now and dinner. Was he really going to leave her here, alone with Rachel?

"Dad?"

Maybe Bel could insist she had to walk into school for the last hour of the day. What would be worse: the stares, or staying here?

A car door slammed outside the house, close enough to prick at Bel's attention. Charlie's too, wandering over to the front window, moving the lace curtain to peer through.

"Great," he muttered, dropping the curtain, looming behind it.

"What?" Rachel asked him, before Bel could.

"A Fox news van just pulled up," he said. "CNN is already here. And so it begins." He wiped his nose on his sleeve. "Keep the curtains shut. Don't let them get anything."

Bel nodded. Rachel didn't.

"Shouldn't I take them something?" she said. "Coffee? They have to stand out there all day."

"Best not to engage," Charlie said, not meeting her eyes. "We've been through all this before, Rachel."

"I didn't say you hadn't," she countered.

Bel swallowed. Toeing the edge of another land mine, all of them. Dad couldn't really leave her here, could he?

"Oh, Charlie," Rachel said, stopping him in his tracks. Her voice wasn't as raspy and rough anymore, closer to normal. Which was worse somehow, because she'd stolen that from Bel too. "Could you leave your credit card?"

He stared at her, hands hidden in his pockets.

"I've been back for two days now," she said in explanation, rearing up from the sofa, a hard step forward on shaky ground. "There's things I need. A phone. Clothes, so I can stop stealing Annabel's. Until I can access my own money again, if it's still there."

"Right." Charlie swallowed. "OK, sure." He dug around in his jeans pocket for his wallet.

"Here." He came over, placed the credit card down on the coffee table with a snap. Retreated again, backtracking through the minefield.

He glanced at the two of them, zipping up his jacket.

"We'll be fine, won't we?" Rachel said, a smile for Bel that was too sweet, too forced, making the knot pull tighter. "It'll be nice to spend some time, just the two of us. We could watch a movie. Make dinner together. Play a board game. Anything you want to do, Annabel. It's your choice."

What Bel wanted to do was keep Dad here, stop him from leaving. Or barricade herself in her room, away from Rachel. That was what she chose.

"Dad?"

She followed him into the hall, watched him approach the front door, reach for the handle.

"Dad, wait."

Bel wanted to cry. She never cried, but she would now, just to stop him from going.

"Do we still have Monopoly?" Rachel asked, behind her.

Dad pulled the door open. "See you later," he said, not looking back, even with Bel's eyes burning in the back of his head. Trying to hold him there.

"What about chess?" Rachel said, oblivious to the storm inside Bel.

The front door clicked shut, taking Dad away, resealing the house behind him.

Bel still standing here, left alone with Rachel.

An eruption of voices outside, muffled through the glass.

"Charlie! How does it feel to have your wife back home?"

"How's Rachel doing? How's the family coping with her sudden return?"

"How does it feel to finally be free of suspicion in your wife's murder? That's a pretty good feeling, right?"

"Can you comment on the—"

A slam. The rumble of his truck engine, drowning the voices out.

"Charlie! Charlie Price!" His own name chased after him as he backed out and drove away.

A strange silence in his wake, foaming at the edges as Bel went back to the living room, avoiding Rachel's gaze, watching the TV as the newscasters introduced another replay of the press conference, a *Breaking News* banner declaring: *Rachel Price found alive after 16 years presumed dead.*

Bel swallowed: she'd been one of those *presumers.*

Rachel turned the TV off without asking, reaching for the coffee table. She slid Dad's credit card off the edge and held it up.

"Hey," she said, turning a smile toward Bel. "If you don't feel like a board game, how about a shopping trip?"

Bel stared across at her. "Huh?"

"Me, you. Go to the mall together." Rachel waved the card, almost fanning herself with it. "That's what moms do with their daughters, right? Shopping? Fashion shows in the living room when you get home. It's one of the big things we missed out on, I think. I'd really like it if we could try. We can get you some things too, of course. Do you need a new jacket?" She pocketed the card, waiting for Bel's response.

Bel hesitated, backing up into the arm of the sofa, trying to think of reasons not to.

"Are you allowed?" she said. "The news only just broke, the police investigation ongoing, the man still out there. Are you allowed to go outside?"

Rachel didn't like the question; Bel could tell by the shift in her eyes. Maybe she wasn't *that* unreadable.

"I was locked inside for fifteen years, Anna," she said, voice gentle, a sad crackle to it. "I don't have to stay inside ever again for any reason. Come on, we'll have fun, I promise."

A sinking in Bel's gut. It took Bel a second to catch up with it, to see past the wrong name, picking up on the other wrong thing.

"Sixteen years," she said, pointing it out for both of them.

Rachel paused, her expression drawn. "That's what I said, isn't it?"

"You said fifteen."

Rachel narrowed her eyes for one more second, then shook her head, her face blank and well guarded. "Did I? Sorry. I meant to say sixteen. Obviously."

Obviously she meant to say that, but she hadn't. Another innocent mistake, like the engine thing. But didn't two mistakes make some kind of pattern? A slip of the tongue or a slipup of the truth? There must be an explanation: like Rachel had lost count of the years in the basement, just as she said. Because the only other explanation was that Rachel was lying for some reason, that she'd never been locked inside for any number of years, and it couldn't be that, right? Just another error; the second time Bel had caught her in as many days. Why was no one else ever around to hear them too?

"What do you say?" Rachel said, studying Bel as hard as Bel was studying her.

"I don't know," she said, speaking carefully. "It's Dad's money. Things are a bit tight at the moment, not sure we should go out and spend it."

A smile pressed into Rachel's cheeks, blank somehow, reinforcing the look in her eyes. "Annabel, sweetie, you don't need to worry about that. Essentials only," she said with a wink. "Besides, he must be getting paid for this documentary about me that he signed up for."

Rachel wasn't wrong there, but that money was for Grandpa.

Bel was running out of excuses, Rachel batting them away one by one.

"We don't have a car." She tried again.

"That's OK. We can get the bus to Berlin. Or a taxi."

That was her last one. Checkmate, Rachel wins. Guess she and Rachel were going shopping then, unless Bel could break her leg in the next few minutes, or Rachel's. They'd be in public, surrounded by other people, but she would still be alone with Rachel.

Wait, that gave Bel another idea.

"I know," she said, backed into a corner, coming out swinging. "We should ask the documentary crew to come along."

Rachel took a step back.

"R-really?" she said. "Is that what you want?"

"Sure." Bel brushed off her knees. "They'd love to get footage of you at the White Mountains Mall, the first place you disappeared, well, *we* disappeared. That's the kind of thing they get excited about. Artsy, you know." Now it was her turn to wink, just as forced as

Rachel's. "Maybe it'll be nice to have a record of our first shopping trip together, mark the occasion. You can't always rely on memory to keep things like that." She smiled, showing teeth.

"Oh, r-right," Rachel stuttered. "If that's what you want. I just thought we could have the day to ours—"

"Cool, I'll call Ramsey." Bel dug out her phone. "He'll be thrilled about this, might even squeal."

She pressed his name to dial, walking away from Rachel, into the kitchen.

Ramsey picked up on the third ring. "Bel?"

"Hi, Ramsey," she said, brightly.

"What's up?"

"Nothing, just wanted to chat."

"Bel?" he said, seeing through her, saying her name sideways.

"I have an idea," she said, loudly, making her voice carry. "Me and Rachel are going shopping to the White Mountains Mall, for some essentials. We wondered if you wanted to come with us, do some filming? Artsy shit."

Ramsey breathed down the phone. "Really?"

"Yeah."

"It's a nice idea, Bel, and I appreciate it, I do. But don't you want to spend time alone with your mum? She's only been home forty-eight hours."

"No, that's OK," Bel said, brighter.

Ramsey paused, his breath and a stronger breeze prickling against the microphone.

"You sure?" he said, not sounding sure himself.

"I'm sure. Tell Ash to wear something normal, we don't want to attract attention."

Ramsey sniffed in her sarcasm.

"We're actually just down the street, filming the media outside your house."

"Good," Bel said. "So you can be here in thirty seconds."

She hung up, cutting Ramsey off. Then she leaned into the living room, shooting Rachel a thumbs-up.

119

"They'll be here soon," she said.

"Great." Rachel attempted a smile, clapping her hands together. "This will be fun. Thank you, Annabel."

"No problem."

"You should eat the rest of your sandwich before we go," Rachel said, pointing to it.

"That's OK, I'm not too hungry. Thanks, though."

Not just words: moves and countermoves, an unspoken battle, sandwiches and shopping.

One mistake was forgivable, it made sense. But two? Two felt like something else entirely. She smiled at Rachel and Rachel smiled back. It looked real, but what if it wasn't? Bel couldn't be sure, she could only trust the knot in her gut. And it told her what she wanted to hear.

Rachel Price might just be lying.

FOURTEEN

The White Mountains Mall had bright overhead lighting that hurt your eyes, tinny uplifting music that didn't work at all. At least not on Bel; she couldn't tell with Rachel.

The camera was nestled on James's shoulder, and Saba held the boom mike over their heads, struggling to keep it steady, moving at this speed. Ramsey walked with the camera, out of frame, and Ash was behind somewhere, citrus bright in a yellow spotted shirt tucked into orange pants.

Rachel was walking too fast, that was the problem, like she was running from something, chased by the camera. Bel was keeping step, side by side but not too close, sometimes even outpacing Rachel, like they were racing to some unknown finish line.

"So, Rachel," Ramsey said, cautiously. "How does it feel to be back here? In this same mall where you first disappeared over sixteen years ago."

"There are certain things I'm not allowed to discuss," she said, "as this is an ongoing criminal investigation." She didn't turn back to say it, didn't give the camera her face.

"Of course, I understand," Ramsey said with a deferential nod. They'd already had this discussion, when Ramsey tried to make conversation on the drive here. Bel had sat in the front next to him,

Rachel alone in the back, closely watching the world go by, smiling when they passed dogs or kids.

Ramsey tried again. "Does it feel surreal to be here, now you know that this place played a huge role in the mystery of your disappearance?"

Rachel did turn back then, cracking open a smile for the camera.

"I'm happy to discuss sitting down with you for an interview another time," she said, not unkindly. "Maybe tomorrow, when Anna is back at school."

Ramsey looked confused by the name; he wasn't the only one. How hard could it be? Take the end of her name instead of the start.

"But for now," Rachel continued, pulling the smile wider, showing more teeth, "I really just want to take my daughter shopping. I've waited a long time for this."

"No, sure." Ramsey backed off. "From now on, you will see us, not hear us. Promise. Pretend we're not here."

"I will," Rachel said, again not unkindly, but it could only be meant one way. Like something Bel would say. A small flicker played on Ramsey's lips, like he'd noticed it too. No, stop that, they were nothing alike.

The mall wasn't busy; it was a Monday afternoon, meandering moms and dads with strollers. But every eye soon fell on them, a sure thing, if Bel had five bucks every time. A growing wasp-buzz of whispers when people recognized *the* Rachel Price from the news this morning, reappeared with a camera crew and going into H&M.

"OK," Rachel said inside, arm brushing up against Bel's. "I just need a few basic things, really. Couple pairs of shoes. A jacket. Some tops, pants. Maybe a skirt, I don't know." She blinked, shy and unsure. "Will you help me look? Tell me what will look good? Everything's a bit more high-waisted than I remember."

"Sure," Bel said again, because Rachel kept trapping her into it. "What colors do you like?"

"Anything, really," Rachel said, voice honey-soft. It didn't match her eyes. "Maybe not red."

They both thought of it then; the red top she'd disappeared in, grainy footage from this very mall, the same filthy red top she'd been forced to wear for the past sixteen years. If her story was real, that was. There were already two strikes against it.

"No red," Bel agreed.

Bel moved off, mission in hand, distracting her from the knot of tension in her gut. Rachel and the crew followed her around like ducklings, weaving in and out of the aisles. Part of her wanted to slip away and hide from Rachel, in a rack of clothing, like she never got to do as a kid. Making moms panic to prove they truly loved you; she assumed that was why children did it. She was too old for that, and the test wouldn't work because Rachel knew more about disappearing than she did. They didn't even know each other, forget about love.

Bel picked out a couple of nice shirts, thin sweaters for daytime, black ankle boots, plain white sneakers—

"Versatile," she said, passing the shoes over.

Some check pants Ash would probably be jealous of. A cropped trench jacket in stone—

"That'll go with everything," she told Rachel, handing her the hanger. "You can layer under it. You don't want something too thick for summer."

Rachel made a sound, in the back of her throat. Eyes twinkling, like she might just cry. The jacket wasn't *that* nice.

A khaki midi skirt buttoned all the way. A black shirtdress—

"You can dress that up, or down to be more casual." Bel added it to the pile in Rachel's hands.

Some sweats.

"You know, for being lazy around the house."

Rachel didn't say anything this time, and Bel looked back to check she was still here. She was, crying, struggling through all the clothes to wipe her face.

"You don't like them?" Bel asked, hovering awkwardly between the aisles.

"No, I love them all, thank you." Rachel finally reached the tear, brushing it away.

Bel felt an ache in her gut, something new, less urgent than the knot. Her face softened, offering Rachel a half smile.

Rachel completed it, making one whole. "Thank you for doing this, Anna."

Anna again. And it was just the knot after all, pulling tighter now Bel had given it her attention. Rachel must have noticed the shift.

"Do you want something for you?" she said, widening her eyes. "I saw you looking at that green top? Something else? And that jumpsuit." She gestured with her head, no hands free. "That would look good on Carter, wouldn't it?"

"I don't need anything," Bel said, turning away.

They headed into the fitting rooms, leaving the crew behind. They had too many items to take in, each carrying several hangers, but the woman at the entrance made an exception. Maybe she recognized *the* Rachel Price. Bel would have to get used to that, she supposed.

"Here." Bel hung the clothes inside the cubicle at the far end, gestured Rachel inside.

Rachel moved slowly now, glancing in before she entered. Bel reached forward to close the door for her, but Rachel's hand darted out, caught it.

"Maybe we don't have to shut it all the way," she said, a breathiness in her voice, close to fear. "It's pretty tight in here."

Tight, like sixteen years in a basement.

Another tug in Bel's gut. Maybe she was being unfair. Two mistakes didn't make Rachel a liar, did it? Things felt strange, and Rachel *was* strange, but she would be, wouldn't she? If she'd been trapped in the dark all that time, alone.

"Sure, we can keep it open a little," Bel said gently, guiding the door back, giving Rachel a few inches.

She sat outside the cubicle, flashes of flesh and material through the small crack in the door.

"Bras are more complicated than they used to be," Rachel huffed from inside.

Bel fought a smile; she lost.

"You OK?" she called.

"Nearly," Rachel replied.

She emerged a few minutes later, the khaki skirt skimming her calves, paired with a ruffled black top and white sneakers. She showed Bel, standing there with sad, subdued jazz hands.

"I like them," Bel said, trying, even though it didn't come naturally to her. "Wait."

She moved closer, bending to her knees.

"What is it?" Rachel looked down at her. "Wrong shape?"

"No, it looks great. It's just your socks," Bel said, reaching forward. She hesitated, seeking permission with her eyes. Rachel nodded above her. "People don't wear them like that anymore. Need to push them down."

Bel rolled the socks down below Rachel's ankles, over the dressing on her left ankle, where she'd been chained. Now she was this close, she noticed something else, peeking over the top of the Band-Aid.

There was a large scar on the inside of Rachel's ankle. A half circle, gnarled and healed, with pearly puckered skin. Where did that come from? When? Dad had never mentioned it, and it wasn't in the press releases that described Rachel's birthmark as her only identifying feature. So she must have got it sometime when she was disappeared.

"Better?" Rachel asked.

Bel straightened up, stepped back. "Better," she confirmed.

Why hadn't Rachel mentioned it in her story? The man never touched her, she'd said, so how had she got that scar? Had it come from an injury you couldn't get if you were locked in a basement all this time?

"Next?" Rachel said, retreating back inside the cubicle, leaving the door ajar.

No, stop it. Bel was trying. She was giving Rachel a chance. It was probably where the cuff used to rub, the same wound as below, an earlier version. She shooed away the knot in her gut; it never listened.

Rachel came back out, now wearing the check pants and a white shirt, with the black boots and the jacket on top.

Bel cleared her throat to try again.

"Looks really good," she said.

Rachel looked up, catching herself in the long mirror, not quite meeting her own eyes.

"You don't like it?" Bel asked.

"I do," Rachel said. "It's just weird, seeing myself." Bel couldn't read Rachel's eyes because they wouldn't stay in one place, darting over the person in the mirror. She spun in a half turn, one way, then the other. "I look . . . nice."

A sound in Rachel's throat, somewhere between a sniff and a laugh. Bel chose for her, laughing quietly too.

"Yeah, you do. Could dress it up more with some jewelry."

Rachel held one arm out, the sleeve pulling taut, looking at her bare wrist.

"Like that gold bracelet you have," she said.

Bel stalled, mouth open. What bracelet did Rachel mean?

"The one with the skulls?" Rachel explained as though she could hear Bel's thoughts.

Bel didn't like that. But there was something else she didn't like more. The laugh staled on her face, the smile turned bitter.

"I don't have that anymore."

It was just one second. Rachel's eyes widened, staring at Bel's reflection, hiding in the back of the mirror. And then it was gone, just as fast, Rachel dropping her arm and rearranging her smile.

"Must be thinking of one Sherry used to wear."

The knot stirred in Bel's gut.

"Yeah," she said. "Must be."

"I think that's everything." Rachel beamed at herself, sharing it with Bel as she stepped back into the cubicle.

The door closed and Bel dropped her smile, unwatched, unguarded.

That bracelet.

The one Sam Blake gave to Bel for her fourteenth birthday. The one Bel threw in the river just a week later, when Sam said what she did about Dad. It wasn't like Rachel could have seen the bracelet lying around the house since she'd returned; it was long gone. So how the fuck did she know about it?

Another question. Another mistake?

Bel didn't want to, but the knot insisted.

She pulled out her phone, swiping until she found the Instagram app. On to her profile, untouched in years. And the last photo Bel ever posted: a selfie of her and Sam, Bel beaming at the camera, Sam's nose nuzzling her cheek. Bel's wrist on the desk in front of them, that gold bracelet catching the light, two small skulls hanging by the clasp. Probably the only photo ever taken of that bracelet, the only proof of its existence before Bel made it disappear.

She checked through the crack in the door that Rachel was still changing. The only way Rachel could have known about the bracelet was if she'd seen this photo after she reappeared. But that wasn't possible either. Rachel didn't have a phone yet, she didn't have access to any device that could connect to the internet. And she didn't have time; Bel had been with her since she returned, apart from at the police station and while she was sleeping. There was no way Rachel could have seen this photo online since Saturday. So how the fuck did Rachel know about the bracelet if she came out of the basement just two days ago?

The answer was clear this time: she couldn't.

Something Rachel knew that she couldn't possibly know if her story was true. Which meant it wasn't. Not some of it, maybe not any of it. That wasn't just a mistake. That was a lie. Which meant the other two weren't mistakes either.

Three lies.

Bel had caught her now.

And if those were lies, what else could she be lying about? Some of it? The rest of it? All of it? Was that all it was, a story, crafted to fit the details it needed to, to fill in the mystery? It didn't even make sense: Why would the man just let Rachel go after all these years? What if there was no man?

Rachel Price had disappeared and reappeared. And now Bel knew for sure, she was lying about some of it, maybe all of it.

The door nudged open and Rachel came out in her old clothes, oblivious or pretending to be, a mountain-pile of new ones in her arms, nearly blocking out her face.

"You OK?" she asked Bel, trying to read her eyes.

Bel blocked her out, looked down. The board had shifted again, rerighting the sides, Bel and this stranger now exactly where they belonged, on opposite ends. A liar and the one who knew about it.

"Fine," she sniffed.

Rachel didn't let it go. "You need water?" she asked. "You look warm."

"Shopping . . . ," Bel said, as though that explained it.

They stood at the back of the line for the register, the camera crew waiting for them at the front of the store.

An iron fist took hold of the knot in Bel's gut, twisted it, tightened it, winding up her insides along with it. A breaking point, and Bel couldn't ignore it anymore.

Rachel was distracted, looking at the rack of socks, now was her chance. Bel's hand snaked out, toward the nearest shelf, wrapping around one of those tiny pots of lip balm. She slipped it up her sleeve, then into the pocket of her denim jacket, safe there.

The little lip balm fed the knot in her gut, sating it. A reprieve, an undoing, cooling and necessary, pull and push, another secret fight where Bel didn't have to choose a side because she was the battleground.

Bel looked away, accidentally meeting Ash's eyes, standing over there by the accessories, running his thumb over a bright pink headband. He hadn't seen, had he?

The relief didn't last long, standing this close to Rachel, shuffling forward until "Next, please." The knot redoubled, pulling at Bel's threads while Rachel pulled out Dad's credit card. The hot prick of shame, right on time.

Ash didn't say anything, even if he had seen.

The mall was busier when they left H&M. Was that normal for a Monday afternoon, or had word spread? People coming down to see for themselves. Not everyone recognized Rachel right away, but they knew she was someone to be stared at: *Is she that actress from the pink lawyer film?* No, she wasn't, but that didn't mean Rachel wasn't acting, even now, a paper bag swinging at her side, matching the one in Bel's hand.

People weren't just staring and pointing anymore. Phones were out, recording Rachel, Bel and the crew as they passed. Taking selfies with them in the background, trading their faces for likes and comments. Bel scratched her nose with her middle finger, to ruin their videos.

Rachel stopped, shoes screaming against the floor, staring ahead.

"Oh. It's a Starbucks now." She chewed the inside of her cheek, turning to Ramsey to explain. She must not realize he already knew everything about her that it was possible to know. "There was a coffeehouse here, the Moose Mouse Coffeehouse. I used to work here after college. They did the best cinnamon buns. I dreamed of having one again. Annabel, I guess you don't remember? Used to get sugar all over your face."

Bel shook her head. No, the cinnamon buns were gone, right along with the memories of Rachel's disappearance and what really happened. Which was not the same as what Rachel said had happened.

"I wanted us to have one together." Rachel's voice shrank, her eyes clouded.

James panned the camera to catch the two of them in front of the Starbucks. Even though the coffeehouse wasn't here anymore, this was still the spot, the last footage of Rachel Price alive, before she and her toddler vanished here, into thin air.

"Starbucks probably do a cinnamon bun," Bel offered.

"It's not the same," Rachel said with a sad sniff, moving on.

Bel had no choice but to follow.

At the corner, Rachel drew closer, leaning in. "Down there," she whispered so the camera and crew couldn't hear, pointing to a *Staff Only* door. "The recycling bins. Where we hid." Her eyes were too close, fusing with Bel's in a way that stung.

Their secret, that only one of them remembered. Bel blinked to break the link and pulled away. Did she have to believe that part of the story at least? How else had the two of them disappeared between security cameras?

Their last stop was T-Mobile, to get Rachel a phone. Ash asked the sales assistant to sign a release form: the guy was helpful, far too helpful, showing the camera his best angle as he talked Rachel through contracts and phones, checking his hair in the glass of the store window.

They settled on the newest iPhone with a monthly contract: unlimited everything. Bel winced on behalf of Dad's card as Rachel went to pay.

"You might find it a little confusing to set up," the guy said, clinging on to his fifteen minutes of fame. "Phones are touchscreen now. I'm sure your daughter can help you."

"Will you, Anna? Sorry, B-Bel. Help me set up my phone?" Rachel looked at her.

"Of course she will," the sales assistant answered for her.

Bel smiled, because the camera was rolling. "Sure."

She left Rachel there, trailing off behind the camera to the back of the store, so she could drop the act. Ash was here too. Just a coincidence, she wasn't trying to stand *with* him.

"So," Ash said in a low voice, hands on his hips, "anything new with you since Saturday?"

Bel smirked. "Nothing of note. Took up knitting."

"Really?" Ash bobbed his head. "I, for one, wouldn't put needles in your hands."

"Why not?"

"You seem like the stabby type," he said, their eyes meeting, a slow blink.

"Thank you." Bel nodded, leaning closer. "You look like a sad tangerine."

"Thank *you.*" He nodded back.

It was annoying, how much he enjoyed her spite, matched her for it with a smile. It got rid of most people, everyone else in fact, so Ash couldn't be right in the head. Bel didn't know how to work with that.

"It's unbelievable, isn't it?" he said, serious now, eyes straying over to Rachel. "This whole thing. Unbelievable."

Bel studied him in secret, the outline of his straight nose down to the swell of his lips, pressed together in thought. She knew how he'd meant it; *unbelievable* to mean extraordinary, shocking, astonishing. But was there a chance he'd left it open to mean the other thing? That he couldn't quite believe Rachel's story, what he knew of it at least, a splinter of doubt hiding there.

If Bel told him everything, would he believe her? Would he be on her side, someone to talk to?

No, she was being ridiculous. Bel moved her eyes away. Ash didn't care. They were just here to make their movie, then they'd fuck off back to England forever. Bel didn't need to push; he was leaving anyway.

"Yeah. Unbelievable," Bel said, but she meant it the other way.

FIFTEEN

"How does it feel to finally have your mom back home, Annabel?"

"I'm not Annabel," Carter said to the baying reporter, following them down the sidewalk with an outheld microphone, a breathless cameraman chasing after.

"Oh." The reporter shifted her attention to Bel instead, reaching across Carter. "How does it feel to finally have your mom back home, Annabel?"

Bel batted the microphone away, then another, like irritating moths slamming themselves against a bulb, never getting what they wanted.

"Come on, now, back up. I said back up!" the officer called, a wide gesture with his uniformed arms, catching the crowd of bleating journalists in an invisible net, pushing them away. "Leave the girls alone, they're just trying to walk to school. I said back up!"

Dave Winter had sent over a couple of patrol officers this morning, to escort Bel past the media circus that had set up outside their house.

"Are you scared that the man who took your mom is still out there? Might come back for her?" another called, escaping the invisible net.

No, Bel wasn't scared of that. He was welcome to her, because he probably didn't exist.

"They aren't going to answer any of your questions," the other officer spoke now, raising her voice. "Out of our way, please."

"GET BACK!"

The reporters gave up by the time they reached the corner of the cemetery, crawling back to their campground outside number 33.

The officers didn't leave, though, walking behind them at a distance, nodding dutifully when Bel looked back at them. Didn't they have some crimes to go take care of?

"How has it been, really?" Carter asked, now they were basically alone. "I saw a video of you at the mall yesterday. Someone posted it online. That must have been nice, huh, to go shopping together?"

"It was fine." Bel shrugged. It hadn't really been fine, but at least now Bel knew for sure, could stop doubting herself. Rachel Price was a liar. She just didn't know what to do with that now, who would believe her. "What else have you seen online?" she asked.

Someone else had to be suspicious of Rachel's story; Bel couldn't be the only one, come on, that was what Reddit boards and Twitter threads were made for.

"Someone posted dashcam footage of Rachel walking along the highway," Carter said. "Came up on TikTok. I didn't want to watch it; she looked hurt. Think it was taken down by the police."

Bel looked sideways at her. "Was it real?"

"Looked it."

"Where?"

"TikTok."

"No, where on the highway?" Bel said, acting like the answer didn't matter.

"Outside Santa's Village."

Santa's Village in Jefferson, about halfway between Lancaster and home. Fuck. So there was video proof of Rachel walking along US Route 2. Maybe she really had walked those eight long hours from Lancaster. Well, she had to have busted up her feet somehow, but that was OK; didn't mean the rest of her disappearance and reappearance was true. The best way to hide a lie was to bury it with some truths, Bel knew that.

"You OK?" Carter narrowed her eyes. Bel had been quiet too long, and Carter knew her too well.

"It's just strange, is all." Could she trust Carter with her doubts? Bel trusted Carter with most things, hardly an unsaid thing between them, but this felt bigger somehow, less easy to come back from once she'd given voice to it. She tried anyway. "Rachel is . . . I mean, there's a couple of things she's said that don't add up. Inconsistencies."

Carter sighed, bumping Bel's elbow. "Bel, you're doing that thing that you do," she said gently, like she was tiptoeing around little land mines of their own. "Trying to see the bad in everything. Looking for reasons to push people away, which means you always find them. This is a good thing. Surely you hoped for this your whole life. It's a miracle she's back, Bel, most people aren't that lucky. And she seems nice, Rachel. Really nice. You have to give her a chance, she's your mom."

It was Bel's turn to sigh. That hurt. More because Carter had looked so deep into her and gotten it all wrong. Bel didn't push people away, she only sped up the process, an inevitable thing. Carter wasn't allowed an opinion, seeing as she would be the one doing the leaving here. She didn't understand because no one ever left her; she was a magnet, long-haired and long-legged.

"Stop it," Carter said, bunching her eyebrows.

"Stop what?"

"Getting mad."

"I'm not mad," Bel lied.

"You're trying to be."

"No."

"Liar." Carter smiled, a less easy smile than her usual. "I'm just saying. Try not to look for reasons. Just get to know her. I think you'll probably like her."

Bel had been right to hesitate about telling Carter, and now Carter got to act like the sensible one, the reasonable one, tempering her wildfire cousin. Bel wasn't the problem, it was Rachel.

"You can hit me if it'll make you feel better."

"OK." Bel's knuckles thumped into the soft flesh of Carter's arm.

"Ow," she whined, rubbing it. "I didn't think you'd do it, God."

"Thought you knew me so well, huh?" Bel replied.

"Right, that's it."

Carter gritted her teeth, disarming Bel with a hard poke to her ribs, wrapping an arm around her neck when Bel bent double, trapping her. Bel swiped with her legs, trying to take out Carter's. Why were they so frickin' long? The cheat.

"I'll let go when you stop being grumpy," Carter laughed, their backpacks crashing together.

"I'm never grumpy," Bel said, grumpily. "Give me my head back."

Carter wouldn't let go.

"Say *please*. And *I love you, Carter Price*."

"Please and I love you, Carter Price."

"Good."

Carter released her neck and Bel straightened up. Her hair static-scruffy, a matching flush in their cheeks.

"I'm gonna murder you in your sleep," Bel said, righting her backpack, walking on.

"The police are right behind us," Carter whispered behind her hand.

"They wouldn't catch me."

The officers walked them down Main Street, all the way to school. They weren't even inside, and already the staring began, not helped by the police escort. They weren't silent stares, paired with excitable whispers, and *Rachel* was a name that carried across a distance, that hard crunch in the middle.

"Don't actually murder someone today," Carter said, holding the door open for her.

"Can't promise."

The pre-bell crowds parted for them, a buzz of voices, growing chain saw loud, students scuffling to see.

"Hey, Bel!" Someone called her name.

Bel looked the other way, ignoring them.

"Bel, what's *she* like?"

Ignored that one too.

The corridor split and Bel and Carter went their separate ways. Bel felt more exposed without her, an army of one. Crossing her arms to protect her chest.

Down the hall past The Rachel Shrine. Shouldn't they take that down now? You didn't keep shrines for not-dead people.

The bell rang just as she walked through the door to her home-room, brimming with chatter when she did, overspilling. She took a seat next to the window, putting her backpack on the chair beside her, to guard it.

"Hello, Bel," said a deep voice, hanging above her.

It was Mr. Tripp, fiddling with the lapels of his blazer, dressed up today, his dark red hair combed back.

"We missed you at school yesterday," he said, a nervous tic in his cheek, blocking his mouth, a semi-smile.

"I went shopping."

"That's OK, thought you'd be taking more time off to, you know, adjust." He pushed his glasses back up his nose. Looked like he was the one who needed adjusting.

"I love school too much," she said.

Mr. Tripp bent closer, resting his elbows on the table.

"How is she, your mom?" He lowered his voice, but of course the other students had gone quiet, to listen in.

"Fine." Then, at the concerned look in her teacher's eyes, she added: "Considering."

He straightened up, removed his creaking elbows. "If you need to talk about anything, Bel, you know I'm right here."

"Yep, right there."

The Rachel fever had got him too, the whole school sick with it. Today was going to be hell, but at least Bel had the next seven hours to herself, without Rachel.

Rachel was here.

She wasn't supposed to be here, Bel had come to school to escape her. But there she was, as Bel and Carter walked out at the end of the day, standing on the grass outside. She was surrounded by a ring of chattering teachers, Principal Wheeler's voice carrying loudest.

Mr. Tripp was there too, hanging back, staring at her. He didn't blink, maybe in case Rachel vanished in the half second his eyes were shut. It had only taken moments last time.

"So, Rachel," the principal crooned. "Will we be looking for an excuse to hire another English teacher? Your old desk has been waiting."

Rachel smiled, shooing him off with a wave of her hand. "I'm not ready to think about any of that yet."

"Of course not," Mrs. Torres said. "You shouldn't have to work another day of your life, honey."

"I don't know about that either. Gas is more expensive than I remember."

That got a laugh from the crowd, somber and polite, shuffling feet.

"Hey, Julian." Rachel spotted Mr. Tripp as her audience shifted. Her feet followed her eyes, pushing through to give him a hug. He held on a little too long, like the hug was proof she was really real. "Been a long time."

"Too long," Mr. Tripp sniffed. "I thought you were dead."

"I'm alive," Rachel said, spinning awkwardly in the middle. "I guess it's stranger for everyone else. I always knew I was alive. Always hoped I'd be able to come back. I wanted to thank you, Jules. For finding Annabel, all those years ago."

"Just happened to be going that way." He wiped his nose. "If only I was there sooner."

"*If only* doesn't help anybody," Rachel said with a smile, sharing it with everyone else. "It would be nice to catch up properly sometime. I just got a new phone. My daughter's gonna help me set it up later." Bel hadn't done it yesterday, pretended she'd forgotten some homework so she could hide in her room. "So maybe you could write your numbers down for me."

"Of course, sweetie." Mrs. Lawrence squeezed her shoulder. "I got a pen and notepad." She pulled them out of her purse and scribbled away, passing the notebook to the others who had worked with Rachel, in the before times. Mr. Tripp went last, then tore the page off, handing it to Rachel.

"Thank you." She held it to her chest. "So nice to see you all. I better find my daughter— Oh, Annabel. Hi! Anna! Carter!"

She waved, breaking through the gang of teachers. Now Bel could see that Rachel was wearing her new trench jacket and check pants, with the sneakers that glowed white, too new.

"Hi," Carter spoke first as Rachel reached them.

"Hi, girls." She smiled, slipping the piece of paper into her jacket pocket. Something jangled when she did, a rattle like keys. "How was school?"

"Good," said Carter.

"Fine," said Bel.

Rachel widened her eyes, waiting for more than a one-word answer.

"How was your day, Aunt Rachel?" Carter asked instead.

"Been very busy," she said, walking toward Main Street, using her eyes to drag Bel and Carter along, forcing their feet. "Turns out there's a lot of admin when you come back from the dead." A small, dry laugh. "More interviews with the police. Appointment with their psychiatrist. Been down to the DMV to get my temporary license. Reopened my bank account, got new house keys. Then my mom came around for coffee." The horsefucker was back in town, then. Would she ever admit that she'd been wrong about Dad, now that Rachel was—you know—alive? "We spoke on Sunday, but she flew in today, she's staying in town for a couple weeks. Then I met with the documentary team."

"That *is* a busy day," Carter said, giving Rachel her full attention. Bel was staring at her too-white shoes instead, only the soles picking up dirt.

"Even busier," Rachel continued, speeding up, Carter keeping pace, Bel lagging behind. Had she come to walk them all the way home? The media circus would be all over that. "This afternoon, Sherry gave me a ride to the car dealer outside town. I bought a secondhand car." She pulled out a set of keys, the dealership tag still on them, dangling from her middle finger. "Nothing fancy. But I thought I'd take it out on its first spin, come pick you two up from school. Here it is."

Rachel pressed the button and a car blipped, flashing at them across the grass strip that bordered the Royalty Inn parking lot. A silver Ford Escape with mean eyes and a teeth-grit grille.

"Come on." Rachel cut across the grass with a skip in her step, Carter following.

Bel stayed on the sidewalk.

"We usually just walk," she said. "It's not far."

"Oh, I know," Rachel said, opening the driver's-side door. "But I wanted to come get you. Never picked you up from school before and if I don't watch out, I'll miss my chance. Don't worry, I remember how to drive."

Bel crossed the grass, stopping before she reached the car. Carter was floating by the passenger side, hand hesitating in the air.

"Front or back?" she asked Bel, deferring to her.

Rachel was waiting too, leaning up on the roof.

"Jump in," she said, sticking with that smile, matching her new car.

Bel swallowed, elbows and jaw locking. Rachel clearly wanted her to sit in the front, right next to her. But would that make it seem like Bel thought any of this was OK or normal? Jump in, simple enough, but nothing Rachel said was simple, there were layers, a push and pull between them. What would Rachel win if Bel said yes?

"Bel?" Carter shot her a look, gesturing between the front or the back, waiting on her answer.

Or Bel could choose the backseat, which was farther from Rachel, a no of sorts, but it was still the backseat.

A choice, binary, this or that, front or back, but Bel wanted neither.

"I just remembered," she said suddenly, shrugging off both their eyes, looking at the sky to fish for the lie. "I said I'd meet someone after school today."

Carter narrowed her eyes. "Who?" She knew. She knew Bel had

no one to meet. Those same nonexistent friends Ramsey wanted to interview last week.

"It's this extra-credit group project thing, for biology. I forgot we said Tuesday after school, with everything going on."

"Oh." A shadow fell across Rachel's eyes, taking the smile with it.

"I should probably go," Bel said, thumb over her shoulder, backtracking from the car. "Don't want to keep them waiting."

"Are you sure?" Carter said pointedly, saying something different with her face, something Rachel couldn't see. Carter knew, or she thought she knew, that Bel was just doing that thing that she did. But Carter wasn't as close to all this; she couldn't see it.

"Yeah," Bel said, giving no secret answers with her face. "Gotta go."

"Sh-should I pick you up later?" Rachel asked, the bed of her knuckles digging into the underside of her face, leaving ghost-white prints behind.

"Not sure when we'll be done. Don't worry, I'll just walk home, thanks. See you later."

Bel raised one hand in goodbye, high-fiving the breeze, turning around when she reached the sidewalk. A car door closed and another opened. She glanced back as Carter climbed in the front beside Rachel, chatting already, pasting over the awkwardness Bel must have left behind. She was good at that, shining harder to compensate.

A twist in Bel's gut, pulling the knot tighter. She didn't like leaving Carter alone with Rachel, but what choice did she have? Carter wasn't listening. It was OK, it would only take a couple of minutes for Rachel to drop Carter home at number 19. But the knot didn't listen to reason, feeding itself on bad feelings, even the small ones.

Bel heard the chug of the engine, joining the noise of those on Main Street as Rachel pulled out, driving Carter away. Blink and they were both gone, blocked by a stream of cars.

Now what?

Dad was at work. Carter was with Rachel. Grandpa didn't remember who she was.

Bel was a homebody, the world the size of 33 Milton Street. But home had been taken over, a slow invasion with a pointed smile, and now Rachel had her own keys.

Bel wanted to stay away, but she had nowhere to go, no one to see, no one to talk to. No one at all.

Except, maybe . . .

SIXTEEN

Ash was just leaving the hotel when Bel got to the door, almost slamming into him and his handheld camera, blinded by her own reflection.

"Whoa, hey." He cradled the camera. "Ramsey will kill me if I break this."

"Would spice up the documentary," Bel said, stepping back, clearing the way for him. "A bit vanilla if no one dies."

"You're in a good mood." He looked her up and down and she did the same. Backward cap and burgundy overalls with a striped top. "What are you doing?"

"Nothing," she said. "I just finished school. School's right there. I was walking past. What are you doing?" she accused him instead.

"Ramsey's had meetings all day, so he asked me to film some reaction stuff in town. How locals feel about Rachel's reappearance and all that. Just heading out again."

"How *do* the locals feel?" Bel asked, using Rachel's trick, starting to walk so Ash had to too.

"Shocked mostly." He shifted the camera to keep up. "But pleased that the story has a happy ending."

"Happy ending," Bel muttered to herself. The police chief said it wasn't a true happy ending until the man who took Rachel was caught. So if he didn't really exist, they had no chance.

"Y-you don't think it does?" Ash asked tentatively.

"Really?" she laughed. "You want to dig into my *mommy issues*?"

"They seem like the most pressing of your issues." He cleared his throat. "It's just, I noticed you maybe weren't OK yesterday, at the mall. If everyone thinks you should be happy and you're not, thought you might want someone to talk to about it. Like, an outsider."

Ash was more than an outsider here, different worlds. Three older sisters and a mom he loved enough to ink on his arm.

Should she try him? He could only be repulsed by her, and that would work in her favor too, finally pushing him away before he got too close and Bel started to think she cared.

Nothing to lose either way.

And no family land mines to tiptoe around, no one who thought they knew Bel better than she knew herself.

"I think Rachel is lying," she said bluntly, watching for a reaction on his face.

"Right." He bit his lip, but Bel wasn't sure what that meant. "Lying about what?"

"About her disappearance. Her reappearance too. Where she's really been the last sixteen years."

Ash's eyes flickered, screwed against the breeze of a passing truck. "And why do you think that?"

Was he giving her a chance? Bel took it, speaking quickly before he took the chance back.

"She's messed up a couple of times, got details in her story wrong. She told me that the man left the engine running when he let her go, on that road, but she told my dad that the engine was switched off first. She accidentally said she was locked up for fifteen years, not sixteen. You would remember that number, right, if it were true? And yesterday, at the mall, she knew about a bracelet I used to have. I threw it in the river, years ago, after my friend . . . Anyway, the only proof that that bracelet ever existed was an old photo on my Instagram. Rachel hasn't been on the internet since she's been back, there's no way she could have seen my Instagram in those forty-eight hours. She shouldn't even know what Instagram is. She must have seen that photo another time. Which means she can't have been locked in a basement until Saturday morning. And the other thing: The man kept her all that time, then just let her go without explanation, and she can't provide a detailed description of him? And . . ." She paused, testing out his eyes. "I guess, I can just feel it. That there's something wrong, that she's not telling the truth."

Ash cupped his fingers around his chin, pulling his head into a nod. "OK," he said.

"OK?" Bel asked him, uncrossing her arms. "You're not going to tell me I'm wrong, that I'm overreacting, that things are supposed to feel strange, or I'm pushing her away because I have latent abandonment issues?"

Ash pressed his lips together, not quite a smile. "Why would I do that? You are absolutely terrifying."

"Thank you." Bel bowed her head. "So you . . . do you believe me?"

The knot clenched; she waited.

"Yeah," he said.

So simple. Not even a full word. But God, she'd needed to hear that, a featherlight feeling in her gut, raising her onto her toes. He believed her, or at least he said he did, and that was good enough for now. Someone on her side, as unlikely and ridiculous as he was.

A family of four passed them on the sidewalk, all staring, not trying to disguise their curiosity, harmonized nosiness. That bright boy who dressed like a clown and the daughter of Rachel Price. Outsiders, but outsiders on the same side.

"If she is lying," Ash said, when the coast was clear, "she'd have to have a motive, right? For disappearing in the first place, and then reappearing after sixteen years. If they were both orchestrated."

"I don't know," Bel said, the first time she could reason it to herself, out loud, using Ash as a brick wall for her thoughts. "If you managed to disappear, so successfully that everyone thought you were dead, what could be your motive for coming back and risk being exposed?"

"I guess the reason behind most things: money," Ash said, holding his camera in the crook of his elbow.

"But what money?" Bel gestured with her empty hands.

"I don't know," Ash replied, the words trailing up at the end, like they were leading somewhere, not a shutdown like Bel's usually were. "Rachel had a meeting with Ramsey today, contracts, for her to participate in interviews and filming. She wouldn't agree to sell her life rights until Ramsey offered up a lot of money. She negotiated some back-end stuff too, that's smart."

Bel stalled, thinking. "How much money?"

"I don't know the exact figure, but a lot more than your dad's contract. I guess that's because *she's* the subject and, with her return, Ramsey knows the documentary will definitely get picked up by a broadcaster. In fact, he's having Zoom meetings with all the big ones today."

A knot in Bel's head, to match the one in her gut, writhing as it spewed out questions and scenarios.

"Seems convenient," she said, "that a film crew just happened to be making a documentary about her when she returned from the dead. What impeccable timing for both parties. Where's Ramsey?" She turned on Ash.

"In the conference room, still in meetings. Why?"

Bel pointed to his camera. "Can I borrow this?"

"Yeah, sure." He handed it over, heavier than she expected, no flinch when their fingers touched.

Bel took off, back toward the hotel.

Ash padded after her, confused. "Actually, wait." Panic rising in his voice. "Why did I just do that? Give it back. Mate, it's expensive."

"Don't worry, I won't drop it or smash it in a rage."

She approached the main door.

"Why would you say that? That sounds exactly like the kind of thing you would do." Ash followed her inside the hotel lobby, anxiously chewing his thumb.

"How do I record?" she asked, heading toward the conference room.

"Give it back, where are you going?" Ash hissed.

"Don't be a buzzkill, *mate*. I'm guessing it's this big red button here. Unless that's self-destruct."

She pressed it, and the image came up in the viewfinder on the side, recording. She made an explosion noise, pushing air around her cheeks, pretending to drop the camera to enjoy the raw look of alarm on Ash's face.

"Too easy," she told him; he was supposed to be able to match her. She pushed the door open with one arm.

"Wha—" Ramsey's face emerged from behind a MacBook on the table. "Ash, I told you I was in meetings. You're lucky I literally just finished one."

"All her," Ash said, a double point in Bel's direction.

"'Ello, Ramsey," Bel said brightly, watching his face in the viewfinder, moving from surprise through confusion.

"Remember how I told you to take care of that camera, Ash?" he said.

"Yeah." Ash scratched his hair under the cap, raising it up, elongating his head. "Accidentally gave it to Bel."

"Why?"

"Because she asked."

"You're always sticking cameras in my face," Bel said. "My turn. How was your day?" She smiled, stretching it beyond a grin.

Ramsey widened his eyes. "Good, actually. Had some exciting conversations with broadcasters. Everyone is desperate for the doc, now Rachel has returned. We've officially changed the name too: *The Reappearance of Rachel Price*." He outlined the title with his fingers, drawing it in the air.

"Imaginative," Bel said. "Nice alliteration."

"That's what I thought, all the execs too. Just got off a meeting with the big red N, if you know what I'm saying."

Bel did, but she rearranged her face like she didn't.

"Starts with *N*," Ramsey said, getting to his feet. "Ends in *-etflix*."

"Sorry, never heard of it," Bel replied with a frown, disarming him before she jumped in.

Her trick worked; Ramsey shook his head and smiled at his feet. God, she was lovably infuriating, wasn't she? A girl like that couldn't possibly be smart too, right?

"What do you want, Bel?" He stared down the camera, sensing something.

"Just thought it was your turn to answer some questions. A reverse interview."

"OK, I'll bite." Ramsey leaned against the table, crossing his legs. He'd put on a crisp blue shirt for the big red N. "What do you want to ask me?"

"It's more of a comment than a question," Bel replied. "Just thinking about the incredible coincidence that you were making a documentary about Rachel's disappearance, then she miraculously comes back from the dead midway through your shoot. Great before-and-after material. And all the broadcasters want it, probably throwing money at you. Which is fantastic, because both you and Rachel profit from that. What convenient timing. Suspicious, a more cynical person might say."

Ramsey pressed his lips together; he knew Bel was that more cynical person.

"Go on," he said, pushing her, almost like he was enjoying it.

"Did you and Rachel work together to orchestrate her reappearance, so you could both cash in on the media storm? You were probably desperate, right, after your last documentary didn't sell and no one will ever see it?"

Ramsey winced; that last point had stung him a little.

"No, Bel. We did not," he said softly, a look on his face that was both scolding and impressed, in real life and the miniature version in the viewfinder. "I did not orchestrate anything. The first time I met Rachel Price was when I knocked on your door Sunday morning. I had no prior contact with her; I didn't even know that was a possibility. Honestly, Bel, I thought she was dead, like you did. One hundred percent, no doubt in my mind, Rachel Price was dead. I'm as shocked as the rest of the world that she's back. It's a once-in-a-lifetime thing, to be here to witness it. And Rachel: she was locked in a basement until three days ago, she couldn't have had contact with anyone to orchestrate anything."

"Right," Bel said. "So it's just a coincidence."

Ramsey shrugged. "They happen." He studied her with interest, so different from the shallow way the *locals* stared. Reading, not just seeing, prying with his filmmaker eyes. "Why, do you think your mum *wasn't* locked in a basement for sixteen years?"

"I'm asking the questions here, I'm the one with the camera." It shook in her hands.

"Interesting," Ramsey said, running his hand over his jaw. "Why do you think your gut reaction is to think your mum is lying, Bel?"

"It isn't," she said.

"Is it less painful for you to think she had control, that she left on purpose? Came back for a reason?"

"Stop asking questions, *I'm* asking questions." Bel breathed in. "Why did you choose Rachel, then, why did you choose us to be your next subject?"

"Honestly?" Ramsey said, crossing his legs the other way, glancing at Ash. "I hadn't really heard of the Rachel Price case before. I know it's a big deal *here,* but you know, America has a lot of murders and missing people. I only started looking into it last year when I was in Maine; I tweeted something miserable about having to abandon the shoot on my last doc. Someone replied that the Rachel Price case would make an interesting documentary, if I was looking for my next idea. I Googled it out of spite, really, and the rest is history. So it's all down to that random person in my comments. No conspiracy here, yeah? We cool? But let's get back into why you wanted there to be one."

"No, let's not," Bel said sharply, dancing with him now. "And in all of your research, have you found anything that contradicts what Rachel says happened to her?"

Ramsey studied her again, and she wished he would stop doing that. He could psychoanalyze her, but she could do it right back. Go for the jugular; make another comment about his failed documentary.

"I mean," he said, "we're interviewing her tomorrow and Thursday, so I don't have her whole story yet, or the story as far as law enforcement will allow. But no, as far as I can tell. There are no contradictions, no reasons to not believe every word. Well, unless you

148

count all those imaginary sightings across the years. Brazil. Paris." Ramsey laughed, a breathy, dismissing sound.

"Wait." Bel stopped him, searching her memory. "You said there was a recent sighting, one in New Hampshire. Where was that? Who was it?"

"Really?" Ramsey asked.

"Really," she replied.

"OK." He gave in, slapping his thighs. Bel followed him with the camera as he returned to his laptop, clicking and typing.

"It was in North Conway," he said. "Let me just search my documents for that. Aha. Yep. North Conway. A woman called Alice Moore. She posted on Facebook, in January, that there was someone in her store who she swore was Rachel Price."

"Where can I find her?" Bel asked. "What's the store called?"

"She's the owner of a small independent clothing shop," he said, checking his notes. "Called *Baa-Baa Boutique*. But—"

"Cool." Bel stepped forward to place the camera—still recording— on the table, trapping Ramsey inside it. "Text the address to Ash."

"Eh?" Ash said, at the sound of his own name.

"Bel," Ramsey began, "I'm not sure you sh—"

"Come on, Ash," Bel said, slapping him on the back. "Let's go. You're driving."

"I'm—what?" He looked aghast. "But I don't have a—"

"Here," Ramsey said, changing his tune suddenly, a new light in his eyes. He dug in his back pocket and threw a set of keys across the room. Ash caught them clumsily, gaze darting between the two of them, deer in their headlights. "Drive on the right-hand side, remember?"

"But—"

"Ash!" they both said, Bel waiting by the door, clapping her hands impatiently.

"Take the camera," Ramsey hissed, bundling it up and pressing it into Ash's chest, with a wink he thought Bel couldn't see. A whispered: "Steady hand, make sure you frame the shot."

"Oh, O-OK," Ash stammered, catching on.

"Wait!" Ramsey darted back to the table. "Release forms. People have to sign these," he said, shoving a few into Ash's hands. "Have you got a pen?"

"I've got a fucking pen," Bel said. "Now, let's go before I change my mind. Fucking thank you."

SEVENTEEN

Horns and *hey watch it*s as Ash pulled off the main road, into a parking spot by the North Conway library.

"American roads are hell," he said, waving an apology out of his window, turning off the engine.

"To be fair," Bel said, "you're a terrible driver."

He glared at her, pulling his cap back on. "To be even more fair, you're a terrible passenger. Could give a bit more warning before yelling at me to turn."

"That wouldn't be as fun." Bel grabbed the backpack between her legs and opened the car door.

"You are something else," Ash muttered under his breath, though he never specified what that something else was, climbing out the other side. He collected the camera from the backseat, running his fingers over the fluff of the microphone, checking the battery. Then he grabbed his bag, one of those mini leather backpacks. It looked stupid on him.

"Nice bag."

"My mum's," he said. "Get the best hand-me-downs from her and my sisters."

Bel nodded, eyes wide and unkind to contradict her smile. She'd never had or given hand-me-downs, only hand-me-sidewayses to Carter when they were kids and Bel outgrew her jeans.

They crossed the road, Bel looking ahead at Baa-Baa Boutique. A quaint storefront: wooden slats painted seaside white and blue, though the sea was a very long way away. Next door to a store called World Magic Gifts, with window displays full of dream catchers and antlers, sculptures that stared as Bel and Ash approached.

Ash pressed record on the camera, centering the shot on Bel, panning up to show the name of the boutique and the little sheep logo.

"Don't you need to say *Action,* or *Rolling* or something?"

"Action, or rolling or something," he said with a lopsided grin.

Bel pushed open the door, a small bell jangling above her head, not holding the door for Ash, letting him struggle with it. She walked past a rack of clothes, a cropped yellow T-shirt at the front reading *Pugs Not Drugs* with a sad, chubby pug in the middle. The kind of thing Ash would probably wear. She turned back and caught him eyeing it, reaching out.

"Focus," she hissed, batting his fingers away. "We're not here to shop."

"He just looks so sad, little guy." Ash stuck out his bottom lip. "Needs a loving home."

Bel rolled her eyes at the camera lens, the two of them in cahoots, right under Ash's nose. She led them up to the register, where a woman in her forties was writing out labels, wearing a white-and-blue-striped top that matched the front of the store.

"Welcome to Baa-Baa Boutique," she said, bored, glazed behind the eyes, until she saw Ash. Then she straightened up and lengthened her neck, pushing her dark hair to one side. "How may I help you?" she asked him.

"We're here to see the owner, Alice Moore," Bel said, failing to get the woman's full attention back from Ash.

"That's me," she said, lines forming around her mouth as she finally noticed the camera in his hands. "What's—"

"We're filming for a documentary," Bel explained. "*The Disappearance of Rachel Price.*"

Ash coughed. "Actually, *The Reappearance of Rachel Price* now."

"Oh, I, the news, it's just amazing, really . . . ," Alice trailed off, finally looking at Bel, eyes circling. "But you look so much like . . . you must be h-her . . ."

Bel let Alice stutter, left her and her aborted sentences hanging there.

"Yes, this is Bel," Ash stepped in. "Rachel's daughter."

"Oh, sweetie." Alice gave Bel her full attention now. "You must be so happy to finally have your mom back home with you."

"Yeah, I must be," Bel said, leaving another awkward gap for Ash.

"Could I get you to sign one of these release forms?" he said, pulling one out of his comically small backpack. "To consent to having your face and voice in the documentary."

"Yes, of course." Alice took the form, signing it after one quick glance, without reading it, handing it back. "Though I'm not sure why you're filming me. I don't even know anyone who knows Rachel."

"Actually," Bel said, taking charge, "we're here to talk to you about something you posted on your Facebook in January. That you thought you saw Rachel Price here, in your store."

"Oh yes." Alice dropped her face, a breathy laugh, letting them in on the joke. "Obviously I was wrong, it couldn't have been her, now we know where poor Rachel really was."

"But could you tell us about the sighting, about the woman you saw? Even though we now know it can't have been Rachel," Bel pushed.

The woman narrowed her eyes. "I don't understand."

"You know," Bel pulled back, speaking behind her hand like they were old friends. That was how old friends spoke, right? "It's just filler for the documentary, some background stuff to pad out the juicy bits, show how widely known Rachel's case was before she came back." Bel didn't leave her any more room to not-understand, pushing again. This woman might have the answers that unlocked Rachel's lies, and Bel was damn well going to get them. "So what can you tell us about this woman you saw?"

Alice paused to clear her throat. "I mean, I couldn't see a lot of her, maybe that's why I convinced myself it had been Rachel. She was wearing a mask, you know, a surgical mask, a Covid mask, so I could only see her eyes, really. And she was wearing a beanie; it was freezing out. Her hair was long, though, almost down to her waist, a darkish blond, like Rachel's when she disappeared. We didn't interact much, just when she came up to the register, there was nothing remarkable about it. But I looked at her eyes, and I just had this thought, like 'Oh my God, she looks like Rachel Price.' I didn't say anything, and I kicked myself later when I convinced myself it was her. I had to tell someone, just in case, so it didn't feel like a secret. So I put it on Facebook. Although, now I *would* be kicking myself if I'd said anything to her, because it clearly couldn't have been your mom."

"Sure," Bel said, but she didn't mean it, because it was possible that that woman might just have been the real Rachel Price, and who was supposed to kick themselves then? But if it was Rachel, Bel needed proof. Evidence. "Do you have any cameras in the store? Would they have recorded this woman?"

"Yes," Alice said. "I checked the footage the next day to see if I was going crazy."

"Can we see the footage?" Bel pressed.

"I don't have it anymore; it gets written over every week."

Bel deflated.

"But I took a screenshot of the clearest image, when she was standing right where you are now. Not the best quality, but it might still be on my phone, hold on."

Bel and Ash held on, exchanging looks while Alice pawed at her screen. "Sorry, lots of my puppy," she said, swiping up. "Here it is."

She held out the phone to show them the photo, Ash zooming in on it, then out to catch Bel's reaction. She crouched closer, screwed her eyes. A woman in a dark puffer jacket and a mask, hair a similar color to Rachel's, long enough to catch in the crook of her elbow as she readjusted her mask, frozen that way. You couldn't see much of her face, the beanie covering where the birthmark might be. It could have been Rachel, there was nothing that counted that out, using the mask and hat as a disguise, blending in in plain sight. Or it could just be another pale woman with the same color hair. They weren't in short supply around here.

"Can you AirDrop that photo to me?" Bel said.

"Please," Ash added for her.

Alice stared blankly. "I don't know what that means."

"Here," Bel said, impatiently, taking the phone out of Alice's hands. She pressed the blue spiral button, waiting for it to find her, then clicked to accept the photo on her device. Handing Alice's phone back without looking.

"Thank you," Ash filled in again, but Bel was only half listening, zooming in on the pixelated face, barely a third uncovered. It was impossible to tell for sure, her gut swaying between yes and no. There was one way she wanted to push it. But if this was Rachel, what was she doing here?

"She came up to the register?" Bel asked, but that wasn't her real question. "Did she buy something?"

Alice nodded, like that was answer enough.

"And?" Bel said, annoyed that she had to. "What did this woman buy?"

"Just two things, if I remember right." Alice rubbed her face like Bel's gaze had burned her. Oh, if only. "She paid in cash, even though we have a sign saying we prefer card." She paused to point at said printed sign. "I think she bought a pair of jeans and a top, that was all."

Bel's ears pricked, so did the ball of tension in her gut, listening in. "What kind of top?"

"A plain long-sleeved top. Red, I believe. I don't do boring colors."

Bel's heart picked up. "A red long-sleeved top," she said, repeating it to make sure she'd heard right.

"Yes."

"And were the jeans black?"

"I think so. Bit more versatile than blue, isn't it? Can wear them in the evening too."

Bel stalled, thinking it through. Alice didn't realize what she'd just said. Maybe she only recognized Rachel Price from that one

155

photo, the one they used on the missing posters and the news: Rachel wearing a white shirt. She couldn't see the significance of a red long-sleeved top and a pair of black jeans. The clothes Rachel was wearing when she disappeared. The same clothes she had on when she reappeared, falling apart; tattered and stained.

"Bel?" Ash said, not understanding her pause, or understanding it and checking she was OK.

Bel ignored him. "Do your items have labels in them?"

"Of course." Alice beamed. "Baa-Baa Boutique, too good a name to not put it in all the clothes. Can I help you look for something, sweetie? Is it for your mom?"

Bel didn't speak, so Ash did again, awkward and shuffling. "I like that pug shir—"

"Actually, we need to go," Bel said, holding on to Ash's overalls to spin him around, camera getting an undershot of her chin. "Bye, thank you, bye," she called behind her, falling into the door, the bell clattering above them, frenzied and shrill.

They didn't speak until they reached the car, and Bel realized she'd been holding on to him all the way. She let go and they climbed in. Ash was still recording, camera pointed at her from his lap.

"What?" he sniffed. "Did you think it was her? I thought the photo was too blurry to tell for sure, and she's so covered up."

"No, yes, no," Bel said, unsure which word should come first. "Yes, the photo isn't clear, could be her, could not. Obviously had to have cut her hair off since. But the things she bought?"

"Red top and black jeans?" he asked, unsure.

"Ash—no offense, well, a bit offense—have you been paying any attention to this documentary you're making?" She rounded on him, the camera a barrier between them. "Those are the clothes Rachel was wearing the day she disappeared. The same clothes she was wearing when I found her walking home on Saturday. Dirty, ripped, full of holes, like she'd been wearing the same clothes for the past sixteen years. Except what if she hadn't? What if that's just what she wanted it to look like?"

Ash's eyes changed.

"So you're saying . . ."

"I'm saying what if she no longer had those original clothes she disappeared in, she would have needed to buy some as similar as possible, for her grand planned reappearance. If so, then it's possible that *was* her, here, in January. Close by but in disguise. A Covid mask. That could explain how she's been moving around—at least for the past four years—hiding her identity. Could you distress a top and jeans that much—get them to rags in just a few months?"

"Probably," Ash said. "If you were motivated enough. But it's not, you know, solid evidence, what that lady remembers that unknown woman buying."

Bel knew that, she knew she'd need more, something more concrete if she was going to expose Rachel as a liar. Convince Dad and the police. But this was stronger than a coincidence, she was sure. She could allow one fluke: the timing of the documentary and Rachel's return. But she couldn't allow another. The clothes meant something; a match lit under her, burning in her belly, proof enough that her gut feeling had been right all along.

"Tell me what you're thinking," Ash said.

"I think you sound like Ramsey," she replied, a surge of new energy climbing up her spine. She rolled her head to let it out, cracking her neck. "I don't know about her disappearance yet, but it's starting to look like Rachel planned her own reappearance, that she's been back for more than just a few days. Which means the basement can't be real. The man can't be real. And for some reason, she wants the world to think they are." She hesitated. "Does that sound crazy?"

Ash shook his head. "No. I mean, you *are* definitely crazy. But not for that."

She smiled at him, a real one that she didn't think twice on.

"Mate, I reckon we did an all-right job back there, you and me," he said, scratching his nose. "The old good cop, bad cop routine."

"Which one's the bad cop?" Bel asked, still smiling, on purpose this time.

Ash gaped at her. "Come on. Seriously?"

EIGHTEEN

Bel wasn't smiling anymore when Ash dropped her home.

Rachel had taken Dad's spot, her new car parked in front of the garage, where his truck lived. The truck was nowhere, so Dad wasn't home from work yet. Fucking great. No Dad, but CNN, NBC, ABC and FOX were all here.

"I guess I'll see you," Ash said as she climbed out.

"I guess," Bel said. "As I'm contractually obliged to."

"Always a pleasure, Bel." He flattened his hand, saluting her as she shut the car door. Trying to out-smartass her; she'd show him, next time.

Bel tramped up to the front door, ignoring the four floating reporters shouting questions at her, protected by their property line, an invisible border they weren't allowed to cross. She pretended sound couldn't cross it either.

Bel eyeballed Rachel's car. Three days back and she was already taking over, muscling the rest of them out, claiming territory. Bel had made progress today—an ally, a clue—but not nearly enough. She'd need more evidence than that to reclaim her home from Rachel Price. Because that was what it would come down to, wouldn't it? One or the other.

She slotted her key into the lock. At least she had her bedroom; the last safe space that Rachel couldn't claim. She'd go there right now, shut herself away until Dad got back, pretend she had home-work.

Bel opened the door, holding her breath, preparing to face Rachel again, though she never felt ready enough.

The hallway was clear.

Bel locked her jaw and walked through to the living room. Rachel wasn't here either, or in the kitchen, though the oven was on, rattling in that way it did. Was Rachel not home? Maybe she went out on a walk?

Something sparked in her gut, that instinct you got in an empty house to call out, make it un-empty, but Bel pushed the feeling down, overrode it. Why would she call out for Rachel? She didn't want to find her. This was a lucky break; she could go hide in her room without having to make excuses.

She started up the stairs, skipping the one that creaked. She paused at the top. The door to the spare room—it was important to think of it like that, not as Rachel's room—was open, and it was empty. The bathroom door was closed, though. No sound of running water, but maybe Rachel was in the bathtub?

Bel lightened her steps, tiptoeing now, just in case. She didn't want Rachel to know she was home, force her to reappear again.

She reached her bedroom door and nudged it open.

Someone gasped and Bel caught it too, sealing off her throat, coughing through it.

Rachel was standing in her bedroom, by the bookshelves.

"Oh, Anna," Rachel said, her gasp breaking into a shy laugh. She'd been holding a book, now clutched in front of her heart, like a shield. "I didn't hear you come in."

That was because she wasn't supposed to. And she wasn't sup-posed to be here, in Bel's room, in her safe space.

Bel dropped her backpack to the floor with a heavy thunk.

"What are you . . . ?" she began, unsure how to end that question, because *What are you doing here?* went much deeper than just her bedroom.

"Sorry," Rachel said, feet shuffling on the carpet. "I was looking for a book, Carter said you're a big reader. I thought I could borrow one. Hope you don't mind."

Bel did mind, and right this second, she didn't know how to pretend otherwise. Rachel had thrown her off, being where she shouldn't, heart thudding against Bel's ribs, fight-or-flight fast.

Rachel held up the book in her hands, spinning it so the jacket flapped like trapped wings. "This is a good book," she said. Bel recognized the green of the cover: *The Memory Thief.* It was one of her favorites, had been all her life. "One of my favorites," Rachel said then, stealing that from her as well.

"It's OK," Bel said. "Bit boring in the middle."

Rachel glanced down at the book, fingers running over the sharp corners and ridges of once-folded pages. "Did someone give you this book, or . . . ?" she said, stilted, trying to make conversation. Maybe Bel had thrown her off too.

"No, I bought that copy a few years ago. Grandpa used to read it to me when I was a kid, I wanted to read it again myself, as not-a-kid."

"That's sweet." Rachel slotted the book into the empty space on the shelf, recompleting the row. "That your grandpa used to read to you."

"He started when Dad was in jail, for your murder," Bel said, finding her footing again, stepping forward.

Rachel nodded, chewing on her secret thoughts alone, face guarding them closely. "I should go visit him, Charlie's dad."

"He probably won't remember you much," Bel said, scoring points where she could. "He's forgotten who me and Carter are, and we've always been here."

Rachel chewed harder, the inside of her cheek, then she blinked, changing her face. "You just missed her; Carter was here. She's very sweet, isn't she? Couldn't stay for dinner, but she helped me set up my new phone, actually. All done, just have to practice using it." She moved her hands behind her back, hiding them, a click in her shoulder. "I know you were too busy yesterday. But it's done now, anyway, and she put your number in for me."

Thanks, Carter.

"I'll text you, so you have my number," Rachel continued. "You can call me anytime. You know that, right? Anytime."

"Sure," Bel said. Anytime, just not the last sixteen years, the years people tended to need their moms most.

Bel stepped forward again, clearing the doorway. She wanted Rachel to leave, though she wasn't sure her bedroom would ever feel safe again now, Rachel's mark left behind on everything she'd touched and looked at. How long had she been snooping around in here? Had she sat on the bed? Had she opened the nightstand drawer, or the closet? Had she found Bel's collection of stolen things?

"I'm filming my interviews the next two days," Rachel said, finding something else to say, another reason to stay.

"Cool."

"I called Ramsey, actually, tried out my new phone." She rubbed one eye. "He had an idea, for us to have a big family meal on Friday night, the whole family: us, Jeff, Sherry, Carter, my mom, your grandpa too, and the caregiver. What's his name again?"

"Yordan."

"Yordan. Ramsey will organize caterers to come in, so we don't have to cook. You can help me pick the menu if you like. They'll film the dinner for the documentary. That'll be fun, won't it? All of us together again."

Fun wasn't the word Bel would have gone with. But at least the house would be busy, full of voices, not this uncomfortable give-and-take alone with Rachel.

"Will be nice to have everyone around."

Rachel smiled at her. "We could ask for anything. Steak? Paella?"

"Dad doesn't like shrimp. Got food poisoning one time."

The smile faltered on one side. "How was your extra-credit thing?" Rachel asked.

"Yeah, fine."

"Ramsey mentioned that he saw you today, after school," Rachel said.

Fuck. Bel might have caught Rachel in some of her lies, but she was about to catch her back. Unless Bel thought fast.

"Oh yeah, I went into the hotel," Bel said, making it up as she went. "I had five minutes before the meeting, and I remembered I'd left my scrunchie there when I filmed my interview. Went to check if it was in lost and found."

Convincing enough. No holes, unless Rachel really went looking. Rachel nodded. "Any luck?"

"No, no luck."

Ramsey wouldn't have told Rachel what they talked about, right? That Bel was onto Rachel, starting to unpick her lies. No, he wouldn't, Bel could tell from the light in his eyes; he'd seen opportunity in Bel's suspicions. And he couldn't be taking advantage of her if she was actually taking advantage of them. Using them to document any evidence she found, a permanent record. Scratching each other's backs, using Ash to do it.

"Will your dad be back for dinner?" Rachel asked, finding something new to say, which meant Bel must have convinced her, covered her own tracks.

"He normally gets home earlier than this," she said.

"It's lasagna tonight. Store-bought. Didn't have time to make it," Rachel said, almost guiltily. "Do you like lasagna?"

If Bel had to answer one more time whether she liked something or not, she might just scream.

The front door slammed below.

"Hello?" Charlie's voice rang out. "Kiddo?"

Thank fuck for that.

Dad was home, and that was good, because it wasn't really home without him.

NINETEEN

Only FOX, CNN and ABC outside the next day when Bel got home from school. Dwindling, one news channel at a time. If they followed nursery rhyme logic, they'd all be gone by Saturday, old news. Until something new broke—like Rachel had made it all up—then they'd all come scurrying back, start the song again. *Ten white news vans, sitting on the curb.*

"Have fun at dancing!" Bel called to Carter as she continued down Milton Street, pulling her hood up to ignore the reporters.

Bel scrambled for her keys in her pocket. She didn't realize until she looked up. Dad's truck wasn't here, but neither was Rachel's car.

Was Rachel out? Maybe she was still at the Royalty Inn, recording her interview with Ramsey. Bel should have checked the parking lot when they walked past.

She unlocked the front door and stepped inside the house, heart picking up, just in case she needed it.

"Hello?" she called out, to double-check.

No one answered.

She walked through the living room. Tried again. "Hello? Dad? Rachel? You here?" Hand resting on the banister, looking up. "Rachel? Mom?" she said, just as a test. "Mommy dearest?"

Nothing. Not a sound. She was home alone.

She sighed, hand to her chest to slow her heart. She kicked off her shoes and dropped her bag, leaving them where they fell. Rachel kept tidying things away, even though she didn't know where they lived: putting plates where the bowls lived, mugs where the glasses lived, and Bel's shoes in the hall closet. So Bel would enjoy leaving them right here while Rachel was gone, the house to herself.

The house to herself.

Bel was an idiot: she hadn't realized what that meant. Not just a chance to leave her shoes in the way, but a chance to search for answers without Rachel's prying eyes. Rachel had done it first, snooping in Bel's room yesterday, so it was her turn now, a fair and equal retaliation. She might have left something in her room, something real, concrete, that Bel could use to unravel her lies.

She'd waited too long already; Rachel could be back any moment.

Bel thundered up the stairs, even the creaky one, and hurried over to the spare room door. She grabbed the handle and pushed it open, stepping inside. If there was an invisible barrier here too, it wasn't strong enough to keep her out.

The bed was made, almost too neatly, like it was a prop and not a real place where someone slept. Afternoon sun spilled in through the open curtains, capturing the room in a static yellow glow, claiming Bel too as she stepped farther inside, bending to check under the bed. Nothing but dust.

To the dresser first. On top were some new things: a can of deodorant, two moisturizers and a scented candle. Bel pulled open the top drawer. Underwear, bras and socks; their haul from H&M. She patted around, checking if Rachel had hidden anything underneath or between, but she felt only fabric.

The next drawer had folded tops, new and the old T-shirts Dad had dug out.

Skirt and pants and jeans in the one below. Rachel must have been wearing the shirtdress for her interview.

Nothing in the drawer at the bottom.

Bel turned and caught movement in the corner of her eye. She twisted toward it. A shape, phantom dark, looming there. Bel blinked and let out her breath. It was just a towel, charcoal gray, hanging on the back of the door, still seesawing gently from when she'd shoved it open.

Bel looked beyond, into the hallway, focusing her ears, checking for any sound. The reporters outside should act like an alarm, shouldn't they? Warning her when Rachel returned with their desperate, shouted questions. It was true, but it wasn't much comfort. She felt jumpy, even at the sounds her own body made, screws tightening in her gut.

She walked over to the nightstand.

There was an iPhone charging cable wrapped around the base of the lamp, plugged in behind. A glass of water on top, at least two stale sips left behind. No book, but a folded piece of paper, a pen resting on top at a diagonal to keep it down.

Bel moved the pen aside to see what was written there in Rachel's scrawl.

> To-do list:
> ☐ Choose menu for Friday
> ☐ Book eye test
> ☐ Book dentist
> ☐ Insurance
> ☐ Annabel

Bel's eyes circled her own name there, at the bottom of the list. Ran her finger across it. Well, what the fuck did that mean? Her name as something to be done, below insurance and dentist. Empty checkboxes, so nothing had been completed yet. And what exactly did Rachel mean by that, what was she planning to do to her?

A shiver passed up Bel's spine, uncanny and cold, even though the room was warm. She placed the pen back where she'd found it and her eyes settled on the handle of the nightstand drawer. A place for secrets—where Bel kept hers—and the only place left where they could be. Her fingers pinched the air, closing around the rectangular handle. She pulled it open, the wood grating against its carved grooves.

The empty iPhone box was inside, receipt on top. A lip balm. A small packet of Kleenex. That was it. No, that couldn't be it. Bel had checked everywhere else in the room. There had to be something; she needed something.

The drawer wouldn't pull out any farther, creaking as Bel tried. She slid the iPhone box to the side to check the dark space behind it.

Wait, there was something here. Something small and pink, buried right at the back.

Bel reached in, closed her fingers around it, tiny and soft.

She pulled it out and held it up to the light.

Light pink, frilled at the top.

It was a baby sock, almost weightless, curled in the palm of her hand.

Bel studied it, held it up and let it dangle. She couldn't believe her feet had ever been that tiny. Because this was her sock, wasn't it? It had to be, from before Rachel disappeared. But what was it doing here?

This drawer had been empty that first night after Rachel reappeared, when Dad set up the room for her. Bel had been here when Dad checked the nightstand, blowing dust from the top. This sock was not there. So how was it there now?

There was only one real explanation: Rachel must have brought it with her. Put it in the drawer herself, tucked it right at the back, like she was trying to hide it.

But how was that even possible? If Rachel had the sock when she reappeared, in her pocket maybe, the police would have taken it into evidence, along with the rest of her clothes. But the sock wasn't in evidence, it was right here. Rachel could have stashed it somewhere before they went off with the police? Somewhere inside the house, or somewhere in town on the way. She'd had plenty of time in the days since to go collect it, bring it back and hide it in the drawer. That was the only possibility, unless Dad kept some of Bel's baby things around the house—in the attic maybe—and Rachel went searching when she was home alone.

But if Rachel *had* brought the sock into the house, why was she keeping one of Bel's baby socks? And how long had she kept it? From when she disappeared?

Bel ran her fingers over the tiny sock, examining it. It felt old, thinning and worn, like this wasn't the first time fingers had stroked it, trying to take something from it.

Bel couldn't see any other way, any other origin for this baby sock in her hand. And if that was true, if Rachel had taken a keepsake from Bel the day she disappeared, then that proved it, didn't it? That she knew she was going to disappear, that she'd planned it, chosen it. You didn't take a souvenir from your baby daughter if you didn't plan to leave forever, abandoning her in the backseat of your car.

The sighting in North Conway three months ago: the black jeans and red top gave it away, that Rachel had planned her reappearance. And here, this tiny baby sock betrayed the other half of the story. That Rachel had also planned her disappearance, that she'd chosen to go, like Bel had always known deep down.

It didn't hurt now, facing the truth, it felt like victory, a confirmation. Rachel cared just enough to keep Bel's sock, but not enough to stay. The sock was proof, still too flimsy for anyone else, but enough for Bel to keep going. To work out why Rachel chose to disappear, then reappear, and what she'd done with those sixteen years between, other than hold on to Bel's sock.

The knot writhed in her gut, pulling at its strings.

Bel closed her fist around the baby sock, locked her fingers under her thumb.

Well, why not? It had been hers in the first place, wasn't Rachel's to keep. She took the sock with her, leaving the spare room as she'd found it.

Into her bedroom, no longer quite as safe.

Hid the sock in her nightstand instead, buried deep under all those other little secrets.

TWENTY

Letting go of something you love is too hard. Don't know if I'll ever make another documentary. Six hundred and twenty-nine likes, forty-one retweets, eleven comments.

Bel's eyes lit up. She'd found it, finally, the tweet that @DirectorRamseyLee posted last October. This must be the one.

It was Thursday evening, and she was sitting on her bed, laptop buttressed against her knees, stomach snarling because she hadn't eaten enough at dinner.

She clicked onto the comments and scrolled down.

Don't give up!

I loved Snow Dog—it made me cry!

And then:

Have you heard of the Rachel Price case? If you're ready for your next story, it would make a great documentary. Can't believe it hasn't been done already.

By a Lucas Ayer, no profile photo. Bel clicked the name. He had zero followers and followed no one. That tweet had been his first and last, joining Twitter in October 2023, like he'd made the account just to do that. Bel narrowed her eyes, studying Lucas's empty gray face, finding nothing.

The laptop juddered in her hands, rattling as an awful sound filled the house, grating and high-pitched, cutting out suddenly.

Someone was drilling. Upstairs. And it wasn't Dad, because the TV was on down below.

The drilling started up again.

Bel let her laptop slide off her lap, got up to follow the noise.

She opened her door, hesitated in the hallway.

Rachel was on her knees outside the spare room door, holding the drill up to the latch hole in the frame, carving out the edges. There was an open box on the floor beside her, a new silver door handle poking out. *Door lever handle: locks both ways,* said the box.

Rachel stopped the drill and blew at the sawdust.

"What are you doing?" Bel asked.

Rachel flinched, her finger pulling the trigger, the drill growling once in response.

"You scared me, Anna—Bel, sorry. Bel."

But Rachel had scared her more times.

"Putting a lock on your door?" Bel trailed forward, nudging the box with her toe.

"Yeah." Rachel pulled out the new handle, showing her. There was a switch to turn for the inside, a keyed lock for the outside of the door. "I haven't been sleeping very well," she said, rubbing her eyes on her sleeve. "I guess because I know he's still out there, could be anywhere. The man who took me. Thought it would help me sleep, knowing I can lock myself in. Worth a try."

Bel nodded, like that made sense, avoiding Rachel's eyes. "This one locks on the outside too." She pointed down at the box. "With a key."

"Oh, so it does," Rachel said, like she hadn't noticed until now, returning her attention to the drill, avoiding Bel's eyes too. She changed the setting and started it up again, removing the screws from the existing door handle, making the house shake again.

Rachel *had* noticed it was a double-sided lock, though, hadn't she? That was the reason she bought it. It wasn't about being able to sleep. It was about being able to lock the room when she wasn't here, keep intruders out. She must know Bel had been in her room yesterday, that she'd taken back her pink baby sock.

Did Rachel now know that Bel knew she was lying? Or at least that she suspected it? Bel didn't want to hang around to find out. She backtracked to the stairs and hurried down.

Dad was in his chair, beer in one hand as he watched baseball reruns, the volume on high.

Bel paused at the back of his chair, wanting to be close to him without him knowing, pretend it was just the two of them again, without the shifts and distances Rachel had created.

"You got back late today," she said. "Missed dinner."

He took a sip.

"Work was busy." His eyes on the TV.

"And yesterday?"

Bel leaned over and gave him a hug, arms around his warm neck, face squished against the back of his head. She'd have to let go soon, before he asked what was wrong, but she didn't want to. He was avoiding the house, working later and later every day. Soon he might just stop coming home at all. Bel knew why. They all knew why, and she wouldn't let that happen.

"Work *is* busy," he said. "I can't help it."

No, he couldn't. But Bel could. Dad didn't need to be the one who worried, for once. Bel could do the worrying, the fixing, the planning. Rachel had only been back five days and she was pushing him away, Bel could sense it. Dad said he believed Rachel's story, every word. But there was no doubt that her return had changed something for him.

Part of Bel had known, the instant she saw his face when he realized Rachel was back, that it would come down to a choice. One or the other. Now she knew they couldn't exist in this house together and for Bel, it wasn't a choice at all. That was why she had to fight: find proof that Rachel Price was a liar, get rid of her before she got rid of Dad.

"OK, kiddo?" Charlie said, tapping her arm until she let go. "What's she doing?"

He meant Rachel.

"Fitting a lock on the spare room door."

"OK," he said. Was that all? So calm, like he didn't even know he was part of this war.

Bel sat on the sofa, the side closest to him.

"Someone left the window open down here last night," he said. "I don't know if it was you or her."

Bel didn't either. "Sorry," she said, just in case. "Hey, Dad."

"Hey, Bel." He saluted his beer at her.

"Have you got any of the stuff from when I was a baby? Toys or clothes? Are they up in the attic?"

"No." His eyes tracked the baseball. "Don't have anything like that. Gave it all to Goodwill, or to Jeff and Sherry for Carter. Why?"

"Oh, nothing. Film crew were asking if we had any," she lied easily, even though it was Dad and she didn't do that to him.

He grunted, taking another swig of his beer.

The drill started up again, shuddering and growling. Building to a high-pitched rattle of a scream.

Dad grabbed the remote, turned the volume up.

And again, both getting louder, one in each of Bel's ears, commentators bellowing over the screech of the drill.

Up and up, pushing and pushing.

TWENTY-ONE

The house was unrecognizable, the entire living room taken over, rearranged around them.

The sofa and Dad's chair had been removed to make way, the table from the kitchen now in here, extended to seat nine, four more dining chairs borrowed from Jeff and Sherry's house. Grandpa didn't need one, he came with his own.

Two cameras were set up, to record both sides of the elongated table. Ash was behind one of them, the smaller camera that he was trusted with, fiddling with the tripod legs. Flared jeans and a fluorescent green T-shirt covered in happy apples: happles. James was opposite, cameras strategically placed so they didn't get each other in the shot. Bel had watched as they worked it out, enjoying when Ash was ordered around, how he carried his shoulders, how he closed one eye to study the viewfinder. They hadn't had time to say one word to each other, which was fine, because it was hard to be rude to someone with just one word.

Ramsey was hovering around the softbox lights, shifting them by millimeters, seeing what no one else could. Saba was at the back with her headphones and audio equipment: everyone already miked up.

The two caterers were bustling around in the kitchen, heating up the pre-prepared meals in the oven. Rachel watched the chaos and

Bel watched her, movement and chatter everywhere, fifteen people in a house meant for two.

Grandpa was already positioned at the head of the table one side, Yordan crammed in beside, to help him with his food. Grandpa looked just as lost as Bel felt.

She fiddled with the new bracelet on her wrist, the chain cold and strange where it pulled against her bone. Rachel had surprised her with it, before everyone arrived. Said she had a lot of birthdays and Christmases to make up for.

"Hey," Carter said, finding her way to Bel through the mayhem.

"Hey."

"OK?" Carter nudged her, elbows clashing. "Things feeling more normal yet?"

Absolutely fucking not, *things* were less normal than ever, and she was even more convinced now that Rachel was a liar. But Bel couldn't answer that, because she was wearing a live microphone, and Saba was listening in.

"Sure," she said, which obviously didn't sound sure enough, because Carter bristled. "Thanks for helping pick out the bracelet." Bel held it out, gold chain against the pale flesh of her wrist. No skulls on this one, but it was a message of some kind, after Rachel slipped up about Bel's old bracelet at the mall.

Carter nodded. "Rachel wanted to get you something she knew you'd love. And I know you best. She's really trying, you know."

"Oh, I know," Bel said, because whatever she had to say about Rachel, she couldn't say she wasn't trying. You had to *try*, to get away with a lie like how you disappeared for sixteen years and reappeared again. It wasn't just a bracelet, was it? It was a countermove, after Bel snooped in her room, stole back that sock. A lock to keep her out, and a bracelet to keep her quiet.

"Starters are ready," Ramsey called, reemerging from the kitchen. "Everyone please take a seat. Ash, James, let's get rolling. Rachel, could we get you in the middle, on this side?"

"Sure." Rachel smiled, dropping down on the chair, bringing her glass of red wine with her.

Bel knew what was going to happen, so she moved faster than Ramsey could, taking a seat on the other side, opposite Rachel. Ramsey caught her with his widened eyes. He came over and bent down to whisper to her.

"I was thinking we'd put you next to your mum," he said, treading carefully.

"I've already sat down." Bel beamed up at him. It was too late anyway, Rachel's mom had already taken the seat to Rachel's left, and Carter on her right, the rest of the family milling toward the table.

Ramsey chewed his lip. "Opposite works better, actually," he said, low and secretive, trying to take the win away from her. He moved out of Charlie's way, already on his third beer, labels peeled off for filming.

The chatter settled down, everyone waiting to be told what to do. Jeff was at one end of the table, then Carter, Rachel, Grandma Susan (horsefucker), Yordan and Grandpa on the other end, then Dad, Bel and Sherry.

"It's nice to see you again, Pat," Rachel said, breaking the awkward silence, watching Grandpa as she took another sip of her wine.

Grandpa's eyes darkened. Yordan whispered something in his ear.

"Ray-chul," Grandpa repeated it, hacking it into two, like it wasn't a name at all.

The caterers appeared, holding two plates each, working from the middle out, Rachel and Bel first. Goat's cheese and red onion tart. Bel had suggested this one, didn't think Rachel would go for it. She glanced up, caught Rachel smiling at her. Bel raised her knife and fork in response.

"Dig in, everyone," Rachel said, like this was her house and she was the host.

Carter took the first bite. "It's delicious."

"Anna picked it," Rachel said. "Sorry. Bel. Still getting used to that."

"Oh yes." Sherry turned to Bel beside her. "I forgot you used to be Anna, it's been so long." Back to Rachel. "She was about six when she insisted on Bel instead, headstrong girl. Seems like she's been Bel forever, honestly."

"Well," Rachel said, "I didn't get the memo."

"No, course not." Sherry smiled. "Lots of new things to get used to. The world too, very different now. Honestly, you can't say *anything* these days without upsetting somebody." Sherry's fork paused on the way to her mouth. "That's a nice outfit, Rachel." A peace offering of some sort.

Rachel's eyes darted down to her top. "Thanks. Anna—fuck—Bel chose it for me." One of her hands balled into a fist, knuckles pushing out like hilltops.

Grandma flinched at the *fuck.* Oh come on, her daughter had supposedly been kept in a basement for sixteen years, and the part she found unpalatable was that four-letter word?

"No, you look really great, Rachel," Sherry continued. "So skinny. I guess sixteen years of captivity is the best diet there is."

Someone dropped a fork.

Carter's face fell open. "Mom," she hissed, eyes wounded, staring across the table at her. "You can't say that!"

Sherry looked at the camera for a moment, then pushed out a laugh. "Oh, don't be silly," she said. "Rachel knows I'm only joking, don't you?"

Rachel grinned back, something sharp about it, Bel felt it, even though it was aimed at Sherry. Seemed the Price family had more land mines lying around, live and ticking even after sixteen years. They hadn't even finished their starters and one had already blown up. What happened to those happy tears and hugs of a few days ago?

"Anyone for any more wine?" Rachel grasped the neck of the bottle. "Jeff? Yordan? Nice to meet you, by the way, Yordan. Is it Bulgaria you're from?"

"Can I drink?" Bel said, throwing out a bomb herself.

"Um, I . . . ," Rachel began, just as Dad huffed, "No."

"Maybe another time," Rachel added.

"I said no," Charlie hardened his voice, stabbing his last piece of tart, avoiding Rachel's eyes.

Bel remembered that thing Dad told Ramsey, about Rachel lighting up rooms for him. Well, she didn't light them up anymore, in fact, he mostly left the room whenever she walked in. But now they were trapped together by the whole family and two cameras, sitting on opposite sides of the table. Bel had chosen her side.

"So, Susan," Charlie said, a glare in his eyes from the closest light box. "I wondered if you had anything to say to me and the rest of my family, now that Rachel has returned, un-murdered."

Grandma put her fork down delicately. "That I'm very happy, very grateful my daughter is alive and well. My only regret is that Edward didn't live to see Rachel come home." Her eyes misted, patting Rachel's shoulder.

"Is that it?" Charlie doubled down, an incredulous smile. "No apologies?"

"Don't bother, Dad," Bel said quietly.

"What's going on?" Rachel put her wine down, gaze flicking between the two sides of her family.

"You can tell her, Susan," Charlie said.

"Nothing, sweetie." Grandma gripped Rachel's arm. "This is meant to be a happy evening, a celebration."

"You can't do it, can you?" Charlie laughed. "Too much pride to say sorry even now. I didn't kill Rachel, did I? She's sitting right there next to you."

"Mom?" Rachel looked at her.

Grandma fiddled with her lace scarf. "I was so sure he'd killed you. There were no other answers. It just had to be him." She wiped a tear that Bel couldn't see.

"It's OK," Rachel said gently.

"It's not OK," Bel stepped in, less gently.

Grandpa's eyes followed the conversation, a loaded fork hovering by this mouth, Yordan distracted too.

"I'm sorry, Charlie, OK?" Grandma dabbed her face with the scarf. "You would understand if something ever happened to Annabel, if she vanished into thin air."

"I wish," muttered Bel, and right now she did. She'd thought this meal would be a cease-fire, everyone on their best behavior, but course one of three and look where they were already. Ramsey hovered by the kitchen door, watching intently; he must have been thrilled.

"It's OK, Mom. Charlie would never hurt me," Rachel said, no, she announced, like he wasn't right here. Dad tensed; Bel could feel it in the air around her. That was confusing: Rachel defending Dad. That had always been Bel's job. Always.

"Now everyone thinks I'm the bad guy." Grandma blew her nose into the napkin.

"No, they don't." Rachel rubbed her mom's back. "It must have been very hard for you all these years, to be around him, if that's what you thought happened. I understand."

"Well, that wasn't much of a problem," Charlie said, finally drawing Rachel's eyes.

"What do you mean?"

"We hardly ever saw your parents."

A shadow crossed Rachel's face; a hurt Bel didn't understand. "Mom?" Rachel said, voice rough at the edges. "You never visited them? Not even for birthdays? Not even once a year?"

Grandma pulled back from her daughter, sensing the shift, the danger. "It would have been too difficult, to see his face, when we thought he—"

"What about Annabel?" Rachel snapped.

Grandma flinched, but Rachel wasn't finished.

"I can't believe this. Annabel was so young; she needed you. You should have been there for her when I couldn't."

"We thought he was a killer," Grandma protested.

"Well, he's not!" Rachel spat. "But that means you chose to leave my daughter alone with the man you were sure had killed me, doesn't it?"

"I'm sorry. I did think about suing for custody, but . . ." Grandma's head dropped, breaking eyeline. A disconnect between them, greater than sixteen years.

Bit rich of Rachel, to be mad at everyone else for abandoning Bel.

"Is everyone done?" Jeff piped up, awkwardly rubbing his elbow. "Food, I mean."

The caterers came in to carry the plates away, the table breaking into small, tentative side conversations, Dad checking that Grandpa didn't need to go home already. Any excuse to leave, to get away. Sherry was talking to Jeff, so Bel had no one to turn to. She unclipped the microphone from her collar, raised it to her mouth.

"I think the meal's going really well so far," she whispered into it. "Happy families."

At the back corner, she saw Saba react. Ash too, hands cupped around his headphones behind camera B. He coughed, stifling a laugh, which was good, because she'd said it for him.

Carter was on her own too, Rachel and Grandma Susan still exchanging hissed words. She looked upset; Carter didn't like confrontation, even when she wasn't in it. Bel kicked her under the table, praying it was her leg and not Rachel's. Carter jerked, looking across at her. Her frown became a smile, but it didn't fix the look in her eyes.

Two huge silver platters arrived, loaded with paella, serving spoons to help themselves.

Charlie picked up one spoon and dropped a load on his plate, staring down at it.

"I did tell her," Bel said, under her breath.

"It's OK, kiddo. I can pick out the shrimp." He smiled sadly. "Don't have much of an appetite anyway."

Opposite, Rachel passed the platter to Carter first. Carter smiled politely, spooning two piles into a mound on her plate, rockfalls of rice and peas.

"Not too much, honey," Sherry said across the table. "Rehearsals this weekend. Don't want to give Ms. Dunn an excuse not to put you front row."

Carter said nothing as she passed the platter back to Rachel. Rachel returned her polite smile, an exchange, but hers seemed more forced, struggling at the corners.

"Dancing this, dancing that," Jeff said, waiting for one of the platters to circle around to him.

"It's important to her, Jeff," Sherry said sharply. "You could give it more attention."

"I give it plenty of attention," he sniffed. "Just let her spend two hundred bucks on my credit card a couple days ago for something *dancing*. What was it, Car, new leotards or something?"

Carter stared at her plate, nodding her chin up and down in a tiny movement.

"Look, you're putting her on the spot now and embarrassing her, Jeff." Sherry snatched the platter out of Bel's hands. "It's an investment in her future."

"I didn't say anything," Jeff said, laughing uncomfortably. "Just that if I'd known how expensive all this dancing stuff would be, I'd have become a criminal mastermind on the dark web instead of working at the Sport Center. My friend Bob from Vermont, he makes . . . oh wait, cameras are on. Never mind."

Sherry sighed, sound like a sprung snake, turning her shoulders to abandon Uncle Jeff on the corner. No part of the table was safe from outbreaks and flare-ups, clearly. They were everywhere since Rachel returned, her fault though Bel didn't quite know how yet, tension simmering just below the surface. Why were they doing this dinner, again?

Bel looked across the table; Rachel was hiding her eyes, making tracks through her paella with the underside of her fork. Good, at least she wasn't having a good time either.

No one was really eating, except for Grandpa, slow, steady forkfuls, in his own world, unaware of the explosions going on around him. Carter was eating too, on her last mouthfuls already, maybe so she didn't have to talk and get drawn into anything.

Rachel followed Bel's eyes to Carter and, without a word, she reached over for the serving spoon and tipped another load of paella onto Carter's plate.

Sherry flinched, raising her finger, trying to swallow her mouthful. But she retracted the finger, didn't say anything, just another sigh, sharper this time, two coiled snakes.

"Thank you," Carter said to Rachel quietly, a twitch by her mouth as she dug into her food.

"No problem, Carter." Rachel's voice echoed as she lowered her face into her glass of wine.

Sherry took a large gulp of her own.

"Is anyone else getting hot?" Jeff fiddled with the seam around his neck. "Should I open a window?"

Ramsey was wide-eyed, entranced. He must have been loving this: didn't have to direct or nudge at all, the dinner party was on a downward spiral all on its own.

"So, Charlie." Rachel speared a piece of chorizo. "Carter tells me you had a girlfriend for two years, you haven't mentioned her yet. Even moved her into our house for a few months?" The words dipped up like a question, needling him on purpose. Why would Carter tell Rachel anything like that? Whose side was she on?

Charlie took a sharp swig of his beer. "I hadn't found the right time to bring it up yet, in *private*." He leaned into the word. "Happened a very long time ago. Bel was ten."

"Eleven," Bel stepped in, eyes on Rachel, locking her elbows to put a shield up around both her and Dad, readying her acid tongue.

"Apparently this woman was the head juror at your trial for my murder," Rachel said, chuckling to herself, a shrimp pirouetting on her fork.

Charlie put down his empty beer. "Just a coincidence. Ellen and I bumped into each other years later. She recognized me."

Ellen was nice; Bel liked Ellen. And that was the problem, because she knew she would leave eventually, everyone always did. So Bel pushed her first, told her she didn't need or want a new mom. Kids could be cruel, and Bel could be the cruelest. Ellen packed her bags the next day.

"Must have looked pretty strange, though," Rachel said, crunching down on the shrimp. "Dating the woman who found you innocent of your wife's murder."

"Least *he* waited until after you were gone," Sherry muttered under her breath, wiping her mouth with her sleeve. No one else at the table heard, waiting for Charlie's response, but Bel had heard, sitting right next to her. She turned and studied her aunt, lips pressed in a tense line. What had she meant by that? That Rachel had been with someone else before she disappeared? There'd been no mention of a relationship in any of the media coverage. Wouldn't that have been huge news? A viable suspect? What had Sherry meant? Bel tucked that away, inside the knot in her gut, let it feed on her near-empty stomach.

"I was lonely," Charlie said, keeping his voice measured and even. "I'd grieved you for years. Everyone kept saying I had to move on. It was hard and it didn't last, so I'm not sure why you need to bring it up now."

"Just making conversation." Rachel let her fork dangle, scrape the plate. "That's what you do at dinner. You've hardly been in the house since I returned, so we haven't had many opportunities to talk in *private*." She leaned on the word the same way he had.

Dad's hands dropped into his lap, tightening into fists, a muscle ticking in his jaw.

Bel didn't know what to say, how to defend him, because Rachel was right, Dad was avoiding the house, but whose fault did she think that was?

"Maybe we should call it a day," he said, looking over at Grandpa.

"Dessert's just coming out," Ramsey interrupted for the first time, surprising the caterers, keeping Dad in his place.

He set his jaw, like he could make it through dessert, which meant Bel could too, as uneasy as she felt. That ball of tension spinning in her gut, gorging itself on all the unsaid and half-said things. What had Sherry meant?

Her plate was cleared away and another put down in front of her, apple pie with a thick dollop of cream. Another thing she'd suggested. What was Rachel's game?

"So, Pat." Rachel turned back to Grandpa. "You turn eighty-five in a couple of weeks. I can't believe it, where has all the time gone?"

Yes, where exactly did all that time go, Rachel? Grandpa stared blankly ahead, like he hadn't even heard.

"Please stop asking him questions," Charlie said. "He can't remember. It will distress him."

"I only asked about his birthday."

"Someone wants the yard, don't they? The Realtor . . . ," Grandpa croaked.

"Carter," Sherry hissed quietly.

Carter hesitated, put down her spoon.

"It's good with the cream," Rachel said to her.

"Sherry?" Jeff said.

The knot in Bel's gut grew, pulling tighter, the opposite of an explosion, like she might crumble and collapse around it.

"Where's Maria?" Grandpa said, a switch, eyes hard and mean.

"Dad." Charlie rested his hand on Grandpa's arm. "Mom isn't—"

"Carter," Sherry hissed again, or the snake inside her.

"She's just having her dessert, Sherry," Rachel said.

"Rachel, I think . . . ," began Grandma Susan.

"Maria?"

"Dad, it's OK."

Bel couldn't take it anymore.

"Hey!" she shouted over the noise, bringing all eyes to her. "Hey. How about a toast, everyone?" She stood, chair scraping against the floor, picking up her half-drunk glass of lemonade.

"An excellent idea, well done, *Bel*," Sherry said, using her name as some kind of weapon, aiming it at Rachel.

Rachel ignored her, picking up her wineglass, smiling up at Bel.

Bel waited for them all to join in, holding their glasses, except Grandpa, who was still looking for Maria. She looked around at everyone, even those behind the cameras, and raised her glass up high, squeezing too hard.

She cleared her throat.

"To the most fucked-up family in America. Cheers!"

TWENTY-TWO

Bel swallowed her drink in one go, knocked the empty glass against her head.

"Annabel," Grandma Susan gasped.

"Cheers!" Yordan smiled, because he must not have heard the first part.

"That's not funny, Bel, sit down," Dad said.

"Don't speak to her like that!" Rachel snapped, eyes ablaze, slamming one hand against the table.

Her wineglass tipped over, spilling a pool of blood over the white tablecloth, a red fork in the stain, reaching for Bel.

Grandpa burst out laughing and Sherry burst into tears.

"Dinner's over." Charlie got to his feet, waving off the cameras.

"Dad?" Bel called after him. But he'd disappeared into the hallway, two more seconds and the front door slammed behind him. Bel was sorry, because maybe she'd been the one to push him out. No, it was Rachel. This whole thing was Rachel. Bel glared across at her.

"Come on, Carter, let's go," Sherry sniffled, taking Carter's arm, pulling her up from the table.

"It was supposed to be a nice evening," Rachel said, quietly, almost to herself. Almost, if there wasn't a microphone attached to her.

Saba went after Sherry and Carter, catching them in the hallway.

Yordan stood up, reaching for the handles of Grandpa's wheelchair.

"Don't worry, Yordan," Jeff said, hurrying over. "I'll get Dad settled in the car. You stay, finish your dessert. No rush."

Jeff wheeled Grandpa off, toward the side door with the ramp. "Here we go, Dad," he said loudly, guiding him outside.

Grandma Susan left next, pausing just long enough to shake her head in Bel's direction.

"Always a pleasure." Bel raised her hand.

Rachel moved off into the kitchen, speaking in a low voice to Ramsey and the caterers.

"Good pie," Yordan said to Bel, awkwardly, the final two at the table.

"The best," Bel replied, walking away, leaving Yordan the last man standing, and he wasn't even family.

Bel narrowed her eyes at Ash, gestured toward the hallway. He abandoned the camera, three steps behind her.

Sherry and Carter were gone now, the front door left open behind them.

"Hey," Ash said, sounding almost breathless. "That was—"

"Can you turn me off?" She spun around to show him her ass.

"What? Oh."

Ash fiddled with the radio pack attached to her jeans. He spooled it up and unclipped the microphone from her shirt, fingers brushing against her collarbone. Bel shivered; the breeze from the open door.

"That was—" he tried again.

"I know." She chewed her lip. "Keep flirting with me and you'll have to marry into that family."

"Wouldn't dream of it," Ash swallowed.

"I need air," Bel said, heading for the dark rectangle of outside.

"Yes, I—I also breathe air." Ash followed her out here too.

There were two news vans still parked in the street outside, no sign of any reporters.

Up the road, Uncle Jeff had gotten Grandpa inside his yellow car, the one Yordan now used, since Grandpa couldn't drive. Jeff was folding up the wheelchair, leaning over to speak to Grandpa.

Across the street, Bel could see Ms. Nelson silhouetted against the yellow glow of her front door, standing there shamelessly, watching. Enjoying the show, as always.

"This way," Bel said, down the steps, leading Ash past the garage and into the backyard.

"That was—" Ash said again.

"I know it was, you can stop saying that," Bel replied. "Listen, I found something else a couple days ago."

"What?"

"One of my baby socks, in Rachel's nightstand. Which means that *A:* She hid that somewhere when she returned, so the police didn't take it into evidence. And *B:* If she took a souvenir from her daughter sixteen years ago, kinda makes it look like she planned to disappear in the first place, doesn't it?"

"Kinda . . . ," Ash said, parroting her. "Or it could mean that she had the sock on her when she was taken, in her pocket or something, kept it the entire time."

Bel glared at him.

"Just playing devil's advocate," he said. "If you're looking for evidence, that still isn't it. You need something that can't be explained away."

Bel glanced at the glow of the kitchen windows, the shape of Rachel and Ramsey moving around inside.

"How did her interviews go this week?" Bel asked.

Ash cleared his throat. "No inconsistencies," he said, knowing what she was *really* asking. "No details changed when Ramsey repeated questions. She got emotional in the right places. Explained when she couldn't answer something because the police told her it would interfere with the investigation. Talked a lot about you, actually." Ash paused to scratch his head, like he was almost sorry about it.

"About me?"

"That thinking about you and needing to get back to you is what

185

kept her going. Her motivation for staying alive, for fighting. That she's missed so much of your life, but she's determined to make up for every day she lost."

"Bullshit," Bel hissed, turning back to the dark silhouette of Rachel in the window. "You can tell, can't you, something's not right since she returned?"

Ash stood beside her. "Everyone in the family does seem to be on edge, yes. But I guess it's a tense situation."

"I need to get her out of the house." Much more urgent, now she could feel her dad pulling away. She chose him, she would always choose him, so Rachel had to go. "The only way to do that is to prove she's lying. Expose her. If I can't prove that she planned her reappearance yet, then I need to shift focus. Concentrate on her disappearance."

"No offense," Ash said, which was a shame because Bel liked trading offense, especially with him. "But didn't hundreds of police officers and federal agents and journalists already try that? They couldn't find anything; that's why her disappearance was always such a big mystery."

Bel ignored that, a flash in her eyes, like they might just glow in the dark. "What would you need to truly disappear for that amount of time? Money." She checked off one finger.

"Quite a lot of it," Ash said, "at least initially. But Rachel didn't have any money when she vanished. Her wallet was left in the car with you, her bank cards at home, and she hadn't taken any cash out of her accounts for several weeks."

"Maybe she gradually took money out over a longer period of time," Bel said, "so it wouldn't raise any flags. Or maybe she got the money from somewhere else. Someone else. Next: A new identity?"

Ash nodded. "She would have needed a new identity with a new name. To live freely for sixteen years, to earn money. Change her appearance too. A driver's license. Maybe a passport if she wasn't in America. All that would have cost money to set up."

"So we circle back to money," Bel said. "What else? Someone who maybe helped her?"

"A reason," Ash said, darkly.

"Huh?"

"She would have needed a reason, Bel, to go through all that effort. People don't just decide to disappear. She'd need a motive. A reason." The word fizzed like a trapped bee. "Something she'd done, or someone else had done, or was about to do. Something she was running away from," he added.

Bel thought of Grandma Susan, of the Gorham Police Department, and where that kind of thinking had taken them, wrongly pointing the finger at Dad.

"Maybe she wasn't running *away* from something, but running *to.*"

"What do you mean?" Ash ran a hand up his tattooed forearm, rubbing it against the evening chill.

"Did you hear what Sherry said, when Rachel was grilling Dad about Ellen?"

Ash shook his head.

"She said: *At least he waited until after you were gone.*"

Ash's mouth dropped open. "Definitely missed that."

"Hopefully the microphones didn't. And that makes it sound like—"

"Like Sherry thinks Rachel had a relationship with someone else before she disappeared," Ash completed it for her.

"Exactly," Bel said. "A reason." The word fizzing in her mouth now, another trade. "I need to know who she was talking about. Sherry knows something, something she's kept secret all this time. She didn't tell the police, but I bet I can get her to tell me. I know exactly what buttons to push."

Bel had spent her whole life learning how to push people, and there was already something between Rachel and Sherry, buried beneath sixteen years. She just needed to find it.

Bel slotted her fingers together, cracked her knuckles like a snapped twig, watching the shadow in the shape of her mother. Another silent promise made in the dark.

TWENTY-THREE

Dad was already gone when Bel woke up. *At work,* he'd texted. But it was a Saturday, and he might as well have said *anywhere but home.* Bel knew.

"I'm going out," she said, grabbing her shoes from the place they didn't live.

"Where?" Rachel jumped up from the sofa, like she might come too.

"Seeing some friends." Bel shot her down. "Will be nice to do something normal." Shooting her farther. They hadn't talked about last night.

"Oh," Rachel said, sitting down, covering her wounds with folded arms, because she knew just as well that *normal* didn't include her. "I have the day to myself, then. Call if you need anything, Anna. Shit. Bel. I'm trying to get that right, I promise. It's only been a week since I found out."

Bel crinkled her face at her, an approximation of a smile. "Bye, Rachel."

She slammed the front door behind her, harder than she needed to.

One news van outside. No sign of any reporters. But there was something else, a police cruiser parked outside Ms. Nelson's house. Bel could see Police Chief Dave Winter, talking to Ms. Nosy herself at her front door, scribbling in a small notebook.

Bel needed to talk to him, actually. Push the police to work on the

188

reappearance while she looked into the disappearance, trap Rachel in the middle. She crossed the road.

Ms. Nelson eyed her warily. Why? Didn't like seeing her up this close, or didn't like when Bel watched back?

"Hey." Bel raised one hand in greeting. "Everything OK?"

Dave's head tracked over his shoulder, eyes falling on hers. "Annabel. I was going to stop by afterward. How's everything going? Everyone settling in OK?"

"Oh yeah," Bel said, hiding her hands in her pockets. "She's made herself right at home."

"Good." He chewed the end of his pen. "Ms. Nelson was just telling me that she's seen a man standing on the street, watching your house. Late at night."

"He was there." Ms. Nelson pointed, gray flyaway hairs bristling in the breeze. "Hiding under that tree. I saw him at four a.m. when I let the cat out. Not the first time this week. Wears a baseball cap to hide his face."

"Thank you, Ms. Nelson," Dave said, the politest way of telling her to shut up. "Have you seen a man like that—Annabel—hanging around outside your house?"

"Yeah, loads of them. They're called reporters. The news vans." She gestured to the last remaining one. "This is the first day it's been quiet."

Ms. Nelson shook her head. "No, he wasn't with them. Standing there for hours, watching the house."

"OK, Ms. Nelson." Dave closed his notebook. "How about you go inside, make some coffee? I'll be in in a minute to get your full statement, OK?"

"I only have decaf," she huffed, padding back inside, pushing the door to.

"Decaf," Dave muttered, stepping down to the sidewalk. "Seriously, though, you seen anyone suspicious hanging around the house?"

Oh, only the woman now living inside it.

"Nope," Bel replied.

189

"Because that man is still out there. And until we catch him, he still presents a danger to Rachel and your family."

Didn't he know—the danger was already inside the house. And that man didn't exist. But another man did, and Bel was on her way to finding out who.

"Haven't seen anything. Sorry," she said. "Hey, did our DNA tests come in yet? She definitely Rachel Price?"

Dave snorted, stopping when he saw her face. "Sorry, thought you were joking. Yeah, yeah they have. One hundred percent her. But you already knew that, right?"

"Right. I was joking, got me." She raised her hands, eyeing his gun. "Did you find the tote bag yet? On the road in Lancaster where the man left her?"

David scratched his hair. "Yeah, right where she said it was."

Fuck.

"Anything?"

Dave thought for a moment. "Her DNA is on it, but so far it's the only profile we can find. No leads to the man who took her yet."

Because nonexistent men didn't have DNA. Dave must have read her disappointment as dread.

"Don't worry," he said, "we're exploring every avenue to find this guy. Tracking license plates. Something will turn up."

"What about her clothes?" Bel asked. The police were no good to her if all they were doing was looking for a man they'd never find.

"Only Rachel's DNA on those too. Well, and yours. From when you found her."

"But what about the labels inside the clothes? Could you see where they were from?"

Dave furrowed his brows, not sure what to make of her. "Long gone, I'm afraid. They're so damaged and old; she wore them most days since she disappeared. Your mom couldn't remember where she bought them."

Fuck again. The labels were conveniently gone, were they? That was because Rachel had bought them from Baa-Baa Boutique a few months ago. She'd certainly covered her tracks for her reappearance, all these little details. If she'd messed up anywhere, it had to be with her disappearance; she must have had less time to plan that.

This had been a pointless conversation, the chief of police wrapped around Rachel's little finger. Didn't matter, Bel could damn well do it on her own.

"I gotta run," Bel said.

She did run, just a little, to get away from him, down the road past numbers 30 and 28. Crossing to get back to the odd side.

It took another forty seconds before she pulled up in front of number 19; Jeff and Sherry's house, painted teal on the bottom half, white up top, shutters to match. She rang the doorbell in the way she did, so they'd know it was her, to the tune of "Baby Shark," which no one found annoying.

"Bel, that's annoying," Sherry said, pulling open the front door. Her hair was unbrushed, face plain and harassed, scrubbed free of last night's TV-ready makeup. "I'm taking Carter to ballet in an hour."

"Sounds like plenty of time for a visit from your favorite niece." Bel pushed her way inside the house, winding around to the kitchen.

"Two seconds," Carter's voice called from upstairs.

"Take your time," Bel called back. She meant it. She wasn't sure Sherry would open up the same way in front of Carter. But it was hard to find a time when Sherry was in the house and Carter wasn't; she tended to follow her daughter around, even though she didn't have sixteen years to make up for.

Bel went to the refrigerator, an old photo of a girl in a ballerina tutu pinned there by a SpongeBob magnet. Sherry, not Carter; you couldn't mistake them. Bel pulled out a Diet Coke.

"So . . . ," Sherry said, leaning in the doorway. "You spoken to your mom much since last night?"

"Not much." Bel sipped the foam that erupted out of the can. "She was quiet at breakfast. Dad left early again."

Sherry nodded. But Bel needed much more than that.

"So last night was *interesting*," she said, offering a smile and a raised eyebrow so Sherry knew Bel was on her side.

"Yes," Sherry said, those snakes hissing in her voice again. "Dinner probably wasn't the smartest idea. Bit too soon. Emotions are bound to be running high, aren't they? God knows how you feel, in that house, no escape from it all."

Well, God didn't know. But Carter and Ash did.

"Yeah," Bel said. "It's been *interesting.*"

"What's been interesting?" Carter appeared around the corner, sliding in past her mom.

She held out her hand, silently asking for a sip. Bel passed the can over.

"All of it," Bel said, annoyed she'd wasted those seconds without Carter. "Since she came back."

"She's trying," Carter said quietly, fingers denting the can. "I think everyone else can try too."

"Oh, we are, honey." Sherry straightened up. "It's not quite as easy as that, when someone's been gone for sixteen years. Rachel's disappearance wasn't just about her, it affected all the people around her. There's bound to be . . ." She trailed off.

"Tension?" Bel suggested.

"Yes," Sherry said. "It's an adjustment."

That word again.

"Well, it's—" Carter started, cut off by the doorbell, one long held note. She shoved the can back into Bel's hands. "That's my package." She darted out of the kitchen ahead of her mom. "Dancing stuff," she yelled back, pulling open the front door.

The low murmur of a voice.

"Yes, that's me, thank you." Carter's, crisp and clear. The front door latched shut again. "Just going to sort these out," she called, bounding up the stairs.

Perfect, now was Bel's chance to swerve the conversation, lay pressure on the breaking points.

"Carter always tries to see the good in people," Bel said, because she wanted Sherry to know she didn't think Rachel was all good either. And Bel knew she'd been upset last night, Rachel stepping on her toes, using Carter to do it. Although who had Rachel been trying to upset, Sherry or Bel?

"She does." Sherry sighed, eyes wandering to the ceiling, taking her mind with them.

"I don't think my dad is happy, you know," Bel said, pushing just a little harder.

"No?" Sherry looked at her.

"Not really. I think things might be a little more complicated than just starting off where they were sixteen years ago."

"Well . . . ," Sherry said, circling it, Bel could tell, the way her mouth twitched, almost giving in. Come on, Aunt Sherry. She needed one more push.

Bel cut straight to it; she didn't know how long they had alone.

"I think we're on the same side, Sherry. Dad's side. We both want him to be happy, right?"

"Right?" Sherry held on to the word, narrowing her eyes.

"I heard what you said last night, to defend him."

Sherry covered her mouth with her hand. "I hope it wasn't recorded. I shouldn't have said it."

"No, you should have." Bel stepped closer, lowered her voice. "It sounded like you thought Rachel was seeing someone else before she disappeared?"

More a shove than a push.

Sherry looked behind her.

"Please, Sherry." Bel stepped forward again. "I'm not a two-year-old anymore. It's my family. I want to be there for Dad, he needs me. How can I get to know Rachel if people keep secrets from me? I want to understand her."

Sherry sighed, the snakes deflating inside her throat. "I don't know anything for sure. Just something I saw, a feeling I had, back then."

"What did you see?" Bel said, stepping back now she'd cracked Sherry open, giving her space.

The change in Sherry's face was instant, voice dropping into whisper-talk. Sherry loved to gossip; her eyes bad at keeping secrets, spilling every time she blinked.

"There was this guy. They were friends, well, Rachel *said* they were just friends. He obviously wanted more, like a lovesick puppy, honestly. I saw them together, maybe a couple of days before she vanished. Walking from school to his car, through the snow. Looked pretty cozy if you asked me, like a line had been crossed. That's all I saw."

"Who was he?"

"That's the thing," Sherry hissed, enjoying this even more. "Why I always wondered if he was the one that killed her. It's not just that they were friends, saw each other at work all the time. It's that he was the first one on the scene when she disappeared. The man that found you."

"Mr. Tripp?" Bel's throat felt gummy, trapping her breath there. Something that felt like betrayal again. She pictured him, his thinning red hair and tortoiseshell glasses, as he'd asked her: *How is she, your mom?* Which was a fucking joke, because he obviously knew way more about Rachel than Bel did.

"Why didn't you ever say anything? Tell the police about Mr. Tripp? They must have asked you questions like that, right?"

Sherry bristled, leaning against the refrigerator. "The police had looked into him already. Of course they had; his prints were all over the crime scene from when he found you. They cleared him."

"Still," Bel doubled down. "Shouldn't you have told them?"

"There can be value in *not* talking, Bel, honey. Think it through."

Bel tried to think it through, coming up blank.

Sherry sighed. "If I'd told the police what I thought about Julian Tripp, it would have only hurt *us,* your dad. Given the police another reason to point the finger at Charlie. They were already looking at him as a suspect, and I didn't want to give them more reason to, a potential motive to have killed Rachel. Family first. Always."

"Family first," Bel agreed, grateful that Sherry's first instinct had been to protect her dad. That was what Bel was trying to do now.

"Besides," Sherry said, "it doesn't matter now. Julian Tripp clearly didn't kill her. Nobody did."

But Aunt Sherry was wrong there; it did matter now. No, Mr. Tripp hadn't killed Rachel, but he could have been involved some other way. Maybe he was the reason Rachel faked her disappearance, or maybe he'd helped her, kept it secret all this time. Either way, Mr. Tripp was the key to unpicking Rachel's lies, Bel was sure, and so was the knot in her gut.

If you need to talk about anything, Bel, Mr. Tripp had said, *you know I'm right here.*

Turns out, they did need to talk. And unlucky for him, Bel knew where he lived.

TWENTY-FOUR

"Can you tell me that again?"

"Seriously? Am I just talking to myself here?" Bel pulled her eyes up, a reverse blink at Ash, swishing along the sidewalk in his flared tartan pants and a backward cap. "You are the shittiest sidekick."

Ash shook his head, hiding a crooked smile from her. "It's not for me, it's for the camera. Ramsey said if we're going to hang out like this, talk about Rachel, investigate her, is it OK if I keep recording it?" He raised his handheld camera, popping his lips twice. "If that's not too exploitative." He tripped awkwardly over the word and over his own tongue.

"The entire documentary is exploitative." Bel shrugged, taking them down a side road. "But you can't exploit me if I'm exploiting you back."

"OK . . . ," he said, blinking, unsure. "Just trying to do a good job for Ramsey. He's relying on me, since I'm the one you trust."

"I don't trust you," Bel sneered.

"I reckon you do a little bit."

"No."

"A sliver?"

"No."

"A smidge?"

"Nope."

"Well, you're the one that came to find me today," he said, a flush in his cheeks, a curl of hair poking out over the strap of his baseball cap.

"Only because I *want* this recorded, could be evidence." Bel matched his smile, sweeter, deadlier. "I don't trust you, and I don't like you, and I definitely don't need you." Ash flinched; right on target. "But I could use your help, and you and Ramsey want to make a great film, right?"

"Right . . ."

"Good, glad we settled that." She sniffed. "You can press record."

Ash's lips stretched into a half smile. Seriously? Still smiling after that, what was wrong with him?

He pointed the camera at her and flipped out the viewfinder, a beep as he pressed record.

"What do you want me to say, then?" Bel asked, picking up her pace.

"Catch us up on what's happened, what you're feeling. What your goals are now?" Ash said, a poor imitation of Ramsey.

"We are looking into Rachel's disappearance. She's not telling the truth about what happened to her; I think she planned them both, her disappearance and her reappearance. At the family dinner last night—which went super well, not awkward at all—my aunt Sherry let slip that Rachel might have been in some kind of relationship before she went missing."

The trees shivered above her on the house-lined street, whispering unknown things, giving up their secrets to the wind.

"No one ever knew about this," Bel continued, close to breathless, walking and talking. "I went to see Sherry this morning and she told me she was talking about Julian Tripp, a teacher at my school, and also the man who found me in that car sixteen years ago. He and Rachel were colleagues, friends, but it might have been more: Sherry saw him and Rachel looking 'cozy' getting into Mr. Tripp's car

197

a couple of days before Rachel disappeared. So we are on our way to his house to ask him about it."

Ash nodded, like she should keep going.

"And my goal?" Bel said. "My goal is to find the fucking truth and get that liar out of my house. Enough?"

Ash swallowed, looking up from the Bel on the camera screen to the one in real life, finding her eyes and latching on. "That was definitely enough, yeah."

Bel raised her hands in victory, tapping the invisible trophy to each of her shoulders.

"But Mr. Tripp didn't disappear too, obviously," Ash said. "So it's not like they ran away together or something."

"Gee, thanks, Sherlock." Bel's trophy vanished and she clapped her hands. "But maybe he's the reason she left, or he helped her. He'll know something, he has to. It's that house, on the end." Bel gestured with her eyes.

Ash panned the camera there and back. "How do you know where your teacher lives, anyway?"

"He did a yard sale a few years ago. I was with my friend, Sam." Bel had stolen something from the yard sale; she couldn't remember what now. Just like she couldn't remember how Sam used to make her laugh.

They approached the path up to Mr. Tripp's house, the front yard overgrown and unkempt. Mailbox sad and rusted.

Ash lowered the camera, following her to the door.

"What are you doing?" Bel clicked at him. "Keep recording."

"I can't," Ash said, torn between the two of them, Bel and the camera. "He has to agree to it first. Sign a release form—"

"He's already done one interview. I'm sure he'll be delighted to do another. Keep rolling."

"Keep rolling," Ash parroted her, raising the camera again, capturing her in it. "For the record, Ramsey," he whispered into the fluffy microphone, "I'm being made to do this against my will, if this goes terribly and someone sues us. But this was your idea, so . . ."

Bel flashed her eyes at him, then knotted her fingers into a fist, knocked it against the door. Six knocks, hard and urgent.

Ash grabbed her hand before she made it seven.

"Stop," he hissed. "Why can't you do anything nicely?"

A muffled cough behind the door, the scrape of a chain. It pulled open, just a crack, Mr. Tripp's gray face. Eyes downcast, the sun reflecting against his glasses.

"I don't have it ye—" he began, cutting off when he glanced up and saw the two of them standing there. "Oh." His face cracked into a cautious smile, opening the door the whole way, shoulders reconnecting to his neck. He wore a grubby yellow T-shirt and gray sweats, hiding his hands in the pockets. "What are you doing here, Bel?" he said, the hard rock of his Adam's apple flitting up and down. "Is there a problem? Is Rachel OK?"

"Just peachy." Bel flashed her teeth as her eyes strayed from Mr. Tripp to the hallway behind him. A dark stain on the carpet, under his bare feet. A tower of cardboard boxes almost as tall as him, stuffed with empty cans of beer. Ghostly finger dents in the metal.

He saw Bel looking, gripped the door again, blocking their view.

"We were wondering if we could do another interview with you, for the documentary," she said. "Now that Rachel has returned, we're reinterviewing everyone, isn't that right, Ash?"

"R-right," Ash coughed, the fabric of his elbow brushing hers.

"I'm not sure I have time right now," Mr. Tripp said. The stale tang of alcohol hung in the air around him. The dark circles under his eyes made more sense now, the gray tinge of his skin. Bel never cared to notice the signs before.

"Sure you do, it's a couple of minutes," Bel said.

Mr. Tripp swiped a finger against the lenses of his glasses. "I was just stepping out."

"You don't look it." Bel cocked her head. "Besides, people might think it's weird if you were willing to talk when everyone thought Rachel was dead, but not when she's alive. Like you were happy she was dead, or something." She laughed.

Mr. Tripp blinked; eyes magnified by his glasses. "That's not—"

"So how did you feel when you first heard Rachel Price was back from the dead?" Bel asked, steepling her fingers, like Ramsey sometimes did.

Mr. Tripp eyed the camera, blinked some more. He smoothed down his hair. "Well, I was shocked, like the whole world. Thought there had to be some mistake, that it must be another woman. Then when I saw Rachel at school, a couple days later, I felt . . . happy. Very happy that she's alive. I didn't think it possible. But it just goes to show you, sometimes, even after something terrible, good things can happen to good people."

Good people didn't orchestrate their own disappearance, put their families through hell.

"How close were you with Rachel before she went missing?" Bel said, aware of Ash's presence just behind her. "Did you spend time together outside of work?"

Mr. Tripp's glasses slipped down his nose. "Not really. She was a coworker, and I'd like to think a friend, but we didn't see each other outside of work."

"Really? Not even *right* outside work?"

"What do you mean?"

"Did you ever give Rachel rides home from work? Spend time in the car together?"

He chewed his back teeth. "No," he said. "She's never been in my car."

Liar.

"Weird." Bel puffed out her cheeks. "My aunt Sherry saw Rachel get into your car just a couple of days before she went missing."

"She must be mistaken."

"Or you must be lying," Bel said, a toothless smile. "Suspicious, isn't it? When you were also the first person on the scene when Rachel disappeared, the one who found me. Your prints all over the car. Is that because you helped Rachel disappear? Do you know where she was all this time? Are you still in love with her?"

Ash tensed.

There was a shift in Mr. Tripp's face: jaw jutting forward, brows furrowing, eclipsing his eyes.

Bel waited, ready for the fight. Didn't he know, she'd spent her whole life fighting?

"I'll see you Monday morning, Annabel," he said, low, through gritted teeth. Said like a threat.

Mr. Tripp stepped back, one last look at the camera before he slammed the door in their faces, a thunderclap without a storm.

TWENTY-FIVE

"You've been out all day." Dad spoke from his chair, balancing a beer on his shoulder.

"So have you," Bel said.

"Work's crazy at the moment, kiddo." He didn't take his eyes off the television.

Well, so was home.

"Did something happen today?"

Bel stalled. What did he mean? A lot had happened today, but nothing he should know about. "I don't . . . ," she began.

"Mug was broken." He finally looked up at her. "My favorite one." "Santa?"

"Just had to throw it away. Did one of you break it?"

Bel didn't like that, being lumped into the same *you* as Rachel. But Bel was the one who'd drunk out of that mug this morning; Rachel had made her a coffee, still hadn't learned that Santa was Dad's mug. Had Bel broken it? She couldn't remember, gulping it down, rushing to get away from Rachel. She'd done things like that before, careless, forgetful. Unless Rachel *did* know it was Dad's favorite and broke it on purpose, pushing him a little farther every day.

"I don't know, sorry, Dad." Bel sat down. "I'll get you a new one."

"Doesn't matter," he said.

But it did.

"I gotta talk to you about something." Dad leaned over for the remote, paused the TV. "I just got a call from your principal. He says you went to a teacher's house today. Mr. Tripp. That you harassed him."

Bel's eyes darkened, her gut clenched. "Fucking rat," she spat, picturing him, stamping on his glasses.

"Apparently you were asking strange questions about Rachel. What's going on, kiddo?" he said, hands motionless in his lap.

Bel was caught.

But that was OK. She didn't have enough evidence for the police, but she had enough for Dad. He was on her side, always. Bel glanced toward the stairs. "Where's Rachel?"

"She's taking a bath."

Bel squeezed her fingers, lowered her voice. "I think she's lying, Dad. About all of it." Dad sat up, chair creaking beneath him. "Her disappearance, her reappearance. She planned them. I don't think a man ever took her. There have been inconsistencies in her story, things she knows that she couldn't know if she'd spent the last sixteen years locked in a basement. She was in North Conway a few months ago, out and free, buying clothes to match the ones she disappeared in. It was all planned. I think Mr. Tripp knows something. Rachel's a liar, Dad, and I don't know what she wants, but we have to find out what really happened so we can—"

"That's enough, Bel," he said, gentle but firm, cutting her off. "We talked about this already. Rachel isn't lying."

"But—"

"I don't want to hear it." He peeled the corner of his beer label. "Rachel is telling the truth about what happened to her. Of course she is; how else could she have been gone for so long?" His gaze hardened, the sharp rip of the beer label coming free. "Trust me, I know her better than you. I believe her, OK, kiddo? That should be enough for you too. I want you to drop this. Please?"

A punch to Bel's gut, knuckle prints in the knot that didn't fade. Dad was supposed to be on her side. How could he not see it?

"You know something's wrong," she tried again, desperate. "You haven't been the same since she came back, avoiding the house, working all the time. I've hardly seen you."

Dad sighed. "Things are just complicated. Real life is, kiddo. It's only been a week, takes longer than that to get used to such a life-changing thing. For me, and for you. Please, Bel, let this go. You'll only make things harder. Promise me?"

Bel had already made a promise: to get rid of Rachel, to go back to their life before Rachel reappeared and ruined everything, back to when they were both happy. Bel chose Dad. He was her constant, the one who'd never leave. She would always choose him. But he wasn't asking her to choose, he was asking her to let it go, to accept Rachel, to make a new promise.

Maybe they could all exist together, in this house.

Bel had to try, because Dad was the one who'd asked. Dad believed Rachel; and that should be enough for her too. Should be.

Bel deflated, but the knot grew, pulling tighter. "OK," she said quietly. "I promise."

Dad smiled at her, raised his beer in a sad salute. "Principal Wheeler said you were with someone from the film crew today?"

"Yeah," she said. "Ash. The camera assistant."

Dad coughed. "I would be careful, spending time with him. They are trying to tell the most interesting story, sensationalizing it, using us to do that. Orchestrating tense situations where they know we'll react in front of the camera. They're trying to manipulate you, kiddo, all this stuff about Rachel. I think you probably shouldn't see Ash again, on your own."

Bel sniffed. "You're probably right," because Dad always was. And Ash was getting too close, anyway. There had to be a reason he was the only one who'd believed her about Rachel, didn't there?

"Just trying to protect you." Dad reached for the remote, finger hovering over the button.

"Can we do something tomorrow?" Bel spoke quickly, before he could un-pause it. "You and me. Rachel too, I guess. The three of us. Maybe a hike or something? I've missed you." He wouldn't know it, but that was one of the hardest things to say, baring everything, chest pried open rib by rib, heart beating and unguarded. She was trying.

Dad's face softened around a smile. "Sure, kiddo. Anything you want."

Upstairs they heard the bathroom door swinging open. The soft pad of Rachel's bare feet, creeping against the carpet. Them down here, her up there. Had Rachel heard any of that, what Bel said about her? Was she trying to listen in? Maybe she . . .

No, stop it. Bel was letting it go.

Really trying to let it go, to override that bad feeling in her gut.

Bel held her breath, waiting, listening. It came; the click of the spare room door shutting, the double click as Rachel locked herself inside.

TWENTY-SIX

Bel awoke with a start, something hard against the inside of her cheek. A face hovering inches above her own in the morning gloom.

She blinked and so did they.

Bel spluttered, rubbing the sleep from her eyes.

"Hello, sleepy," Carter said, sitting on the bed, Bel's body dragged toward the dip she made.

"I thought you were fucking Rachel." Bel clutched her chest, relocating her jumped-up heart. "Did you just poke me in the mouth?" she said, feeling around with her dried-out tongue.

"You poke me all the time," Carter said, her back now turned.

"Not in the mouth while you're sleeping, you freak." Bel kicked her, cushioned through the comforter. "I think maybe I've been a bad influence on you."

"I said your name twice and you didn't wake up, so I had to resort to drastic measures."

"I'll show you drastic measures." Bel kicked her again, double-footed until Carter had no choice but to tumble off the bed.

She stood up, holding on to the strap of her yellow backpack, the bulk of it trailing on the floor.

"How was ballet yesterday?" Bel asked, gathering her static hair back into a ponytail.

"Fine," Carter said, sharply, cutting that off. "I thought we could hang out today. My mom's driving me crazy."

Carter didn't know the true meaning of that phrase.

"Thought we could bake cookies with Rachel or something," Carter continued. "Or go to the movies. Just, please, entertain me."

Bel swiveled her legs, climbing out of bed. "Me and Dad were planning to go on a hike today. You can come if you want." She picked up the hoodie lying crumpled on the floor, pulled it on. "Is he downstairs?"

"Haven't seen him." Carter headed for the door. "Rachel's down there. Said she might attempt pancakes this morning."

"Sounds ominous."

"Bel," Carter said, elbowing her in the ribs.

They walked down the stairs together, Bel pushing Carter in front, a shield as they entered the kitchen, and the sputtering sounds from the stove.

"Morning An–ah–Bel, almost had it that time," Rachel said, cautiously lifting the edge of one chunky pancake, glancing back to smile at them.

Rachel looked tired, darker circles under her eyes, like that lock on her door had done her no good and she still wasn't sleeping.

"Morning." Bel cracked the bones in her neck. She, on the other hand, had slept too hard.

"Coffee's in the pot, help yourself," Rachel said. "Carter, pancakes for you too?"

"Yes please, Rachel." Carter grinned, sitting at the table. Her smile faltered. "I-if that's OK?"

"Of course that's OK. You can even have the first batch." Rachel slid the pancakes onto a waiting plate.

"Where's Dad?" Bel asked, pouring coffee into her favorite mug, plain with a yellow *B*. *B* for Bel, not *A* for Anna.

"Haven't seen him." Rachel turned back to the pan, pouring more mixture.

"Is he in the house?"

"Don't think so."

Bel didn't trust her answer.

"Dad?" she shouted, wandering away to the bottom of the stairs. "Dad?!" she called up.

Nothing.

"Not here." Bel returned to the kitchen, Rachel handing her a plate with a stack of three pancakes, chocolate chip.

Maybe he'd gone to get sandwiches for their hike. Bel sat down, pulled her phone out of her hoodie pocket. No texts from Dad. Just one from Ash: *Let me know if you want to do anything today.* She shouldn't have given him her number, that was a mistake. Dad was right: the film crew couldn't be trusted.

She took one bite, the batter turning into a thick paste in her dried-out mouth. She swallowed and stood up again, chair screeching against the tiles.

"Where are you . . . ," Rachel began, sitting down herself.

Bel didn't answer, heading for the front door, the knot in her gut making itself known, stretching and yawning. She pulled the door open, standing on the threshold, looking up and down the street, as though she could summon Dad over the horizon. He would be back from the store any second, if that was where he'd gone. The road was quiet, too quiet, like something was missing: there were no news vans parked outside. Not one. Rachel Price had officially tipped the scales into Old News, eight days in. Was this the beginning of the end?

Bel's eye caught on something else, something that wasn't missing, but should have been. Dad's truck. It was right here, parked in front of the garage in his usual spot, Rachel's car tucked beside it. So . . . he hadn't gone to the store.

"Dad?!" Bel called through the house again, shutting the door behind her.

"Annabel, your breakfast will get cold," Rachel's voice rang out in response.

Bel wandered through, hanging in the doorway, neither in the room or out.

"Doesn't make sense," she muttered, more to herself. "Dad's truck is here, but he isn't."

"Eat your pancakes or I will." Carter swung her legs as she ate.

"Did you see him this morning?" Bel stared at Rachel.

"No." Rachel swallowed. "He must have left before I got up. Didn't hear anything."

"But his truck is here."

Rachel split a pancake in half. "Maybe he had plans with someone."

"He did have plans," Bel said, "with me. We were supposed to go on a hike today. He promised."

They'd both made a promise last night, and Bel was keeping hers. So where was he?

She called him, gripping the phone too hard against her ear.

It didn't even ring.

*"Hello, you've reached—*Charlie Price,*"* his voice cut in, gruff and prerecorded, *"who is unable to take your call right now. Please leave a message after the tone."*

"That's weird. Straight to voicemail."

Bel brought up their message thread. Texted: *Dad, where are you? Call me back.*

It didn't deliver, the blue bubble of text waiting in the ether, stuck somewhere between her phone and his.

"An–B-Bel, your pancakes."

"Not hungry." Bel turned away. There was no room in her stomach, the knot spinning and growing, feeding itself on every bad thought, and one question: Where was Dad?

She sat in Dad's chair, and she waited.

She tried another number.

"Hello, this is Bryson Auto, Gabe speaking. How can I help?"

Bel cleared her throat. "Hi, Gabe. This is Bel Price, Charlie's daughter."

"Hi, Bel. How're you doing?" Gabe said, voice whistling through his back teeth.

"Just wondering if my dad's there, if he's working today? He said he'd be home today, but I can't find him."

Two rattling breaths leaked out the speaker, into her ear. "Your dad's not in today. He doesn't usually work weekends."

209

"Right." Bel chewed her thumb. "But you've been busy, he worked late yesterday, and he's been working late all week, so I just thought—"

"If anything, he's been leaving early. Family stuff, he said," Gabe replied, some tool clattering in the background. "Wasn't in yesterday either. But hey, if I see him, I'll tell him to give you a call, OK?"

"Y-yeah, thanks." Bel stared down at the phone before she hung up. Stared afterward too.

Dad hadn't gone into work yesterday, hadn't been working late all week like he said, missing dinner every night. Telling Bel he was at work and telling work he was at home. So where had he really been, and was he there now?

"Still can't get hold of him?" Rachel's voice cut in behind her, making her jump.

She shook her head.

"Well . . . we can go on a hike, you, me and Carter," Rachel said. "If that's what you wanted to do today. We could do the Mascot Mine trail."

"They've got barriers up around there," Carter said, standing on Bel's other side, trapping her between. "Some kids from school broke open the grate into the mine shaft. I wasn't there," she clarified, holding up her hands.

"You guys go ahead," Bel said, removing herself. "I'm going to wait for Dad. He said he'd be home today. He'll be back."

She had no reason to believe that other than he had to, because Dad was the one who always came back. And Bel would wait right here for him to prove her right.

Carter and Rachel played Monopoly. Bel was supposed to be playing too: she rolled the dice, but she bought no properties, happy to sit in jail for three turns.

She tried Dad's number every thirty minutes. Voicemail. Voicemail. Voicemail. Her text still hadn't delivered. Why was his phone off? He never turned his phone off.

Carter left and Rachel stayed, hovering around her.

"I'm sure he'll be back later." She reached out, like she was about to rest her hand on Bel's shoulder.

Bel jumped up before she could.

"I'm going to go look for him," she announced, thundering upstairs to get dressed.

Bel walked past the Royalty Inn and her school, both Sunday quiet. All the way up to Bryson Auto, to see if Gabe was somehow wrong. There was someone else working there too, tinkering beneath a red car, a set of legs and boots.

"Dad?"

The man rolled out; it wasn't him.

"Sorry."

She stood outside, called Jeff.

"Have you heard from Dad?" she said when he picked up. "Since last night."

"Hello to you too. No, I haven't. Why, he not home?"

"Or at work," Bel said. "Not picking up his phone."

"I'm sure he's fine. Stop worrying," he said, which was pretty perceptive for Uncle Jeff, because Bel *was* worried now, heart nudging up her throat, on a fast track toward panic.

Where was he? Where was he?

She tried every bar and coffeehouse in Gorham, tried them a second time: "You again, you're underage, get out."

Sent another text. Called him again, body betraying her, soothing itself at the sound of his recorded voice, "Charlie Price." Fucking idiot, that wasn't the real him, riling her heart up again.

Dialed the landline at Grandpa's house, asked Yordan if he'd seen him.

"Not since Friday night. Sorry."

What was Bel going to do?

She headed back toward home, just in case they'd missed each other, coming and going. Ramsey was on the street outside the hotel when she passed, zipping up his jacket.

211

"Hey." A smile split his face, familiar and overfriendly. "What a coincidence. Do you have a sec?"

No, she didn't.

"Sorry, can't." She barreled past. "I'm looking for Dad."

"Why?" Ramsey's voice floated after her. "He disappeared?"

Said like a joke, but it doubled Bel over, giving shape to her worst nightmare.

"No," she called back. "He'll be at home."

He wasn't at home.

She waited another hour. Then two. Giving Rachel one-word answers, watching the front door, willing it to open.

"He'll be back for dinner, I'm sure," Rachel said, eyes fixed on Bel's hands, jangling in her lap, pressing against the knot in her stomach. "Do you like salmon?"

At seven, Bel went to check Dad's room.

The bed was unmade. That wasn't unusual; Dad often left the sheets in a bundle, telltale signs of where he'd climbed out. Bel traced her fingers along his pillow, as though she could get some sense of him through the fabric. Where he'd gone after he got out of bed this morning, what was in his head.

To his closet next. She studied the hangers: some were empty, swinging when she ran her hand past, but those sweaters and shirts were probably just in the laundry basket. Something else was gone too. The khaki canvas bag Dad packed whenever they went on a weekend away. The bag was gone, wasn't in its usual place on the floor of the closet. Wasn't in any unusual places either. It wasn't here.

"Fuck." The knot outgrew Bel's stomach, looking for other soft places to make its home.

Where was the bag? Dad couldn't have packed a bag, because that sounded like someone who wanted to leave. And Dad wouldn't do that. Dad didn't leave.

"Found anything?" Rachel asked at the bottom of the stairs.

"No." Bel shrugged her off, avoiding her eyes.

She went to the sideboard in the hall, where Dad kept his keys and wallet. The wallet wasn't here but his keys—both truck and house—were. Bel picked them up to be sure, studying the key ring: a grinning photo of the two of them, at Story Land for her twelfth birthday. Dad hadn't taken his truck, but wouldn't he need his house keys, so he could come back home when he was ready?

Bel opened the drawer of the sideboard. Papers and bills. She dug her hand to the back corner, where they kept their passports.

There was only one here. She checked, patting her hand around the rest of the drawer. She pulled the passport out, flicked to the photo page. *Annabel Price* and her own stony face, staring back.

Where was Dad's passport? It should have been here, right here with hers.

No, no, no. The knot twisted, pulling its deep-buried strings, Bel's fingers twitching with it. Her heart had bulleted through panic, kicking harder and harder.

Something was wrong. Something was really, really wrong.

"You ready for dinner?"

No, because she was waiting for Dad. He didn't have his keys, so he'd need someone to let him in. Bel would wait right here by the front door, to be that someone.

She watched the darkening street out the window, face between the slats of the shades, eyes flickering to any sign of movement: a woman walking a dog with a green LED collar, a kid on a scooter, an older kid chasing after him, a man hurrying past, pulling at the peak of his baseball cap.

Bel checked the clock on her phone. He would be back by nine for dinner, with an easy smile and an even easier explanation of where he'd been, why his phone was off. Nine was the deadline; he had to be back by then.

But that ticked by too.

"Do you want me to heat this up for you, Anna-sorry-Bel? You should come sit down."

Bel waited until 9:59 p.m.

Then she unlocked her phone, called a different number.

The one for Police Chief Dave Winter.

The sound chimed through Bel, echoing in her empty chest, a click when he answered.

"Hi, it's Bel, Annabel Price. My dad is missing."

TWENTY-SEVEN

"His passport is missing too?"

Dave Winter eyed her across the table, tapping a pen against his notebook, flickering in and out of a beam of morning sunlight.

"Yes, I've checked everywhere," Bel said, breathless from explaining. "But—I'm trying to tell you—my dad wouldn't leave. Trust me. Something has happened to him, something bad."

"And it looks like a bag has been packed? Clothes missing? His wallet?"

"Yes." Bel held on to the word, borrowing Aunt Sherry's snakes. Hands squeezing each other, fingernails leaving half-moon imprints. "But again, I'm saying he wouldn't leave me. It's completely out of character—that's what you ask, isn't it? What all the reports said about Rachel at the time. Something bad has happened and I want to file a missing person report. You need to look for him. It's urgent. You've already left it too long—we should have done this last night."

Dave Winter sighed, unclicked his pen. "Annabel, I understand this feels like an emergency to you. But as an adult, your dad has a legal right to disappear without telling his family, if that's what he wants to do. I gotta tell you, all the signs are looking like he left voluntarily, no sign of foul play. Bags packed, passport and wallet gone."

Bel shook her head. "Someone just wants us to think that. Why wouldn't he take his truck, if he'd decided to leave?"

Dave sighed again, picked up his pen, flicked a couple pages back. "When did you last see him?"

"Ten o'clock Saturday night, when I went to bed." Bel leaned forward, separating her hands. "I don't know when he went missing, sometime before morning. But that means it's been almost thirty-six hours since he was last seen. No one has heard from him, and his phone's been off the whole time. You need to start looking for him. Now."

Her leg juddered against the underside of the table, just nine days since she was last here, talking about a reappearance, not a disappearance, tables turning, sides shifting again. And Dave Winter still wasn't listening.

"I'm not sure there's anything I can do."

"What do you mean?" Bel straightened up, locking her jaw, the knot in her gut spitting sparks. "You can do exactly what you did last time one of my parents went missing. Look for him. Track his phone. Get search dogs. Do it all."

"I can't justify a full investigation like that," he said, trying to be understanding, failing. "Your mom's disappearance was different; the circumstances were suspicious and it was evident she was in danger. Your dad . . . a grown man has a right to take off for a day or two if he wants. It's understandable, given the situation. Rachel's return probably hasn't been easy on the family. Ms. Nelson told me it sounded like there was a family argument at your house on Friday. She saw your dad storming off down the street. It's just stress, blowing off steam. I'm sure he'll be back in a couple of days."

"You're wrong." Bel slammed one fist against the table, making his notebook pages fan back. "You've already been wrong; you said he'd probably turn up last night. He didn't. Something bad has happened to him. The circumstances *are* suspicious and he *is* in danger."

"In danger from who?"

"Rachel!" The knot in her gut exploded and Bel did too, her new promise to Dad shattered and forgotten. "It's something to do with Rachel! She's back for just one week, and now my dad disappears? It's connected. It's something to do with her."

Not just something; it was everything to do with her. Rachel was a liar; she'd orchestrated one disappearance, and now she'd made Dad disappear too. Bel should have worked harder, faster, to find evidence and remove Rachel from their lives. Now it might be too late; Dad was already gone, the worst had already happened. The last thing he'd asked her to do was to trust Rachel, and now Rachel had taken him from her.

"I'm sure it *is* connected," Dave said. "Rachel coming back after being presumed dead all this time was an unprecedented event. And the stress of knowing the man who took her is still out there. I think *I'd* want a break if all that happened to me."

"My dad didn't leave!" she shouted, both fists on the table.

"Annabel, you need to c—"

"Don't tell me to calm down." She took aim with her eyes, blinking the fire his way. "*You* need to do your job. File the missing person report and look for him."

Dave's mouth opened silently, building up another sigh. Anger wasn't going to push him, but something else might.

"You owe him," Bel said, darkly, lowering her voice. "You owe him, and you know it. You've been wrong about him before. Convinced he was the one who killed Rachel. Locked him up, made him face trial. You were wrong and you put him through hell. Here's your chance to do the right thing. You owe him. Please. Help me find him."

Dave's mouth stayed open, but there was a shift in his eyes, and a shift in his shoulders.

"OK," he said gently. His fingers drummed the table, dancing spiders. "I'm going to need a written statement from you for the report. I'll need all his details: phone number and carrier. It will take a few days to subpoena the records. I need bank details, if you have them, papers at home."

"Yes," Bel said, breathless again. A new feeling too: hope. It was small and fragile, and she fed it to the knot in her gut. "I can do that. Right now."

"An officer will have to come out to the house, do a search. And we'll need a statement from Rachel too."

"Thank you," she said, throat dry and scratchy. Eyes too, from fitful bursts of sleep, fighting it all night, watching the door in case Rachel came for her too.

Dave stood up from the table, knocking his knuckles against it once. "Don't thank me," he said, holding his notebook against his chest, eyes heavy and sad. "Like you said, I owe him."

Bel nodded. They all did.

Bel didn't go home again until it was dark. She closed the front door, wincing at the sound of the latch, giving her away. Home, except it wasn't anymore; the air was different, it got trapped in your ears, amplifying every creak and sigh that a house was supposed to make. And the ones it wasn't: footsteps from the living room, muffled and creeping.

Rachel's head appeared around the corner, the rest of her body following, trapping Bel in the hallway.

"An-B-Bel. Where were you?"

Bel shrugged off her jacket. "Jeff and Sherry's. Where were you?" She shot the question back at her.

Rachel's mouth twitched, sharpening her chin. "After the officers finished their search here, I went to give my statement to the chief of police, told him the last time I saw Charlie, before I took a bath that evening. I didn't hear him leaving, but he must have, during the night."

Bel took one step forward, forcing Rachel to take one back, freeing her. "I thought you weren't sleeping well," she said, heading for the kitchen. Rachel tailed her. "Strange you didn't hear anything." Using one lie to un-flip another.

Bel reached for the refrigerator, pulled out the carton of apple juice Rachel had bought. Said she'd missed it while she was in that basement.

"He must have been quiet," Rachel said, from the doorway.

"Must have been." Bel took a sip, straight from the carton.

Rachel didn't react. "It'll be OK," she said instead. "I promise."

Bel tipped her head up and drained the carton, wiping her mouth on her sleeve.

"Where were you the rest of the day? Doesn't take six hours to give a statement."

"Driving around," Rachel said, "to the places I thought he could be. Looking for him."

Bel squeezed the empty carton, caving it in. She dropped it into the trash can, on top of a red takeout coffee cup, a logo with a cartoon cow, pursed lips to blow a steaming mug. Rachel must have stopped at a coffeehouse while out *looking for Dad*.

"You didn't find him, then?" Bel spun around.

Rachel had moved into the room while Bel's back was turned, feet silently tracing the floor. Both of them circling the other, pushing and pulling. Getting ready.

"No, I didn't find him," Rachel said.

"I will." Bel met her eyes. "I'll find him, bring him home." Said as a promise, meant as a threat.

Rachel blinked.

"Risotto for dinner. Do you like risotto?"

"I already ate."

TWENTY-EIGHT

The doorbell rang, a scream that split the house in two, riding along the fault lines, daring them to fail.

"I'll get it!" Bel thundered down the stairs, claiming that side as hers. Rachel might move quieter, but she could move faster.

She pulled open the front door, Dave Winter on the threshold, in his dark uniform.

"Annabel!" A reporter screamed from the street. "Why do you think your dad has gone missing?"

The same one Bel told to fuck off earlier, directly into his outheld microphone.

The white vans came back yesterday, when news broke about Charlie Price disappearing just one week after his wife came back from the dead. One parent in, one parent out, a revolving-door family. Quite the story, seeing as there were now seven vans on the curb, the BBC too. A *source close to the family* was the one who told the press. It was probably Grandma Susan; she had previously, and she was a fucking horsefucker.

"Off the property, sir. Don't make me come down there!" Dave shouted, hands flailing as he conducted the horde of yapping journalists.

"Hi," Bel said to the back of his twisted neck, flushed red.

He untwisted it, mouth in a grim line. "Annabel. Good, you're here. Is your mom home? I have an update."

Her heart jumped, bracing against the base of her throat. Was an update a good thing? Or the worst thing imaginable?

"Come in." She beckoned him through, wishing he would move faster, the knot spiraling in her gut, chewing off a piece of her each time.

"Hello, Rachel," Dave said, mouth turning up at the corners in an almost smile. Would he smile if he was here to tell them they'd found Dad dead? You wouldn't smile if he was dead, right? Fuck.

Bel searched his face for other signs, searched Rachel's too. Did she already know what Dave was here to tell them? If Rachel had killed him, Bel would kill her; that was another promise.

"Do you want a coffee or . . . ?" Rachel offered.

"What is it?" Bel couldn't wait any longer. Dad had been missing almost four days now, straight to voicemail every time: "*You've reached* Charlie Price," even though he was unreachable.

"Couple things." Dave slid his hands into his pockets. "We put in a subpoena for your dad's cell phone records. Still waiting on those, these things don't happen overnight." Dave removed one hand, dropped it by his side. "But we have managed to access Charlie's bank account."

"And?" Bel said, blocking him in, making him tell her, not Rachel.

"There's been activity over the last four days. He's withdrawn money and made some purchases . . . in Vermont."

"Vermont?" Rachel said, voice climbing at the end.

Dave turned to her. "We're working with the State Police now, using the hits to try track him down. But this is good news." He looked at Bel for that last part, the grim line of his mouth less grim now. "This means your dad is OK, that he's in Vermont to blow off steam, get some space. Like we thought. He'll probably come home when he's ready."

Bel stalled, mind whirring over what he just said. Dad was in Vermont? That was good news, wasn't it, like Dave said? Much better

221

than the worst news possible. So why was there a sinking feeling in her gut, feeding on that flash of hope? Because Bel knew him best. Dad wouldn't leave her, wouldn't go to Vermont without telling her, wouldn't have his phone off and let her worry this much, he just wouldn't do that. And maybe none of this was as simple as *blowing off steam* or *getting space*. Disappeared without a trace, except now there was a trace . . . in Vermont.

"That is good news," Rachel said, quietly.

"But you'll keep looking for him?" Bel said, not quietly.

"Like I said, we're working with the Vermont State Police to track him down when he next uses his card. And we're waiting on those phone records. A person's phone can tell you a lot about them."

Bel's eyes followed her mind, alighting on the black rectangle on the coffee table.

Not Dad's phone, but Rachel's.

Dave was still talking to her. "I'll keep looking for your dad, but you don't need to worry, can stop putting missing posters up all over town. Though I appreciate the help. You should probably go back to school, get back to normal."

"I went today," Bel replied. For one reason only: not to be normal, but to corner Mr. Tripp, force answers out of him. He wasn't there. Off sick, apparently, had been all week. How long could he keep that going, to avoid her?

"I'll be in touch, when we know anything more." Dave dipped his head like he was bowing to Rachel. "You let me know if those reporters outside are giving you any trouble."

"Thank you, Dave," Rachel said with an empty smile. "I'll walk you to the door."

The quiet murmur of their voices, moving away into the hall. Bel didn't follow, listening to her gut and listening to her head, because sometimes they weren't on the same side. *If* it was a possibility that Dad had chosen to leave, that he'd gone to Vermont, then he'd done it because of Rachel, to get away from her. And maybe he wouldn't come back until Rachel was exposed as a liar and removed from the house. Maybe he was afraid of what happened last time, all those fingers pointing at him, and he'd rather run than face that again. So either way you looked at it—head or gut—the way forward was the same: prove Rachel was lying, find out how and why she really disappeared and reappeared sixteen years later. Rachel was the way back to Dad.

And if Bel couldn't get the answers from Mr. Tripp, then she'd have to get them from Rachel herself.

Maybe avoiding her had been the wrong thing to do, keeping out of the house, barricading herself in her bedroom. Maybe it was time to shift focus. Study Rachel. Show interest, spend time with her. Wait for her to show her hand and slip up. You know what it is they say, about enemies and friends.

The noise of the reporters swelled as the front door opened, Dave calling back his goodbyes. Bel looked at Rachel's phone again, unguarded. *A person's phone can tell you a lot about them.*

Her fingers itched at her side, splaying and stretching, testing the air. Rachel had Mr. Tripp's number, they must have talked. So maybe the answers were right there, behind that glass screen.

She took one step toward the phone, reached for it, then stopped, sensing a change. Rachel had appeared in the room, soundless and watching.

"That's good news, isn't it?" Rachel said. "About the bank account. I know you've been worried. Been a bit quiet, distant."

Bel nodded. She was about to be the opposite of distant. Closing in instead of running away. She needed to get Rachel away from her phone long enough to go through it. And she had to unlock it to do that. Lucky for her, both problems led to the same person.

"Hey, Rachel," she said brightly, switching on a smile. "I was thinking I'd ask Carter to come around tonight. Distract us," she said, when she meant just *distract you.* "We could bake cookies or something. Spend some time together, the three of us."

Rachel's eyes glittered, chin pulling her mouth down into a grin.

"That's a great idea, A . . . B-Bel. I'd love to."

* * *

223

"What?" Carter hissed as Bel dragged her inside.

"I told you to come *now,* not in ten minutes." Bel let her cousin go, turning the corner into the living room. Heart kicking against the cage of her ribs, echoing in her ears. Could Carter hear it too?

"I was in the shower." Carter gazed at her, reading her nerves as something else. "You didn't say it was an emergency. Is there news about U-Uncle Charlie?"

"No. Well, y-yes, I'll explain later." They didn't have to be quiet, but they had to be quick. "Rachel's at the store, she could be back any second."

Bel had insisted they make peanut butter cookies, because she knew they were out of peanut butter, and she knew Rachel would offer to go get some, for the olive branch Bel was dangling in front of her.

"You helped Rachel set up her new phone, right?"

"Yeah," Carter answered, narrowing her eyes. "Because you were avoiding her."

"Do you know what her passcode is?"

Carter narrowed her eyes farther, two suspicious slivers of whipped-up blue. "Why?"

But judging by the tight set of her mouth, she already knew why.

"I need you to tell me the passcode."

Carter sighed, stretching her neck, eyes up to the ceiling. "Bel, why?"

"I need to look through her phone."

"Why do you *need* to look through her phone?" Hovering somewhere close to annoyed.

"Because," Bel lowered her voice, even though Rachel wasn't in the house. It didn't feel like something that could be said loud, it belonged to whispers. "I still think Rachel is lying about her disappearance, and I'm pretty sure she's the reason my dad is now missing."

"Bel, that's—"

"Sometimes you have to trust your gut, Carter. I know that's what happened, I just need to prove it, and the answers might be on her phone. I need your help, for my dad."

Carter hesitated, eyes circling Bel's.

"You've known him a lot longer than you've known Rachel," Bel continued, trying to be gentle, trying to push but not push her away. "Please. For me?"

"Bel, I should tell y—"

Bel shushed her, ears pricking to a new sound. The rasp of wheels against the gravel in the driveway, the reporters stirring, reanimating. Her alarm, her warning siren.

"Rachel's home," Bel hissed. "Quick, Carter." She grabbed her arms. "Tell me the passcode."

A car door slammed, voices shrieked like circling birds.

Carter broke with another sigh, a low warning in her voice. "It's *five six seven eight.* Like when you count in music."

"*Five six seven eight,*" Bel muttered, committing it to memory. "Thanks. Love you."

Carter grumbled.

"One more thing," Bel spoke quickly, racing the click of Rachel's shoes to the front door. "We're baking cookies. I just need you to distract her, while I take her phone and look through."

"Bel," Carter hissed.

"Just keep her busy, you're good at that."

Carter opened her mouth to protest, but it was too late. The sound of the front door swinging open, the rustling of grocery bags.

"I'm back!" Rachel's voice floated through.

"Great," Bel replied. "Carter's here and she's insisting on being head baker." She winked at Carter, just as Rachel came around the corner.

Flushed cheeks and a smile that reached into her eyes. "Hi, Carter," she said. "That's fine by me, totally happy for you to boss me around."

"No bossing," Carter said, "we will work as a *teeeam.*" Baring her teeth with that last word, showing them to Bel. Attagirl.

Carter went to help Rachel with the bags.

"I found a recipe online. We can use my phone," Bel said, pulling it out, unlocking it with her face.

A text popped up on-screen, from Ash: *I'm here.* Bel had messaged him the same time as Carter: *Come to my house now, bring the camera. Wait in the garage—side door is open. Make sure reporters don't see you.*

To which Ash had replied: *Are you going to murder me? On my way.*

"Got it?" Rachel asked.

Bel glanced up. "Yeah: flour, butter, peanut butter, eggs . . ." She reeled off the rest of the ingredients, following Rachel and Carter into the kitchen.

She kept one eye on Rachel as she dumped a bag on the counter, her keys beside it. But where was her phone?

"Got some new flour," Rachel said. "Wasn't sure how long your dad had kept the old one."

Rachel patted the pockets of her trench jacket. She dipped her hand inside and pulled out her phone. Bel stopped moving, only her eyes. Rachel took one quick look at the screen, then placed the phone facedown on the kitchen table.

"I'll just hang my jacket up." Rachel pulled it off, draping it over one arm. "A-B-Bel, can you find the mixing bowl? No idea where your dad moved it to."

"Sure." Bel headed toward the cupboard, using it as an excuse to move closer to the table, to study the phone's position. It was halfway between Bel's usual place and Dad's, at a jaunty angle a few inches from the edge. She blinked to look at it with fresh eyes, remembering the exact spot.

Carter was watching her while Rachel was out of the kitchen.

Bel pressed a finger to her lips before Carter could say anything.

"Alexa!" Rachel called, back in the room, making Bel flinch. She'd only just grasped the concept, that you had to pause after the name. Or she was faking all of it. "Play happy, chill music."

"Here's a playlist for happy, chill music."

Bel handed her the mixing bowl.

"Thank you, sweetie. This was a nice idea."

Bel nodded, surprised that Rachel had fallen for *nice*.

"How much butter?" Carter asked, heading for the refrigerator.

"One cup. I'll leave the recipe here on my phone." Bel placed it on the counter. See, Bel would leave her own phone here with Rachel. A trade, of sorts. Her eyes flicked to the other one. She couldn't just take it; Rachel was standing right there, looking at her.

"If there's any left over, girls, should I take some to your grandpa?" Rachel handed a new pack of sugar to Carter.

"He'd like that," Carter said, wrapping her hand around the sugar, not wincing when her fingers brushed against Rachel's.

"Just wondering," Rachel continued, "while your dad's away, Annabel, whether I should see if Yordan needs any help with Pat. Anything I can do, clean the house or something? Does Yordan take him out every day, for a walk or something?"

"Grandpa can't walk," Bel said, forgetting she was playing nice, adding an awkward smile to soften it. "Don't worry, Yordan's got it. And Uncle Jeff can do more."

But this detour into Grandpa had given Bel an idea.

"But it's a good idea, to take cookies around. Grandpa's probably confused about where Dad is. I'll get a Tupperware; you won't know where they live."

Bel opened the cupboard, Tupperware lids already slipping and sliding from their unsteady piles. She grabbed two containers, one clear, one dark blue, and their matching lids.

"Here." She carried them over to the kitchen table, placed them down in front of the phone, obscuring Rachel's line of sight to it.

And just like she had hundreds of times before, with small insignificant things to feed that knot in her gut, she reached for the phone. Her fingers around its cold edges. She bracketed her hand to slide it up her sleeve, all the way in until it was gone. Hand to her chest to hold it there.

Got it.

Rachel wasn't the only expert in disappearing.

Carter gave Bel a knowing look, a half roll of her eyes.

"Gotta pee." Bel slipped out into the hallway. Out of sight, she transferred the phone into the back pocket of her jeans.

She waited, trying to think of something, anything, that could keep her away longer than *gotta pee.* Bel looked around for inspiration.

227

Could she say she felt sick? No, that wouldn't work, Rachel would want to stay close, pretend to mother her.

Come on, something, something. Pile of her shoes by the door. Hum of reporters outside. A letter on the sideboard, addressed to *Charlie Price,* because the missing still got mail.

Wait, an idea.

Bel grabbed the letter, making sure the address faced her, not out.

She headed toward the kitchen, rearranging her face to someone without a plan.

"Hey," she said from the doorway. "A letter's been delivered here for Ms. Nelson. Looks important, could be something medical, insurance." She pretended to study the front. "I'll go drop it over now. Back in a minute," she said, turning away before anyone could protest.

"Should we preheat the oven?" Carter's voice rang out, bringing Rachel's attention back to her.

"What temperature?" Rachel asked.

Everyone playing their role perfectly. Bel dropped the letter back where she found it and opened the front door.

Reporters tumbled out of their vans, cameras and microphones and hopeful looks in their eyes.

"Annabel *this.*"

And:

"Annabel *that.*"

Bel ignored them all, down the steps and toward the garage, pulling Rachel's phone out of her back pocket, capturing her own face in its dark, unlit screen.

TWENTY-NINE

"Fuck, you scared me," Ash said, clutching one hand to his strawberry-covered heart, backing into a rake. Gasping and backing away from that too.

"What, the reporters screaming my name didn't give you any pre-warning?" Bel stepped carefully around the tarp-covered lawn mower. "So," she said, cradling the phone. "My dad's missing."

"I saw on the news."

His eyes clouded, catching hers when she glanced over, like he was hurt somehow, that she hadn't told him first.

"What happened?" he asked.

"Went missing Saturday night. His phone is off. Looks like he packed a bag and his passport, but he didn't leave because of the stress, he wouldn't do that." She didn't pause, leaving no gap for dissent or Ash's devil's advocate, the devil playing for Rachel's side. "Rachel is behind it, I know she is, and he's in danger. We have to find the truth, we have to save my dad."

"He's really gone?"

"He's gone." Her deepest fear made real in two tiny words, bottomless and cruel. Her lip quivered, a bite behind the surface of her eyes. She held it back. Not here, not in front of Ash, for fuck's sake. "Guess the Prices have a thing for disappearing," she said with a cynical sniff, hiding behind it. "Be my turn soon."

"I'm sorry, Bel."

He reached for her hand, but there was no time to hold hands, no reason it would help.

"Are you recording?" she asked, stepping back.

"Should I be?"

Bel nodded, waiting as he flipped out the viewfinder, the beep as he pressed record, giving her a thumbs-up with his spare hand.

Bel held up the phone, showing the camera.

"Rachel's phone," she said.

Ash's eyes widened. "How?"

Bel enjoyed that look on his face. "Carter's inside distracting her. We don't have much time. Have to find whatever Rachel and Mr. Tripp are hiding. He knows something, why else would he lie, slam the door in our faces? He's been sick off work all week; maybe he knows what Rachel did to my dad, maybe he helped her."

"OK." Ash stretched the word across a few trailing seconds. "So now you want me to capture evidence of *you* committing a crime?"

"I've done worse." Bel blinked. "I'd do much worse to find him."

She tapped the phone screen. The background lit up, an old photo they had in a frame; Rachel with baby Bel balanced on her hip, looking at each other, a smile creeping across Rachel's younger face. It was that woman's secrets Bel wanted, pre-disappeared Rachel, as well as the older one inside the house.

Bel swiped up. It tried Face ID first, the screen juddering when it didn't recognize her, prompting for the passcode instead, bringing up the keypad. Bel's thumb moved across, pressing 5, 6, 7 and 8.

The phone unlocked.

"I'm in," she said, Ash drawing closer, pointing the camera down to record the screen.

Bel pressed the green speech bubble to open all of Rachel's text conversations. An unopened message from Sherry ten minutes ago: *Can you make sure Carter is home for dinner, thx.*

Moving down the list, she saw Carter, Jeff, a few notifications about Amazon deliveries. Bel's name below those, and she was surprised to see that Rachel had entered it right, *Bel,* not *Anna.*

And then—bingo—Julian Tripp.

Bel opened the message thread, straightening the phone so the camera could see too. She scrolled up to the start, eyes circling.

The first was from Rachel, last Tuesday: *Hi it's Rachel Price, I got my new phone set up, just texting everyone so they have my number.*

Mr. Tripp had replied four minutes later: *Hi, Rachel. Was so nice to see you, pretty surreal actually. I hope you're settling back into normal life, let me know if there's anything I can do. Would be great to meet up, we've got sixteen years to catch up on. I was even married for a while!*

"Sixteen years to catch up on," Ash read out from the screen. "And he tells her he was married. Sounds like they weren't in contact while she was disappeared, doesn't it?"

"I guess. *But . . .*" She sharpened the word into a point. "He's clearly hiding something about Rachel. About her disappearance." She read out Rachel's response: *"Yes, we should catch up sometime."*

"Pretty blunt," Ash said. "Like she doesn't want to see him."

Mr. Tripp texted again, two days later, a large gray bubble. Ash read it out: *"Was great bumping into you at the store. Hope you've figured out that lock! I don't want to bring this up again, but I do really need it back ASAP. I know things are probably complicated right now, but let me know."* Ash finished, staring down at the screen through the camera. "What's he talking about? What does he want back?"

"I don't want to bring this up again, but I do really need it back," Bel read it out again, leaning on the words differently to see if the meaning was any clearer.

"Something he gave Rachel, before she disappeared?" Ash said. "And now he wants it back."

Bel moved on to Rachel's reply, her final message to him. *"Let's talk about this another time."*

Julian had sent one last message, Friday morning. *"OK,"* Ash read, *"but it's pretty desperate. Let me know."*

"Fuck sake," Bel groaned. "This is it? Why can't people label their cryptic conversations better? How are we going to find out what they're talking about?"

"Text him?" Ash said uncertainly. "We could text him now, as

Rachel. He won't talk to you but he'll talk to her. The old catfish routine." He looked at her, over the camera, eyes glassy and wide, dropping for half a second to look at her mouth.

Bel thought about it. "No. He might take too long to reply. I have to head back soon or Rachel will think something's wrong. And then if he replies later, when Rachel has the phone back, she'll know I took it, what I did. She can't know I'm onto her." There was more to say, but she didn't want to say it, didn't want to put it into words and make it real that way. That Rachel was dangerous, that Rachel scared her, that Rachel had already taken too much and Bel didn't want to give her a reason to take more.

But Ash nodded, as though she had said all those things and he understood. Which was stupid, really, because he didn't know her at all and she wished he'd stop pretending. But still he kept nodding, a new glint in his eye.

"No, but you can *call* him," he said.

"Are you on crack?"

"No, listen. You'll probably punch me for saying this, but you and Rachel sound almost exactly the same. You literally have the same voice. You can call him as Rachel, pretend to be Rachel, and he won't know, as long as you play it right."

"I can't *be* Rachel."

"Yes, you can, you can do this." He sought out her eyes in the gloom. "You delete it from the call log after and Rachel will never know. There's nothing to lose if he doesn't buy it. But you only have a few minutes and you need these answers."

She did need these answers, for Dad, but there was no way . . .

"Scared?" Ash said, pushing her and she knew it, but she was pushed all the same.

"I ain't scared of shit." She unlocked the sleeping phone. "I can be Rachel," she said, more to herself, as she clicked on Julian Tripp's contact info, thumb hovering over the blue call button. "I'm Rachel," she whispered as she dared herself and thought of Dad, pressing her thumb down.

Calling Julian Tripp . . .

The double ring of the dial tone against her ear.

"Put it on speaker," Ash hissed, steadying the camera. "It'll help muffle your voice."

Bel pressed it onto speakerphone, a click as she did, the dial tone cutting out. A buzzy silence in its wake.

"Hello, Rachel?" Mr. Tripp's voice rattled from the speakers.

Bel cleared her throat, watching Ash as she became Rachel, taking her cues from him. "Hi, J-Julian. Sorry I haven't gotten back to you yet, been a crazy few days. I don't know if you've heard about Charlie—"

"I did hear about that, actually, I'm sorry. Any idea where he's gone?"

That meant they could rule Mr. Tripp out, didn't it, for having anything to do with Dad's disappearance? Ash noted her pause, nodded her on.

"No," she said, "I think it's just been a very stressful situation for everyone. The police think he'll come home soon."

"Well, that's something then, I guess," Mr. Tripp replied, and it was working; he really thought she was Rachel. "So . . . ," he said, leaving a trail for her to pick up.

But Bel didn't know how. She glanced at Ash, his lips parted, half formed around a word that might have been *message.*

"So about your message," Bel said, "I thought it would be better to actually talk it through."

"No, I understand." Mr. Tripp sniffed. "And I'm sorry to ask again so soon. It's just, it's a lot of money, you know."

Bel's heart thudded against her ribs, eyes snapping to Ash. *Money,* she mouthed. Mr. Tripp had given Rachel money before she disappeared. This changed everything.

How much? Ash mouthed back, jabbing his finger toward the phone.

"Rachel, you OK?" Mr. Tripp's voice chimed through.

"No, it's fine," Bel sniffed. "I understand. Um . . . it's been a long time, a lot has happened, I can't remember how much it was exactly . . ."

Ash screwed his eyes and Bel crossed her fingers that she hadn't messed up already.

"It was three thousand bucks, Rachel."

Her heart abandoned her ribs for her throat. She thumbed the mute button, hand shaking.

"Holy fucking shit!" she shouted, a laugh getting in the way, breaking up her voice.

Ash caught her laugh, stifled it. "Keep going," he whispered, just as Mr. Tripp said:

"Rachel? You there?"

Bel unmuted it, wiped the smile off her face.

"Sorry—" she said, but Mr. Tripp didn't let her finish.

"I know it's awkward . . . embarrassing to ask for it, but I always thought you'd pay me back when you could. Then I thought you were dead, like everyone else. But now you're not . . . you know, life hasn't been the easiest. I got medical bills to pay off. Debts. Borrowed a lot of money too. It would really help, if you could pay me back."

"No, sure," Bel said, "I understand," even though she didn't, even though a tiny part of her wanted to take Rachel's side over his, a man more interested in getting his money than his old friend back from the dead. "Things are a bit complicated, I've only been back a week and a half. But you'll get everything you're owed, I promise."

An intake of breath down the line, too deep, almost on the verge of tears. "God, that's such a relief. Thank you."

"Sure." Bel bit back what she really wanted to say, what Rachel might have too. "You didn't ever tell anyone, about the money, did you?"

Ash screwed his face again, eyes and mouth.

"No, course not. I didn't tell the police, I was scared they'd think I had something to do with you going missing, which I obviously didn't. Especially as I'm the one who found your car, who found Bel. But it wouldn't have helped anyway, the money had nothing to do with that man snatching you out of the car, right?"

"Right," she said, running it over in her head, her thoughts becoming Rachel's. "No, it's good you never told them." Bel took a breath, stepped out onto shakier ground. "When did you give me the money again, it wasn't long before, was it?"

"That's why I kept it secret. You asked me on the Friday, and I gave the cash to you after school on Monday, when I drove you home."

That was it, the moment Aunt Sherry had seen, a line being crossed. But maybe she'd read it wrong, and the reason they'd looked *cozy* was because one was passing a huge amount of cash to the other, their little secret.

"That was only two days before sh—I went missing?" Bel said. Ash flapped his hands, and she flapped hers back, mouthing for him to *shut up*.

"Exactly," Mr. Tripp said. "So you aren't mad, that I didn't tell anyone?"

"I'm not mad, Julian." Bel pulled a face.

Silence, saliva ticking around his mouth, down the other end of the phone.

"Rachel?" The sound of her name cut through Bel.

"Yes?" she answered to it.

"I know it's not really important, after everything you've been through. But it's always played on my mind, the not knowing. You never told me what the money was for. Only that you couldn't access your own money, and you needed it, it was an emergency." He sniffed. "When I gave it to you, you said I was a *lifesaver,* which I thought was just one of those things people say, a thank-you. But after you disappeared, I wondered if it meant something else, and that you'd been wrong, that the money hadn't saved your life."

Bel stalled, searching Ash's eyes for what to say. He didn't know either, shrugging behind the camera. "I can't say."

"Come on, Rachel." Mr. Tripp sniffed. "I knew something wasn't right. You hadn't been yourself for weeks, months, even. Jumpy, paranoid. Losing weight, your clothes getting baggy. Stopped coming to Wednesday Wine Night after school. You needed the money and you were scared. Who were you scared of, Rachel? You didn't know the man that abducted you. I always thought it was Charlie, it made sense when he was arrested for killing you. I was so concerned that Monday, I put a tra—"

"You're wrong," Bel snapped, speaking from her own gut, not Rachel's. "I was not scared of Charlie."

Mr. Tripp paused. "Well, you were afraid of someone. Who was it? Charlie's brother?"

"Jeff?" Bel narrowed her eyes. "Why would I be afraid of Uncl—" She stopped herself, slapping a hand to her mouth.

Ash screwed his face, one eye open, staying very still.

Bel tried: "I mean, I don't think—"

"Annabel, is that you?" The speakers rattled with his voice, a dark, crackling edge to it.

Bel jabbed the red button to hang up, holding the phone away from her, like it was counting down to explode.

"Oh well," Ash said, somehow out of breath, standing still. "You were bound to fuck up at some point."

Bel navigated into the call log, deleting the top entry to Julian Tripp, disappearing all trace of what they just did, her skin alive and electric.

"You don't think he'll tell Rachel?"

"Probably not," Ash said. "We just caught him, he admitted to withholding information from police so he wouldn't look suspicious. I reckon he'll want to keep this as quiet as we do."

Bel felt some comfort in that *we*. A comfort she resented immediately, feeding it to the knot in her stomach. There was no *we*. Bel only had one person, and he was missing.

"Worth it," she said, clicking the bones in her neck. "Three thousand dollars in cash two days before she disappeared. That's a slam dunk, right? Enough to start a new life somewhere, isn't it? To disappear yourself?"

Ash's mouth twitched.

"We just proved it, didn't we?" Bel's eyes glittered in the dark. "That Rachel Price wasn't abducted; she chose to leave. She planned her own disappearance."

Ash hesitated, chewed his lower lip. "Not enough for the police or a court of law. I actually think it's illegal to record someone on the phone without their consent in the US. We'll let Ramsey worry about that. But . . . yeah, I think we maybe just did."

A smile pulled at the edges of Bel's mouth. She gave in, shooting a wink at the camera in Ash's hands. "I knew it."

"But we still don't know where she went. Why she left. How. Why she's back."

"We will. We have to, to find my dad," Bel said, tucking Rachel's phone up her sleeve. "I should go, already been too long."

"OK." His lips parted like he wanted to say more, but he stopped himself.

"See ya later, alligator." Bel waved him off like he was anybody else, heading for the door.

"In a while, crocodile," Ash responded, recording her as she walked out of the garage, into the low evening sun.

The reporters scrambled.

"Annabel, *please.*"

"Annabel, *wait.*"

She ignored them, unable to shift that smile, covering it with her other sleeve.

"Where's your father gone?" CNN shouted.

Up the steps, Bel unlocked the front door and pushed it open.

A sweet vanilla smell wrapped her up as she walked through the house.

"Back." She hung in the kitchen doorway, watching as Rachel and Carter both turned, a similar look in their eyes and warm flush in their cheeks. "Sorry," she said, before anyone could ask. "Ms. Nelson wouldn't shut up. Lonely, I think. How are the cookies?"

"Done," Carter said stiffly. "Already in the oven."

Bel shifted her face, pretending to look disappointed. Rachel smiled at her.

"Well, you didn't miss out on the eating part," she said.

"Or the cleaning up," added Carter.

Bel took the hint, stepping into the room, edging toward the table.

"How long do they have left?" she asked, hoping the right person would answer.

Rachel bent to look at the timer on the oven and Bel didn't hesitate. She straightened her arm and slid Rachel's phone out, placing it where she'd found it, shielded behind the Tupperware, rotating it to a diagonal.

Bel snatched her hand away just in time.

"Four minutes," Rachel said, turning back.

"Smell amazing already."

Bel joined Carter at the sink, rolling up her sleeves. Carter shot her a look, and Bel shot one back, blinks instead of words.

She heard a huff of air behind her, not quite a sigh, not quite a gasp, just a breath that hitched halfway through.

Bel turned back.

Rachel was standing beside the kitchen table, looking down at it. At her phone.

Bel stopped breathing.

Rachel's fingers trailed along the wooden surface, over to her phone. And in one small movement, she spun the phone from one diagonal to the other, finger tapping beside, studying it.

Rachel glanced up without warning, catching Bel's eyes.

She gave her a smile, vanilla sweet and warm.

Bel smiled back, tight-lipped, without teeth.

THIRTY

Bel stopped outside number 39, Ash's hotel room. Patted down her hair, pushed up her eyebrows.

The door opened before she had a chance to knock.

It was Ramsey, ducking his head as he left the room.

His eyes latched onto hers as the door latched shut. "Hi, Bel."

"Hi yourself," she snapped, suddenly awkward that he'd caught her standing here. "Ash told me to come over, that he's found something," she explained.

Ramsey nodded, a knowing half smile. "I know," he said, to hammer the smile home. "We found something we wanted to show you."

He moved past her, down the corridor.

"You aren't coming?" she asked.

Ramsey turned, smile on the other side now. "Nah. A good filmmaker knows when he's getting in the way of his own film." He clicked his fingers at her, tiny guns made of skin as he walked away, disappearing around the corner.

Bel hammered her fist against the door.

It opened, barely, Ash's pale face appearing in the crack.

"Why do you knock like a serial killer?" his floating head grumbled.

"Are you naked?"

"No." His eyes tracked back and forth, confused.

"Open the door, then," Bel said, pushing it.

She walked in, the hotel room dingy, curtains framing the evening sky. A laptop open on the desk, glowing ghostly white, small camera hooked up to it. A spiderweb of cables beside. The desk chair and the room's armchair pulled in front.

"You've left boxers on the bed." Bel pointed, trying to embarrass him.

Ash nodded, trying not to be embarrassed. "Those ones live there, actually."

He wandered back to the desk, muttering to himself. "Need a fresh card for the camera." He sorted through a stack of clear plastic cases, some labeled with a red X. "That's why it's important to label them, says Ramsey. Aha." He pulled one open and popped out the SD card, slotting it inside the handheld camera.

"Is this all the documentary footage?"

"All the stuff I've shot," he said. "Ramsey's editing the early footage for the broadcasters, but he wants to keep this stuff with you under wraps, until we know what we have. I'm supposed to rotate the memory cards, remember which ones are full, which ones I've already uploaded and wiped." He pointed, fingers taking her on a tour of the untidy desk. "All gets saved onto this bad boy here." He tapped two fingers against a black external hard drive, plugged into the laptop.

"Memory storage, exciting stuff." Bel clicked her tongue.

"Well, I can't spend all day running around with you."

"Not that you'd want to," Bel said.

"No, you're awful company."

Bel's phone vibrated in her jacket pocket, saving them from the awkward-on-purpose moment. She pulled it out and gasped.

"It's the chief of police. About Dad."

"Answer it," Ash said, turning away and averting his eyes, as though that meant he couldn't listen in.

Bel pressed the phone to her ear, spoke before Dave Winter could. "Do you have any news? Have you found him?"

The line crackled with Dave's breath. "Hi, Annabel. No, we haven't found him, but we have an update. His phone records finally came through."

Bel backed away, boots skidding against the rough carpet. "And?"

"Your dad made one phone call the night he went missing. In the middle of the night, actually, three-twenty a.m. The call lasted only a few seconds, but it pinged off a cell tower near Danville, Vermont. So that's where he was when he made the call."

"Who did he call?" Bel said, trying not to rush him, taking everything in.

"He called a number belonging to a Robert Meyer, who lives just outside Barton, Vermont. I wanted to ask if you know who he is? Heard that name before? Is he a friend of your dad's?"

Bel searched her memories, lining them up against that name. "*Robert Meyer.* No, I don't think I recognize it," she said, annoyed that she didn't, for Dad's sake.

"That's OK," Dave said, "Rachel didn't recognize it either."

"You've spoken to Rachel?"

"I called her first," Dave said, unaware of his betrayal, calling Rachel, letting her know that her plan was working perfectly. "State Police are going to talk to this Robert Meyer, see what he knows, I'll let you know if he tells us anything useful. Danville would have been on the drive to Barton, so it seems like that's where your dad was heading."

But how was he heading there, when his truck was at home?

"Anything else?" she said, voice slipping, clawing back up her throat.

"Huh?"

"The phone records. Did he make any other calls?" There was only one name she cared about: her own. For her to have been the last person Dad tried to reach, even though she'd had no missed calls.

"No," Dave said, not realizing how big that *no* was. "Looks like he turned the phone off after making that one call. Been off since, no activity."

Bel's heart sank, curdling in her gut, buddying up to the knot that always lived there now.

"He's been gone six days," she said, not a question, but a reminder of Dave's promise, what he owed Charlie Price, here on the other side of all their history.

"We're working on it. There's been a couple more hits on his bank card, one on Thursday, one today, so we're tracing him that way too. Won't be long, Annabel."

"OK." She hesitated to let him go. Should she tell Dave about Julian Tripp? About the three thousand dollars? "Officer Winter—"

"You can call me Dave, sweetie. Known each other long enough."

And that was long enough to change her mind. No, she shouldn't tell him. She wanted Dave to focus on finding Dad; he had the tools to do that and she didn't. She shouldn't distract him with Rachel. It was Bel's job to take down Rachel, her responsibility.

"Will you call me first with updates, not Rachel? She wants me to deal with this; she's still feeling overwhelmed."

The line crackled again. "Sure," he said. "Hope you two are holding up OK?"

Oh, they were holding up just fine.

"I gotta go," she said, Dave's goodbyes growing faint as she pulled the phone away from her ear, pressed the red button.

"Who's Robert Meyer?" Ash asked, facing her again.

"I don't know. Lives in Vermont. He was the last person Dad called, the night he went missing."

"So your dad's in Vermont?"

"Or that's where Rachel wants us to think he is."

A text pinged up on Bel's screen. God, she was Miss Fucking Popular today: Ash, then Dave Winter, now Carter:

Can I come over for a sleepover? Mom is being a nightmare again.

Bel typed out a reply:

Can't sorry, I'm out!

She slid her phone back into her jacket pocket, stared at Ash expectantly. "So . . . I didn't come here just to insult your hideous sweater. You said you'd found something?"

"Yes, we did, when we were editing the dinner party scene. Hold on, I should have the camera on."

He flipped out the viewfinder and pressed record, snapping his fingers in front of the lens like a makeshift clapper board. There were books on the desk, *The Woman who Disappeared Twice* on top, an old true-crime book about Rachel. Ash placed the camera on the pile, pointing it back at them.

"You sit here." He patted the cushioned chair closest to the camera, a spew of dust as he did, floating around her.

Bel sat.

Ash did too, pulling his chair in too close, leaning across her to reach the laptop.

He froze, her breath on his exposed neck.

Bel looked at the shape of his mouth and he looked at hers. A second dragged by, Bel's heart out of its place, beating too many times, finding his green eyes again.

Oh fuck.

She blinked and pulled back, leaning into her chair. Ash coughed into his fist, fiddling with the camera's position. Just in time too, like they'd been about to cross some unseen line. Lucky the camera was there between them, to hold the line. Because that would have been really fucking stupid. Pointless too. Ash would leave forever when this film was done. That was all they were to each other. Subject and Camera Assistant.

Bel shifted her chair a few inches away. His Side and Her Side.

He better stay out of hers.

"Is it about my dad?" she asked instead, Ash turning back to the laptop. He clicked into a folder labeled *Dinner Party*. "About Rachel?"

"You'll see." He double-clicked on an audio file. "Or, rather, you'll *hear*."

The on-screen arrow hovered over the play button, twitching in tandem with Ash's finger on the trackpad.

"I was going through the audio from the dinner party, to see if your dad said anything when he stormed off, if he gave any clues as to where he's gone now."

Bel leaned forward, forgetting about Her Side. "Did he?"

Ash shook his head. "He said *for fuck's sake,* nothing else, then turned his mike pack off. But there was someone else who didn't. Someone who forgot they were wearing a hot mike, that they were being recorded."

Bel blinked the question at him.

"Your uncle Jeff," he answered. "Jeff went to help your grandpa into the car, after everyone left the table."

"I remember," Bel said.

"This is the conversation they had, what the microphone picked up."

Ash pressed play.

Rustling.

Heavy breathing.

"Are you in, Dad?" Jeff's gruff voice, breathless with effort. "Let me get the seat belt."

"I—I," Grandpa stuttered.

"Don't worry, I'll get that."

More rustling.

A click.

"Dad," Jeff's voice dropped lower, into whispers. Bel closed her eyes to focus her ears. "I have to ask you something, and I need you to remember."

The swish of movement, a cacophony of clothes crackling against each other.

Ash paused quickly. "There's audio here, but it's too quiet to hear over the rustling, I've tried."

He un-paused.

A grating click from the back of a throat; the sound her grandpa made when he was searching for words.

"I don't know who that is," he rasped.

Jeff's voice came back clearer. "You do, Dad. You do know. Where was she? Where did they find her?"

"I don't know."

"Dad, I need you to try. It's important."

"I don't . . . I want to go home," Grandpa said, voice frail, every syllable an effort. "Where's . . . Y-Y—"

"Yordan?" Jeff sighed, the scratch of fingernails against stubble. "I'll go get him. You stay here, Dad."

"That's it." Ash stopped the file, the abrupt silence buzzing in Bel's ears. "Saba took the microphone off him when he came back inside."

Bel's mouth opened and closed, chewing the air while she searched for words, no more luck than Grandpa. "What?" was all she came up with.

"I know," Ash spoke low and light. "I messaged you as soon as we heard it."

"Where was she?" Bel quoted her uncle. *"Where did they find her?* He's talking about Rachel, isn't he?" She looked for confirmation in Ash's eyes.

"That's what we thought too."

Bel thought that through, forking paths of *if*s and *but*s, her head racing down each way and backtracking.

"Wait a second," she said, telling herself too. "So Jeff thinks Grandpa knows something about Rachel. About where she was those sixteen years, and her reappearance. *Where did they find her?* It sounds like she had to come back because someone found her— who's *they*?"

Ash looked at her; too much eye contact, then not enough. "Seems Jeff didn't get the answers he wanted either."

"But why does Jeff think Grandpa knows something about Rachel? He has dementia, he doesn't *know* anything."

Ash shrugged. "Your uncle seems convinced he has the answers, you can hear the desperation in his voice."

Bel chewed on that too. "Well, fuck." She sat back in her chair, burying her fingers in her hair.

"Made me wonder," Ash said, "if it had anything to do with what Julian Tripp said. Rachel's comment about *you're a lifesaver* and that she was scared of someone, him bringing up Jeff's name."

Bel tried to sort through it all, drawing lines in her head. Rachel scared of Jeff? Rachel planning her disappearance, taking money from Mr. Tripp so no one would suspect she left willingly? Grandpa

245

knowing something about Rachel? Jeff knowing Grandpa knew something but not what it was? How did all of this fit together?

"Whatever Jeff thinks Grandpa knows about Rachel, he's kept it to himself, and now Dad's gone." Bel set her jaw. "But he won't be keeping it much longer. He's going to tell me, tomorrow."

Bel could do it; get Uncle Jeff to crack, just like Sherry. Because there was something else hiding between the members of the Price family, something Rachel's return had disturbed.

Beneath the land mines, there were secrets too.

THIRTY-ONE

Key to the lock, Bel hesitated. A shiver up her spine, picking up the hairs on the back of her neck. That pre-warning, that primal response to danger.

Bel checked over her shoulder, searching through the darkness, eyes catching on the trees across the street, their dancing shadows, shaping them into looming faces. But her eyes were wrong, the danger wasn't coming from that way, it was behind the door.

She slotted the key in and shoved the door inward, opening onto the waiting war zone.

Laughter and warm voices, the smell of something buttery and sweet. She hadn't expected that.

"An-Bel, is that you?" Rachel's voice rang out, finding her around the corner.

Bel dropped her bag, kicked off her shoes, leaving them in the way.

"Honey, I'm home," she said darkly, to herself, following the sounds of the TV into the living room.

"Hi, sweetie." Rachel's eyes shone in the dark room, settling on Bel. The television threw light on her face with each frame, flashes of bright white into a green afterglow.

She was on the sofa, legs tucked up under a checkered blanket. And she wasn't alone.

Carter was on the other end. Legs hidden beneath the same blanket.

A bowl of popcorn between them, half empty already.

Rachel took another handful. "We're having a movie night. Come join, there's plenty of space." She moved the popcorn to her lap.

Bel's eyes darted to Carter, her face flashing the same colors as Rachel's.

"We're watching *Knives Out*," Carter said, even though she must know that wasn't the question in Bel's eyes.

"I told you I was out tonight." Bel stood dead still in the same spot.

"I know." Carter's hands disappeared under the blanket too. "By the time you replied, I was already here. Rachel said I could sleep over. She didn't have anything to do either, so we decided to watch a movie. Have you seen this one, Bel? I think you'd like it."

Bel didn't care if she'd like the movie, she didn't like this at all. The two of them together, without her. A churn of acid in her gut, the knot paddling around in it. This was a calculated move somehow; Rachel shifting the pieces on the board, trying to take Carter onto her side.

Bel wouldn't give her up that easy.

"What's it about?" Bel brightened her voice, moving toward the sofa, blocking the TV for Rachel, throwing her into full shadow.

"It's a murder mystery," Carter said, "about a fucked-up family."

"I like it already."

Bel took the middle seat, between them, her body a barricade between Carter and Rachel, reclaiming her cousin, who couldn't see what Rachel truly was.

She tucked her legs under the blanket, pulling until one of Rachel's feet was exposed.

Rachel offered her the popcorn.

Bel hesitated, then took a handful. The pretense of it all: mother and daughter, and Carter.

"Its's definitely him." Rachel pointed at the screen, trying to catch Bel up, or showing her that she was better at this kind of thing.

"No news vans outside." Bel spoke over the character.

"They packed up earlier," Rachel said. "Guess they have to sleep sometime."

"Or they don't care as much about Dad disappearing as you reappearing," Bel said, eyes ahead, because she wouldn't be able to hide which one *she* cared about most, and she was trying to keep Rachel close, study her to work out how to destroy her. Look how well she was doing; so close that she could hear the way Rachel's breath rattled gently.

"He'll be back, Bel." Carter pressed the underside of her foot against Bel's, matching them up. "Cops in Vermont will track him down soon, and he'll come home. Won't he?" She leaned forward to speak across Bel, looking to Rachel.

Rachel's hand paused above the popcorn, eyes darting between Carter and Bel. "Yes, I'm sure he will," she answered. Bel could read Rachel better now, could tell Carter had put her on the spot. Maybe Carter wasn't lost after all. And maybe Dad wasn't either.

"He better be," Bel added, like a threat, because it was.

Rachel returned her gaze to the television. "It's your grandpa's eighty-fifth birthday next Friday," she said, not a question. "Carter said your dad hosts a family dinner here every year. That mac and cheese is the tradition. We can still do that, you know, even if he's not back by then."

Bel swallowed. She tried not to move her head, eyes straining to study Rachel side-on. The flicker of the TV against the glass of her eyes. What had she meant by that? Had Rachel given something away; did she know Dad wouldn't be back next week? Wouldn't ever be back, because she'd made sure of it?

"Yeah." Bel sniffed. "That would be nice."

Rachel reached for another handful of popcorn. Bel flinched at the bone-crunch sound of it in her mouth.

"Does Yordan ever take your grandpa out for walks?" Rachel asked. Bel was too close; could smell her buttery breath. "Not good to be inside the house all day."

Bel was about to answer but stopped herself. It wasn't the first time Rachel had asked about Grandpa and Yordan, about their routine. Bel noticed things like that, now she wasn't avoiding Rachel all the time. Was there something in that, or was Rachel just trying to make it look like she cared?

"Grandpa's fine," she said, shutting that down, whatever Rachel was trying. A curveball to throw her off, flipping Rachel's questions back to her: "Do you like mac and cheese?"

A smile played across Rachel's lips. "Yeah, I do."

The movie finished, only crumbs and unpopped kernels at the bottom of the bowl.

"We should do this again," Rachel said, a sheen across her eyes, matching the sheen across her bared teeth. "If you want? Movie night. Us three. I had fun."

"Me too," Bel said, at the exact same time as Carter. They laughed, and Rachel ruined it by joining in.

"Maybe once a week? I've got a lot of movies to catch up on." Rachel stood, kernels rattling in the bowl as she picked it up. "Carter, where would you like to sleep? I can make up Charlie's bed for you?"

Bel stiffened, and Carter must have felt it, through their feet.

"That's OK." Carter smiled up at her. "I'll go in with Bel, like I normally do."

"Perfect." Rachel beamed, and maybe Bel was getting worse at this, because her smile didn't seem fake at all.

Bel ventured back from brushing her teeth, hurrying down the hall so Rachel couldn't catch her, those eyes glowing in the dark.

"Good night, girls!" Rachel called from the spare room, her door left ajar; not locked, not even shut.

Bel winced, a shiver, even though the house was warm.

"Night," Carter called from Bel's room. Bel said it too, half a second later; a deeper, darker echo.

She reached her bedroom and closed the door, leaning up against it. Carter was already in bed, tucked up on her usual side.

"So?" Bel turned off the top light, climbing in under the comforter.

"So what?" Carter replied.

Bel put her cold feet on the exposed skin of Carter's legs. Carter kicked back.

"So *Rachel*?" Bel said, voice dropping into whispers. She didn't trust Rachel or her half-closed door; she could be creeping around outside, listening in.

"*So* what about her?" Carter said, not following suit, not lowering her voice. "She said she had no plans and how about we watch a movie and wait for you to get back. I didn't want to be at home. It's not a big deal. We had fun, didn't we?"

Bel couldn't say she did. "Why are you getting defensive?"

"I'm not," Carter snapped, hands crossed over her chest.

"Yes you are."

"Because I know you're going to find some reason to be annoyed about it."

"No I'm not," Bel said.

"Yes you are," Carter hit back.

"Not annoyed, no. We just have to be careful around her, OK?" Bel hissed.

"Why do we have to be careful? Rachel is nice. She's nice to both of us and she's been through hell. Why do you always have to do this?"

"I'm not *doing* anything," Bel said. "It's Rachel. She's doing everything. She's back for just a week with a made-up story about where she's been for sixteen years, and then my dad goes missing? Of course she wants you to think she's *nice*."

"Bel." A warning.

"Carter." A warning back. "Did she say anything to you?"

"About what?" Carter recrossed her arms the other way, staring up at the ceiling.

"About anything? About my dad? About your parents? About why she chose to disappear and lie about it? Any slipups?"

"Maybe." Carter chewed her bottom lip. "She told me she was an evil mastermind with a plan for world domination."

"Carter." Bel turned to look at her, a final warning, eyes sharpening with it.

"No, nothing," Carter sighed. "She asked me questions about school

251

and dancing and then we talked about the movie. Nothing suspicious, sorry, Bel," said like she wasn't sorry one bit. She raised one arm and dropped it against the comforter, a straight line between her and Bel, her own barricade.

Bel turned the lamp off, throwing them into darkness. It was her turn to stare up at the ceiling. Who could she convince if she couldn't even convince Carter? Had Rachel already won?

No, because Bel still had a plan, a next move. Jeff knew something about Rachel, or he believed that Grandpa did. Uncle Jeff was the way to get what she wanted: Dad back home and Rachel gone, like it was always meant to be.

Bel hadn't been studying her uncle since Rachel returned, but maybe she should have been.

"Has your dad said anything?" Bel said, treading lightly, something she could only ask in the dark.

"About Rachel?" Carter shifted, the comforter too. "No. Well, I mean, of course he's talked about her: about her return, about the stress of it all and that's why he thinks Uncle Charlie took off for some space. But he was happy she came home."

Bel thought about that. She could play her the clip, what they caught Jeff saying to Grandpa. But what if Carter then told Rachel, took away their advantage?

"Has he been acting strange at all? Since Rachel returned?"

A pause, the crackle of Carter's hair against the pillow.

"No," she said. "Why?"

"No reason, just wondering."

The whites of Carter's eyes glowed across from her. One slow blink took them away.

"Well, maybe a bit," Carter said. "But everyone's been acting strange since Rachel returned." Another blink. "Especially you."

Carter rolled over, turned her back on Bel.

"I'm going to sleep," she said.

THIRTY-TWO

The bell above the door jangled, catching Bel's nerves.

She headed through the store, down the aisle of camping gear, past hockey, toward the break room door, ignoring the *Employees Only* sign, shoving it open.

Uncle Jeff was inside, making a cup of coffee, the machine sputtering.

"Bel," he said. "What are you doing? You're not allowed back here."

"Came to talk to you." She set her jaw.

"Uh-oh, am I in trouble?" he asked, adding milk to his coffee.

"You tell me."

"Is it about Carter?" He took a sip. "She stayed with you last night, right? She and Sherry have been . . . well, you know teenage girls."

"Well, I am one," Bel said. "But it's not about Carter."

"Your dad?" Jeff looked up, lines crinkling around his eyes. "I bet he'll be back tomorrow. That makes sense. Full week away to clear his head. Cops don't seem worried."

"Not about Dad either," Bel said. "It's Rachel."

Jeff took another sip, like it was on purpose, to give himself time.

"What about her?" he said.

Bel wasn't sure how to best approach this: all guns blazing or only half, keep some back for later.

"I think you know something about her that you're not saying."

His mouth opened and closed. "I know as much as you do," he said, ending in a cough, catching it and the lie in his fist. Because Bel knew her uncle was lying to her, and she could prove it.

"Let me show you something." Bel gestured toward the table, where Jeff's phone was lying face up. She took a seat and pulled out her own phone, waited for him to take the chair opposite. "Last week, when we had the family dinner, you helped Grandpa into the car."

"Yes," Jeff said, eyes up, coffee down. "And what—"

"You were wearing a live microphone. It recorded everything you said."

Bel watched Jeff as he swallowed hard, one of his hands curling into a fist, the bony mountain range of his knuckles pushing through skin, giving him away.

"Would you like to hear it?" She didn't wait for the answer, scrolling to the audio file and pressing play, turning the volume all the way up.

"Are you in, Dad?" Jeff's voice from last week, metallic and tinny through her phone speakers.

Bel watched the uncle in front of her, as the one from last week spoke. He fidgeted, ran a hand around his neck.

"Let me get the seat belt."

"I—I," Grandpa stuttered.

"Don't worry, I'll get that."

Rustling. A click.

"Dad." A pause. *"I have to ask you something, and I need you to remember."*

Jeff dropped his head into his hands, elbows propped on the table. The crackle of material rasping against the microphone.

"I don't know who that is," Grandpa croaked in reply.

"You do, Dad," Jeff insisted, the one from now still hiding his face. *"You do know. Where was she? Where did they find her?"*

"I don't know."

"Dad, I need you to try. It's important."

She stopped the clip, the room too quiet. Bel used the thickening silence against Jeff, staring him down until his face emerged from his hands.

"Bel, I can explain," he said, eyes wide in the headlights of her hard stare.

"Can you?" She cleared her throat. "Why do you think Grandpa knows where Rachel was? That he knows who found her, and when?"

Jeff hesitated, a quick burst of blinks, muscles twitching around his mouth.

"Um . . . ," he said. "Yeah, I asked him about Rachel. I don't know anything, I swear. But Dad had mentioned something strange about her, so I was pushing for details. Now I think he was just confused."

Bel narrowed her eyes. "We don't hear Grandpa say anything about Rachel before you bring it up. It's all recorded."

"No." Jeff shook his head, too long and too fast, obscuring his eyes. "Not then. A couple of days before, when I was at his house."

"What did he say?" Bel pushed.

"I can't remember exactly." Jeff coughed. "Something about Rachel. About f-finding her. Maybe he was recalling an older memory and it just sounded like it was about her reappearance. He's confused. We can't trust his memories. But I wanted to check when I had him alone, after he'd seen her, see if it sparked anything. Obviously, he couldn't remember. I shouldn't have done that, not fair."

It felt like he was still lying to her, another cough to cover it, holding eye contact with his reflection in Bel's phone screen, but not with her.

"So does Grandpa know something about Rachel or not?" She hardened her voice, trying to catch his gaze.

"I don't know. I don't think so."

Bel dropped one hand to the table, a thud that finally drew his attention. "And you don't know anything more about her disappearance or reappearance?"

"No, I don't know anything," he said, and maybe he was lying or maybe not. Jeff didn't like confrontation and Bel lived for it; they couldn't be more different. But she didn't like the way he'd leaned on the word *know,* like maybe he suspected something, or half believed another, and she'd only chosen the wrong word.

"You sure?" She gave him another chance.

"Sure."

"Did Rachel ever have any reason to be afraid of you?"

Jeff's face clouded over, eyebrows eclipsing the whites of his eyes.

"Of me? No," he said quietly. "Why would you ask that? I always liked Rachel. She always liked me, I think."

"And now?"

Jeff shrugged. "She's family, of course."

"Family first," Bel said, echoing Sherry's words. But Rachel was less family than others, much less than Dad. And if Jeff knew anything that could help bring him home . . .

"Do you know where Dad is? Did he mention wanting to leave after Rachel came back?"

Jeff shook his head. "I don't know where he is, but I know he'll be back. He's the heart of this family. He never said anything, but you could see how overwhelmed he—"

Jeff was cut off by his phone, vibrating against the table, rotating as it did, an angry bug on its back.

They both glanced at the screen.

An incoming call from *Bob.*

Jeff's friend, who he always dropped into conversations even when he didn't fit. *Bob from Vermont.*

Bel's heart jumped to the base of her throat.

Wait a fucking second.

Jeff moved to reject the call but Bel swatted his hand away.

"Bob from Vermont," she said, voice urgent, grating in her throat. "Is his full name Robert Meyer?"

Jeff narrowed his eyes.

Bel clapped her hands to shock him out of it.

"Yes."

"Fuck!" Bel grabbed the phone before her uncle could.

"Hey, give—"

Bel swiped to accept the call, raised the phone to her ear.

Jeff got to his feet and Bel jumped back from him.

"Hello?" a gruff voice said down the line. Bob from Vermont, not just a name, but a voice too. "Jeff, I gotta tell you something."

"Hi, Bob," Bel said, moving away from Jeff, a two-step dance, hand splayed to hold him back.

"This isn't Jeff."

Bob from Vermont was observant, she could give him that.

"No, it's not," she said. "I'm Bel, his niece."

"Charlie's kid?"

"Charlie's kid," she repeated. "Now that you mention him, I need to ask you something."

"I already know what you're gonna say." A sigh that tickled the speaker.

"You're the last person my dad called before he went missing," Bel continued anyway, pushing through. "At three in the morning last Saturday, the night he disappeared. What did he say, Bob? I really need to know," she added, voice tight and desperate, clinging to the walls of her throat.

Another sigh. Observant and a mouth-breather, Bob from Vermont. But he might be the only person who knew where Dad was.

"I've been through this with the State Police. Just got back from an interview with them, thought Jeff should know."

Bel didn't care about any of that.

"What did my dad say on the phone? It's important."

Jeff had backed off now, listening, eyes rotating.

"He didn't say anything," Bob said, sharpening the consonants. "The call only lasted a few seconds. I picked it up, said *Hello, who's there,* and no one answered. I could only hear the wind, like someone was there, just not talking. That's it. I don't know anything else, like I said to the police."

Bel held a breath, trapped it in her cheeks, thinking. If Dad didn't talk, maybe he wasn't the one making that call, it could have been Rachel using his phone. Or option three: Bob from Vermont was lying to her.

"What's he saying?" Jeff asked in a stage whisper.

She ignored him.

"My dad made the call from Danville, Vermont. He must have been on the way to see you?" Not a question, but Bel made it one.

"Well, he never turned up, and I never heard from him. And I don't know why you've got me messed up in your family stuff. Now I got cops asking me all kinds of shit."

"What kinds of shit?" Bel looked at Jeff, trying to remember all the scraps he'd dropped in about Bob over the years. Hadn't he said something about the dark web?

"Just because I choose to live off the grid," Bob was rattling on.

"What about your *online activities*?" Bel asked, phrasing it as nicely as she could.

"Now you sound like one of them cops," Bob scoffed. "And no, before you ask me too, I did not sell your dad a fake identity. I never saw him, you have my word."

Bel paused. She might have Bob's word, but she had something else too, something much more valuable.

"You sell fake identities?" she asked, grasping at the thread he'd left.

A pause.

"No . . . I do not."

"OK, but if you did know about that kind of thing, how much would it cost someone to buy themselves a whole new identity? Passport? Driver's license?"

"I'm telling you, I don't know anything about that *kind of thing*," Bob replied, way too strong in his denial.

"What if you had three thousand dollars?" Bel said, chancing it. "Would that be enough?"

Bob breathed out, the line crackled.

"I think that would be more than enough," he said, carefully.

Bel's stomach flipped, the knot landing heavy with it.

Her dad hadn't gone to Bob from Vermont, Bel had his word. But someone else might have.

She chanced again, nothing to lose, even though Uncle Jeff was right here. "Sixteen years ago, did Rachel Price come to you to buy a new identity? She would have had the cash to pay you."

A shadow crossed Jeff's eyes, waiting for the answer to play out on Bel's face.

Bob coughed, and Bel couldn't help thinking that a lie would follow, if he was anything like Jeff.

She waited.

"No, she did not," Bob said, slowly, clearly. "I've never met Rachel Price. You don't think I would have told Jeff if she had? Saved your family all that pain, all these years? She never came to me, you have my word on that too. Neither of your parents, so I don't know why your dad called me and dragged me into all this. But I want to be kept out of it, you hear?"

Bel deflated. Could he be lying about one and not the other? She either trusted his answers or she didn't.

"Loud and clear, Bob from Vermont," she said.

The line beeped, went dead.

"He's cheerful." Bel chucked the phone back to her uncle.

He fumbled, catching it against his chest. "What did he say?"

"A lot of nothing." Bel sniffed. "Dad called him that night, but he didn't say anything, apparently. Bob never saw him."

Jeff nodded. "I trust everything Bob says. He wouldn't lie."

"Course not. Dark-web criminals are as honest as they come, Uncle Jeff."

He hesitated, one slow blink. "Why do you think your mom is lying about her disappearance?"

"I don't." Bel shrugged, feigning surprise. "Do you?" Threw it back at him.

"No . . ." Jeff's voice trailed away from him.

"Good, glad we agree."

Jeff coughed into his closed fist.

"Don't tell Rachel about that call," Bel said, grabbing her abandoned phone. "Or I'll tell her you think you know where she really disappeared to."

Jeff shifted uncomfortably, shoulders rising to his ears.

"Deal," he said, speaking to the floor.

"Good." Bel pushed the door open with her heels, setting Jeff free. She gave him a pointed thumbs-up. "Family first."

Each giving up a little more of Rachel, bit by bit. And even more of themselves.

Family first, and Grandpa was next.

THIRTY-THREE

"Hi, Yordan."

Bel bared her teeth in a smile, too fierce, judging by Yordan's alarmed face.

"Hello, Annabel," he said, pulling the door fully open. "We weren't expecting visitors. I'm just doing your grandpa's lunch."

"Great, I'll join you." Bel gave him no choice, foot crossing the threshold, bumping the door out of Yordan's hands. She stepped inside, a wave of dry heat enveloping her, stinging her eyes.

Yordan nodded as she winced, understanding. "Your grandpa feels the cold."

Bel followed him down the hallway, stairs snaking up to the right.

Grandpa couldn't go upstairs anymore, the house cut in half for him. The study was his bedroom now, and Yordan slept upstairs, in the room Dad had grown up in. A lot of history here, the building blocks of the Price family. The grandmother Bel never met died right there, after a fall down the stairs, hit her head just the wrong way. Bel and Carter used to try and summon her ghost, before the idea of ghosts became something to fear. *Hey, Granny Price, watch me do a handstand. Hey, Granny Price, is the devil real?*

Grandpa was in the living room, in his armchair, the one they used to sit in to read together.

261

"Pat, someone's here to see you." Yordan overenunciated every word. "Your granddaughter Annabel. Isn't that nice?"

Bel walked into Grandpa's eyeline, dropping onto the sofa opposite. "Hi, Paw-Paw, nice to see you." She followed suit, leaning hard on every consonant.

"I'll be in the kitchen," Yordan told her. "You want anything? Coffee?"

"I'm OK, thanks."

Yordan slipped out, steps silent on the thick carpet, leaving them alone.

Bel hadn't been alone with Grandpa, not since his first stroke last summer. Dad was always here to take the lead, to step in when Grandpa got confused, to be a familiar face through all the broken memories.

"Warm in here, isn't it?" Bel said, starting to sweat.

Grandpa made a sound in his throat.

"Did you enjoy the family meal last week, Grandpa?" she said loudly. "The paella?"

Grandpa raised a shaky finger, finally looked at her. "Charlie?"

"Dad's not here." It wounded her to have to say it. "He's gone away for a while, remember? He'll be back real soon, I promise."

Grandpa nodded upward instead of down, straining the loose skin of his neck.

"Are you looking forward to your birthday dinner next week?"

Grandpa stared at her blankly. Maybe she'd spoken too fast. Or maybe it was as Dad said: Grandpa didn't remember Bel, she belonged to that lost time. Maybe Rachel did too. Bel knew more than anyone what that was like. Ain't memory a bitch, huh? Gone was gone, no matter how you asked. But Bel was going to ask anyway; she had to.

"Who are you?" Grandpa asked her, right on cue.

"It's Bel. Annabel. Charlie's daughter."

"Rachel?" Grandpa said, and the hairs picked up on the back of Bel's neck.

"No. I'm Rachel's daughter." Strange to state it as simple as that when it was anything but.

Grandpa's eyes sank down her face. "Rachel?"

"Rachel's my mom." Bel tried another way, and it felt just as wrong, that forbidden word. "Do you remember Rachel?"

His head moved; not quite a nod, but maybe on the way. Bel would take any sign she could get. It was stupid to pin your hopes on an old man who couldn't remember, but here we were. The same hopes had been pinned on Bel once, as a baby who could hardly speak.

"Rachel disappeared, do you know that?" Bel asked, slowing down, trapping her hands between her knees.

A flicker in Grandpa's eyes. One hand dropped to his lap.

"Charlie?"

"Yes, Charlie's wife, Rachel."

Grandpa looked over his shoulder, into the hallway. Was he looking for Yordan?

"Paw-Paw?"

". . . it was an accident?" he muttered. "No one meant to kill her."

"No one did kill her, Grandpa," Bel said, feeling the heat of frustration and knowing it wasn't fair. "Rachel's back, remember? You've seen her."

Grandpa's mouth twitched.

"Do you know where she was before she came back, Grandpa? Did someone find her? Do you remember?"

Bel needed him to remember.

Grandpa pressed his eyelids together. "I'm hungry."

"Grandpa, please." Bel shifted to the edge of the sofa. "Tell me what you know about Rachel. I can't help Dad if you don't help me."

Grandpa stared at her, unfocused, unseeing, mouth moving but no sound.

"Rachel?" she tried one more time.

No reaction.

This was pointless and she knew it, so did the knot in her gut, twitching on its strings. Grandpa didn't know anything, and even if he ever did, it was lost now, along with the rest of his broken memory, along with his two forgotten granddaughters. Jeff must have read too much into Grandpa's confused mutterings. Fucking Jeff, sending her down the wrong way.

"Never mind, Grandpa." Bel gave up, wiping the frown off on the back of her hand. "I'm sorry."

Yordan's head appeared in the doorway.

"It'll be a few minutes until lunch, Pat," he called, glancing over at Bel, a wary look in his dark eyes, a reluctant twist to his pursed lips.

"What?" Bel snapped, scaring it out of him.

"S-sorry." He tripped back, stumbled forward. "I couldn't help overhearing."

"Couldn't you?" she said, disappointment turning stale and angry.

Yordan raised his hands in surrender. "Small house, you were talking loud, wasn't trying to." He moved farther into the room. "I'm sorry your grandpa isn't able to answer your questions, I'm sure you were trying, weren't you, Pat?"

Grandpa grunted.

"Can we talk out here?" Yordan asked her, thumb over his shoulder.

Bel stood up, followed him into the small kitchen where the microwave burred, Grandpa's lunch parading under the yellow light.

"Sorry." He raised his thick eyebrows, making ripples up his forehead. "I don't like talking in front of him like he's not there. I would say don't take it to heart, he doesn't remember me most days either, but he's not my family. It must be hard."

"It's fine." Bel sniffed. It wasn't like Grandpa had chosen to forget her. Choosing to go was much worse: ask Rachel.

"He gets confused, struggles most with the long-term stuff. But you wanted to ask him about Rachel, didn't you? I thought maybe I could help instead."

Bel tilted her head, wordlessly asking him to go on.

"He does remember Rachel," Yordan said, checking the timer on the microwave. "Maybe a younger version of her, before she disappeared. He brings her up sometimes. Mostly it's 'Charlie's girlfriend, Rachel,' and that she likes books, that she's an English teacher. She actually came around yesterday, for coffee. Also unannounced." Yordan pressed his lips into a toothless smile. Bel wished he wouldn't;

group her and Rachel together like that. "Pat did seem familiar with her, like he knew who she was. So that answers one of your questions."

The knot stirred in Bel's stomach. "Rachel was here?"

Yordan nodded. "She wanted to visit Pat to see how he was getting on without Charlie. Asked to come in for coffee."

"What did they talk about?"

"Just small talk. How the house looked exactly the same the last time Rachel saw it. I made them coffee, then went to fold laundry, to give them some time alone."

"And you didn't hear what they talked about?" Bel asked. "Thought it was a small house."

"I was upstairs," Yordan countered. "I only left them for five minutes. But . . ." He paused, screwing his lips again, like he was trying to stop himself.

"Yordan?"

His mouth untwisted. "Not saying anything bad, it was just a little strange. I came downstairs and Rachel wasn't here, where I left her." He gestured at the small dining table. "Your grandpa was in here with the two coffees but Rachel wasn't. I called her name and she didn't respond."

"Where did she go?"

An insistent beep filled the room, blaring three times. Yordan's attention snapped to the microwave. Bel cleared her throat to bring it back.

"I found her in the living room," he said. "I asked what she was doing, if she was looking for something, and she said she was just looking to see if anything had changed. Then she thanked me for the coffee—which she hadn't finished—and she left."

A clicking sound in Bel's ear as her jaw locked, back teeth pushing against each other, biting on nothing, biting on something.

"Where in the living room was she?"

Yordan turned to the microwave. "Near the fireplace, but she left as soon as I entered."

"Did she take something?"

"No, of course not," Yordan hissed, pulling the hot plate of food out of the microwave. Carrots and a slice of chicken potpie.

Bel tried to re-create the scene: the fireplace at the back of the room, beyond the sofa and the bookshelves. She couldn't think of anything around the fireplace that Rachel would be interested in. It was just a normal living room where a family once lived, now an old man who only remembered half of them.

What had Rachel been trying to do? Because it wasn't just the sneaking off during the unannounced visit yesterday, was it? No, it was the number of times she'd asked Bel and Carter about Grandpa's routine, whether Yordan ever took him out of the house. Both led to the same inevitable conclusion: there was something in this house Rachel wanted, or needed, something she wanted to keep secret. And if it was important to Rachel, then it was important to Bel.

"Yordan," Bel said, trying to sound sweet, failing immediately.

"Yes?" Yordan replied, because he didn't know her well enough.

"I guess my dad didn't have a chance to tell you this, with everything going on," she said, thinking on her feet. "But for Grandpa's birthday, he'd always take him to Moose Brook State Park. Hiking, fishing." It was a lie; they'd only done that once their whole life. "Dad was planning to take him again this year. I know it's different, since his stroke, and you couldn't do the trails, but there's the roads around the campground his chair could go on. It's supposed to be a nice day tomorrow. I was thinking you could still take him, for an hour or two. A walk, grab some lunch. Grandpa would really like that, I think. Hopefully it'll distract him, from Dad being gone." That was the only part Bel didn't have to fake, the way her eyes overstretched, overfilled, at the thought of Dad being gone.

Yordan pressed his lips together in a way Bel couldn't read: she didn't know him well enough either. "If that's what your dad would want," he said, or he asked, teetering between the two.

"Yes." Bel jumped on it. "It is." Dad holding everything together, even when he wasn't here. "Jeff could come too. Grandpa should have one of his boys with him."

"OK," Yordan said, reluctantly, splitting the word in two, like maybe he knew he was being lied to, but was happy to go along with it because saying no was harder. And Bel would have made saying no very hard indeed. "What time?"

"Maybe if you leave at eleven?" Bel suggested, counting it through, working out the timings. "Yeah, eleven tomorrow. I'll tell Jeff to meet you there."

Fuck Uncle Jeff: he'd been wrong, so now he had plans tomorrow. So did she and Ash.

And Rachel.

Busy, busy day, tomorrow, for all of them.

"OK, sounds good."

"Good," Bel said too. Better than good.

"Rachel!" Bel shut the front door behind her, the double click of the catch, like it was ticking down to something. "I'm home!"

Bel waited, listening throughout the house, for the creaks and sighs of a living person. Rachel moved quietly, steps delicate and deadly. Bel was learning more about her every day. The way she walked, the way she blinked when she was tired, the way she fiddled, pressing her fingers against her thumbs when she wasn't thinking.

Rachel appeared around the corner, soundless, face split with a smile.

"Having a good day?" she asked, stepping back to let Bel into the living room.

Bel dropped her jacket on the sofa. She was having a great day.

"It's OK," she said.

Rachel nodded. "Hey, was Carter OK this morning? Seemed a bit quiet at breakfast."

"She's fine." Bel knew what Rachel was trying to do, trying to use Carter against her, but Bel refused to play her game. "Think everyone is just worried about Dad. I miss him," she added, playing her own game.

Rachel dropped her eyes, fiddling with the fabric lines in her jeans, pushing denim mountains into valleys, popping down and up. "I know, sweetie," she said. "I'm sorry."

Sorry for what, Bel wanted to say, but she knew it would be a mistake. Rachel couldn't know that Bel doubted her, not until it was far too late.

"Grandpa misses him too," Bel said, watching her closely. "I went to visit him today and he just keeps saying Charlie, doesn't understand."

Rachel swallowed. "Must be hard," which might as well have been nothing.

Bel cleared her throat. "Especially with his birthday coming up. Dad normally takes him to Moose Brook for a hike every year. Yordan says he's going to take Grandpa anyway, as a birthday treat." There was a twitch behind Rachel's eyes, balls rolling under the thin skin of her lids. "Supposed to be a nice day tomorrow and there's roads his wheelchair can go on. I'm not going, Grandpa doesn't remember me, it confuses him, but Jeff's going. Obviously, it doesn't replace Dad, but . . . it's something."

Now was Bel's turn to drop her eyes; she didn't want Rachel to feel watched.

Come on, take the bait, fall into her trap.

This was exactly what Rachel wanted: Grandpa and Yordan out of that house for a couple hours, so she could get inside and do whatever it was she needed to do. Bel would know she'd fallen for it if she asked what time they were going. Come on, Rachel.

"That's a nice idea," she said, pressing her thumb to her bottom lip, creating a valley there too. "Maybe I should go too. What time are they going?"

Got her.

Bel tried not to smile. "Yordan said they were leaving at eleven-thirty."

Rachel nodded again, small movements like it was absent-minded, but Bel knew better.

"I might have a doctor's appointment at twelve," she said, making her excuses already. "I'll check my calendar."

Rachel walked silently out into the hallway, toward the stairs.

Bel waited a few seconds, then pulled out her phone. Typed a message to Ash:

Do you have an even smaller camera? One someone wouldn't notice?

It was delivered and read within seconds, Bel's gut tightening as three dots appeared on-screen.

His reply came through.

Fuck's sake, what are we doing now?

"Who are you smirking at?" Rachel asked, in the room again, a smirk of her own. Bel hadn't heard her coming.

"Nothing." Bel put her phone away. "It's just Ash," because she couldn't think of a better lie.

"From the film crew?" Rachel asked, the smirk becoming a grin. "Oh, he's handsome." She winked.

Heat rose in Bel's cheeks, staining them pink. "No, he's not."

Rachel laughed.

"Shut up, Rachel," Bel said, laughing too, only because Rachel was.

Rachel stopped, ending in a sigh, the laugh still there in the lines around her eyes. "You know, B-Bel," she said, hesitating. "I know I've only been back two weeks, and everything must still be very strange for you. But you know, you don't have to call me Rachel. You can call me Mom." She fiddled, pressing her fingers to her thumbs. "Only if you felt comfortable doing that."

An awkward silence in the no-man's-land between them. A line had been crossed, and Bel wasn't sure what to do now. She fiddled too, with the ends of her hair. It wasn't the worst idea: Bel wanted Rachel to trust her, needed her to, so she wouldn't see the end coming. And it was coming. Tomorrow, Bel would catch her.

Bel cleared her throat, took one step toward Rachel, crossing the border. "Shall we make dinner together tonight, Ra-M-Mom?"

Rachel beamed.

THIRTY-FOUR

A leaf trailed into Bel's eye. She rubbed it away, knocking elbows with Ash.

"Watch the camera," he hissed, dodging a branch. They were hidden in the trees that lined Madison Avenue, opposite Grandpa's squat white house. "What time is it?"

Bel checked her phone. "Eleven-oh-one. I told Rachel eleven-thirty. We won't have long to set up."

"We won't need it." Ash turned the camera, catching the nervous look on her face.

"Hurry up, Yordan," she whispered, watching as Yordan finally got Grandpa into the passenger seat of the yellow car. He folded up the wheelchair and put it in the trunk, before climbing in himself. The engine started.

"Enjoy your walk, Grandpa," Bel said as the car backed out, drove past them. "Let's go."

They crossed the empty street, Bel, camera, Ash. A darkened line before the front yard; a shadow from the telephone line overhead. They crossed that too, no going back.

Beside the steps to the front door was a wooden barrel of plastic flowers, and an ugly ceramic toad, holding a fishing rod.

Bel picked the toad up by his head; a small silver key waited there, in its dirty outline. She scooped it up. "Everyone knows Grandpa keeps the spare key under the toad, always has."

She was counting on Rachel knowing that too.

"Budge," she said, knocking Ash out of her way on the steps. She slotted the key into the front door and pushed it open. "Need to re-member to put the key back before we leave."

"Roger."

"The toad's called Barry, actually." She walked ahead into the sti-fling, airless heat of Grandpa's house. "Carter named him."

"No, I meant . . . ," Ash began, falling for it. "You know what I meant." Un-falling. "Fuck, it's hot in here."

He closed the door behind him, fumbling with the camera.

"This way." Bel beckoned him down the hall and into the liv-ing room, even warmer somehow. "Yordan caught Rachel sneaking around in here, the living room," she said for the camera's sake. "Over by the fireplace." Bel traced her steps that way, looking around, from the basket of logs beside it, to the TV stand, to the sideboard beneath the window on the far wall. "We need to know what she's looking for. It's important, I know it."

She waited for Ash to join her across the room. She'd told him to dress incognito, which, for Ash, meant a thin yellow turtleneck and denim overalls. Like a Minion.

"Best place to put the camera is on the bookshelves." Bel pointed to the double-framed bookshelf, hundreds of books piled sideways and up, in an order only Grandpa understood. Lots she recognized, from when he used to read to her. "She's less likely to spot it there, right? Do you have the small camera?"

"Of course." Ash dropped his backpack, unzipped it one-handed. "But has no one ever told you it's rude to ask a guy about the size of his camera?"

Bel snorted, then regretted it, because Ash was smirking, too pleased with himself. "Hurry up," she snapped instead. "Rachel was still at home when I left, but we have no idea when she'll turn up."

"Hurrying." He pulled out a small black square with a tiny lens eye, trailing a black cable. All of it no bigger than his hand. "Small enough for you?"

"It'll do." She ironed out her face, taking it from him.

"For *discreet* filming, Ramsey said. Let's set it up," Ash said, placing the handheld camera on the coffee table to free his hands, still recording, pointed at them. "We need a plug."

"There's one behind the bookshelf, I think."

Ash knelt down, pulled out a few hardbacks on the lowest shelf. "Here it is. Perfect, we can chase the cable behind all the books. Where shall we put the camera?"

He took it back from her without asking, fingers brushing hers.

"I am the camera assistant," he explained, at the sour look on her face.

"And I am the brains."

"We'll see about that."

Ash placed the camera on the second-highest shelf, about head height, tucked between two horizontal piles of books. The spines were dark, mostly black, and the camera blended right in, lost in their clutter. You'd only see it if you were looking for it. And Rachel wouldn't be looking for it, she'd be looking for something else.

"Good?" Ash said, checking.

Bel nodded.

"I'll just chase this wire down the back here." His tongue between his teeth, concentrating.

"Like when you felt up my top the second time we met," Bel said, trying to make him uncomfortable, because it was fun, and she needed a distraction from the knot in her gut.

"That's not what happened," he said coolly. "I'm far too awkward for that."

"Played with my ass too."

"Bel, I'm trying to concentrate," he said, feeding the plug head down. "I'll need the Wi-Fi password to set it up. You go find that."

Sending her away, because he couldn't send himself.

"Found it," she said, because she already knew where to look. On

272

the TV stand was a piece of paper with Dad's handwriting, double its usual size:

Wi-Fi Password: PatPrice123

Bel stroked her finger across his words, something he had touched.

Ash replaced the books in front of the socket, standing back to admire the setup. "Pretty good spies, we are. The name's Maddox, Ash Maddox."

"The name's *Hurry the fuck up and turn it on.*"

"All right, grumpy," he said, voice pitching higher. "Shouldn't speak to your spy-husband like that."

"You bring it out in me, darling." She gave him a sickly grin, still trying to push him away, even though there was a tiny part of her that no longer wanted to.

"Ah, because you're so *tough*," Ash said with a knowing look, pulling out an iPad. "Tough girl that eats feelings for breakfast."

"And lunch," she added.

"Children for dinner," he said, voice deep and rolling.

Bel smirked but she didn't like that; that Ash thought he knew her. Knew her well enough to know the thing that she did.

"Password?" He opened the settings on-screen.

"PatPrice123."

He typed it in. "Hold on."

He pressed a button on the small camera. It beeped, just once, no LED light to give it away.

"We're connected," he said, eyes down on the iPad screen, bringing it over so Bel could see.

They stood shoulder to shoulder, looking down at two people standing shoulder to shoulder, looking down at an iPad. One dressed like a Minion. The other with a secret smile.

Bel waved, the miniature version of her copying after a one-second delay.

"That's us," she said. You could see most of the living room, from the fireplace at the far end over to Grandpa's armchair and the TV, the picture quality better than she'd hoped.

She glanced up from Ash on the screen to Ash just inches away, eyes circling his. "We're going to catch her, aren't we? Proof, on video. Ruin her documentary too."

"Well." Ash scratched his nose. "It's not *her* documentary."

"*The Reappearance of Rachel Price*?" she said, voice hardening, because Bel didn't suffer fools, and Ash was definitely a fool.

"Oh thanks, I know what it's called." He smiled. "The documentary isn't about Rachel. It's about you."

Bel blinked at him.

"Ramsey said he realized after your first interview that there was something about you. That actually, even after Rachel came back and everything changed, you were still the subject."

"What do you mean?" Her gut tightened, forgetting about the knot.

"You're the heart of it, Ramsey says, and he's the expert." Ash paused, biting his lip, looking at hers. "Your name might not be in the title, but the subject is the person who will be most changed by the story. Ramsey says that's you."

Bel's heart thudded in the base of her throat, skin alive and electric with it, sparking where Ash's arm brushed hers.

"Ew," she said, trying to ruin it. She failed.

Bel's eyes fell to the iPad, and she saw the way Ash looked at her, the soft curve of his open mouth, the slow burn in his eyes. Ridiculous, wasn't he? On-screen, one of Ash's hands floated toward her. Bel watched herself reach for the front of his overalls, pulling him in.

She looked up.

Their eyes met.

Then their lips.

Ash's warm hand cupped the back of her neck, a different kind of shiver, one that moved down instead. Bel's bottom lip slid between his, parting, like this was the easiest thing in the world. It didn't feel pointless, it felt like everything had always been building to this, a glow that made her forget the knot ever existed. Ash's nose bumped against hers, the hard corners of the iPad pushing against their bellies.

Bel pulled away first, eyes heavy, lips stung.

"Uh-oh," Ash whispered, breath brushing against her cheek.

His voice brought her back into her skin, into this too-hot room, and Bel remembered how unguarded she was, how defenseless, how stupid. She wished for the knot to return and it did, hollowed her out.

"You're right." She stepped back, not looking at him. Why should she look at him? He would be leaving soon, leaving her behind. Caring was the stupidest thing she could do. And she didn't care, trust her. "We shouldn't have done that."

Ash's eyes clouded. "That's not what I meant."

Bel wiped her mouth on her sleeve. "I was just messing with you," she said. "You know how we do. Mutual unpleasantness."

"That wasn't unpleasant for me."

She stared him down.

"OK, Bel." A weak, one-sided smile, eyes drawn. "You're right. I find you thoroughly unpleasant, but I have to put up with you because it's a job and I'm helping my brother-in-law."

"Good." That was better, much better. "We should go outside; Rachel could be here any minute."

Ash tucked the iPad under one arm, shouldered his backpack and picked up the camera. Bel could offer to carry something, but she was trying to be unpleasant, to undo what they'd just done. Besides, he *was* the camera assistant. And Bel was the heart, which was stupid now she was thinking with a clear head. Ramsey was wrong; she wasn't going to be the one to change. In fact, if Bel had her way, everything would go back to the way it was before these cameras showed up. Rachel gone, just Bel and Dad, the way it was supposed to be. He'll see.

Bel closed the front door and followed Ash down the steps, circling around to replace the key under the ceramic toad. Ready for Rachel.

They crossed the road again, scrambling through the bushes and trees that lined the other side, under the constant hiss of cars from Main Street.

Ash dropped his backpack when they'd clambered in far enough.

"Can you hold the iPad?" he said, not making eye contact, passing it over. "So I can record you watching it?"

"Sure, I'm the *heart*," she said, no eye contact either.

The screen showed the empty living room, waiting. Bel and Ash must be there somewhere, tiny and hidden, through the pixelated wall of green out the front window.

"What's the time?" Ash asked.

Bel checked the top of the screen. "Twenty-nine past. Lucky we didn't waste any more time," she said, another stab, and Ash staggered back.

Her eyes flicked from the image of the living room to the time in the upper corner, counting the minutes on.

"She's going to turn up, I know it."

Eleven-thirty.

The knot spiraled, eating away at her. Was she wrong? She couldn't be wrong, come on, Rachel.

Eleven-thirty-one, and a shushing sound of tires peeled toward them, breaking away from Main Street. Ash breathed in and Bel breathed out.

Please don't be Grandpa and Yordan, she thought, hoping she didn't see bright yellow through the leaves.

She didn't.

She saw silver. A silver Ford Escape, with mean eyes for headlights.

The fuzzy shape of Rachel behind the wheel.

Yes.

Bel and Ash exchanged a look, a wicked smile she didn't share with him.

"Guess you know her pretty well," Ash said, and Bel couldn't tell if he was trying to be unkind back.

Rachel parked, two wheels on the grass in front of Grandpa's house.

Ash turned the camera, zooming to capture Rachel as she stepped out of the car and closed the door.

Bel strained her eyes, heart pulsating behind them.

Rachel approached the house, not checking over her shoulder, acting like she belonged. She dipped around the handrail, toward the ceramic toad. She bent down, out of view, blocked by the silver car, but when she straightened up, her hand was curled around something small.

"She has the key," Ash whispered. "Well done, Barry."

Rachel took the steps up two at a time, slotting the key in and pushing the front door open. She snaked around and shut it behind her, the noise not reaching them across the street.

"She's in." Bel dropped her eyes to the iPad instead, tilting it so Ash and the handheld camera could see.

The empty living room.

Bel counted ten seconds until Rachel appeared in the frame, walking past Grandpa's leather armchair.

She paused there, reaching up to tie her hair into a ponytail, opening her collar.

She started moving again, beyond the sofa.

"What do you want in there, Rachel?" Bel asked her through the screen. A feeling deep down that whatever it was might be the beginning of the end for Rachel. For all of them.

Rachel grew larger on the screen as she walked toward the camera. Right toward the camera.

Her face and eyes turning, fixing that way.

"Fuck, she hasn't . . . ," Ash began.

Rachel paused, one hand in the air. She moved another step closer, head tilting as she stared right at them, through the hidden camera. Eyes locking on.

"Fuck, she has," Bel replied, a shiver as she and Rachel stared at each other through the screen. No, no, no. How could she have spotted it so soon? It was well hidden.

Rachel frowned, her face engulfed by her hand as it grew monstrously large, reaching out for the small camera. Covering the lens with the glowy pink of flesh, taking over the screen.

The view tipped up into blackness, the dark underside of the shelf above.

She'd found it. It was already over.

THIRTY-FIVE

"No, no, no." Bel looked down at the black, empty screen.

"Shh," Ash hissed. "She might hear you."

"This isn't fair, this was supposed to be it."

"I'm sorry," Ash offered, but it wasn't enough, not nearly enough.

"No." Bel handed him the iPad, useless to her now. "She's not winning."

"Where are you going?" Ash grabbed her hand.

"I have to know what she came here for."

"Bel," her name shaped by a gasp, but she was already running from him, across the road. Jumping over the line of shadow to the left side of the house, crouching below the front windows.

She curved around the corner, hand to the wooden slats to steady herself, heart trying to drag her back. She wouldn't listen, her head winning out, telling her this was her chance to take Rachel down.

Bel hurried three more steps, then dropped to her knees below the window, the one on the far wall of the living room, beside the fireplace, over the sideboard.

If Rachel was distracted, looking for whatever she was looking for, she wouldn't see Bel. She planted her feet and slowly, slowly, rose up, straightening her legs.

She stopped when her eyes broke above the ledge, looking through the very bottom corner of the glass.

Her own reflection got in the way, obscuring the room beyond.

Bel moved closer, pressed her nose against the window, cupping her hands around her eyes.

The room came into view.

And so did Rachel, dead still, staring right back at her.

Bel's heart told her so, escaping out her chest.

Rachel angled her head.

"Annabel?" she called, voice muffled by the glass.

Fuck.

Bel stood up the whole way, eyes still cupped against the window. "Hi!" she leveled her voice, smoothing the fear out of it. "I thought someone was inside."

Rachel smiled. It didn't reach her eyes.

"Come around." She gestured toward the hallway and the front door, her fingers walking through the air.

Double fuck.

"OK!" Bel smiled, backing up until she could only see herself again, and that smile didn't even convince her.

She walked around the corner, planning her excuses, discarding the ones that wouldn't do, the ones Rachel would see through.

Ash must have spotted her now. Bel waved her arm in his direction, telling him to get out of here. Swiping her hand across her neck twice to tell him it was over, she was dead, double dead. Rachel had taken the bait, but the plan had fallen apart.

She trudged up the steps and the front door opened, Rachel standing in the heat beyond, an unreadable look on her face.

"Hi." She moved back to allow Bel in.

"Hi," Bel said, brighter, to throw her off. "That's funny," she said, still not sure what she was going to say or how it was funny.

"What are you doing here?" Rachel asked.

Bel was backed into a corner, came back with a lie.

"I couldn't find my water bottle. I thought maybe I'd left it here yesterday. Did you see it inside?" Bel wandered through into the living room. "Wait." She narrowed her eyes on purpose. "What are you doing here? You had a doctor's appointment?"

Because Rachel might have caught Bel, but Bel had also caught Rachel here. A stalemate, a trial for both of them. Bel felt like she'd passed. Rachel's turn.

"Oh, I got the day wrong," Rachel said, leaning double-handed on the back of Grandpa's chair.

"Did you?"

"Yeah. So I came over for Grandpa's walk. Guess I just missed them."

Bel nodded, like that made sense. Then she stalled, chin pointed up, like a new thought held her there. "How come you were inside, then?"

Rachel shuffled, clammy hands against the leather. "When I realized they weren't here, I let myself in with the spare." She paused. "It's Pat's birthday next week and I wasn't sure what to get him. I thought I'd have a quick look around, see if I could figure out what he'd like."

Bel completed the nod. Not quite as good a lie as hers.

Rachel pointed toward the bookshelf. "Although I think I've been caught. I noticed there's a camera on the shelf."

Bel's eyes followed the line of Rachel's finger, spinning, searching, as though she didn't know exactly where it was. "Oh, that." A dismissive wave of her hand. "Dad put that in months ago, to check up on Grandpa during the day, before the second stroke. I think it's disconnected; hasn't been turned on since Yordan got here."

Rachel flexed her chin. "Makes sense."

Yes, it did. Bel was pleased with that.

"Why were you at the window?" Rachel said, throwing it back to her.

"I thought I heard someone inside," Bel countered. "And the spare key wasn't under the frog." Rachel wasn't going to trip her up.

"You didn't see my car parked out front?" Rachel narrowed her eyes.

"I saw a car, didn't realize it was yours, don't know the license plate yet. Lucky it was only you," she said, with a breathy laugh, as though Rachel was safe, as though Rachel wasn't the most dangerous person to her.

"Yeah, lucky." Rachel glanced behind her, through the open doorway into the hall. Her eyes fixed on the stairs, climbing them one by one, as the silence stretched between them, growing teeth.

Bel studied Rachel's face, looked for the signs she was learning, the twitches, the lines. Did Rachel know? Who had really caught who here?

"We should probably head home, hey?" Rachel said, breaking the deadlock, offering a way out. "Want a ride?"

Bel couldn't say no.

THIRTY-SIX

"Thanks for coming in, Annabel."

Dave Winter sat across from her, the garish light of the interview room reflecting off his badge.

"What's happened? Is it bad?"

It was bad, Bel knew it. Knot tumbling through the empty pit of her stomach, nothing to catch on.

Dad had been missing for ten days now. It was temporary, a test, a problem Bel knew how to fix. They couldn't take that away from her, Bel didn't know how to live without him.

"This is going to be pretty hard for you to hear, Annabel."

Harder if he didn't hurry the fuck up with it.

Bel locked her jaw, readying herself.

If Dad was dead, then so was Rachel.

"We tracked down his credit card," Dave said, shoulders tensed by his ears. "We got a new hit at an ATM, and Vermont State Police were able to get to the scene. It wasn't your dad using the card. It was a college student, age twenty-two, called Matthew Abbey. Police questioned him about his connection to Charlie Price. There isn't any." He sniffed. "He says he found the credit card under a table in a diner he went to last Monday."

"What diner?" Bel asked, hooking her hands together, holding on.

Dave glanced down at his notes, flicked a page. "In Vermont. The How Cow Café, near Barton."

Bel recognized the town. "That's where Robert Meyer lives."

Dave nodded. "He claims he didn't see your dad that night, and that nothing was said on that final phone call. But the credit card being found there does point to your dad being in the area."

Which still left it up in the air: whether Bob from Vermont had lied to Bel or not.

"Matthew Abbey is being charged with credit card fraud, but it didn't give us any other leads on Charlie's whereabouts, other than he'd been to that diner last Monday. No cameras, before you ask."

"OK," Bel said. That was one update, and it wasn't so bad. Good, even; it showed that Dad wasn't traveling around Vermont, spending money on burgers and beer, like he'd chosen to be gone. "What else?"

Dave sighed, took a moment to run his fingers over his mouth. The worst was yet to come, clearly. The bad news and then the very bad news.

"What?" Bel broke, a tightening at the back of her throat, that tremor before you cried or before you threw up, somewhere between the two.

"We didn't just find the credit card," Dave said carefully.

Bel's mind skipped ahead of him, got lost there. Fuck. No, what else did they find? Not his body. No, no, no.

"We found his phone and his passport. The phone was switched off, as we knew. They were found together, by a janitor, in a trash can at a private airfield in Vermont." Dave paused. "Right up by the Canadian border."

He left it there, as though that were enough, the full story: beginning, middle, end.

"What are you trying to tell me?" Bel angled forward, trailing shadows on the table from her hair, her stomach an endless cliff drop to the end of the world.

"Annabel," he said, even softer. "I don't think your dad's in the country anymore. Looks like he wanted to go, left voluntarily. The credit card hits threw us off for a while, but he probably crossed the border last week." Dave cleared his throat. "Got on a small, private aircraft and we didn't know about it, because, well, our running theory is he ditched his old passport because he'd acquired another one, under a new identity."

Bel shook her head.

Dave continued. "We believe that's why he might have gone to see Robert Meyer. An individual who has ties to online criminal activity, who may be involved in that kind of thing."

"No."

"I'm sorry, Annabel," Dave said, and he did look it, eyes slumped and heavy, a troubled fold in his chin. "I really wanted to help you find him, after . . . everything. But all the signs point to the fact that Charlie left voluntarily, that he's left the country, potentially using a different name. It's not a crime to leave your old life behind, as much as it hurts."

"No," Bel said, voice finally catching, shedding its skin, coming out as a whisper.

"He's outside of our jurisdiction now. Way outside. I'm sorry, but we can't look for him anymore." Dave's eyes darkened farther. "I want to be honest with you, Annabel, because we've been through it all, you and me. Your mom's disappearance, and you were a big part of the reason it stuck with me so long, that tiny little girl left alone in the backseat. Then what happened with Phillip Alves, and everything since Rachel came back. I want you to be able to trust me when I tell you. We can't look for Charlie anymore and, if I'm being honest, it seems like he doesn't want to be found."

Bel slammed the front door, an explosion of sound, echoing down the hallways and trenches of number 33. Slammed her bedroom door too, falling face-first on her bed, burying her head between the pillows.

There was no reaction to the double explosion, no creeping feet, no quiet knocks on her door. Rachel must not be in. Good, because

Bel couldn't see her right now. If she did, she knew their cold war would catch fire, started by her.

Dad did not choose to disappear to Canada, to leave his old life behind with Bel in it. Dave Winter was wrong. Unbelievable, asking him to trust her. Bel didn't trust him; she didn't trust anyone.

Bel punched the pillow with a closed fist, then the other. It was Rachel, it was Rachel, it was all Rachel, and she was the only one who could see it. The alternative was to side with Dave Winter, to believe Dad chose to go, to leave her, and Bel would never go that way. That way hurt much, much more.

Bel rolled over, stared at the ceiling.

The credit card left in a diner, for someone to find, to distract the police: That must have been Rachel, right? She must have staged the phone call to Bob from Vermont too. She must have planted the phone and the passport to make it look like Dad had crossed the border. Rachel was the expert in disappearing, after all; maybe she'd simply had to re-create her own. But how could Bel prove it, now the police had given up on him, now she was all on her own?

They didn't know when the phone and passport were dumped, but the credit card had to have been left last Monday, or the Sunday before, for the student to have found it Monday afternoon.

So where was Rachel in those first two days after Dad disappeared? On the Sunday she was here, at home. But Monday . . .

A memory stirred. In the kitchen that evening. Bel throwing away a carton of apple juice; she'd only drunk it to piss Rachel off. There had been a takeout coffee cup in the trash, hadn't there? That was what she was catching on, her mind trying to pull back, to remember the logo. Wait, what was the name of the diner again, where Dad's credit card was found?

The How Cow Café; she heard it back in Dave Winter's voice, snapping to attention.

Bel scrambled for her laptop at the end of the bed. Pressed the button, willing it to wake up faster.

She typed *How Cow Café Vermont* into Google and clicked enter, the laptop dipping up and down with her touch.

A page of results.

The diner's website, and an image of their logo.

A red background. A white cartoon cow against it, pursed lips to blow a steaming mug of coffee. This was it, wasn't it? The same thing she saw in the trash downstairs last week. Her memory wasn't that clear, hadn't held on to it because she hadn't realized it would ever be important. But she remembered enough, and this couldn't be a coincidence.

Last Monday, Rachel planted the credit card in that diner in Barton, Vermont, on her way to dump the phone and passport farther north at the airfield. Thought she'd grab a cup of coffee to keep her going. Had it in the car on the drive back to Gorham. Took it inside the house to throw it away. She'd planned everything, but she hadn't planned on Bel seeing it.

That was evidence. Real evidence that Rachel was the one making it look like Dad disappeared. If Bel found it, then Dave Winter would have to trust her right back, wouldn't he?

Bel didn't waste another second.

She darted out of her room, heavy down the steps like rolling thunder.

Into the kitchen, she pulled the cupboard handle, the double trash cans rolling out, crashing at the end of the hinge.

Both were almost empty. Their contents buried at the bottom, hidden by the waves and surges of the trash bag.

Bel pushed her hand inside. Grabbing handfuls and bringing them to the light so she could see.

Eggshells and banana skins.

Plastic food wrappers.

Used coffee grounds, bleeding brown all over her fingers. The cup wasn't in this one.

The other side held more promise; cardboard toilet rolls and bits of paper. But Bel dug both hands through and couldn't find the cup.

Rachel must have taken out the trash. It would be in the garbage cans outside.

Bel was on her feet again, flying through the house.

She collided with the front door, leaving it open as she sprinted down the steps to the garbage cans. They were both left out, by the sidewalk, because it was always Dad's job to bring them in.

Bel skidded to a stop in front of them.

The metal can first. Bel unhooked the elasticated cord from the lid. It was black bear season, didn't you know?

She pushed the lid off and it fell on the path, clattering, spinning on its rim like this was just a game, a building sound of drums.

Bel looked; there was only one black trash bag here, crumpled at the bottom. She lowered her arm inside. Cold metal pressed into her armpit as she reached. She grabbed the top of the bag and pulled it out.

Fingers clumsy as she undid the knot.

It released and so did the smell, a sour undertone to the spring air.

Bel pulled the opening wide, sorting through with her hand, flinching every time it touched something wet.

It was too dark inside the bag to see anything, and she trusted her eyes more than her fingers, who lied to her, turning everything into spiders and slugs.

Bel stood up and upturned the bag, trash falling all around, a wrapper clinging to her boots.

She bent down in the middle of it all, sweeping her hand through the mess. Apple cores and broccoli stumps—dinner last night—slimy bits of plastic, crumpled paper towels with orange greasy stains, the hard outer skins of an onion, a lump of cheese fuzzy with mold. Bel checked everything; the cup wasn't here.

But she wasn't giving up. Rachel could have put it in the recycling instead. She must have.

Bel flipped the lid off the recycling bin, folded bits of cardboard and paper and cartons shifting in front of her eyes.

Her heart double time, a pressure building behind her face, reaching for her eyes. Bel gripped the bin and turned it over, spilling everything to the grass. Shaking it for the shy bits stuck at the bottom.

She dropped to her knees, checking under and inside folded boxes. Flipping through cartons and packaging, eyes moving faster than her hands. They knew before her. The cup wasn't here either.

Bel went through it all again, trash and recycling, filth soaking into the knees of her jeans, grime embedding under her fingernails, hoping she could change the answer if she hoped hard enough. It had to be here. Please, please.

She dropped to the ground, sitting in the middle of the desperate swirl of trash, cascading and shifting around her, hands dirty and stained and empty.

It wasn't here. It wasn't here and Rachel had won again.

Bel kicked out at the trash, a growl breaking free from her throat, sparking the red hot inside her again.

"What are you doing there?" asked a small voice behind her. Frail and familiar.

Bel's head whipped around.

Ms. Nosy from number 32, being nosy, living up to her name. Standing on the sidewalk with her arms tucked behind her, watching Bel in her pile of trash, a scowl on her face.

"I'm taking the trash out," Bel said, near hysterical, her arms wide, encircling her throne of garbage.

"You shouldn't have them out." Ms. Nelson tutted the final word. "It's Tuesday today. Trash gets collected on a Monday morning."

A sinking feeling in Bel's gut, beside the well of red hot. And there it was. The cup would have been right here. But Bel was too late. A day and a half too late, and her evidence was gone, lost forever.

"Fuck," she erupted, kicking out again.

Ms. Nelson bristled. "It's all right, dear. They come again next week."

Bel couldn't cry so she laughed instead, staring down at her filthy hands.

Ms. Nelson laughed nervously too, rocking on her heels.

"You should clean that up, seal the trash cans. Don't want to attract bears. It's black bear seas—"

"I know it's black bear season," Bel snapped, wiping her hands on her jeans.

"Yes, well." Ms. Nelson inspected her own clean hands. "I wanted to ask: It's your grandfather's birthday this week, isn't it?"

"Friday," Bel mumbled, not looking up. Because it was some kind of deadline in her mind. A small voice in her head that said if Dad wasn't home by then, he never would be.

"You know, he used to be one of my best customers," she said, like it was Bel's fault somehow. "Pat would be in the bookstore every other week. Don't see him around anymore."

"No," Bel said, because she didn't want to be having this conversation, any conversation, while she sat here in this stinking pile of trash with no way to bring Dad home.

"I wondered whether I should drop a few new books around, for his birthday. Is that a nice idea?" Ms. Nelson said, looking down at her.

"Really nice idea, Ms. Nelson, except you know he can't read anymore. Can't even remember who I am."

Forgetting was just another way of leaving, and everybody left eventually. Hopefully Ms. Nelson would too, because it was hard to fall apart with her standing over you.

"Oh." She drew a sharp breath, whistling between her teeth.

Still, she didn't go. Stepped even closer.

"I tried to call Chief Winter today," she said. "Have the police done anything more about that man?"

"What man?" Bel asked, pressing her teeth together until they hurt.

"The man who's been watching your house."

"There is no man!" Bel exploded, the red hot behind her eyes now. "There is no fucking man! Rachel made him up, OK? She made my dad disappear, and it's my fault, I shouldn't have let her out of my sight!"

Ms. Nelson took a step back, blinking slowly at her.

Bel let out a long breath, trying to bring herself back from the edge.

"It was just someone from the press, Ms. Nelson. You know those news vans? There were lots of men watching the house. They've all gone now."

Bel pushed up to her knees, reaching for the discarded trash bag, filling with the empty breeze as she held it out. "Nice seeing you, Ms. Nelson," Bel said, hoping she'd finally take the hint and leave her alone. But Bel couldn't let her go without one last swipe, without sharing some of that rage simmering so close to the surface. "And maybe you should stop watching our house too. Everyone knows you do. I've actually heard some of the neighbors refer to you as Ms. Nosy."

Ms. Nelson's face fell, mouth pulled into a thin line, and it didn't make Bel feel any better.

She did leave then, turning on her heels without a goodbye as Bel started picking up handfuls of trash, dropping them inside.

She had to clear this all up, before Rachel got home. Because if Rachel didn't know anything was wrong, then there was still a chance. Dad wasn't in Canada, Bel and her gut knew that, but he must be somewhere, just like Rachel was somewhere for those sixteen years.

What she'd said to Ms. Nelson was true: she shouldn't have let Rachel out of her sight. Bel had made a mistake, avoiding Rachel so much at the start, keeping out of the house and out of her way. All she'd done was give Rachel time alone to plan, to carry it out, and now Dad was gone.

Not anymore.

Bel had already let Rachel in, spending time together, pretending to bond, mother and daughter. It had gotten her closer to the truth, but she had to take it one step farther.

Watch her every second of the day, stick to her side, become her shadow.

Because Rachel would lead her right to Dad.

"Won't let you out of my sight."

THIRTY-SEVEN

Bel was awake before her eyes opened, forced out of sleep with a gasp in her throat.

She sat up in bed. Checked the phone on the nightstand: 2:04 a.m. Something must have woken her, but was she pushed out or was she pulled? A bad dream or—

There was a noise downstairs.

A rustle, a quiet press of steps.

Rachel was awake, moving around.

She must be trying to go somewhere, thinking Bel would sleep through.

Well, Bel hadn't, drinking too much coffee today, and the last two nights, to make sure she slept shallowly, dipping in and out. To make sure Rachel wasn't going anywhere in the middle of the night. But now she was.

Bel swung her legs out of bed, moving as quietly as she could.

She thought Rachel might try something like this. Bel hadn't given her another choice; she'd been her constant companion the last two days. Faked a cough to stay home sick from school, wouldn't let Rachel leave the house on her own.

"I have to go to the bank."

"I'll come too."

If Rachel caught on, she never showed it, never hesitated.

"That's OK, B-Bel. I don't like being on my own either."

Bel heard another hushed swipe of shoes downstairs. A muted thud; something picked up and put down.

She threw on a hoodie and grabbed her phone, navigated to her message thread with Ash; they hadn't texted since Tuesday. She typed:

Hope this wakes you. Rachel is sneaking off somewhere, I'm going to follow her. Meet me with the camera. I think this is it.

She slid the phone into the front pocket of her hoodie and tiptoed to the door, feet as light as Rachel's.

Though Rachel wasn't silent now; Bel could still hear her, shuffling around down there, skulking, shaping the darkness with the sound of her feet. She must have thought she didn't need to, with Bel being asleep and Dad being gone.

Bel opened her door slowly, cursing where the bottom edge scuffed against the carpet. She stepped out into the hallway. Rachel would be heading toward the front door soon, Bel was sure. Then probably her car, which was Bel's first problem. But she could follow on her old bike; it was in the garage and she could be fast, she had everything to lose if she wasn't. Or if Ash left right now, maybe he'd get here in time with a car, pick her up and follow Rachel's trail.

See, she could make plans too.

Bel was a shadow among shadows, a dark shape among dark shapes, standing at the top of the stairs. She walked down them, weight in her toes before lowering her heels, a quiet sound among quiet sounds.

She stepped over the one that creaked and stopped three from the end. Looked toward the living room.

Rachel was in there still, the scratch of shoes on the rug, the rustle of fabric, the beating of Bel's heart inside her own ears.

If Bel headed to the kitchen, she could circle around, try see what Rachel was up to, from the open doorway that adjoined the rooms. Get herself ready to follow as soon as Rachel left.

Bel crept down the final steps, across the hall and into the kitchen, the tiles cold through her socks. It was pitch-black in here too, no lights on downstairs, only the weak silver glow of the moon. If Rachel thought Bel was asleep, why hadn't she put on a light?

She slid along the counter, hidden from Rachel by the wall between them, past the dining table, stepping over chair legs. Bel pressed herself against the wall, wrapped three fingers around the edge of the open archway. Leaning into them, she pulled herself closer, silently, head floating just around the corner, eyes wide and searching.

Rachel was standing with her back turned, by the TV cabinet. She was holding something in both hands, looking down at it. Bel recognized the swirling gold photo frame. She knew exactly what picture that was: her and Dad, taken during a family meal out at Rosa's Pizza, his arm draped on her shoulder. Carter was a blur, walking through the background.

Why was Rachel so interested in this photo now? She'd had weeks to study it if she wanted.

Rachel bent to replace the photo, a gentle clunk as it touched down.

She straightened up in the darkness, standing tall, too tall, half a foot too tall, her shoulders shifting, growing wider than they should.

Bel's heart broke free, the flush of its fight-or-flight heat beneath her skin. She blinked to break apart the darkness, to see what she was scared she'd see. Moved out a little farther to be sure.

It wasn't Rachel, it was a man.

Bel couldn't help it, the noise in her throat, her sock slipping under her.

The man whipped around, head snapping her way. He looked just the same, darkness stealing all sense of direction. They stared at each other, these two dark shapes, her here, him there, frozen and unmoving.

Until Bel did move, instinct taking over. Eyes still on the figure, she snaked her hand along the wall, fingertips alighting on the cool plastic of the light switch.

A brief flash of hope before the flash of light, that the shadow standing in front of her would be Dad, finally home.

She flicked the switch, eyes watering in the sudden yellow glare. Bel blinked.

It wasn't Dad.

But it wasn't a stranger either; she knew that face, that look in his eyes.

A man in his fifties, ten years older than the last time she saw him. Dark close-shaved hair, graying in orbits around his long ears, covered with a baseball cap. The wide-set eyes with too much white that made him look forever shocked.

"You're not supposed to be here." Bel tried to keep the fear out of her voice. She failed. "We have a restraining order against you, Phillip."

Phillip Alves smiled, finally coming to life in the light, unlocking his arms, swinging them at his sides.

"Oops," he said, splitting into a laugh that sounded like a dog in pain, wheezy and unnerving. "In my defense, you weren't supposed to be here either. Thought the house was empty."

Empty? The word flipped over in Bel's head. The house wasn't empty, and Bel wasn't alone, because if Rachel wasn't the one sneaking around the living room, then she had to be upstairs, in bed.

"Rachel," Bel called, across the kitchen, toward the hall. "Rachel!" Louder now. "Mom?!"

"She's not here," Phillip said. He'd moved closer, while Bel's eyes weren't there to hold him in place.

"Mom?!"

"Rachel's not here, I said." Phillip raised his voice, over her shouting. "I wish you'd listen. I saw her drive away twenty minutes ago."

Bel stalled, lips half formed around the next *Mom,* swallowing it down, thick and gelatinous. Rachel wasn't here. Rachel had snuck out, and Bel had missed it, missed her chance. Rachel was gone and now Bel wished she wasn't for a different reason.

"You been watching the house again, Phillip?" Bel lowered her voice, softening the edges, almost friendly, trying to undo the damage her shouting had caused. The air pulsed with the presence of this man, pushing against her ears. Bel didn't know what he was capable of, and she didn't know if her sharp tongue would set him off.

He nodded. "Since Rachel returned."

Bel nodded too, cursing Ms. Nelson for being right, herself for not believing her.

"OK, well, as you said, Rachel's not here right now, so maybe you can come back another time."

That wheezing, hitching laugh again, eyes frozen nightmare-wide.

"How's she been, your ma?" he said, wiping his mouth on his sleeve. "Since she's been back?"

"Um . . ." Bel didn't know what to do, how to make him leave. Maybe she should keep him talking, keep it friendly. She'd texted Ash and he might be on his way here right now. Unless he was asleep, his phone on silent. Or maybe good old Ms. Nelson had seen Phillip breaking in and already called the cops. Fuck, no, Bel had just told her to stop watching their house, to stick her nose out. She hadn't realized she'd need it so soon, lashed out and only hurt herself.

"Hello?" Phillip waved at her.

"Sorry." Bel swallowed. She shouldn't keep him waiting. She could talk about Rachel while she figured out what to do, speak his language. An obsession sixteen years couldn't shake, because here he was again, right where they started.

"She's been fine," Bel said.

"Fine?" Phillip didn't like that answer.

"It's been an adjustment," Bel said, reusing everyone's word. "But she's OK."

"OK?" The word cracked open in Phillip's mouth. Didn't like that answer either.

"Well," she said, trying, "it hasn't all been good. It's strange, some-one coming back after all that time. There's been disagreements, old things coming back up, you know."

Phillip made a sound in the back of his throat. "She told you any-thing? About where she was?"

"She was kept in a basement." Bel swallowed. "She didn't know the man who took her."

Phillip laughed again. "OK, OK," he said, hands up, fingers twitching. "And what about where she *really* was?"

Bel scratched the back of her head, gave herself time to think. What did Phillip want to hear? What would make him go away?

"She was in a basement."

"OK," he said, cartoonish and mean, mocking her, head bouncing around on his neck. "So why'd your dad run away, then, huh?" He took a step toward her. "Rachel Price comes home and then a week later Charlie Price takes off. Seems suspicious, don't it? Don't tell me you think that's just a coincidence, thought you were a smart girl."

Bel felt the red-hot surge in her gut, told it that now wasn't the time. She had to keep a cool head.

"My dad didn't run away," she said, coolly.

"Yes-he-did," Phillip retorted, words in one quick slur, enjoying himself.

Bel took a breath to slow her heart. Come on, Ash, please be awake, please be close. "No he didn't. He wouldn't do that."

Phillip pressed his lips together, like he was trying not to laugh again. Thank God he didn't.

"Yes he did," he said. "I saw him."

Bel abandoned her next sentence.

"What did you say?" she asked.

He flashed those strange eyes. "Now you're listening."

"What do you mean you saw him?" Bel took a step forward now, regretted it.

"I was watching the house," he said, simply. "It was late, around two a.m., and I saw your dad, walking out the front door. He'd packed a bag. Closed the door real slow, like he didn't want to wake anyone."

Bel shook her head. "When was this?"

"You know when. The night your dad left, Saturday before last. He got into his truck and drove away. I was across the street. Thought he might have spotted me, thought he'd be coming back, so I left."

Bel was still shaking her head, hadn't stopped. "No, that's not right. His truck was still here in the morning, how could he have driven away in it?"

Phillip shrugged, hands hanging in the air by his ears.

"I don't believe you," she said.

"Just telling you what I saw."

"Was he on his own?"

"He was on his own." A swipe of his tongue, wetting his lips.

Bel still didn't believe him. Phillip was a liar. Of course he was a liar: he was a stalker, unhinged, lost everything because he couldn't let the mystery of Rachel Price go. Still couldn't. Still had more to lose.

"So tell me why you think your dad ran away?" Phillip perched on the lip of the sofa, settling in.

"He didn't."

"Rachel must have told you something."

Bel shifted her weight onto her other leg. "She told me a man took her and kept her in a basement for sixteen years, then he let her go."

"Bullshit," Phillip spat in that whisper-yell Bel remembered. "You must know something."

"I don't," Bel said. But she did, she knew a lot more than something. But why did Phillip Alves deserve those answers when no one had given them to her? Fuck him.

"Tell me." He jumped up again, scratching his neck, leaving a swipe of four angry red lines.

"I don't know anything!" She was that eight-year-old girl again, sitting in the backseat, a stranger dressed up as a police officer screaming in her face.

"Come on," Phillip said in that breathy shout of his, so much worse than if he just screamed. "You've been living in this house with both of them. You must know something. Seen something, heard something?"

"No." Bel watched the change in Phillip, the rage, red spreading from the scratches up his face.

Come on, Ash. Come on, Ms. Nelson. No one was coming, were they? Bel was on her own.

Not quite on her own: her phone was right here, in the front pocket of her hoodie. Could she call 911 without Phillip seeing? Not really, it was touchscreen, she couldn't try without seeing the screen. Still, she slid one hand into the pocket, touching the phone, to know it was there.

"You have to know something. I need to know what really happened. I've waited so long."

He hadn't waited as long as Bel, it wasn't his parents, it wasn't his life falling apart. A flash of anger, building in the knot in her gut, but she couldn't let it out, she listened to her fear instead.

"Why don't you believe what Rachel says happened to her?" Bel asked instead, trying to calm him down.

"I need a better answer. The truth. If her story was true, your dad wouldn't have taken off."

"Or maybe Rachel did something to him?" Bel said, the truth escaping anyway.

"Why would she do something to him, if he hadn't done something to her first?" Phillip grinned, thinking he'd trapped her with that one. "I saw him leave, remember. She wasn't with him."

Bel exhaled. "My dad didn't have anything to do with Rachel's disappearance, Rachel has said that herself. He had an alibi."

"Sure." Phillip mocked her again.

"He was found innocent," Bel said, holding it in when she wanted to explode at him, this man who'd made her story his own, who didn't deserve any part of it. "You didn't see his face when Rachel returned. He didn't know she was alive, I can promise you that. I know him better than anyone. He was at the hospital that day, then he drove home. He wasn't involved."

Phillip lurched forward, doubling over with that terrible, wheezing laugh, the sound creeping through her.

She gripped the phone harder.

"What are you laughing at?" she asked, not sure she wanted to know, scared that Phillip Alves was the end point of the way she'd chosen for herself. Did she sound like this when she talked about Rachel?

"You know," Phillip said, still laughing, "this isn't the first time I've been inside this house. Almost got caught then too."

"What are you talking about?" Bel shifted her weight again, legs fizzing.

"I was here sixteen years ago. Got in the same way. The catch on that window is broken, by the way." He pointed over his shoulder. "You should get that fixed. Anyway." His eyes stretched wider somehow, unblinking. "I thought I'd find some clues while nobody was in. The police were starting to look at your dad, April I think, before his arrest. I knew it was supposed to be me, to find out who killed Rachel. I was in the kitchen when I heard a car pull up. I didn't have time to make it outside, so I went upstairs. Into the first door I saw. Turned out to be your bedroom, a crib in the corner."

Bel's safe place. Maybe it had never really been all that safe.

"I hid in your room, listening. Charlie came in the front door. He was with someone, another man. I didn't recognize his voice. I couldn't hear everything but they were arguing about something. *Shh, don't wake Annabel,* your dad said, so you must have been there too."

Phillip wasn't looking at her, he was staring at a point just beyond her shoulder, lost in the memory. Maybe now was Bel's chance, while he was distracted. She shuffled back, hiding one arm behind the archway into the kitchen, swapping the hands in her front pocket.

"I didn't hear a lot, they were being quiet for your sake," Phillip said, like it was her fault. Bel closed her fingers around her phone, started to drag it slowly out the other side.

"But Charlie was angry, because he knew the police were looking at him as their main suspect. He shouted one thing and I heard. I'd never forget."

Phillip still hadn't blinked, his strange eyes watering over. Bel glanced down, sliding the phone screen clear of her pocket. It couldn't see her face, asked for a passcode instead, but Bel thumbed the emergency button.

Phillip still wasn't watching, clearing his throat for the next part. "Your dad said, *I don't care if you're sorry. We agreed two o'clock. You didn't keep to the time and now look what's happened.*"

The keypad was open. Bel pressed 9, thumb floating toward the *1*, eyes darting up to check she was clear.

She wasn't.

She stifled a gasp, turned it into a cough. Phillip was staring at her, waiting for a response. But he couldn't see what her left hand was doing behind this wall.

"That could have been about anything." Bel held his gaze, but she wouldn't find the *1* without her eyes. "He was probably talking about something that day, someone being late for lunch or something."

Phillip's neck cricked, a one-sided twitch in his cheek. "They were talking about Rachel. About the police investigation," he said, like he thought he'd trapped her again.

"Rachel disappeared around six o'clock," she countered, eyes itching to look down, watering. She let them, finding the *1*, pressing it twice as she returned her gaze.

"But your dad's alibi began at two o'clock, didn't it?" Phillip smiled. "That's when he cut his hand."

Bel pretended to think about that, dropping her eyes, but they didn't reach the floor, catching on her phone instead. She found the call button at the bottom, thumb following her gaze to it.

"Hey! What are you doing there?"

A rush of heavy feet and Phillip was on top of her. He slammed his hand down into hers and the phone crashed onto the tiles.

"What were you doing there, trying to call the police?" His eyes were on fire now, fingers gripped around Bel's wrist, squeezing too hard.

"No." Bel struggled against his iron grip, the adrenaline hiding the pain from her. "I was trying to show you something. Evidence I found. About Rachel."

"Oh." Phillip pulled back, mouth still formed around the ghost of the sound as he let her go. He turned to where the phone had skidded, reached down for it.

"Fuck you," Bel growled, locking her bones and charging at Phillip. He shouldn't have turned his back on her, she wasn't eight anymore, or that abandoned baby in the backseat. She shoved him and he fell, rolling with the momentum.

Bel didn't wait to see the look of shock in his eyes. She flew toward the back door, forcing the handle down.

Phillip had got up too fast; she felt the disturbed air behind her.

She pulled the door as he grabbed her ponytail, jerking her head back, exposing her neck.

Bel's arm shot up, elbow first. She slammed it into his face, right between those eyes. Heard a crunch.

Phillip shrieked, slapping his hands to his bleeding face.

Bel slipped outside the open door, into the dark night. Crossed the patio in three strides, onto the wet grass, soaking through her socks.

"Help!" she screamed. "Hel—"

Her ponytail jolted back again, ripping at her scalp.

She slipped with the force of it, falling to the grass, the air knocked out of her in one desperate rasp.

Phillip dropped too, pinning her wrists to the ground.

"What evidence do you have?" he panted, blood dripping from his nose onto her face, sliding into her hair. "What do you know?"

"Help!" Bel screamed. "Ms. Nelson—"

Phillip let go of one of her wrists, slapping his palm against her mouth to silence her, the salt of blood and his clammy hands. But he couldn't hold her mouth and both her hands at the same time. She reached up, fingers outstretched, scrabbling at his strange eyes. Her nails scraped something soft and wet.

Phillip screeched, squinting, holding both her wrists again, releasing her mouth.

"Tell me what you know!" he roared.

"I don't know anything!" She pushed against the grass, trying to buck him off. Come on, Ms. Nelson. Come on, Ash. Help her. Please.

"I need to know!" His scream pulled at the tendons on his neck, sinewy and red-raw.

"Fuck you," Bel spat in his face, forced a knee into his chest. "You don't need to know. I do! Why the fuck do you deserve the answers?"

301

"Tell me!"

"No!"

A scream. But it wasn't Bel and it wasn't Phillip.

Two pale hands shot out of the darkness.

Phillip was thrown off her, rolling in the moonlit grass.

Bel looked up, breath fast and ragged.

Rachel was standing there, against the starless sky.

Her eyes were glittering and mean, mouth bared, showing all her teeth. She glared down at Phillip and roared again. A desperate, terrible sound, but Bel wasn't afraid anymore, wasn't alone.

"I'll kill you!" Rachel screamed. She doubled back, grabbing the rake from the patio. "Touch my daughter, I'll fucking kill you!" She raised the rake above her head, stumbling toward Phillip.

She was going to do it, she was.

Rachel swung but Phillip scrabbled back, the rake catching one of his ankles. He screeched. Rachel dragged it back to go again.

Phillip didn't give her the chance. He pushed up to his feet and bolted, across the dark grass, into the trees at the back, disappearing into the night.

Rachel dropped the rake.

Bel sat up.

Rachel's eyes whipped back to her, not mean anymore, still glittering. She hurried over, falling to her knees at Bel's side.

"Are you OK?" she said, gently holding the sides of Bel's head. "You're hurt."

Bel glanced down at her gray hoodie, stained with spatters of red.

"It's not mine," she said. "Think I broke his nose."

"Are you OK?" Rachel asked again, and maybe she didn't mean the blood after all.

"Fine." Bel's voice cracked. "Where were you?"

"I'm sorry." Rachel pulled Bel closer, arms around her, one hand pressed to the back of her head, like it was made to fit right there. "I'm sorry."

Bel wanted to push her away, but she also wanted to stay like this for a moment longer, exhausted, the shakes coming on, Rachel warm against them. Bel's body betraying her, forgetting that it was Rachel they were supposed to be scared of.

"It was Phillip Alves," she said, giving herself a reason to pull away. "The police told you about him, right? The one who was obsessed with you, with the case. The one who took me when I was eight."

Rachel watched her closely. No stars in the sky but there were in her eyes.

"I won't let him near you again, I promise," Rachel said. "My job to protect you."

"You weren't here." Bel's voice shrank.

"I need to call the police," Rachel said, wiping her eyes. She rubbed a hand down Bel's sleeve and straightened up. "Then we'll get you inside, OK?"

Rachel swiped at her phone, raised it to her ear.

Bel could hear the dial tone ringing, splintering the quiet night like their screams must have done.

A click.

"Officer Winter?" Rachel turned, facing the back of their house. "It's Rachel Price. It's an emergency. Phillip Alves was just in our house. He attacked Bel."

"I'm fine," Bel called in the background, standing up, wiping wet grass from her legs.

"Yes," Rachel said, an answer to some unheard question. "Yes." Another. "He ran off through the backyard. Send officers now. You have to get him."

Rachel turned back, eyes picking Bel out of the darkness. The yellow glow of inside lit up half her face, the gray light of the moon on the other. She breathed in. "It's him, Dave. Phillip Alves. The one you're looking for. The man who took me."

THIRTY-EIGHT

Rachel switched off the engine, pulled out the key, holding it up like it might unlock something else.

"We can cancel your grandpa's birthday dinner today, B-Bel. After last night . . ."

Bel shrugged. "No, I'm fine," she said, because she didn't quite know what she was. She thought of Phillip's wild eyes, his hitching laugh. Phillip was the man, the one who kept Rachel in his basement for sixteen years and let her go.

"It's over," Rachel said, reaching out to her, squeezing her hand. Bel didn't flinch, she was too tired, didn't know what to believe anymore. If they'd found the man, did that mean Rachel wasn't lying about any of it? Had she been wrong?

"Come on." Rachel climbed out, Bel mirroring her on the other side.

Ms. Nelson was standing in her open doorway, watching, like she had last night when the cops showed up. Bel nodded at her. An apology, a truce.

"Bel?" A voice sailed down the street.

It was Ash, hurrying toward them, navy sweater with white birds.

Bel glanced at Rachel.

"I'll go inside," Rachel said. "Start clearing up."

Bel waited for the front door to close behind her.

Ash cut in first.

"I was waiting for you. I got your text. Sorry, my phone was on silent." Worry pulled at his eyebrows. "What happened? Did you follow Rachel? Where did she go, what was she doing? Someone said the cops were here. What did you find?"

Bel took a breath, knowing she'd have to explain everything, not sure how. She gestured for him to follow her, away from the house, toward the cemetery.

"The cops weren't here for Rachel. They were here for Phillip Alves."

"Phillip Alves?" Ash hissed. "That crazy guy obsessed with the case? The one who kidnapped you?"

"He broke into the house when he saw Rachel leave. Looking for clues. But I was there. He thought I knew something about Rachel. He got mad."

Ash shifted, steps falling in time with hers. He almost reached for her hand. "Did he hurt you?"

"He might have," Bel said. "If Rachel didn't come home in time. She threatened him, he ran off."

"She saved you?" he asked.

Bel didn't want to answer that. Rachel shouldn't have been gone in the first place. And if she wasn't lying, then why was she sneaking out of the house that late? Things were too unclear now, where were the battle lines? Who was on whose side?

"That's not all," Bel said instead. "We just got back from the police station, from giving our statements. Rachel says it's him. Phillip Alves was the man who took her."

Ash stopped, stared at her.

"It's Phillip?"

"That's what Rachel says."

His eyebrows drew together now, pulling across his nose. "But . . ." He trailed off. "Wasn't Phillip in prison for three years after he kidnapped you?"

Bel's heels dragged, grating on the sidewalk. "Rachel says there was a long period of time when the man didn't come close enough for her to see, kept the lights out and his face covered when he left her food. It could have been someone else and she didn't realize at the time; a brother, a friend."

"Phillip Alves." Ash sounded it out on his lips, faltering, like it didn't quite fit.

"The police showed her Phillip's mug shot when she first returned, asked if he was the guy," Bel said. "She said no at the time. She didn't recognize him until she saw him in person, the way he moved, the way he breathed."

"Unbelievable," Ash said, but which way did he mean it? They walked the path through the cemetery, red leaves dotted on the grass. "So now they have to find him?"

"They already did. State Police picked him up a few hours later, walking down the highway, Route Two. He's been arrested, being questioned by the feds now. I broke his nose, by the way," she said, so he knew she hadn't needed Rachel, she might have been fine on her own.

"Phillip Alves," Ash said again, leaving the name there, floating in front of them, walking into it.

"Why do you keep saying it like that?" Bel snapped.

He stopped walking. "I guess, it's just . . . do you believe her?"

The knot twisted in Bel's gut. She went back to an answer that was safe, hiding behind it. "I don't know."

"But what about everything we've found? If the answer is just that Phillip Alves—a stranger—abducted her, why did she borrow that money from Julian Tripp right before she disappeared?"

"I don't know." Bel hid farther behind it. "Maybe the three thousand dollars was for something else? Not running away."

"What about the sighting in January? The red top and black jeans?"

"Maybe it wasn't Rachel."

"What was she so desperate to find in your grandpa's house?"

"I don't know. Maybe it doesn't even matter." And maybe the cup she'd seen in the trash was just another coffee cup with a cow. They couldn't be rare.

Ash stared at her, like he didn't understand, and maybe Bel didn't either. Why was she defending Rachel now, taking her side even when it felt wrong to say it? Because the other option, if it wasn't Phillip Alves, was to trust what he said instead, who he thought had taken Rachel after obsessing over it for sixteen years. Dad leaving with a packed bag in the middle of the night, Dad talking to some unknown man about his alibi in the months after Rachel disappeared. Bel could choose to believe Rachel or to believe Phillip Alves, and Rachel was the easier choice, didn't hurt as much.

"Phillip Alves," Ash said one more time.

"Stop saying it like that."

"I'm sorry." He looked at her, under the shade of the red tree. "I guess I just thought the answer would be closer to home."

Bel tilted her chin. "Closer to home? What do you mean by that?"

"N-nothing," he backed off. "It just seemed—"

"You mean my dad, don't you?"

"I didn't say that," Ash said, hands up, tiptoeing around a land mine he'd already set off.

"But you meant it, didn't you?" Bel locked her jaw, hardened her eyes. "Why does this always happen? He had a fucking alibi." Her mind battened down, shutting out Phillip's deranged rambling. "It has to be Phillip. My dad didn't do anything. I know that, Ash." Knew it, had to believe it. She was alone in the world without him. "And maybe I'm wrong, maybe he did leave me, run away to Canada. Maybe he thought—with Rachel back—that people would start suspecting he was involved in her disappearance, just like you're doing now. Maybe he knew people would turn on him again, and he was scared. And now when the news breaks about Phillip's arrest, when there's finally an answer to the Rachel fucking Price mystery, he can come home. He'll finally be free, from people like you."

Charlie Price, a name forever marred after Dave Winter arrested him for something he didn't do. That made sense, Dad leaving for that reason, Bel could shift things around in her head to accept that.

"That's not what I meant, Bel, pl—"

"He told me to stay away from you, right before he disappeared, did you know?" Bel said, going for his weak spot. She knew Ash now, and he knew her. And that meant she knew exactly how to hurt him, how to lash out and make it last. "He warned me. Said you were using me for the film. Manipulating me about Rachel. I'm surprised you don't have a camera on you right now, wouldn't this be great footage for your little film, huh? My name's not in the title, but I'm the heart, remember, or maybe you just told me that to manipulate me. So you can impress Ramsey, make him think you aren't a total waste of space."

Her eyes stung. It wasn't working, not the way it should, because it was too late; she'd let him in too close, and now it hurt her too.

"Where's your camera, Ash, huh?" She pushed him in the shoulder, jabbed him with two fingers. "That's all this is supposed to be, isn't it, you and me? It's pointless, it doesn't matter. You're leaving, you were always leaving. You don't really care apart from making a great film for Ramsey. Plotty, twisty, one the big broadcasters will pay a bunch of money for. Come on, where's your camera?"

"Bel, stop." Ash's voice cracked in two, eyes glazed with un-cried tears. "That's not fair. I know what you're doing—"

"Then it's done, OK?" Bel's breath hitched, hands shaking. "It's done."

She left him there, standing by a row of graves, under the bleeding tree.

Waited until Ash couldn't see her anymore to wipe her eyes.

"I bought a birthday cake, you don't think he'll mind?" Rachel asked, stirring the mac and cheese on the stove. "Didn't think we'd have time to make one."

"It's fine. He won't remember." Bel stared out the back door as the evening darkened, her reflection as Phillip snatched her hair back, baring her throat.

"You OK, Bel?" Rachel paused, adding salt to the pan.

"Yeah." She sniffed. "Are . . . are you OK?"

Rachel turned. She seemed surprised by the question. So was Bel, if she was being honest. A smile flickered onto Rachel's face, unsure at first, until she met Bel's eyes. Across the room from each other, but it wasn't such a great distance anymore.

"Yeah," she said too. "I'm OK."

Bel nodded. "I should probably get ready. We told everyone seven-thirty, right?"

Rachel checked the clock on the oven. "Twenty minutes to go. Perfect timing."

Bel went upstairs, changed into jeans and a cardigan, brushed her hair. She'd washed it twice since Phillip had touched it, left his blood behind. It still didn't feel clean.

She put the hairbrush down on the windowsill, beside the photo frame. Her and Dad beaming for the camera, the same one he had on his keys, Story Land for her twelfth birthday.

Bel's thumb passed over the photo, her face reflected in the glass, young Bel in one eye, Dad in the other. He'd been missing thirteen days. But now, because of Phillip Alves, everything was going to be OK, Dad could finally come home. Bel was ready for it. Ready for peace, a truce, to put the house back together again, leave her armor outside.

Bel and Rachel could be on the same side, if it was Dad's side too. A family.

Family first.

Her eyes trailed away to her nightstand. She followed them, opening the drawer to her collection of stolen things. She realized something, looking down at the pens and lip balms, that one unusable AirPod, the queen chess piece. Bel hadn't taken anything in a couple of weeks. The knot had been there in her gut, but it hadn't asked to be fed, hadn't needed it. She must have been distracted, so consumed with Rachel.

She reached inside, fingers closing around something small and soft. She pulled it out, her tiny pink baby sock, cradled in the palm of her hand. Bel could return this to Rachel, put it back where she found it. It clearly meant something to her. An olive branch. A first step.

Bel took that first step, and a second, walking out of her room and down the hall.

She paused at the closed door into Rachel's room. Tried the handle. It was unlocked. In fact, Bel hadn't heard Rachel lock it at all, these past couple weeks.

She went inside, padding quietly, so Rachel wouldn't hear from downstairs. Rachel hadn't made her bed, hadn't had time. Bel moved over to the nightstand and slid out the top drawer.

The iPhone box was still inside. A lip balm, rolling toward her. A packet of Kleenex.

Bel pinched the small sock and pushed it to the far corner, where she'd found it.

But there was something else there now. Hidden in the shadows, a cold touch of metal against the skin of her knuckles. Bel couldn't help herself. She let the sock go and scrabbled for the small piece of metal, pulled it out.

It was a ring. A plain gold ring. A wedding band. Too big to be Rachel's, it had to be a man's.

Bel brought it closer, studied it, moving it so it caught the light.

It was engraved on the inside.

July 23 2005

The date her parents got married.

This was Dad's wedding ring.

The one he still wore. The one he couldn't take off.

And it was here, in Rachel's drawer.

Bel's heart fell into her stomach, the knot took a bite. No, no, no. He couldn't take this off. Which meant . . .

Everything wasn't going to be OK. Dad didn't run away, Rachel had done something to him, something final. Answers unraveled again, that last speck of hope swallowed whole. And a new feeling, that Dad was never coming home.

Bel broke apart, following her heart down, down, down. Finding her own land mines, setting them all off at once.

"Rachel!" she screamed, burning down the house.

Bel burst out of the room, the ring hot in her fist, catching fire too. "Rachel!"

Down the stairs, the thunderclap of her feet building into something worse.

"Mom!"

"Just fluffing the cushions," Rachel called back.

Bel followed her voice through the door, into war.

"Don't know why, no one cares if the cushions are fluffed." She smiled to herself.

"I can't do this anymore!" Bel shouted, voice shaking the room.

Rachel dropped the cushion.

"Bel, what's—"

"I can't do it! You're lying to me! You've been lying since you returned!"

Rachel blinked, mouth falling open. "Bel, I—"

Bel cut her off, storming forward. She slammed the ring down on the coffee table.

"That's Dad's wedding ring." She pointed. "He couldn't take it off!"

Bel's eyes hooked onto Rachel's, steadied, took aim.

"What have you done to him, Rachel?"

THIRTY-NINE

Rachel staggered back, staring down at the ring between them.

"Bel," she said calmly, though her eyes betrayed her. "I can explain."

"No!" Bel shouted. "No more lies!"

"I don't want to lie to you," Rachel said, hands up, unarmed.

"Then don't. What have you done to Dad? Where is he?!"

"I don't know," Rachel said, but Bel knew that trick all too well, blowing up Rachel's wall so there was nothing for her to hide behind.

"You have his ring. Did you kill him, Rachel? Mom, did you kill him?"

Rachel didn't say anything, couldn't lie quick enough.

"He was the only one who'd never leave me." Voice scratchy and raw as tears finally broke, rib cage empty, her heart dropping all the way, she might never get it back. "Everyone always leaves. He was the only one I had and you've taken him from me."

Rachel's eyes filled too, watching Bel split herself open. "Bel, listen—"

"No, I'm not listening to you, you're a liar!"

"Bel."

"Phillip Alves didn't take you, did he?!" She wiped the tears, rebuilding the barricade, gritting her teeth. "You'd never even seen him before last night, had you?"

Rachel swallowed.

"Say it!" Bel roared.

"No." Rachel hugged her chest, shielding it. But they were only arms and Bel could break through those. "But he tried to hurt you. I panicked. It wasn't part of the plan, I just wanted to protect you, keep him away from you. No one touches my daughter."

"So there is a plan?" Bel said, catching on that, holding on with both hands. "There's always been a plan, hasn't there? Phillip Alves didn't take you, because no one took you. Where were you all this time?"

"Bel, I can't—"

"Tell me where you were!" Another land mine. "You weren't locked in a basement, so where were you?!"

"I can't tell you!" Rachel said, Bel's explosion setting off hers, eyes broken open. "I wouldn't do that to you!"

"You've done far worse!" Bel shouted back, louder. "You left me behind in the backseat of your car! I was just a baby!"

Rachel's head shuddered side to side, shaking free her tears. "No, Bel. I would never leave y—"

"Don't lie!" Bel pointed at her, stabbing the air. "You borrowed three thousand dollars from Julian Tripp days before you disappeared. You chose to go!"

Rachel stepped back, the blow hitting her right in the chest, hands pressed to the wound. "No, no, that's not—"

"Yes, you did!" Bel closed in on her. "You knew you couldn't withdraw it yourself, because everyone would know you'd planned to run away, so you took it from Mr. Tripp. You left me! Where did you go? Did you go to Jeff's friend Bob in Vermont for a new identity? Is that how you hid, how you knew to make it look like Dad had done the same? Why did you leave? Tell me the truth!"

Rachel winced at every shot, shrinking, eyes fast and desperate. "No, no, Bel. Please."

"Stop saying *no*, tell me where you were!"

"I can't!" Rachel shouted, coming back stronger, closing the distance. "I can't tell you the truth! I wouldn't do that to you. It's my job to protect you. I can do this on my own. I was on my own for a very long time, I know how it works."

Too entrenched, Bel couldn't move her, not even by falling apart in front of her.

"Please, Mom! Tell me where Dad is. What did you do to him?"

Rachel said nothing, shook her head instead. She didn't care, caring wasn't part of the plan.

"It's my fault," Bel cried. "I knew from the start you were lying. I should have tried harder to prove it before you got to Dad. Now he's gone and it's my fault."

Rachel's eyes flashed, simmering with new tears. "Nothing is your fault, Bel. Do you hear me? Not one thing. Listen to me. I had fifteen years to imagine who you would grow up to be, and you're more perfect than any version I could think up." Tears pooled at the crack in her lips. "Nothing is your fault, it's everyone else, and I will protect you from them."

But Bel saw between the tears. She tilted her chin up, sharpened it to a point. "It was sixteen years you were locked up, Rachel. Not fifteen. You've lost count of your own lies."

Rachel's breath shuddered in her chest. "I'm sorry," she said.

And that tripped another one. "No you're not!" Bel shouted; fight left in her still. She kicked out at the armchair and it jumped back, screeching against the floor. "If you were sorry you would tell me the truth. Tell me!"

"No." Rachel's voice cracked.

Bel gave up. But if she was going down, then Rachel was going down with her. Her breath hitched as it built within her.

"I wish you'd stayed disappeared!" she screamed, the words clawing at her throat. "I wish you'd never come back!"

The doorbell went, trilling through the house.

Rachel wiped her face, her eyes dulled, like something had broken behind them.

"Bel, sweetheart," she said softly, voice worn thin. "Should I tell everyone to come back another day? We don't have to do this now."

"No." Bel caught her own tears on her sleeve, face stinging and raw. "No. I don't want to be alone in this house with you ever again."

She left Rachel behind, heading for the front door, pulled it open.

Sherry was standing there, holding a plate with a home-baked cake. Rough blue icing spelled the words: *Happy 85th Birthday!* Carter was behind her on the steps, Jeff on the path.

"Everything OK in here?" Sherry said, eyes wide and probing. They must have heard the shouting, must be able to read it all over Bel's face. Carter definitely could, eyebrows drawn, a small nod, asking if Bel was OK in their own secret way.

"Yes, fine," Bel said, but another voice had said it too. Rachel, standing right behind her. Speaking together, both liars now.

It didn't faze Rachel. "Come in," she said.

Everyone had arrived now, Grandpa tucked in at the head of the table, Yordan beside. They were in the kitchen, the table extended to seat eight. But there weren't eight of them, because Dad was missing. No one had even mentioned him.

Rachel served out the mac and cheese, squelching as it hit the plates, long sinews of cheese clinging to the spoon.

"There you go, Bel, sweetie." She handed her plate back, hand tracing over Bel's shoulder before she moved on.

Bel didn't understand that, or the softness in her voice. Shouldn't she be angry? Bel had just said the worst thing imaginable to her, both of them at opposite ends of rock bottom, and yet here Rachel was, soft and kind.

Rachel must be a better liar than she'd thought. She admitted it, she'd lied about Phillip Alves, which meant everything else she'd ever said was on the table too, everything about her disappearance and reappearance. Bel asked her for the truth, gave her a final chance, and Rachel had refused. They couldn't ever come back from that, couldn't pretend anymore, couldn't play house or mother and daughter. So whatever happened tonight, this was a last supper, an ending of some kind.

"So it was Phillip Alves all along?" Sherry asked, fork raised. "I knew he was crazy when he came into our house pretending to be a cop. Asked all kinds of bizarre questions about you. And all that time, he knew exactly what happened to you, because you were in his basement. Sicko. I knew it all along, I swear, had a feeling."

Jeff coughed, eyes shifting from Sherry to Rachel.

"You must be relieved it's finally over?" Sherry asked. "You too, Bel. That must have been scary last night."

"Yes," Bel and Rachel said together, again, and that had to stop.

"It's good to finally know the whole truth." Bel frowned at Rachel, who had taken the seat across from her. Rachel met her eyes.

"It is," Sherry agreed.

Jeff coughed again, knocking his fist against his chest. "Maybe we should talk about something a bit lighter. Meant to be a celebration. Happy birthday, Dad." Jeff raised his beer, took a large glug of it, swallowing four times.

Grandpa didn't notice, spooning macaroni into his mouth, one tiny tube at a time.

Carter was eating just as slowly, twirling her fork, goring bits of pasta, then letting them go. Maybe the other half of the Prices had an argument before this meal too; Carter too quiet, Uncle Jeff too fidgety, finishing off his first beer already.

Sherry was oblivious, or better at hiding it.

"It's just good to know that things can go back to normal." Sherry gave her husband a pointed look, eyes drifting to the empty beer. "Sorry we were a couple minutes late, by the way. It was this one." She pointed her fork at Carter. "Doing science homework. At her computer looking at graphs instead of getting ready. Got annoyed at me for dragging her away. I just said: *You don't need biology to be a dancer, but you do need to learn to be on time.*"

"That's more than OK." Rachel answered to Carter, not Sherry. "I'm bad at keeping time too."

Maybe that was the first true thing Rachel had said. She *was* bad at time; twice she'd accidentally said fifteen years when she should have said sixteen.

"Yes," Sherry cut in again. "Weren't you late for your own wedding?"

Rachel glanced down at her plate. Not a lot of appetite at this table. "Only ten minutes."

It was a good thing Sherry was here to steer the conversation, steer the family. Dad normally did that, when he was here. No one had brought him up still, the eighth empty space, his wedding ring tucked in the pocket of Bel's jeans.

"You finished, Bel?" Rachel asked, eyes glittering in a way that wasn't easy to fake.

"S-sure." Even though Bel had hardly touched her food either.

She didn't understand, how Rachel was being nice to her. Was it just a show, for everyone else here? Bel had said the cruelest thing to her, to cut her as deep as she could, a fatal blow. And Rachel hadn't left, even though she knew she was caught, even though Bel had all but wished her dead. She was still here.

Bel rubbed her cried-out eyes. She'd never had an argument like that with Dad, not once her whole life. He would threaten to leave the house at the first sign of raised voices, to go for a drive. Bel never wanted him to leave, so she relented, she always gave in. It worked every time. They had never shouted at each other across the room like that, never had to work anything through. But now Bel wasn't sure; was that a good thing or not? Had it felt good to scream at the top of her lungs, her deepest, darkest feelings, to share them with someone?

"We actually have two birthday cakes, thanks, Sherry." Rachel nodded at her.

"Mine's low-cal," Sherry announced to the table, eyes lingering on Carter. Carter fiddled with her tights, pulling the material out, letting it fling back against her knees.

"Before we get to cake," Rachel said, taking charge, wrestling it from Sherry, "I thought we could do gifts."

Sherry sniffed. "That's fine. We normally do gifts after cake, but you wouldn't know that; missed a few birthdays." An amused exhale of breath.

Rachel ignored her, disappearing into the living room for a few moments. She came back with a present wrapped in blue-and-white-striped paper, in the shape of a hardcover book. A red ribbon tied around it.

"This is from me and Bel, Pat," she said, leaning over Grandpa to hand him the gift. Did she do that because she knew Bel hadn't had time to get him a gift? Was she being nice or was she picking up the fight somehow? "Happy birthday."

"R-Rachel?" Grandpa looked up at her.

"Yes," she replied with a sideways smile.

"Charlie's girlfriend."

"That's right, Pat," Sherry cut in. "Well done."

"Let me help," Yordan said, removing the ribbon for Grandpa.

"I've got it, Charlie." Grandpa snatched it back.

He pulled at the corners with his bony, spotted fingers, ripped the paper off.

"A book." He spun it in his hands and Bel recognized the green cover before she even saw the title. *The Memory Thief.* One of her favorite books, one Grandpa used to read to her when she was little.

Sherry leaned into Jeff. "A little insensitive," she whispered, loud enough that Bel and Carter could hear. "Giving the man with dementia a book called *The Memory Thief.*"

"I thought you'd like it," Rachel said loudly, retaking her seat. "Ms. Nelson at the bookstore recommended it."

But Bel's mind snagged on something else, dragging it to the surface. Rachel snooping in Bel's bedroom, flicking through her copy of this exact book. Bel caught her. Rachel said it was one of her favorites, and Bel hadn't wanted to admit it was one of hers too. Rachel asked if anyone had given her this book, which—now she thought about it—had been a strange thing to ask. But everything about Rachel was strange in those early days. Bel told her that Grandpa used to read it to her as a kid, that she bought her own copy a few years ago. So Rachel knew Grandpa already had this book, sitting on his shelves at home, Bel had told her so. Did she forget?

"That's very thoughtful of Rachel, isn't it, Pat?" Yordan said. "I can read this to you at home."

Grandpa let the book slip out of his hands, like it was gone from his head already. He glanced at Yordan, then over to Jeff.

"Charlie?" he said, an edge to his voice, almost accusatory.

"Charlie's not here, Dad." Jeff shifted. "Remember? Charlie went on a little trip. He'll be back soon."

Dad's wedding ring burned a hole in Bel's pocket, searing her skin. A secret she didn't share but it felt like her burden now too. That maybe Dad was never coming back. A black hole where her heart used to be.

"You think he's coming back?" Bel asked Jeff, watching Rachel's reaction.

Her eyes were empty.

"Of course he's coming back." Jeff's eyes widened, pupils large: from the beer or from their attention? "He's the center of this family, always has been. Holds us all together."

The heart, you might say: Ramsey was wrong about that. It wasn't Bel, it was Dad. Wasn't it?

"But you know," Jeff continued. "With Rachel coming back— sorry, Rachel– there was obviously a lot of stress, and media attention again, and I think he just needed to get away."

"All the way to Canada? Without his passport?" Bel pressed, gaze switching between him and Rachel.

"Well, if the cops think he took off to Canada, I can't say it's out of character." Jeff finished off his second beer. "Charlie can be spontaneous sometimes. Drove me crazy. You know he left for Costa Rica when he was twenty without telling anyone, no contact for six weeks? Skipped out on his job at the logging yard when things were already bad. Dad was furious." Jeff nodded in Grandpa's direction. "I mean, he proposed to you, Rachel, after what, three months?"

Rachel nodded, no change in her face.

"So I'm saying, Charlie sometimes just does things, especially when feelings are involved. His way of coping. I mean, there was the Taco Bell woman, a couple weeks after Ellen left him. You'd think that was out of character, but he was obviously hurting. It's the same when Rachel returned. A lot of strong, confusing emotions. I think he'll be back this weekend; two weeks away feels right. Something else to celebrate." He raised his beer bottle.

But Bel couldn't *cheers* to that, three words circling in her head, something Jeff just said.

"What Taco Bell woman?"

Jeff's face flushed, putting down his bottle with a dull thud. "Probably not something you want to hear, Bel."

"I do want to hear it." She needed to hear it, the knot spiraling, feeding on her near-empty stomach. "What Taco Bell woman?"

"I don't—"

"Uncle Jeff." Bel bared her teeth.

Jeff ran an awkward hand through his hair. "Just that Charlie was in line at Taco Bell. North Conway, I think he said. It was a couple weeks after Ellen left him. He got talking to a woman in line and— sorry, Rachel—they went to a motel down the road and, you know."

Bel didn't know; she could guess. But there was something more, something bigger, her heart hammering, waiting for her to find it. Taco Bell, North Conway, two weeks after Dad's girlfriend Ellen left them, because Bel made her, pushed her away. Wait. That was it. The trip to Story Land for her twelfth birthday. That photo of her and Dad. They stopped at Taco Bell on the way home, and . . .

The knot twisted, leaving a knife-shaped hole, Bel bleeding around it.

Dad had lied to her.

All this time.

Bel said it was three hours, enough time to piss herself twice, sobbing in the backseat like the world had ended, because part of it had. But Dad told her it had been only fifteen minutes—max—that she was just being silly. Bel had believed him, she'd rewritten the memory in her head, turned it into a funny childhood anecdote.

Bel might be sick, heart making a break for her throat.

Because it wasn't funny. It was the one thing, the very thing Dad must have known she'd be afraid of. After Rachel, after Phillip Alves. The backseat was a bad place, where bad things happened.

Jeff had no idea what he'd just done, what he'd undone.

Dad had lied to Bel, betrayed her. Abandoned her in the backseat for hours, to go off with Taco Bell woman, unpicking a scar that would never heal.

And if he'd lied about that, what else had he lied to her about?

FORTY

Bel pushed her chair away, its feet screeching against the tiles, cutting the room into shreds. Grandpa slapped his hands to his ears.

"You OK, Bel?" Rachel asked. Could she see something, read the undoing behind Bel's eyes?

"Need some water."

But she didn't go for the glasses. She opened the cupboard below, where they kept the overspill of mugs, not the ones in daily rotation. Chasing a hunch, a feeling in her gut, the knot leading the way. Sherry was talking about herself, reclaiming the focus, as Bel hid behind the cupboard door.

Her hand dug through, moving rows of flowery and patterned mugs aside, searching for a specific one. Dad's favorite. The one that she or Rachel had broken, that he'd thrown away. Bel couldn't remember breaking it, apologizing just in case.

It was here, hiding in the shadows at the back. Santa's beaming face and cracked skin. Unbroken. Never broken in the first place. Bel blinked to make sure.

She'd believed it because Dad told her so. Just like the Taco Bell story. Like everything else: forgetting to seal the trash cans even though it was black bear season and she remembered sealing them. Leaving windows open, even though she had no memory of it. Faucets running.

Bel came apart, sorting through her memories, the ones Dad had obscured, tried to change. She unpicked them all, going back years, separating herself from him, sorting the true from the only-true-because-Dad-told-her.

When she was done, fully undone, she built herself back, in a new shape. Bel straightened up into it, the mug dangling from her fingers.

It was Rachel too, Dad always said. Front door left open. Oven forgotten, burned food. It used to terrify Bel, to share something with that ghost of a mother, to be like her in any way. But now she realized, nothing like that had happened in the house, not once, since Dad went missing. Because the link wasn't between her and Rachel, it had been Dad all along. Lying to them, making them doubt their own memories so they'd need him all the more. And Bel had needed him, maybe too much, the second voice in her head, not truly herself without him.

Fuck.

One of the last things Dad said to her was a warning, that she was being manipulated. But it was much closer to home than that.

Bel pulled out the trash can, dumped the Santa mug inside, where it belonged.

She didn't bother with another excuse, leaving the kitchen, eyes ahead, finally knowing the way.

Up the stairs, to her room.

Her parents were liars. Rachel wasn't who she thought she was. But Dad wasn't either.

Something came back to her, in Phillip Alves's feverish voice. *Why would she do something to him, if he hadn't done something to her first?*

Bel knew where she was going, her gut leading the way.

To the bookshelves mounted on the wall.

The green hardcover spine she knew too well.

Bel pulled out her copy of *The Memory Thief,* flicking through the pages, something staring her in the face, but she didn't know what. She just knew it was important, a sign Rachel had given that she was finally able to see.

She went back to the very start, the page with the copyright and publisher information, eyes scanning.

She found it, about halfway down.

Originally published in hardcover and ebook March 2008.

She ran her finger over the date.

March 2008. After Rachel disappeared. One month after.

Rachel had told Bel it was one of her favorites, but she couldn't have read it before she went missing. The man hadn't let her have books in the basement, but Bel knew there never was a man or a basement. So unless Rachel was lying about having read the book at all—and that didn't feel like the answer—then Rachel had read this book sometime in those sixteen years when she was disappeared.

And there was more, the way forward. But it wasn't about this copy here, in Bel's hands. Or the new one downstairs that Rachel had wrapped up. It was about the one in Grandpa's house. *Did someone give you this book?*

Bel knew that was the way, to finally solve the mystery of what really happened to Rachel Price. But to find it, she had to accept where the truth would take her. That the answers to Rachel's disappearance and reappearance led back to Dad somehow, she knew it in her gut, as tangible as the knot. All the hints she'd rejected, pushed away to find another lead, hiding from it, clinging to that alibi as the answer to anyone's doubt, even her own. What Grandma Susan said. What Mr. Tripp said. What Phillip Alves said. The lock on Rachel's door that she hadn't locked since Dad went away.

Bel replaced the book, glanced at the photo frame on her windowsill. Her twelfth birthday. Story Land. Dad beaming, arms wrapped around her. She picked it up, searched Dad's eyes.

Who was he really, this man? Someone who would leave his daughter alone three hours in the backseat, wet from tears and her own piss because she thought she'd been left all alone in the world again. Bel couldn't be on his side anymore, because he'd never been on hers.

She put the photo back, face down, making Dad disappear, and that sad, lonely little girl too.

Bel accepted it and she was ready. Knew what she had to do.

She darted out of her room and to the stairs.

But she wasn't alone.

Carter was there, coming up as Bel was going down.

"Hey," Carter said, quietly, blocking the way.

"Hey yourself." Down three more steps to meet her.

"You OK?" Carter looked up at her, eyes glittering from the ceiling lights.

"Fine. You?"

Carter opened her mouth, a delay before any words came. "Can I talk to you about something?" Adding: "It's important," when she saw the look on Bel's face.

Bel could hear the hurt in Carter's voice, even though she'd tried to hide it. She knew Carter better than she knew herself, because Bel hadn't done a great job of knowing herself.

"You can always talk to me," she said. "But I can't do this right now, sorry. There's something I have to do. Will you cover for me? It's important."

Carter breathed out. Not a sigh, something deeper. "OK," she said in a small voice, moving her arm to let Bel through. "I'll cover for you."

"Thanks, love you." Bel hurried down the stairs, into the living room instead. Over to the sofa, where Yordan had placed his bag for Grandpa, everything he might need when away from the house.

Bel reached inside. Incontinence pads and wet wipes. Spare clothes. More than one bottle of pills. She pulled one out, studied it. Painkillers. No, not these. Put them back, tried again. Found another orange pill bottle, squinted to read the words on the label. *One after every meal,* it said. This was what she was looking for.

Bel slipped the bottle up her sleeve, her fingers well practiced at this. Not because the knot told her to. Because she needed a reason to leave here and go to Grandpa's house, without Rachel catching on.

Her chance came, when Grandpa finished his slice of cake, pushed his plate away.

Bel waited, willing Yordan to move faster. Unknowingly playing a part in another of Bel's plans. She wouldn't fail this time.

"You're all being very quiet tonight," Sherry commented, which didn't help the silence, only a temporary fix.

Yordan stood up, excusing himself from his own slices of cake—one from each, to be diplomatic—wandering into the living room.

He was gone a whole minute, reappearing in the archway. "Sorry, I can't find Pat's digestion pills. I must have left them at home. I'll go get them quickly now."

Bel was ready. She stood up. "Don't worry, Yordan. I'll get them, you haven't finished your cake."

"No." Yordan smiled, hand up to refuse. "It's my job. I left them behind."

"Really, I don't mind," she insisted, doubling down with her eyes. "You stay here with Grandpa. I need some fresh air anyway. Stuffy in here."

Yordan pursed his lips. Did he know? "Well, if you want?"

Bel nodded. "It's no problem."

Rachel pushed her chair back. "Bel, you can't drive. Maybe I should—"

"I'll take my bike." Bel cut her off. If Rachel got to the house before Bel did, then maybe she'd never find it, the truth. Rachel didn't want her to have it. "I'll be like twenty minutes max. Where are the pills, Yordan?"

"Should be in the cupboard above the coffee machine," he said, retaking his seat. They were hidden in Bel's back pocket, actually, sorry, Yordan.

"Be right back," Bel said, before Rachel could dissent again.

Rachel watched her go, something more in her eyes. Carter too.

Bel waved, leaving them in silence again, heading for the front door.

She closed it behind her, the cool evening breeze playing in her hair, throwing it across her face, stinging her worn-out eyes.

She hurried to the garage, through the side door. Ash wasn't waiting in here for her anymore, but her old bike was, too small but it would do. She wheeled it out into the night, onto the sidewalk, stepped one leg over.

Bel pulled her phone out, held it up until it recognized her face. It didn't, maybe because it was dark, or maybe because she had changed. She unlocked it with her passcode and scrolled to her messages with Ash.

I was wrong, I'm sorry, she typed, pressed send. She never said sorry, because she never wanted anyone back after she'd pushed them away. *I know how to find the truth. I need you. Meet me outside my grandpa's house. Bring the camera. This is it.*

Bel placed her feet on the pedals and pushed off, sailing down the moonlit street, finally on her way.

The wind howled in her ears, like it knew as well.

It all ended tonight.

FORTY-ONE

Grandpa's street. The road rough against her wheels, a grating that sounded like whispers, urging her on.

No streetlights, only the silver of the moon, looming over the dark mountains. But it was enough. Bel could see a figure outside the house. She recognized the curve of Ash's shoulders, his awkward wave.

He'd driven here, in Ramsey's rental car, that was how he beat her, riding as fast as the wind.

Bel gripped the brakes. She skidded and jumped off, ditching the bike on the grass outside.

"Hi," Ash said, another awkward wave, like the first hadn't counted.

Bel moved closer until he was more than an outline, the camera cradled in the crook of his arm.

"I'm sorry," she said, chest tight, wrapped around her heart. She hadn't lost it forever, then. "I didn't mean what I said. I was just trying . . . I was wrong."

Ash's eyes hooked onto hers. He broke into a smile. "Wow. Bel Price apologizing. Should have had the camera on for that one. No one will ever believe me."

Bel exhaled, a laugh in there somewhere. She closed the gap between them, tiny punch to his arm.

"Thought so." Ash's breath was warm on her face, leaving the heat there. "I'm sorry too. I shouldn't have said that *closer to home* thing. I didn't mean your dad, but—"

"No." Bel cut him off. "You were right. The answer is closer to home. It's not Phillip Alves. My mom just admitted that herself. Said she couldn't tell me the truth, that she wouldn't do that to me. But I know how to find it. And I think the answer . . ." She trailed off, trying to find the words, trying to find the strength to say them out loud.

"Bel?" Ash said, voice soft, helping her cross the line.

"I think the answer leads back to my dad, somehow." She paused. "I'm not sure he is who I thought he was. Guess it took me a lot longer than everyone else to see it."

Ash chewed his lip, glanced over at the house. "Why are we here, then?"

"This is where the answer is. What Rachel was looking for. Something that would lead us to the truth. That's why she wanted to get to it. She doesn't want anyone finding the truth."

"But we don't know what she—"

"I do know what she was looking for," Bel spoke across him, looking at the dark house. One of the three houses she called home, part of her history, part of the Price family. But the houses had kept secrets from her too. "Rachel didn't just happen to spot our camera as she walked past. It was too well hidden for that. She found it because we'd hidden it exactly where she was heading. She was going for the bookshelves, Ash."

Ash's eyes narrowed, like that made perfect sense, and none at all.

"It's a book." Bel tried to explain, all the pieces she'd now put together, the feeling in her gut holding them there. "*The Memory Thief.* My grandpa used to read it to me. Always told me it was a *very special book.* That's what he said: *very special.* I caught Rachel in my room, a few days after she returned, looking through my copy of the book. Said it was one of her favorites, but it was published after she went missing. She asked me something too, I didn't realize what it meant at the time. She asked if someone had given me that copy. She meant Grandpa, I'm sure of it. And today, for his birthday, Rachel gave him a new copy, like it was a message for him, even if he can't remember.

That's why she wanted Grandpa and Yordan out of the house, why she went straight for the bookshelves. She wanted that book, that specific copy of this book."

Ash was nodding, with her now, holding those pieces together too. "But why?"

"Let's find out."

Bel hurried past the steps, lifted the ceramic toad up by his cold head.

"You should turn the camera on. I think we're about to solve the mystery."

Bel had waited long enough. Only her whole life.

"Are Yordan and your grandpa out?" Ash hovered behind, a beep as he pressed record.

"They're at my house." Bel scrabbled for the key. "With Rachel."

Up the steps, a finality to the sound, echoing in her chest. She unlocked the door and pushed it open.

The wall of heat tried to push her back, drying out her eyes and her ragged throat. Bel fought through, carving a path, the heat folding her in, pulling Ash in after her.

He closed the front door and Bel switched on a light, glancing back, eyeing the camera. No longer recording to catch Rachel. Recording to hold on to the truth, to have the answer be a physical thing that no one could take away from her, like memory had the day Rachel disappeared. An answer Bel must have seen but never held on to. A way back to that tiny girl who was too young to understand, too young to speak.

Bel walked into the living room, the air staler in here, drier. A room that had seen a lot of living, decades and generations of Prices. Ash was right behind her, flicking on the light.

"You ready?" he asked, both staring across the room, at the wooden bookshelf.

Bel finally was.

Her feet followed her eyes. Stopping, standing before the chaotic shelves, books piled sideways and up. So many books, no sense to their order.

Bel's gaze ran backward and forward, up and down, looking for that green spine she knew so well.

Her heart kicked up, a sharp breath in.

There it was. *The Memory Thief* by Audrey Hart. Second shelf down, level with her eyes. Just a few inches from where they'd hidden the camera.

Bel reached for the book.

One finger hooked on to the cover, a shiver passing from the book's spine up her own, creeping and cold. She pulled and the book tilted, breaking ranks. She dragged it out, books sliding and falling to fill the space it left behind.

Bel stared down at it, in her hands, opening the front cover.

She looked at the title page. Then chapter one, the first line of the first page about a man in a made-up world, cursed to never have his own memories, stealing other people's by cutting open their heads.

"Dark shit." Ash read over her shoulder.

Bel flicked through the first chapter, then the next, eyes darting across the double-page spread, so dried out she could almost hear them scratching as they stirred in her head.

She reached page one hundred and started skimming, then flicking, pages fanning a breeze up at her. A snatched look at every single one, right to the acknowledgments.

"Nothing," she said, confusion giving way to despair, emptying her out. "I thought . . ."

"What?"

"I thought there'd be a message in here, or something . . . I don't know." It was too hot in here; her despair caught fire, rolling into rage. She slammed the book shut, slapping both halves together. "This was supposed to be it." Her mouth hung open, breathing out her last hope.

Ash reached with his free hand, tucked her hair behind her ear.

"Let's look again," he said gently. "Slowly. You might have missed something."

Bel inhaled, pulling her last hope back.

She opened the book again, to chapter one, paused there for a long moment. Ash shifted closer, looking with his eyes and then through the camera. Bel didn't just look, she read, the voice in her head speaking the first sentence, dipping and pausing the way Grandpa once had.

"Wait," Ash said, spotting something in the viewfinder as he zoomed in. But Bel couldn't wait, because she'd noticed it too, reading on to the second sentence, something tripping up her eyes.

He had no past, only now and what was to come.

"That *h*." She stroked the tip of her finger to it. "It's thicker than the other letters. Like someone wrote over it." A slightly gray shine as Bel moved it under the light, like it was overlined with pencil, thickening its edges, making them stand out, but only very slightly, not drawing attention to itself.

"Very faint," Ash said. "Very subtle. But yeah, looks like someone went over that. Unless it's a printing error."

"No, see." Bel pointed at the final line of the page.

I don't remember you.

"The *e* in *remember,*" she said, voice tripping over itself as her mind raced ahead, flicking to the next page. She squinted. There were more highlighted letters here too, now she knew to look for them, hiding inside the words, so faint you might not have seen them, not if you didn't know this was a *special book.*

"There *is* a message here!"

Bel moved, clutching the book to her chest, rushing over to the coffee table. She placed the book down, open to that next double page.

"I need a pen and paper." She clicked her fingers, glancing around the room. Something white caught her eye. The sheet of paper on the TV stand, the one with the Wi-Fi password in Dad's oversized handwriting. That would do. Bel grabbed it, turned it over to the clean side.

"Pen, pen, pen," she said, darting around. "Yordan, where would you keep a motherfucking pen?!"

She found one in the kitchen, a pot beside the microwave. Sprinted back, crashing to her knees in front of the open book, Ash hovering over her with the camera, one hand on her shoulder to calm her, to let her know he was here. He was leaving, Ash was always leaving, but he was here now, and that meant something too.

h e

Bel wrote those two letters at the top of the sheet, then turned her eyes back to the book.

This might just be hell.

She added that *l*.

He gulped.

And that *p*.

h e l p

help

Bel looked up at Ash, eyes wide and circling, heart beating so hard she thought he might hear, might catch it too.

"Keep going," he said, finding his voice again.

Bel did. Finding *m y n a* on the other page.

She flicked to the next double page, finger up and down, hunting for the highlighted letters.

m e i s r a c

Turned to the next, the pen trying to keep up with her eyes.

h e l p r i c e

"Help. My name is Rachel Price," Ash read aloud, sorting the jumbled letters into words. Bel's skin flashed cold against all sense, throat constricting, squeezing her out-of-place heart.

A message from Rachel.

And it wasn't finished yet.

Bel turned to chapter two.

He couldn't see over the hill.

i a m b

Turning the pages, mind emptying out, focusing only on the letters. A message from the past, from her mom, one she didn't want Bel to find. Next page and the next, rows of letters building up, nonsensical, shifting under her gaze like they were slipping down the paper. More highlighted letters and more, her eyes attuned to them now.

All the way to page forty-two. There was nothing after that, Bel checked; the book was clean, no more pencil marks. She wrote down that final *e* hidden inside *wept* and then breathed again, blinking until her mind returned to her. Ash's eyes were narrowed, scanning the lines of scattered letters, but Bel had to be the one to read it first.

She picked the pen up again, placing the tip against the page, below the last row, and she began sorting through the letters, splitting and grouping them until they made words, rewriting the full message below.

Help. My name is Rachel Price.

I am being kept by Patrick Price

in a red truck on Price logging yard.

Call police.

FORTY-TWO

The pen dropped from Bel's hand, a ghost line meandering down the page.

"Oh my God," Ash whispered, somewhere above her. Somewhere far above her, because she was falling, following her heart off that cliff edge inside.

It was Grandpa.

Someone did take Rachel, she hadn't lied about that part, but it wasn't a stranger. Grandpa was the man. He took Rachel from the car on that frozen February evening sixteen years ago, leaving Bel behind. Doors closed, heater on, so his only granddaughter wouldn't freeze on the backseat as he disappeared her mom, his daughter-in-law.

A lump lodged in her throat, jagged and bitter.

"It was Grandpa." Her gaze darted over his name in her handwriting, the letters sharpening, growing thorns to prick at her eyes. Patrick Price. Pat. Grandpa. Paw-Paw.

She gasped, but it didn't make it past the lump in her throat. Mr. Tripp had told the police that Bel seemed fine when he'd found her, that she was babbling made-up words, the same nonsense sound over and again. Now Bel wondered; had she been trying to tell him? Those sounds she'd made, had they really been: *Paw-Paw, Paw-Paw*?

"I'm sorry, Bel." Ash ran one hand up her back, against the shiver.

One tear made it out of her dried-out eyes, falling to the page, to Rachel's message, hidden all these years.

" 'Price logging yard,' " Ash read out, a question in the quiet lilt of his voice.

"Grandpa's yard. It went out of business way before I was born."

"Where is it?"

"Here, in Gorham. Fuck." Bel clawed at her face, raking her fingers through her hair. "She was in town. Rachel was being held right here. I know that red truck. There's a huge junk pile of old sawing equipment and cars and trucks. We used to go to the yard sometimes, when it snowed. There's a hill there, good for sledding. Grandpa used to yell at me and Carter when we got too close to the old trucks. Said it wasn't safe, that we had to keep far away from it." Her breath juddered. "Not because it wasn't safe, it's because he was keeping Rachel there. She was right there, so close to us, and I never knew."

Ash pressed his eyes shut, like he didn't know what to say, no words could possibly fit in that awful space, Bel's memories rewriting around it.

"I never knew," Bel said again, a quiet echo, reverberating in her hollowed-out head. She looked at *The Memory Thief,* lying there, splayed open. "I read from this book, this exact copy." It felt like a confession somehow. "Grandpa must have been taking food to Rachel, gave her books to pass the time. This book." She stroked one finger against the edge of its pages. "She had it in the red truck with her and she hid a message inside it. I read this book and I never found it, never saw the marks." Touching the same book, maybe only weeks or months after Rachel had, her small fingers in her mom's invisible handprints. "Rachel must have been so desperate. Hoping someone would find this message. That Grandpa would give the book away, or someone else would read it and rescue her. She waited all those years for it. It could have been me. Should have been me. But I never saw it. I never knew."

Ash still couldn't find the words.

The Memory Thief. A book Rachel had pinned all her hopes on. *A special book.*

Bel tore her eyes away, heading for the bookshelf again. "Rachel was there a long time. Grandpa must have given her more than one book to read."

Maybe there were more *special books*.

Ash followed her with the camera as Bel picked one at random, pulling it off the shelf.

The Hunger Games. Bel flicked to chapter one, hunting through the words. They were here too, the faint pencil marks, picking out the letters. *Help* all on the first page, the *p* in Prim's name. Bel turned to Ash, wide-eyed. "Rachel's message. It's here too."

"Fuck." Ash placed the camera on the coffee table, lens pointed at them to capture it all. He came to stand beside her, shoulder brushing hers, scanning all the books, spines and sideways titles.

He grabbed a paperback from the highest shelf, *The Night Circus*, and flipped it open, eyes glinting as they ran down the pages. *"He-lp. My na-me is Rach . . ."* He broke off, flicking through the next dozen pages. "It's here too. The whole thing."

Bel dropped *The Hunger Games*, grabbed two more books. She checked through them: *Bring Up the Bodies* and *Behind Closed Doors*. The message was in both, all the way to *call police*, ending on page forty-six in one, forty-nine in the other.

She dropped them at her feet, a crash and flutter of pages, and went for two more.

Ash had a pile in his arms now, looking through the one on top. "This one," he said, sliding it off to the floor. "This one." And the next and the next. The mounds growing at their feet, tripping them as they reached for more books.

Gone Girl and *Station Eleven* and *The Vanishing Half* and *The Guest List*. They all had it. *Help. My name is Rachel Price.*

Ash paused on the book in his hands, doubling back, finger on the page. "This one's different. *Help, my name is Rachel Price. We are being kept* instead of *I am being kept*."

"What is it?" Bel stepped over the growing mess of books, heel catching one, bending its spine.

He held it up.

"An old book. *The Green Mile* by Stephen King."

Bel stared down at it, found the two letters. "*We*? You think my grandpa was keeping someone else in there too?"

"I don't know," Ash said. "It's the only one I've found. The rest say *I*."

Bel grabbed more books, searching for the highlighted letters, for any variation. *The Midnight Library*, *A Little Life*, *Six of Crows* and *Game of Thrones*.

"Some of these books are recent." Bel dropped *Malibu Rising* to the growing heap, peaks and valleys of sliding books, the shelves emptying before their eyes.

Ash nodded, holding up a hardcover, eyes dancing around the copyright page. "This was published last year. January 2023, it says."

Bel reached for another book, but she stopped herself, retracting her fingers, losing them up her sleeve. What else was there to know?

"She was there the whole time, wasn't she?" Bel said, missing half her voice, staring around at the mess, the devastation. A row of books fell over by themselves, jumping to their deaths with all the others. The crash brought Bel back. She held out her arm to stop Ash too, resting against his chest.

She looked down at them all, the answers to the mystery, right here the entire time. "I read a lot of these books. These exact copies. No one ever found her message. It should have been me."

Maybe Rachel hoped it would be her own daughter—the Anna she imagined—who'd eventually find the letters, who would be the one to save her. Marking her message in a dozen books. Maybe hundreds. A hundred hopes. A hundred chances. A bookshelf full of them, Grandpa hoarding them here, telling Bel they were special, but never why. Because her mom had read them first.

"I'm sorry," Bel whispered, to the books, to her mom.

"Why is this her favorite?" Ash returned to *The Memory Thief*, picking up his camera.

"Maybe that was the first one." Bel joined him. "It was out here longest. Her biggest hope."

"Fuck," Ash said, softening the hardest word somehow. "This is awful. Poor Rachel."

The truth was awful, but this wasn't all of it. The answer was Grandpa, it was here in Rachel's own words, in Bel's handwriting, but where did Dad fit into this story?

There was only one way forward, the way that hurt more.

Bel decided, knowing bone-deep that the decision had already been made, the moment she'd read her mom's message.

"I have to go there. To the logging yard. The red truck. I have to see it for myself. I need to see what they did to her."

Ash's eyes narrowed. "They?"

"My dad." It hurt just to say it. "Why would she do something to him, if he hadn't done something to her first?"

Phillip's words, now her own.

She turned away, hands empty, out of the living room. She didn't look back: not at the half-empty shelves or the chaos below, the aftermath. Bel didn't need to see any more.

Ash followed her with the camera, out the front door.

Outside was a different world, a silver glow around her fingers, a cool breeze up her spine, another shiver.

Bel threw the key toward the ceramic toad, no time to go back and hide it under. Her heart and her head were on the same side, telling her she needed to go, that she was so close now.

She glanced down at her bike, discarded on the grass.

"I can drive," Ash offered, reading her eyes in the dark.

He started the engine, beams too bright, lighting up Grandpa's house, glaring off the glass like an accusation.

"There's two ways," Bel said. "The yard's on the other side of the river. Quickest from here is the bridge at the mountain trailhead. We'll have to ditch the car and go the rest on foot." The bridge you could drive over was all the way on the other side of town. Neither way hurt less, but one would be faster, and Bel's heart didn't have time for the other, a violent ache in the base of her throat. "Turn right."

Ash pulled out onto Main Street.

Bel gripped the camera, watching the road in the viewfinder as

Ash sped down it. They passed under a flickering streetlight, where the town thinned out, trees taking over. A rush of blood in her ears or maybe it was the Androscoggin River, racing them to the right.

"It's coming up."

The old railway bridge that flew over the road, across the river too, now used only by snowmobiles.

"Slow down."

They passed under the hulking green metal bridge, standing on double concrete legs, making the darkness darker still for half a breath.

"Pull off here."

Ash followed her voice, peeling right into the small gravel lot by the base of the bridge. The car rolled to a stop, Ash parking right in front of the mountain trail sign.

Bel passed him the camera and jumped out, the rush in her ears becoming a roar, a sound inside her own head or was it the river right there?

The headlights switched off and Bel waited for Ash in the pitch black, the moon too weak to reach her. She pulled out her phone for the flashlight, a ghostly white glow on her feet. There were no lights here, and there would be no more the rest of the way to Price & Sons Logging Yard.

Ash scrambled out of the car, fiddling with the camera's screen. "It has night vision mode. Hold on. There we go. I can see now," he said, using the viewfinder as his eyes in the dark.

Bel lit her way up the base of the ramp, her steps hollow and metallic as she followed it around, where the pedestrian walkway had been added, a lower level to the bridge, closer to the churn of water below.

"OK?" she checked with Ash, stepping out over the river.

The metal clunk of their feet on the bridge, out of time as they hurried along, re-creating the beat in Bel's chest. She flicked the light up from her feet, the trestle frame of the bridge caging them in, catching them.

"Fuck." Ash stumbled behind her. Bel turned and he stumbled again, another "Fuck."

340

"What?" she hissed.

"Just, you look scary in the night vision. Your eyes are glowing green."

They reached the other end, Bel's feet speeding up as the metal ramp tilted her down to the ground. The river was behind them now, on the other side, the wilder side, trees growing up around them. Bel raised her phone, branches and leaves dancing in the wind, throwing nightmare shadows along the path.

"How long from here?" Ash asked, sticking close to her.

"Ten minutes, if we walk fast. The yard is near the base of Deer Mountain. We follow the river for now."

Bel kept the light on her feet, watching every step, the only thing keeping the darkness from swallowing them whole. "This goes to an old power station, over the reservoir."

"Are there bears?" he said, turning his camera toward the thick covering of trees.

"Ash. It's New Hampshire."

"Fantastic."

They crossed the small concrete bridge over the reservoir, another rush of dark water they couldn't see.

"This way now."

The road curved left, taking them away from the river, around the hulking shape of the mountain. The path was uneven, an old logging road, churned up by heavy wheels.

Ash tripped and Bel offered her hand, keeping her glowing eyes to herself.

"We're here," she said eventually, lighting up the high metal fence that surrounded the yard, a huge clearing in the trees, cut into the forest. The rusty printed sign, telling them: *Trespassers Keep Out.* Had that always been there, or did Grandpa only add it when he had something inside to hide?

They trudged alongside the fence to the huge gates at the front, a larger sign here, old painted letters, peeling away with time. *Price & Sons Logging Yard.*

Looking through his viewfinder, Ash approached the gates, reached out for the large padlock, a thick chain around the middle railings, sealing them shut. He let the padlock swing back with a clang, echoing in the trees.

"How do we get in?"

"There's a gap in the fence this way," Bel said, guiding him with her flashlight.

They walked beyond the gate, to where the chain-link fence was broken, the bottom corner rolling away from its post.

Bel hauled it up and ducked her head under, holding it for Ash.

"Used to get our sleds in this way," she said, making sure he was through.

Another line crossed, a different world inside the fence than the one outside. This was where it happened, the place her mom had disappeared to for all that time.

Ash followed her, the yard now covered in patches of grass, high and untamed. It was flat until it wasn't, sloping up toward the tree line. She and Carter would race up, dragging their sled behind, jumping on together, speeding down the fresh snow toward the fence and the river. Had Rachel been able to hear their screams? They hadn't heard hers.

"Come on," Bel said, not lighting her feet anymore, but the way ahead, toward the junk pile at the other end. It was about here, right here, this invisible line, when Grandpa would yell, "That's far enough, dangerous over there. Those saws could cut you. Those trucks could fall on you. Come back this way, Bel."

Bel didn't go back that way. She pushed forward, waiting for the hulking dark shapes of the rusted cars, looking up for that frame used for hauling logs, tall as a giraffe, that she and Carter named Larry, from a distance, from behind that invisible line.

Bel's foot nudged something. The light followed her eyes down. It was an old, rusted saw blade, grass growing through the middle hole, teeth in a perfect circle.

"We'll have to find our way through," she said to Ash. "The red truck is in the middle of it all."

Bel pushed on, stopping when she hit a barrier. Two cars, glass and tires gone, just the bones, pressed up nose to nose. She clambered over their hoods, the light disappearing against the metal. Stood on top and helped Ash over.

More obstacles, unseen things catching their clothes in the dark, holding on. A machine Bel didn't understand, interconnecting wheels and gears. Too big to climb over so they went around.

Part of a sawmill; a huge, round blade, growing out of the earth.

"Watch out," Ash warned her.

Bel was lost, in this dark labyrinth of broken, rusted things. Blades, and saws, and axes and metal skeletons that used to be machines.

"Can you see it?" she asked him, checking back.

Ash looked down at the viewfinder, panning the camera around.

"Not sure," he said, voice ragged and tired. "I can see a truck that way, I don't know if it's red. Night vision doesn't show colors."

Bel held up the flashlight, the way he pointed the camera. She squinted, eyes following the beam.

The red truck was right there, thirty feet away, just a pile of tires between here and there, separating them.

A semitrailer with an old shipping container still attached to the bed of the abandoned truck. The head of the truck and its container both red, dull and rusty. But it stood out against the cold grays and browns of everything else Bel's light found, the heart at the center of the metal beast.

Ash gasped; he'd seen it too.

The end of their journey.

Bel walked toward it, stepping in and around the tires.

Ash lagged behind. She turned, a question in her green, glowing eyes.

"N-not sure I should be filming this," Ash stuttered. "It's a crime scene. Doesn't feel right, to show the place where Rachel . . ." He trailed off.

"Wouldn't Ramsey want you to? For the film?"

Ash shook his head, eyes shrinking as Bel lit up his face. He stopped recording, a beep that echoed through the metal maze. He tucked the camera under his arm, pulling out his phone instead, flicking on the flashlight. Two lights better than one. "Some things are more important than the film." He squeezed her hand. "Ramsey would say the same."

"Ash—" Bel began, but the words died before she breathed life to them, her ears pricking to a new sound, carried by the wind.

A shout, muffled and faint.

And again.

Bel followed the sound with her eyes, over to the red truck.

"There's someone in there." Ash's mouth dropped open.

Another shout, dampened inside the metal container, almost in the shape of words.

"Is somebody out there?!"

Bel's heart doubled, kicking up into her throat.

"Fuck," she said, retaking Ash's hand.

Another low shout, one that sounded like, "Help!"

"What do we do?" Ash asked, low and urgent.

Bel knew, didn't need to say it. She had to keep going. The red truck had the answers she'd waited her whole life for.

She dropped Ash's hand, wading through the tires, eyes up on the shipping container, the four metal bars and handles that sealed the doors shut.

A tire flat on its side, two piled up behind it, leading like stairs to the back of the container.

Bel stepped up the first tire, up again, planting her feet against the thick rubber, resting her fingers on the cold metal.

Another shout, louder now that she was right outside, touching it.

She glanced back at Ash.

He was just a pinprick of light, floating somewhere below.

"Somebody help!" from inside.

Bel took a breath, sucking in the darkness, filled herself with it.

She reached for the first lock, hand tightening around the metal lever, stinging her skin. She pulled it to the left and it screeched, blocking out the shouts inside as it unclipped from the door.

She grabbed the other handle, flipping it, the bar releasing, unsealing the left door. It creaked, a crack of different darkness beyond.

Bel held on to the handle, pulling the door toward her, swinging it open.

She knew before she opened the door, before she waved the flashlight inside, before she saw him slumped against the far wall of the container.

He held his hands out to block the light, covering his face.

"Who is it?" he shouted, voice rough and raw.

"It's me," Bel said, hiding behind her ball of light.

"Rachel?"

"It's me, Dad."

He lowered his hands, eyes wide and haunted, staring blindly at the dark shape of her.

"Bel."

FORTY-THREE

The light danced around the inside of the container, bringing it to life in flashes and shadows, moving as Bel did, stepping up into it.

The walls and ceiling were lined with some kind of insulation, panels of corrugated foam. The floor too, underneath rugs and blankets.

There was a mattress in the far corner, pillows and more blankets. A camping toilet the other side, with a removable tank. An electric fan, cable wound around its base. A lamp too, unplugged. Piles of ragged clothes and old towels. Giant vats of bottled water, some empty. A chaotic orbit of food; packets and cans and boxes. A lonely fork lying across an opened can of sweet corn. Toiletries, wet wipes, a box of batteries.

And Dad sitting against the far wall, between the toilet and the bed. There was a metal cuff around one of his ankles, a chain that snaked around him, disappearing through a small hole in the container wall, attached outside somewhere.

"Bel." He stood up, chain hissing as he did, unraveling, following him. He only got two-thirds of the way to her before it pulled tight, stopping him.

A dark shape in his hand. He clicked it on. A flashlight, much brighter than hers. He rested it against a box of crackers, pointed at the ceiling, lighting up the room.

"It *is* you," Dad said, voice steadier now, a shadow of dark stubble on his face that the light couldn't touch. "Thank God it's you, Bel. Not her." Another shadow crossed his eyes. "Thought I heard voices. Talking. Is someone with you?"

"It's Ash." She looked back for him. He was peering inside, a slow blink, like this all might disappear if he didn't look too long.

"Who?"

"Ash, from the film crew," Bel said, louder, finding her voice.

Dad's face shifted, a strange and unfamiliar look, lit from below. "Send him away, Bel. He needs to leave, now."

Bel glanced between the two of them, pinned in the middle.

"You need to leave," Dad barked at Ash instead. "Go away, you hear? And do not call the police. No police. This is family business."

Ash looked at Bel. "I don't think I should leave you."

"Go!" Dad pointed with a ragged finger, his wedding band missing from that hand.

"Wait." Bel held up her own finger. "Ash, come with me."

She stepped out of the container, down the steps made of old tires, Ash at her side.

"Bel," he whispered. "What the fuck? I'm not leaving y—"

"I can do this on my own." She took his hand. "He's my dad. They're my parents. My family. I need the truth, all of it."

Bel couldn't hide behind the film crew forever.

"I can't leave you alone with him, wha—"

"I've been alone with him my whole life. Me and Dad, just the two of us. He's lied to me, Ash. I have to know what he did, what part he played. He owes me the truth, no one else. He won't talk with you here, but maybe he's finally ready to talk to me."

Ash glanced up at the container, glowing in the middle of the metal maze. "Are you sure?"

"Family first, huh," she said. The trouble was knowing who deserved to be family at the end of it all. "I'll be OK. I need to do this. Can you find your way back to the car?"

He slid his fingers between hers. "I'm not worried about me."

"Don't call the police, Ash," Bel said, not because Dad had told them. She needed the truth first, before she decided what to do with it. Her family. Her parents. Her decision. "Go back to the hotel. I'll call you when it's done. OK?"

Ash didn't answer. He pulled her into him, arms tight, the camera trapped between them. She rested her head against his chest, listening to the tick of his heart. "Be safe," he whispered, lips grazing her ear.

"I will." Dad was chained up; he couldn't do anything to her. Then another thought, overlapping that one: Dad wouldn't ever do anything to her anyway, right?

Ash's fingers trailed down her arm as he turned away, raising his phone, lighting up the hulking shapes of saws and rusted-out cars, picking his way through.

Bel watched him disappear, the maze swallowing him.

She inhaled the darkness. She was ready, counting herself down as she climbed up.

Inside the container, across from her dad.

"He's gone."

"No police?" Dad said, the question urgent enough to reach his eyes.

"He won't call the police."

"Good." He shifted, the chain singing as he did. "God am I glad to see you, kiddo. Don't know how you found me, but you've got to get me out of here."

"Dad—" Bel began, but he cut her off.

"She's crazy. Rachel," he said, spitting the name, eyes wide with panic. "She locked me in here for no reason. Told me in the middle of the night she had something to show me. Brought me here, into the truck. Before I knew what was happening, she locked this cuff around my ankle. How long has it been, kiddo? She's brought food and water a couple times, but won't tell me why she did this, said that giving me any answers would be a *kindness*. You've got to help me. Rachel has the key to this." He gestured at his ankle, raw where the metal hugged the skin. "Maybe you can find a handsaw in the junk. Help me, kiddo."

Bel didn't move. "Rachel did this?" she said, using ignorance as a mask. She knew a lot more than Dad expected her to.

"Yes," he said, voice pleading. "Rachel's crazy. Something must have happened to her while she was gone, made her lose her mind. She locked me in here for no reason."

"Why would she do that to you, lock you in here, if you didn't do something to her first?"

Dad's eyes snapped open. "What are you talking about, kiddo? I've never done anything to her. It doesn't make sense."

Bel chewed her lip. "Hm, you know what else doesn't make sense?"

Dad stared at her.

"If Rachel is crazy, if she locked you up in here for no reason, why don't you want me to call the police?"

He took a step back, eyes spinning. "Because," he held on to the word, giving himself more time. "Because you know how the police in Gorham are. Dave Winter would probably find some way of making this my fault. Arrest me again."

"Maybe he should."

"What are you talking about, kiddo?" he said, that last word sharp enough to cut her. "Come on, you need to look for a way to get me out of this cuff. Force it open, cut the chain. Go look for something. Now!"

"No," Bel said, wincing at the look on his face. She'd never said *no* to him like that before, she always relented, anything to keep him happy, to keep him from leaving because everyone left, eventually. Except maybe that was never true to begin with. "No, Dad. I'm sorry, but I need to know why Rachel put you in here."

His mouth gaped, open and shut, shifting the shadows on the ceiling. "I don't know, kiddo. That's the honest truth. She must have lost her mind when she was gone, because this—"

"She wasn't gone, Dad. Rachel was never gone. She was right here, in this red truck, in this container. Chained by the ankle. This is where she was all those years. Right here."

Dad looked around like he was seeing it all for the first time. Bel couldn't trust his eyes, not anymore.

"And I know who put her here." Bel hardened her gaze.

Dad shook his head, the chain rattling behind. "Why are you looking at me like that? It wasn't me. I had nothing to do with this."

He lied too easily, rolling off the tongue. Maybe because he'd been practicing all her life.

"It was Grandpa." Bel studied him, for any twitch of the truth. "Grandpa is the one who took Rachel. He kept her here, on his yard, in this container. Brought her food and water. Brought her books to read to pass the years. All that time she was right here." She breathed out some of that darkness. "You knew."

"No!" His voice cracked, eyes pulling wider, new folds in his skin. "I didn't know. I swear to you, kiddo. You have to believe me."

"I always believed you," Bel said, hers trying to crack too. She built a new wall over it. "You were innocent. You were the only person who really cared about me, who would never leave. I did believe you. I defended you, told everyone they were wrong about you. Because you had an alibi, you couldn't have had anything to do with Rachel's disappearance, right?"

"Yes, that's right. Please. You have to get me out of here."

"And it was almost a good alibi, wasn't it?" Bel kept going, ignoring the plea in his eyes. "Almost worked. You cut your hand at work at exactly two o'clock. Because that's the time you'd agreed with Grandpa, when he would abduct Rachel. A bad cut, needed stitches. Meaning you'd be at the hospital, on the security cameras there, a solid alibi for the next few hours so they could never suspect you."

Dad was shaking his head, blinking.

"Only Grandpa didn't take her at two o'clock, did he? He was late, because Rachel went to the mall in Berlin. Grandpa couldn't intercept until Rachel got to that road where me and the car were found. He didn't take her until six o'clock, right at the tail end of your good alibi. So it wasn't so good anymore, was it? Left just enough time, a few spare minutes, for there to be some doubt, and the police jumped on it." Bel's hand dropped to her side, trigger-finger ready. "You never planned to be arrested, but you were because Grandpa was late."

"Bel, listen to me."

"No, you listen! Someone overheard you, Dad. Talking to Grandpa."

A twitch by his mouth, too late for him to hide it. He wanted to ask who, but he couldn't do that, and they both knew it.

"You planned it all with Grandpa. Rachel's disappearance. You knew she was here!"

"No!" he shouted, hands trembling as he held them up. "I didn't. I didn't know she was here!"

His eyes widened, slipping off her face, mouth dropping open. Couldn't even look at her as he lied.

"Yes you—"

"He didn't," a voice said behind Bel, a voice so familiar it almost sounded like her own.

FORTY-FOUR

Bel blinked and Rachel appeared from the darkness behind, up into the container. Not looking at Charlie, eyes only for Bel. Hand twitching at her side like she wanted to reach for her.

"He didn't," she said again. "Actually telling the truth for once."

Bel angled her shoulders, not facing her dad or her mom, halfway between.

"How did you know I was here?" she asked.

"Waited twenty minutes and you didn't come home," Rachel answered. "I drove over to your grandpa's to look for you, saw the books all over the floor. I saw you found my message. I knew you'd come here, to the red truck. I'm sorry." She dropped her eyes, only for a second. "I didn't want you to find out like that. Find out at all. This is your family, the people that raised you. I saw how much you loved them, and as much as that hurt me, I didn't want to hurt you. I never wanted you to know."

It was too late for that.

"What do you mean he's telling the truth?" Bel glanced back at Charlie. "He didn't know you were here?"

Rachel didn't look at him, spoke about him, spoke around him. "That's true. He didn't know I was here the whole time, in this truck. He didn't know. Because he thought I was dead."

Now she looked at him, eyes full of fire. The chains rattled as Charlie stepped back, but Rachel wasn't done.

"He thought I was dead, because that's what he told Pat to do. That was the plan. You had the rest of it right, Bel. But your grandpa wasn't supposed to just take me at two o'clock that day. He was supposed to kill me."

Dad made a sound in his throat, low and guttural.

"Surprised, Charlie?" Rachel threw the words at him, deadly, like her eyes. "Must have been a big surprise when you found me in your kitchen three weeks ago, after being sure I was dead for sixteen years, huh? Everyone else assumed I was dead, but you were the only one who was sure." She sniffed, a laugh buried there somewhere, deep below. "The look on your face. I thought you'd have a heart attack. Kinda hoped you would."

"I don't know what you're talking about," Charlie croaked.

"Oh, that's OK." Rachel clicked her tongue. "Because I *do* know everything, more than you, in fact. Pat told me everything. Explained it all, so I'd see that it wasn't his fault. That, really, by keeping me here, he was *saving me*. He was so desperate to believe that, your dad. So desperate for me to believe it too. That by not killing me, by keeping me here instead, he'd saved me from you."

"You told Grandpa to kill her?" Bel turned to her dad, almost didn't recognize him. "Why?" There were too many *why*s. "Why would Grandpa agree to that?"

Rachel looked between the two of them, eyes hardening one way, glittering the other. "You going to tell her, Charlie?"

Dad darted forward, a crash as he reached the end of his chain. He winced, clutching his chest. "None of this is true, Bel. She's manipulating you!"

"Right, I'll tell her, then."

"Stop talking, Rachel!" he screamed, face reddening, a shadow monster writhing on the ceiling above him. "Don't listen to her, Bel!"

Bel flicked between her parents, left and right, Mom and Dad.

"She wants the truth, Charlie. She deserves it. And you're never going to give it to her." Rachel turned to Bel, eyes soft, teeth away. "Your grandpa agreed to the plan—at least, as far as your dad knew— because Charlie blackmailed him."

"With what?" Bel asked.

"Another Price secret. What a family, huh?" Rachel said, mouth in a grim line. "When your dad was a teenager, one night, he heard his parents arguing. The night his mom died. He got out of bed just in time to see Pat shove his mom. Maria fell down the stairs, a broken neck, catastrophic head injuries. The coroner reported it as an accident, that she tripped and fell because it was dark. That's the story Pat told them. But Charlie knew it wasn't an accident, that she was pushed, his dad killed his mom, whether he meant to or not. He never told anyone, not Pat, not Jeff. Kept it to himself for years, decades, until he saw an opportunity to use it. You probably thought wife-killing ran in the family, huh, Charlie?" she spat in his direction. Back to Bel. "Charlie told Pat that if he didn't agree to kill me, he would go to the police and tell them what he saw that night. That he'd take it all the way, testify against his dad. That he could make Jeff believe he'd seen it too, and how was your grandpa going to say both of them were lying? That's why Pat agreed to it. Cowards, all of them."

Dad's eyes narrowed on the back of Rachel's head, taking aim.

"Pat told me," Rachel said, unaware, "that if he didn't agree to the plan, didn't take me, he was scared Charlie would eventually kill me himself, so he was *saving* me from that. But Charlie had to believe I was dead. And he did." The chain clattered as Dad started pacing. "Charlie thanked him after, can you believe that? Said he didn't want to know any of the details, how he'd done it, where my body was, just that it was done. He wanted plausible deniability. Pat always said that if Charlie ever showed remorse, if he regretted it, Pat would reveal what he'd really done, that I was still alive. That they'd find a way to bring me back home. Charlie never mentioned it to him once. He thought he'd had me killed and he never had any doubts about what they did, never regretted it."

Dad burst into laughter, hitching and hollow.

"What are you doing, Rachel? Bel is never going to believe you. She doesn't even know you! Bel! Look at me, kiddo!"

She did, but only for a second, his eyes red and wild, stalactites of spit hanging from his teeth. She turned back to Rachel, her face wounded but quiet.

"Why would he want to kill you?" Bel asked, looking at both of her parents, head spinning, because she couldn't see both at the same time.

Rachel sighed. "I'd known for a while that Charlie was going to kill me. It wasn't just when Pat took me. I knew for weeks, months."

"Why?"

"You know your dad," she said, not unkindly, "maybe better than I do. You know how it works. How everything orbits around him, how he's always right. Controls everyone in the family, even if they don't know it. You noticed how everyone says sorry to him, but he never says it back, because he's never wrong. He thought he could control me too. I was too young when I married him, naïve, and he was so much older, so he had to be right about everything. But . . . being your mom changed me, and I started to see how he really was. I think he saw me pulling away from him, so he tried to pull me back. For months, he tried to make me think I'd lost my mind, so I'd need him, so I'd never leave." Rachel pressed her eyes together. "*Oh, Rachel, you left the front door open. Rachel, sweetie, you left the oven on, house could have burned down.* None of it ever happened. I knew that, but he was good at it, I started to doubt myself." She threw a look at him, bitter and cold. "You made a mistake, though, Charlie, a big one. That last Christmas. *Rachel, you left Annabel in the bathtub alone, she could have drowned.* Him holding you, you screaming. That's when I knew. I'd never forget about you, you were my world. I knew he was dangerous, that I had to leave him. I think Charlie could tell he'd lost, that I was going to leave, and he couldn't live with that, oh no. That's why he wanted to kill me. The final way to control me."

"Oh, come on!" Dad strained against his chain, stamping his free foot, the container shuddering. "Do you hear yourself, Rachel? You need help, honestly. These fantasies in your head. Bel doesn't believe any of this! I raised her smarter than that!"

He had raised her, and she was smart, but he was wrong. She believed Rachel, because Bel never left the front door open, or the trash unsealed, she never smashed that fucking mug, and Dad left her in a Taco Bell parking lot for hours, not minutes. But she was smart enough to see something else too, all the things Rachel left out.

"But you *were* leaving, weren't you?" Bel said. "You borrowed three thousand dollars from Julian Tripp two days before you went missing. You were going to use it to leave us, to run away."

Rachel nodded, a sad smile dragging down the corners of her mouth. "You're right, Bel. And you are smart, not because of *him*. Your dad had taken my bank cards off me by that point. For my own good, he said, because I maxed out a credit card and forgot I'd done it. It was a lie. But I didn't have access to my money, and I needed some if I was going to leave. I knew he was going to kill me. It wasn't a question of *if*, it was how long I had left. I didn't think I had enough time to see this credit card thing play out, especially when he then pretended my car was broken, to isolate me more. I couldn't wait. Julian was my only friend; work was the one place I was free from Charlie. I knew if I asked Julian, after school, he'd give me the money. And he did, just a couple days later. Three thousand dollars. It was enough. Then Charlie *fixed* my car for me, and I knew I had to leave, that day, before it was too late. That exact day. Wednesday, February thirteenth. You're right, Bel. I was running away. And I was taking you with me."

Bel breathed out the rest of the darkness, a shudder up her spine, but it wasn't a shiver, it was warm. There they were. The words she'd waited her whole life to hear, never knew it until this moment. Her mom didn't leave her behind, didn't choose to abandon her. Bel had always been a part of the plan; they were supposed to leave together.

A tear broke free, clinging to her lashes.

Rachel reached out, stroked her thumb along Bel's wrist, the warm shiver there too.

"I'd been planning for weeks, Bel. The entire thing. And now I had the money, it was time to go through with it. That's what happened in the mall, why I disappeared twice that day. The first time was planned. It's true, what I told you, how we disappeared in the mall. The recycling bin behind that *Staff Only* door. But it wasn't a coincidence, and it wasn't because I thought a stalker was watching us. I'd been visiting the mall for weeks, working it all out, tracking the cameras, finding a blind spot by that door. What time those bins were taken out the side door every day, where they took them, how long until the recycling was collected, if there were cameras there. I knew if we could get through that door, into one of those bins, and be wheeled out, park the car a few streets over, no one would ever know. The *Staff Only* door wasn't left unlocked; I swiped a key from someone two weeks before. I was ready, Bel. And it worked. We disappeared inside that mall, no trace of us leaving. You were so good inside that bin, like you knew it was important that we weren't caught. I wanted people to think we'd disappeared close to home, an impossible mystery to keep them occupied, so they'd never look for us anywhere else, so Charlie would have no idea where we went."

Rachel paused for breath, eyes darkening with the story.

"I didn't know . . . it was the same day Charlie and Pat agreed to carry out their plan too. Charlie was going to cut his hand around two o'clock, to begin his alibi. That's when Pat was supposed to get me, at home. Pat arrived just in time to see us leaving, heading for the mall, so he followed us to Berlin. Parked near our car, waited for us to get back. We were gone for hours, Bel, hiding in that bin, waiting to be wheeled out. But Pat couldn't call Charlie to tell him something had gone wrong with the timing. Charlie's alibi had to be perfect; no link between them, no phone calls. So Pat waited. Followed us when we finally got back to the car. He thought we were heading home, but we were on our way to disappear for good, to find a new home. That's why I drove the back roads, so no cameras would pick up our plates. I didn't know Pat was behind us the whole way. We were on that quiet road and he saw his opportunity, sped up to overtake us, braking in front. I had to swerve off the road to avoid hitting him. You were OK, Bel. Always such a brave girl. I got out of the car to scream at this other driver. Then I realized it was Pat. I asked what the hell he was doing, he could have killed us. He said he had to show me something, it was an emergency. I knew our plan was already ruined, because Pat had seen us *after* we disappeared. I was distracted, thinking about what the hell to do, so I didn't see the cuffs in his hand. He opened his trunk. Grabbed my wrists, shoved me inside, closed the door. I screamed for him to let me out, kicking against the latch, but then there was this awful moment, when I realized I'd left you with the door open. It was freezing out. I stopped screaming for me and I started screaming for you, telling Pat I didn't care what he did to me but he had to go back and close the door to make sure you were OK. He did, he checked that the heater was on, and he shut the door. He says you saw him, Bel, you called out to him. He gave you a juice box and left you there in the backseat. He wanted me to know he'd never hurt his granddaughter, promised to take care of you while I couldn't. Then he brought me here." She opened her hands, gesturing at the makeshift prison cell.

Bel took it all in again, the grooved foam along the ceiling, to the chain around Dad's ankle that disappeared outside. This small, dark room; her mom's home for all that time. She tried to imagine it as Rachel saw it that first day, the edges growing sharper, shadows deeper, walls closing in. How had she survived all that?

Rachel seemed to read her mind, knowing the look in her eyes, as Bel now knew hers.

"Pat had about a week to put this all together, after Charlie asked him to kill me. Insulated it." She pointed at the foam. "For the temperature, but I always thought it was so no one could hear me scream. No one ever did." She sniffed. "I was cuffed around the ankle. Holes for ventilation, in the walls and ceiling. He put a generator out back, ran a cable through the hole in the wall there. So I had an electric heater in winter, a fan for summer. God, summer was awful in here, so hot I could hardly move. Had a lamp I could use those months when the generator was on, so I wasn't living in darkness. Other times I had flashlights, enough batteries to keep one on the entire time. He came twice a week, with food and water, any other supplies I asked for. Sat with me for a while with the door open; I always thought it was my chance to convince him to let me go. I think I got close, a couple times. But he said it could only happen if Charlie ever came to him, sorry for what they'd done. Otherwise, he said letting me go would be the same as letting me die, that Charlie would kill me himself. He would bring me a new book, every couple of weeks." Rachel found Bel's eyes again, anchoring her to here and now, where she wasn't the one chained up. "But you know that already, found them all. I thought Pat would take them to a secondhand bookstore, or give them to you. Didn't think he'd keep them all this time. He was never much of a reader."

"He used to read to me," Bel spoke around the lump in her throat. "Those same books, after you'd read them."

Rachel's eyes glittered again.

"I asked him to do that. Thought when you got old enough, maybe you'd see the marks, find the message."

"I'm sorry." Bel's eyes dropped to the floor, the guilt too heavy, dragging them down.

"It's not your fault, Bel." Rachel ran her hand down Bel's arm, up the other, until her eyes returned. "You didn't know. I had to make it so faint, barely visible. Honestly, I'm not surprised no one ever found them. There was no other way. Pat had given me a pencil and a notebook, for writing down supplies I needed. Then when he brought me the first book, I just wrote the message out, big letters above chapter one. But Pat flipped through it, found the message right away. He told me he'd burned the book, that he couldn't bring me any more if I tried that again. So I had to be smarter about it, hide a message that Pat couldn't find, because I knew he'd be checking, each time I gave a book back. *The Memory Thief,* that was the second book he ever brought me, the first one I hid that message in. Why it's my favorite. I used to tell him it was a special book, never told him why. Even though it didn't work, it gave me something to live for, it gave me hope."

Bel felt her eyes glaze too, glittering in the same way as Rachel's, un-cried tears for all those missed chances, years of being so close and never knowing.

"So you and me were running away. That's why the three thousand dollars, why we disappeared inside the mall. But then Grandpa intercepted us, took you. That's why you disappeared twice; one was planned, one wasn't."

Rachel nodded.

"But what was the rest of your plan?" Bel asked. The chain rattled, making her jump, and she'd almost forgotten Dad was here, watching them. "Where were we going after the mall?"

Bel had to know what life Rachel had planned for them, what the other way would have been. She'd lived one already, the tiny girl left abandoned in the backseat, her life a mystery for others to gawk at, terrified of ever being left again, knowing it was inevitable. Bel needed to know the other way, the other life she could have had, what Dad and Grandpa took from her.

"A few weeks before that day," Rachel said, "before Charlie cut me off from my money, I'd bought another car. This cheap thing, unregistered, from a couple who just wanted cash. I'd parked it in Randolph, a street with just vacation homes, no one around to report it. We were going to swap cars, sink my old one in Lake Durand. From there, drive to Vermont, a town called Barton."

"Where Robert Meyer lives," Bel said, filling in the gap, knowing where the rest of this was going, because she'd lived a version of it the last two weeks.

"Jeff's friend Bob." Rachel nodded. "He used to drop him into conversation whenever he could. Told me once that Bob sold fake identities from the dark web, that it wasn't as expensive as I thought either. Jeff didn't know how much that stuck with me, how much I'd need it later. I got Bob's number and address from Jeff's phone in that final week. Wrote them down on a piece of paper, actually, because I was going to leave my phone behind in the car at the bottom of a lake. That paper is one of the only things I had in my pocket when Pat took me. That and Julian's three thousand dollars. Pat never found the money, I hid it. But that bit of paper, I looked at it so many times, how close we'd been to our new life. I memorized it all, the phone number, address. Used to recite it sometimes, test myself. We were going to turn up at Bob's house that night, and buy a full new identity for you and me, Bel. We had the money, and enough left to help us start over. From there we'd go to a private airfield, near the border. Convince someone flying a small aircraft to take us into Canada. We would have had our new passports, for the flight plan, for the authorities, and no one would have known it was really us. From there, with our new names, we would make our way to this tiny town, called Dalhousie, in New Brunswick. Only a few thousand people, not a lot of tourists. I looked it up on the computers at school, so there'd be no trace to me. Charlie would never have found us, no one would. That was going to be our new home. We could have disappeared there. We could have been happy there. A family."

Bel blinked. They could have been happy there, a way that would have hurt less than the one she'd lived. Rachel had only forgotten one thing: she didn't just have the paper with Bob's number and the three thousand dollars when Grandpa kidnapped her, she must have had Bel's sock too. The little pink frilly one that she'd brought back when she came back from the dead.

"That's how you knew how to set everything up," Bel said. "Make it look like Dad left the country, ran away with a new identity. Because it was meant to be our plan."

"It was meant to be our plan," Rachel repeated.

"Wait," Charlie spluttered, pulling against his chain, waving for Bel's attention. "What do you mean it looks like I ran away?"

Bel set her jaw. "You ran away, bought a new identity from Robert Meyer, ditched your old passport and phone in a private airfield in Vermont and boarded a small aircraft to Canada with a new name. That's where the police think you are now, they aren't looking for you anymore."

Bel watched the change in his face, the shift in his eyes, the panic he couldn't hide from her or Rachel.

"No one's looking for me?" he said, voice desperate and raw, on the way to a shout.

"I looked for you," Bel said, but Dad must have not heard her.

"No one's looking for me?!" He was shouting now, a flush of angry red creeping up his neck, reaching his eyes. "They think I ran away?!"

"Well, you did run away." Rachel stepped in front of Bel, her body a barricade between them.

"Liar!" he screamed, tilting forward, swiping his arms. He couldn't reach her, chain straining behind him. "Bel knows I would never—"

"You left in the middle of the night, Charlie. Packed a bag and took your passport; I didn't even have to do those things for you."

"Lying bitch!"

Rachel bared her teeth at him, a cruel smile. "I thought it would make you squirm, me coming back from the dead. I hoped it would. Me, alive, telling the world it was a stranger who took me. You couldn't even ask your dad about it, the only other person who knew the truth, because he can no longer remember any of it. I bet you tried, didn't you? Wondering how much I knew, what I was going to do about it. But come on, you only lasted a week. Then you set off in the middle of the night, running away before the consequences could catch up to you. I knew it was a possibility," she said to Bel. "I wasn't sleeping at night, in case he tried it. I set off a couple minutes after he did, caught him before he even got to Main Street. Told him it was time I told him the truth, what really happened to me, but I couldn't say it, I had to show him. Drove us here, led him to the truck. Pretended I only knew it was Pat who took me, working alone, that Charlie must not have known what his father was truly capable of. I saw the glint in his eye, I know how his mind works; he was figuring out a way to save himself, to pin the whole thing on his own dad without a second thought. I showed him where the generator plugged in and while he wasn't looking, I slipped the cuff around his ankle, locked it. The look on his face, when he knew that I knew."

"Liar!" Charlie screeched, a line of spit trailing down his chin.

"Bel knows I wouldn't leave. You're crazy, Rachel! Bel doesn't believe any of this!"

She didn't want to, her gut struggling against it, but she had to believe it. Dad had left her, and it wasn't just his word against Rachel's, one parent against the other, because Phillip Alves had seen it too.

"Bel," Dad said, staring through Rachel at her. "Look at me, kiddo. Don't listen to her, she's crazy. You have to trust me. What proof do you have that anything she's saying is true?"

Bel's heart betrayed her, reacting to his voice, forcing itself against her ribs, trying to get to him. Her eyes flicked between him and Rachel. "The money, Dad. I knew about the three thousand dollars from Mr. Tripp. I found the books at Grandpa's house, the message she left. It's what led me here. And Phillip Alves; he saw you leaving that night."

"You don't think she could have set those things up?" His eyes softened. "She's manipulating you, kiddo. She's unwell. We need to get her help, you and me, OK? But you need to get me out of here, now."

"Charlie—" Rachel began.

"I'm not talking to you, I'm talking to my daughter!"

"Our daughter," Rachel said, something new in her eyes, hard and unmovable, staring him down.

"Rachel has the key to the cuff, Bel. You need to get me out of here. I've been in this hellhole for two weeks, Bel, please help me."

"Two weeks." Rachel forced out a laugh. "You've done two weeks, Charlie. You have no idea what I went through in here. Try fifteen years!"

Dad opened his mouth to respond, but Bel spoke over him.

"Fifteen years." She touched Rachel's shoulder, turned her around. "Not the first time you've said that. Even though it's been more than sixteen years since that day. So you didn't get out of here three weeks ago, when you reappeared?"

"No."

"When did you get out?"

"Last summer," Rachel said. "August. When your grandpa had his first stroke."

Bel stared at her, rewriting everything again. She hadn't stopped to think about it, what had happened to Rachel when Grandpa went to the hospital, when he lost his memory and Rachel along with it.

"He normally came by twice a week, with supplies," she said. "I wasn't worried when he missed one, thought he was just busy. Then he missed another. I started to ration food and water, just in case. I didn't know he was in the hospital, recovering from his stroke. After two weeks, I thought he was leaving me in here to die, that he couldn't go through with this anymore but wasn't strong enough to kill me himself. The food was almost gone, water too. The generator went off, no one to fill up the gas. No fan, no light. It was so hot, I was sweating so much, not enough water to save me from it. I thought I was dying, here alone in the dark. Could feel all my bones. I was so dehydrated, so thin, that I didn't need the key anymore, the cuff slipped right off, over my foot. I was free for the first time, but I couldn't open the door, not from the inside." Her eyes were heavy, reliving it: her slow death, right here. "I tried everything. Tried making tools out of empty cans, the fan, something to force the door. Nothing worked. I was going to die in here. It was twenty-one days since I'd last seen Pat. And then I heard someone moving around outside. I was so weak, but I managed to hit a flashlight against the door, over and over, screaming for help."

Rachel stared at the door, now open into the endless black night.

"It opened. I'd gotten so used to the darkness that I couldn't see anything for a few seconds. Then I heard his voice, Pat's, asking who I was." Rachel shook her head. "I didn't understand, thought it was some kind of cruel joke. He asked me what I was doing here on his yard and who I was. And I realized; he really didn't know who I was. Didn't remember me or that he was the one keeping me here. I figured it must have been a stroke, and there was significant damage to his brain, to his memories. It was my one chance and I wasn't going to lose it. I wasn't chained up anymore and the door was open. I told your grandpa that I was a Realtor, looking for a client interested in buying the yard, that I'd accidentally gotten trapped inside the truck and I'd been there all day. He told me he was sorry that happened. He actually apologized to me. I grabbed some things, the three thousand dollars, and then I was free. Pat even held the door open for me as I climbed out. Asked to give him a call if there were any offers on the yard. He didn't remember me. I didn't even need to run. I couldn't have run, if I'd wanted to. I just walked right out of here. First thing I did, drank from the river until I was sick. Found a car parked by the trailhead, across the bridge. They had food and water, clothes and camping gear. I took it all. Stayed in the trees for a few days until I had my strength back."

Bel nodded, the final pieces coming together now, all the signs and half-truths she'd uncovered, showing her the way.

"You escaped eight, nine months ago," she said. "Why didn't you come home then?"

Rachel bit down on her lip, a ghostly imprint of her front teeth when she let it go. "I almost did. Almost went straight to the Gorham Police, I was so desperate to see you again. But I stopped myself. It was like the message in the books. I messed up the first one, and I knew I needed to be smarter about this. I only had one chance to return, and I wanted to be prepared, wanted to do it right. So I left town, left New Hampshire. Dyed my hair in a gas station toilet, caught a Greyhound, then another. Ended up in small town called Millinocket, in Maine. I thought it was far enough away, and people wouldn't recognize me with my hair, how thin I was. I had those three thousand dollars to get started. Rented a room. Got work as a maid, cash in hand. And I planned. I researched, and I was careful about it. Public computers, not close to where I was staying. I found your old Instagram, Bel. I must have looked at that photo of you with the bracelet a thousand times. More. Kept me going. And I needed it: your grandpa never told me Charlie had been arrested back then, that a jury found him not guilty of my murder. That terrified me; that they had gotten it so wrong, found him innocent of exactly what he

365

had done, or what he'd tried to do. I knew I could never go to the police with the truth, couldn't trust the criminal justice system to punish Charlie for what he'd done. How would it even work? There was no DNA evidence tying Charlie to any of the scenes because he hadn't been there. And the only witness I had couldn't remember any of it, what Charlie told him to do to me. No. The truth wasn't the way to get to Charlie, to get him away from you. So I came up with a different plan, a different story about where I'd been, and what I'd do to those who'd done this to me. There was more . . . something else I needed to find before I came back. Took a while. Turned out it was closer to home than I thought."

"You mean the clothes?" Bel asked. "The red top and black jeans from that boutique in New Conway? That was you, wasn't it, in January?"

A shift in Rachel's eyes, sharper. Not like she was angry, like she was proud somehow. Her well-laid plans and Bel unraveling them all, both living a lie under the same roof. Like mother like daughter.

"Yes. That was me. I'd moved closer, staying in a trailer near Lancaster. *Borrowed* a neighbor's car when they weren't home. That's where I originally bought that red top, those jeans, thought I'd find something similar, remove the labels so police couldn't date them, turn them into rags. Pat threw out the original clothes, burned them, actually. Brought me new clothes every year. For Christmas."

Rachel approached the pile of clothes, taking her within the boundary of Dad's chain. He didn't move, watching her closely as she kicked out at the old tops and sweaters, breaking apart the small mountain of fabric.

"When I was ready, when it was time, I cut my hair off, put on those ruined clothes. Fresh wound on my ankle I'd been working on, like I just escaped the cuff. I destroyed every last trace of me from that trailer. Left a tote bag I'd worn over my face on that road. Then I walked home. I know I messed the story up a couple of times, Bel. It was so hard, lying to your face, like you were being punished too. But I didn't think you'd accept the truth if I told you, you weren't ready. These people raised you, you love them. I thought I had to do it all on my own, the only one who'd ever know. Well, me and your dad, because he had to go, of course. But I'm so glad you're here with me now. That I'm not alone anymore."

Rachel breathed out and so did Bel. There it was; the whole truth. Bel had been right about everything, and wrong about more. Rachel had lied, had planned both her disappearance and her reappearance. Just not in the way Bel could have ever guessed.

"And what's your plan now, huh, Rachel?" Charlie spat in her direction.

"This." She sharpened her chin, opened her arms. "That you go through the exact same thing you did to me, Charlie. Fifteen years, five months, twenty-five days. You've done thirteen days. Bit of a ways to go."

"You're fucking crazy!"

"Think of it like I'm *saving* you, Charlie. The only other option was to kill you."

"Are you listening to this, Bel?" He forgot to take the edge out of his voice, the fire out of his eyes. "She's fucking crazy. Talking about killing me."

"You killed me first, *honey*," Rachel hissed.

"Bel!"

"Stop!" Bel raised her hands, coming to stand between her parents, stopping in the middle. "Stop it!"

Rachel held her hands up too, a flash of fear in her eyes. "Careful, Bel. Don't get too close to him."

There was fear in Charlie's eyes too, but it didn't take the same shape as her mom's. "Rachel has the key," he said. "We can sort everything out, kiddo, OK? Get everyone the help they need. But you have to get the key from her. You need to set me free."

Bel glanced back at Rachel, hooking onto her eyes, so much like her own. She'd always hated that, always wished she'd been born with the Price eyes.

"Bel, get the key!"

Dad's voice in one ear, Mom's in the other.

"It's OK, Bel," Rachel said gently, one hand disappearing behind, to her pocket. She brought it back, opened it. A small silver key on her outstretched palm. "It's right here."

Charlie strained against his chain, swiping toward Rachel, the disturbed air fluttering her hair.

"I can't reach!" he screamed. "Grab the key, Bel. NOW!"

Bel stared down at it, against Rachel's pale skin. Her fingers twitched, Dad's heavy breath in time with her own.

"You've told me everything, right?" she asked, still looking at the key. "No more lies?"

A twitch by Rachel's mouth, the truth in her eyes. "No," she said. "There's something else. There's more I need to tell you, but not here, like this. I promise to tell you everything. I will never lie to you again."

"Bel, grab the key!" Dad screeched. He put a heavy hand on her shoulder, thumb pressing against her bare neck. He gave her a gentle push, one step toward Rachel, out of the middle. "Get the key, kiddo," he whispered, letting her go.

"What do you mean there's more?" Bel stared at Rachel. "What haven't you told me?"

"She's trying to manipulate you. Stop listening. Just take the key."

"I'll tell you everything. Not here. *He* can't know."

"Shut the fuck up, Rachel! Bel, get the key."

His fingers against her back, another nudge, pushing her farther out of the middle, toward Rachel.

"You can take it if you want," Rachel said, a tear falling, catching at the crack in her lips. "I won't try to stop you. It's your choice. You haven't had a lot of choice in your life, Bel. Now you do."

Bel looked over her shoulder at Dad, then back to Mom.

"Take it, Bel. Come on."

"It's OK, sweetie," Rachel said. "I'll understand."

But Dad wouldn't.

Bel took a step forward.

"Yes, that's it, kiddo." His voice hovered behind her, urging her on, her heart throwing itself against the bars of her rib cage, pulling both ways, and neither.

"It's OK." Rachel watched Bel take another step toward her.

"She knows it's OK, stop talking to her, Rachel!" Dad's voice seemed farther away now.

Bel's eyes watered, holding the key in place, there on Rachel's hand.

Take the key or don't.

Choose Charlie or Rachel. Mom or Dad.

Her lies or his.

Eyes on the key.

One way or the other, because Bel couldn't have both. One couldn't exist if the other did. She'd made this choice already, head and heart and gut. Chose the man who'd raised her, because they were a team, always had been. Both had lied to her, Mom and Dad, standing here in no-man's-land between them, lost, the after-ring in her ears, and an ending that was hers to choose.

So choose.

Bel took another step, feet unsteady.

And what would it come down to, in the end? The one she knew more, the one she'd loved longer, loved harder, the one who came back from the dead for her? One all her life, one for just three weeks. Second thoughts pitted themselves against each other, streaming behind her eyes.

But maybe only one truth really mattered, when you took it all away, threw out those memories or the space where they should have been. Who had chosen to leave her behind and who hadn't. Bel tore her gaze from the key, circling Rachel's eyes, the color and shape of her own. Back to the key.

Rachel nodded.

"You have to get me out of here, kiddo. Please!"

Blurred edges, eyes crossing, splicing the key into two. She blinked until her vision righted, because there was only one. She could only choose one.

Mom.

Or.

Dad.

His.

Side.

Or.

Hers.

One.

Or.

The.

Other.

Bel chose. And she chose right this time. Head and heart and gut.

She closed the gap between her and Rachel, eyes fixed on the key, watering because she couldn't blink, blink and everything might disappear. Bel reached out, fingers gliding through the air, a shiver as she touched the skin of Rachel's palm. Warm, not cold.

She closed Rachel's hand around the key, into a fist. Skin to skin, bone to bone. Held it there, tight.

Eyes on her mom's.

She chose her.

"Bel!" Dad screamed. He couldn't see.

Bel let go, though something of her stayed behind, there in Rachel's closed hand. She stood beside her mom.

"No, Dad," she said, darkly, meeting his eye.

"What are you talking about?" He blinked because he didn't understand. She knew he wouldn't. "Don't be stupid. Get the key."

"I said no." And she didn't say sorry.

"What the fuck are you doing?!" he screeched, backing away, chain clattering. "You can't be serious. You have to let me go! She's brainwashed you."

"I've made my choice, Charlie." Bel's heart didn't waver, not at the pleading in his voice. She didn't know this man, not really, and her heart didn't either. Family first, and he wasn't her family anymore. He never was.

"Bel, stop, you must be fucking crazy!"

"Yeah, I must be," she said, shutting him out, doing that thing she

370

did, the thing she'd gotten so good at because she'd had to, to survive. She pushed him away.

Charlie sucked at the stale air. "No, no, no," he said to himself, a crescendo building in his chest. "No!" he barked. "No!" he screamed, strings of spit holding his teeth together, an animal look in his eye. "You can't leave me in here! YOU CAN'T!"

"Why not?" Bel said. He'd left her. He'd decided to kill Rachel. He'd chosen for Bel, that tiny babbling girl, picked the way that hurt less for him but ruined her. The knot in her gut she hadn't felt so much since he'd been gone.

"I'm begging you!" he screamed, hands in front of his chest. "You can't leave me in here!"

Bel glanced at her mom.

A blink, a hidden message inside it. Yes, they could leave him in here. A new family secret, dark only because of the ones that came before, one that bound the two of them together. Mother and daughter. Mom and Bel. A team.

"No!"

A roar as he bounded toward them, chain pulling taut with a crash of metal. Charlie's hand scrabbled the air, fingers closing around Bel's sleeve, pulling her toward him and those desperate, hungry eyes.

Bel dug her nails into his flesh, scratching deep. Rachel stamped on his foot, pulled Bel out of his grip. She bared her teeth, eyes glittering the same way they had when another man tried to hurt her daughter.

"Do not touch her!" She stood in front of Bel. "I can make it even worse for you!"

"Don't leave me here!" he howled, empty swipes at the air, slipping, crashing to his knees. "I'll kill you, Rachel! I should have fucking killed you!"

Mom reached back, took Bel's hand. Gave it a squeeze.

It was time to go.

"I'll fucking kill you!"

Bel turned toward the open doorway, a black frame, the empty night beyond, waiting for them.

But it wasn't empty.

A white ball of light, floating up the tires. A dark shape looming behind it.

A new voice and a pair of eyes, glowing in the night.

"What the fuck is going on here?"

FORTY-FIVE

Uncle Jeff came into the light, the container floor shifting with his weight, tipping away from Bel and Rachel.

His mouth dropped open when he spotted Charlie there, on his knees.

"Charlie?" He hurried over to his little brother. "What are you doing here? You're supposed to be in Canada? What the fuck is going on here?" he said again, eyes catching on the chain attached to Charlie's ankle, gaze shifting around the makeshift room.

"Oh my God, am I glad to see you," Charlie cried, a hand snaking over his brother's shoulder, eyes hooking onto his. "You have to help me, Jeff. Rachel locked me in here, it's been two weeks. She's crazy. Filled Bel's head full of lies. They want to leave me here. You have to help me."

"Why would Rachel . . . ," Jeff began, eyeing Bel and Rachel, standing together, out of Charlie's reach.

"Rachel has the key to the cuff," Charlie said, a growl in his throat, blinking out a tear. "You need to get it, Jeff. Get the key and unlock me."

Jeff straightened up, standing over his brother. "I don't understand."

"You don't need to understand, just get the key." Charlie pushed up to his feet, chain rattling. He stood shoulder to shoulder with his brother, fingers gripping on again.

"Rachel," Jeff said, looking over at her, his eyes crossing sides. "Is that true? Why would you—"

"Stop asking her questions," Charlie barked, guiding his brother forward, his head floating over his shoulder, voice in his ear. "Just get the key. It's in her hand."

Jeff took a step forward, into the middle. "Look, I don't know what's happened here, but I'm sure we can work it out. We're a family, aren't we?"

"Jeff, don't," Rachel said, an edge to her voice, a warning.

"I'm sorry, Rachel." Jeff blinked at her. "But I'm going to need that key."

Rachel stepped back, Bel with her, foot nudging into the cascade of clothes.

"How did you find us here?" Bel asked him, stalling for time.

Jeff's eyes fell on her instead, lines easing, like he thought they were safe there.

"You and Rachel never came back to dinner, so Sherry stayed behind to clear up and me and Carter followed Yordan back to Grandpa's house to see where everyone had gone. We saw the mess. Books all over the floor. We thought someone had broken in. Grandpa was upset, so Yordan went to settle him into bed, and me and Carter started tidying. I saw the note on the coffee table. *Help. My name is Rachel Price,*" he recited, a quick look at her. "It mentioned the red truck here. So I drove right over. Left Carter to clear up the mess. What the fuck is going on?"

Bel shuffled back, a lump beneath her heel. She lifted her shoe. A flash of color against the blacks and grays Rachel had worn during her imprisonment here. Pink. A tiny pink sock, frilly at the edge. The other sock, her other sock. The one in her mom's nightstand, and the one here, a complete pair. Rachel must have had both when Grandpa grabbed her, managed to take one with her when he let her go. Bel picked it up, just as soft, just as small. How was it possible she was ever this small?

"What did the rest of the note say?" Rachel stared Jeff down. "What did it say, Jeff? *Help. My name is Rachel Price . . .*"

Jeff coughed into his fist.

"Say it," Rachel said, voice gentle, eyes anything but. *"I am being kept by . . ."*

". . . by Patrick Price," Jeff said shakily, losing his way, feet dragging to a stop. *"In a red truck on Price logging yard."*

Rachel smiled. It twisted at the edges, turned cruel. "But you already knew that, didn't you?"

The color drained from Jeff's face, lip tucked behind his teeth.

"What?" Bel looked up.

Jeff shook his head. "No, I didn't. I don't—"

"But you do, don't you? You *know.*" Rachel pushed back, taking a step toward him now. "I've seen the way you look at us. You know. Does Sherry know too? How long have you known, Jeff? From the very start? How could you do that to me?"

"No!" Jeff waved his hands, voice tight and jittery. "I never knew, I swear to you, Rachel. It was only when you came back, only when I saw the similarities."

"But you said nothing," Rachel growled.

"What are you talking about?" Bel asked them both.

"It doesn't matter!" Charlie shouted. "Jeff, the key!"

"I'm not giving you this key, Jeff." Rachel's voice was dark and deep, chin sharpened to a point. "You've taken enough from me."

"Please," Jeff begged her, blinking away tears.

"You owe me. You know you do."

"What are you going to do?" Jeff asked, the tears winning, breaking down his face. "Please don't take her away from us."

"You took her away from me," Rachel cried.

"Who are you talking about?" Bel's eyes darted between them, her mom and her uncle, dancing around another secret, another land mine. And there was only one name that fit there, in that space, ready to explode. "Carter?"

Rachel closed her eyes.

Jeff hid his face in his hands.

Bel looked down at the tiny pink sock, dangling between her fingers. A baby sock. Here. But it didn't belong to Bel, it never had.

Bel emptied out, an outward breath that didn't end until it was all gone, a rasp at the back of her throat.

She staggered, hitting the wall of the container, clutching the sock against her empty chest.

Rachel reached for her. "Bel, I'm sorry. I wanted to tell her first."

Bel tried to speak, but she couldn't speak because she couldn't breathe, and she couldn't see for all the smoke.

"What are you talking about?" Charlie barked. "Jeff?"

Her mom touched her hand and her breath came back, tearing down her throat, filling her, a different shape again. A different person. A sister.

She cried, shrinking against the wall, looking up at her mom.

"You were pregnant when you disappeared. You had a baby in here."

Bel handed her the tiny pink sock.

"Carter's your baby."

Rachel pressed her eyes together, twin tears from each eye, racing down her face. "Yes," she said quietly.

Bel wiped her face on her sleeve. "How?"

"I was four and a half months pregnant when Pat locked me in here. I hadn't told anyone. Especially not *him*." She didn't need to say Charlie's name. "It was another reason we had to get away from him, start a new life, before he killed me. I wasn't showing much, but I started wearing baggy clothes, just in case. Julian even thought I was losing weight." She sniffed. "I didn't want that baby to be born into this family. We had to get to our new home. Our family of three. But then I was in here."

She glanced behind her, checking Jeff hadn't moved. Hands on his face, stretching his eyes down, showing the red exposed parts of the socket.

"I told your grandpa I was pregnant that first day. Don't think he believed me. Not until several weeks in, when I started to show. He still wouldn't let me go. Asked me to write down the supplies I'd need. Said he'd be here for the birth, that we could do it together. We had everything ready. Diapers. Clothes." She stroked her thumb over the little pink sock. "He wasn't here when I went into labor. I delivered her myself. Thought I was going to die, but there she was, screaming up at me. Perfect. Mine. The only world she knew was the one inside this container. But she had me and I had her, not alone anymore. We were doing OK. I didn't let Pat hold her, wouldn't let him near." Her breath shuddered. "I only had her for two weeks. Hadn't even named her yet. Pat came in with some scales, said we needed to weigh her, check she was healthy. I only let him close for one second, and he took her, where I couldn't reach her." She glanced at the chain. "I screamed but he wouldn't give her back, said he couldn't let his granddaughter grow up in a place like this, it wasn't fair. That she would go to a good home, she'd be taken care of, he promised. He took her. Closed the door. And I never saw my baby again."

Bel took her mom's hand, hot and sticky, the sock between them. "I'm sorry."

Help. My name is Rachel Price. We are being kept by Patrick Price in a red truck on Price logging yard. Because Rachel wasn't always alone, for just two weeks, for one message in one book. Her and her baby.

Carter was Rachel's daughter, but she was someone else too. Not Bel's cousin, but her little sister. *My baby.* Bel and Carter, Carter and Bel. And somehow, it was the most shocking thing, this final truth, and also not at all, not even a little bit. Her sister.

"I asked about her every time Pat dropped off food. You too." Rachel sniffed. "My girls. Pat wouldn't tell me where the baby went. Just that she was with a good family. I assumed he meant she'd gone into foster care, that she'd been adopted. That's what I was looking for, when I got out last summer. Spent months trying to find records, a baby who'd been born in New Hampshire on the first of July, 2008. I had to find my other daughter, before I came home for you. I didn't even think." She glanced at Jeff, hands only covering his mouth now. "And then I saw a photo of Carter on Sherry's Facebook. Dancing, smiling. I knew right away, that she had to be my baby girl. The ages matched, and her face . . . I checked, I scrolled through Sherry's albums, to photos of Carter as a baby, just a few weeks old. It was her.

My girl. Still wearing the clothes Pat had bought for me. That's when I started planning my reappearance. To come home, for both of you. And what I would do to the Price family, this *family* who took everything from me."

"I didn't know," Jeff cried, mouth uncovered now. "You have to believe me, Rachel, we didn't know she was yours. Dad told me he knew someone who worked at a women's shelter, that there was a woman, six months pregnant, who didn't want the baby, but couldn't go to an adoption agency because she was undocumented, would get deported. So Dad thought of us. We'd been trying to have a baby for more than ten years. Dad and his friend thought this would be the best thing for everyone. Dad told us the baby was due in July, that the parents looked enough like us that no one would be able to tell, same skin color, similar hair. Sherry would have to pretend to be pregnant, so nobody would ask questions, as none of this was legal. We were desperate, Rachel. Sherry wanted a baby so much. We said yes. Sherry started wearing maternity clothes, we bought bumps online, changed the size every couple weeks. Dad told us when the baby was born, that it was a girl, that she was healthy. He said the mother needed a couple of weeks with her, for everything to settle, and then she'd be ours. We laid low, hardly left the house. Charlie was in jail awaiting trial. Bel was living with us, but she was too young to understand. Then Dad brought the baby around, in the middle of the night. And we fell in love instantly. Bel too."

Another dark family secret she'd lived through, that she'd been too small to hold on to, to remember. A birth that never happened, and a baby that appeared from nowhere.

"We told everyone she'd been born July tenth. A home birth, because Sherry didn't like hospitals, or needles. We registered her, named her, promised to give this baby the best life we could. We were careful. Sherry never let a doctor near her with a needle, no blood tests, nothing that could risk exposing she wasn't ours. If I'm honest, I almost started to forget, that Sherry hadn't given birth to her that night in July. She felt so much like part of the family, looked it too. I thought it was just wishful thinking."

He coughed into his hand.

"Then you came back, Rachel. And it was the way you looked at her, the way you were with her. The similarities. Carter looks like a Price, but she also looks like you, not in the obvious ways, but it's there, in her smile. The way you're both always fiddling, always moving somehow. I just had this bad feeling, when I saw you two together. I tried telling Sherry. She told me I was being ridiculous, that it wasn't possible. I think I knew, after that dinner party, for the documentary. I was almost sure."

Bel straightened up, her back against the wall of the container, the foam insulation pressing in like fingers.

"That's what you were asking Grandpa that night." She narrowed her eyes at her uncle. "What the microphone caught you saying. You weren't asking about Rachel. You were asking him about Carter. *Where was she? Where did they find her?* Because Grandpa knew where Carter came from, who her mother really was, but he couldn't remember. He can't remember any of this. I asked you about that conversation. You lied to my face." Her voice found its strength, carrying her forward.

"I'm sorry, Bel. I was protecting my daughter."

"Except she's not your daughter! She's your niece too! My sister!"

Charlie shifted, the chain dancing behind him. "Is she mine, Rachel?"

"Of course she's yours," Rachel spat. "Except she'll never be yours."

"I'm sorry, Charlie." Jeff faced his brother. "I didn't know she was your daughter. Dad lied to us, all of us."

"Don't apologize to him!" Rachel hissed, the fire back in her eyes, now the ghosts were gone. "If you think your dad is a monster, Jeff, take a good hard look at your brother. All of this is because of him. Pat only kept me in here because Charlie asked him to kill me. Pat convinced himself he was saving me, from him. Charlie wanted me dead, which means Carter would have died too. That's your family, Jeff."

Jeff did what Rachel said, turned around, took a good hard look at his brother. So did Bel, and Charlie Price was a different shape now, not the man she ever knew. He was no family of hers. She had a mom, and a sister, and that was all she ever needed.

"Please," Charlie whispered, underlit by the flashlight, upward shadows he cast on himself, silver pooling in his eyes. "Help me, Jeff."

Jeff coughed into his hand. Turned back. Blinked. "I have to let him go, Rachel. Please give me the key."

Jeff had chosen, and he'd chosen wrong.

"Uncle Jeff—" Bel began.

"No, Jeff," Rachel said darkly, eyes hardening, standing her ground. "I'm choosing to believe you. That you didn't know. That you thought you were giving an unwanted baby a home, that you're a good person. You don't always have to listen to him. You can choose."

"Please, help me," Charlie choked.

"I have to let him go," Jeff cried, eyes flickering, torn in two. "I have to. He's my brother. My family."

He chose wrong again.

"No!" Bel held out her arm.

Jeff pushed it away.

"No, Jeff." Rachel backed up until she was against the wall. "You can choose!"

"Please give me the key, Rachel." He reached out toward her, no chain to keep him back.

"No," she whispered, a shift behind her eyes, but it wasn't fear.

Rachel stepped forward to meet him, elbow to his chest.

Before Jeff could grab her arm, she pulled it back and swung, launching the key out the doorway, into the dark night.

It disappeared and Bel held her breath. Heard the tiny clink as it landed, somewhere out there, in the metal maze.

"Noooo!" Charlie howled, kicking out at the boxes of food, the flashlight falling over, a silver streak along the floor, throwing them all into shadow. "You bitch! Find it, Jeff. Find it!"

Jeff stared out into the night, mouth open and shut, chewing the air.

"I'll never find it. It's pitch-black out there, junk everywhere."

"Jeff!"

"I tried, Charlie," he sniffed.

Silence, just the chorus of their breaths, and a ringing in Bel's ears.

"Forget the key." Charlie straightened up, hand on his brother's shoulder, reeling him back in. "Go find a handsaw. There must be hundreds of saws out there. Find something to get me out of this chain, Jeff. Now!"

He shouted that last word, piercing the night, bringing Jeff back to life. Rachel too, arms locking at her sides.

Jeff looked at Charlie, eye to eye, brother to brother. He picked up the flashlight, their faces distorted, eyes glowing white. Jeff turned, pointed it out the open doorway.

"OK," he said, walking through.

Rachel whipped around, found Bel's eyes in the dark.

Then she found her hand, held it tight.

"Bel, run!"

FORTY-SIX

Hand in hand, through the maze.

Running. Bel's phone swinging at her side, lighting the way in nightmare flashes.

Metal shadows loomed, catching their clothes, snatching their hair.

A rusted saw blade in their path, trying to separate them, but Bel would not let go of her mom's hand.

A clatter of sliding metal, somewhere behind, the distant silver of the flashlight in Jeff's hands, sharper, stronger than theirs, a spotlight stalking through the dark shapes.

"I got one, Charlie!" they heard him call.

Charlie's voice, fainter. "Hurry!"

"Keep going," her mom said, moving faster, holding Bel's hand tighter, skin to skin, bone to bone.

Around a burned-out car on its back.

A sharp intake of breath beside her.

Rachel disappeared.

Hand snatched out of Bel's.

Bel swung the flashlight over.

Rachel was on her hands and knees, shoe caught on a metal bar.

"You OK?" Bel helped her mom stand, retook her hand.

"I'm OK," Rachel said, a change in her gait now, a limp on one side, leaning into Bel's hand. It didn't slow her down. "Just got to get to the car."

The way cleared ahead of them, no more shadows, no more metal, just grass, downhill, pushing them faster. Rachel hissed each time her right foot pounded the ground.

They reached the fence.

Bel grabbed the loose panel of chain-link, held it up for Rachel to clamber through. She followed, looking back at Price & Sons Logging Yard. A fence around nothing, just more darkness, except a faint white light, glowing inside the red truck in the middle.

"Come on, I parked in front of the gates."

Running again. Not together anymore, out of time, Rachel's steps growing uneven.

She pulled her car keys out, pressed the button.

A blip as the car unlocked, a flash of white and red, guiding them forward, a map in the darkness. Relief sparked in Bel's run-down heart.

They drew close and Bel's flashlight found it too: Rachel's silver car, waiting, nose parked right against the front gates.

But it wasn't alone.

Another car faced them. Jeff's. He'd parked right behind Rachel, sideways, blocking her in.

Rachel breathed out. "No, Jeff!"

She darted forward, studying the gap between the cars. It was only a few inches, just the span of her hand.

"Fucker!" Rachel kicked out at Jeff's front wheel. It cost her, hissing and reaching for her right ankle.

"Mom?"

"Get in, Bel." She opened her car door, dome light flicking on, a faint yellow through the windows. "Maybe I can turn it. Have to try."

Bel climbed into the passenger seat, shut herself in.

Rachel started the engine, a metal growl in this cold metal place full of dead machines. The headlights flicked on, through the bars of the gates, glaring against the old sign, into the darkness beyond.

Rachel's elbow bumped hers as she put it in reverse.

Taillights stained the night red. Rachel pulled the steering wheel to the right, as far as it would go, tires complaining, grating against the dirt road. She pressed her bad foot to the gas with a wince.

The car juddered back, only half a second before it bumped against the side of Jeff's car.

Rachel sniffed. Put the car in drive. Turned the wheel all the way to the left.

The car shuddered forward, crashing into the gates with a dull thud. They bent inward, as much as that heavy chain around the middle would let them.

Bel looked out the window. It wasn't much at all; the angle of the car had hardly changed. They were stuck here, trapped.

"Mom."

Rachel gasped, leaning forward to peer through the windshield.

Bel looked too.

Two tiny figures crossed one of their headlight beams, into the other, moving fast, out the metal maze, onto the grass. Someone was ahead, a ball of light in one hand, something dark in the other. Heading straight toward them.

"He's free." Rachel's hands dropped from the steering wheel. "We don't have time." Terror reshaped her face. "Run, Bel!"

Bel didn't hesitate this time, heart ahead of her, fight-or-flight fast against her ribs.

She sprinted around the back of Jeff's car, catching up to her mom.

"Don't look back, just run!"

Bel couldn't help it; she looked back.

Both car doors left open, letting the night in, engine running, headlights glaring.

But it was another light she looked for. Moving fast, now reaching the gap in the fence. The ball of light became a long silver beam, hacking away the darkness. The sound of feet behind it.

And a voice.

"Charlie, what are you going to do!?"

The beam of light twisted, following them down the road.

"Hurry." Rachel pushed herself harder, gritting her teeth, breathing through it.

Bel hooked their arms together, taking some of the weight off her ankle.

"I know the way." Bel's voice shook with the patter of her feet. "The reservoir, across the railway bridge to the main road. We can get help there."

"Charlie!" Jeff shouted weakly, some way behind them. "What are you doing!?"

Did Jeff realize already, that he'd made the wrong choice? That he shouldn't have set him free.

Bel wanted to glance back, to see how close they were. But she didn't need to, she only needed to look at Rachel; silver lighting up her flyaway hairs. The beam wasn't just following them anymore, it had found them. Charlie and his flashlight chasing them down.

"Mom. He's catching up."

Rachel looked at her, one side of her face lit up, one eye, losing the rest to the night. Half here, half disappeared.

"Off the road. We'll lose him in the trees."

Rachel dragged Bel into the tree line, then Bel dragged her, the ground growing rough and uneven.

Bel lit the way, much darker now, the trees looming over them, blocking out the sky, roots catching hold of their legs. They moved as fast as they could, darting through and around.

The world tilted, reaching uphill, taking the trees with it.

The breath was tight in Bel's chest, hauling Rachel up alongside her.

"Charlie!" They heard a strangled cry behind them. "Wait!"

He was somewhere in the trees too, hunting them down. Bel couldn't see the silver beam; the trees were blocking it, hiding them.

"This way," Rachel whispered, pointing to where the trees thinned out, a path snaking up. "The hikers' trail."

They climbed together, picking up their pace. Bel could even see the moon through the canopy of shadows, over the mountain. Leading the way, and that way was up.

Bel's hand grew sticky against Rachel's, but she wouldn't let go.

"How's your ankle?"

Rachel squeezed her fingers. "Just have to keep going."

Without warning, the trees broke away all at once, in a clean line, letting the sky have them. The huge track where the forest had been cleared for the power lines, running in and out of town.

They moved out into the open, exposed by the moon.

"Faster," Rachel said, but she was the one who couldn't move any faster.

Bel eyed the tree cover ahead, racing to it, crossing the shadows of the power lines, too clean and straight to belong in this wild place of trees and moonlight.

They were so close. Bel looked back to check how far they'd come.

A silver light emerged from the trees, the dark shape of Charlie behind it, charging into the open ground. The beam shifted, veered over, pointing directly at them, straight through Bel's heart.

"Fuck, he sees us. Go!"

She pulled Rachel into the trees, back on the trail.

Up and up, just keep moving.

Bel had made her choice, she chose her mom, and she chose her again, every single second, fingers around hers, dragging her up as fast as she could, away from the man who was going to kill her.

A howl behind, but it wasn't at the moon.

"Charlie, wait! What are you going to do?!"

Bel knew. And Rachel knew. Jeff must know too.

She tried not to look at her mom, to read the pain in the set of her jaw, the fear in the blacks of her eyes.

"Where are we going?"

"Up," Rachel said, eyes ahead, not sharing the fear, not letting Bel take any of it. "Mascot Mine. We can hide, lose them. Not far now. We can make it."

Up and up, steeper and steeper, Bel's knees screaming, muscles burning.

"We have to leave the trail," Rachel panted. "This way."

The way the trees grew thick and untamed, leaning up the mountain as they fought their way through.

Rachel dropped Bel's hand to climb a steep pass on all fours, checking back for her, flashlight catching the sheen of sweat across her face, a bloody scratch on her cheek.

Bel retook her arm, choosing and choosing again.

There was nothing left, only adrenaline, only fear, working together to keep Bel's legs moving, every breath snagging, ripping at her lungs.

"This way." Rachel veered off. "The mine's here somewhere. It must be . . ."

The trees trickled out, making way for the moon, rocky beneath their feet. Bel held up the flashlight. They were on a ledge, the ground disappearing over there, a sheer drop into darkness.

"No, no, no." Rachel limped, moving closer to the edge, looking down. "We came too high." Her foot nudged a stone and it rolled over the edge, clattering down the rockface. Bel never heard it hit the bottom. "The mine is down there."

Bel joined her, looking down into all that nothing, her light barely scratching the surface, stomach peeling away, toward her spine. She looked ahead instead and saw stars on the ground, reds and whites and yellows, pinpricks of headlights, windows that glowed small as specks. It was Gorham, not quite sleeping, and Bel knew where they were now, wearing night as its disguise. Point Lookout, where you could see the whole town and the mountains beyond in the day. Which meant the entrance to the mine was all the way down there, hundreds of feet below, over the ledge.

"It's OK." Bel took her mom's hand, pulled her back from the edge. "We'll follow the trail down to the other side of Hogan Road."

"No," Rachel said quietly. She dropped Bel's hand, grabbed the other one instead, took the phone out of it, swiped the flashlight off.

"What are you doing?" Bel blinked, eyes adjusting to the moonlight.

"It's the light he's following." Rachel passed the phone back, pressing Bel's hand closed around it, like Bel had done with the key. "Bel," she said, a change in her voice, a break in the middle, like she had just decided something too.

Rachel put her hands on her shoulders.

"No." Bel knew before she said it, shaking her head.

"I'm slowing you down, Bel."

"No, Mom."

"You run that way." She pointed. "Without the light. Be careful. Find the trail again. Keep going. I'll draw him here with my light." She said it fast and she said it hard.

"No, Mom, I'm not leaving you."

"It's me he wants." She shook Bel's shoulders, trying to get her to listen. Bel wouldn't.

"No."

"He won't stop. You keep running, my sweet girl." Her voice cracked, bringing Bel's face closer to hers, hands cupped behind her ears. "Don't look back."

"No." The tears came all at once, blurring Rachel's face, losing it to the darkness.

"Please, Bel. I have to know you're safe. He's coming." Rachel pressed her forehead against Bel's, eye to eye, heart to heart. "Tell the police. Don't let him get away with it this time, don't let him get away with killing me twice."

"Mom," Bel cried, throat seizing around the word. Not a hard word anymore, the easiest one in the world. "Mom."

"Go, Bel." Rachel blinked, tears of her own. "I love you. So, so much. Take care of your sister for me. I know you always have."

"Mom."

"Go."

Rachel pushed her away.

"Go."

Bel went.

Rachel said not to look back but she did, from the tree line. Saw her mom standing out there on the ledge, waving the flashlight above her head, another star where it shouldn't be.

Bel kept going, silent sobs that split her in half, gut ripping open. The knot rolled right out and she lost it forever, in the wild. Running away from Rachel, like the day she reappeared. Scared then and scared now.

"Charlie! Stop!"

Uncle Jeff's voice, somewhere in the dark.

Bel stopped; breath trapped like a windstorm behind her face.

The sound of feet, crashing through the trees close by. That silver beam, pointing toward the end.

And Bel was going the wrong way. The way that hurt far too much, she'd never live through it, leaving Rachel behind.

Rachel had never left her behind.

Her mom had made her decision, but Bel had made hers too. She chose her mom.

And she chose her again, even if Rachel didn't want her to.

She went back.

A scream building in her throat, following that beam of light, chasing it down.

"There you are!" Charlie's voice filled the night, ragged and wild.

"Charlie, don't!" Jeff shouted. "You don't want to do this!"

Bel sprinted, breaking through the trees onto the moonlit edge.

The flashlight was on the ground, that harsh silver beam pointing at Bel, two dark shapes entangled behind it.

"Mom!" Bel screamed.

Charlie had one arm around Rachel's neck, forcing her to the ground.

She fought back, ankle buckling, scrabbling at his face.

Bel jumped forward, but an arm caught her, dragging her away.

"It's not safe, Bel." Jeff held on to her, pinning her arms down. "He's not safe."

"Let me go!" she screeched, struggling against him.

"Not safe." He held tighter.

Charlie roared, tackling Rachel, feet grating against the stone, two dark figures, dancing toward the edge.

"Let go!" Bel struggled.

Jeff was too strong.

Charlie too, bearing down on Rachel. Her legs gave out and she dropped with a dull thud, a few feet from the edge.

Charlie pressed one shoe against Rachel's throat, pushed his weight down into it. His ankle was bleeding, the cuff gone, cut free. She scrabbled and kicked, but he could not be moved.

"Mom!" Bel scratched at Jeff's arms.

Rachel spoke, voice breathy, crushed beneath his foot. "Protect my daughter, Jeff. You owe me."

Charlie didn't look over, only had eyes for her. His arm grew longer than it should, overstretching, inhuman, something dark gripped in his hand. Bel couldn't see what it was, not until he raised it up against the stars.

An axe.

A click in Rachel's throat as she looked at it, hanging over her head.

"If you want me to beg, you're out of luck, Charlie," she croaked. "I've already been dead once."

He shrieked, a sound that wasn't human either, an explosion of rage, no shape to it. A monster standing at the edge of the world, bringing it down around him.

It moved Bel beyond fear, to whatever came next.

"Should have done it myself!" Charlie gasped, like the scream had crushed him too, left only half of him behind. "Now look what you've done!"

He raised the axe.

"No!" Bel screamed, fighting against Jeff.

Rachel turned her head, found Bel. *Don't look,* she mouthed, eyes glittering before she pressed them together, waiting for the end.

"Mom!"

A scream.

But it wasn't Bel.

A blur of coppery-brown hair, shooting out of the trees. Long legs, bounding past.

Jeff's arms loosened.

"Carter?" he said, confused, letting Bel go. "Carter!" he screamed, running after her.

But she was ahead, and she was too fast.

"Carter!"

That wrenched Charlie out. He glanced over, just as Carter bounded into him, a double-handed push, shoving him away from Rachel.

He stumbled, tripping over Rachel's arm. Dropped the axe and tripped on that too, staggering back.

Jeff reached them, skidding, wrenching Carter away from the edge, throwing her behind him.

Charlie was still moving, too much momentum, stones skidding under his feet.

His eyes widened.

He reached out for Jeff, grabbed a fistful of his brother's shirt.

One of his heels dropped over the edge, the rest of the foot slipping with it.

Charlie tilted.

Falling back, into all that nothing.

The other foot went.

Bel blinked but she didn't miss it.

Charlie disappeared over the edge.

He didn't let go, dragging Jeff with him.

One of them screamed, all the way down.

FORTY-SEVEN

Carter was on her knees.

Rachel on her back.

Bel, her feet.

Carter screamed into her hands, trapping it there, rebounding into her.

"Carter!" Bel closed the distance, crashing to her knees. She wrapped her arms around Carter, held her head until the scream gave way.

"They're gone," Carter cried, voice echoing back through Bel's ribs.

Rachel stood up, shakily, resting her weight on her other ankle. She picked up the flashlight Charlie had dropped, the silver beam in her hands now, lighting the way. She limped toward the edge, where Charlie went over. Bel joined her mom, feet firm, as Rachel pointed the light down, crags of rock sticking out like teeth below. The light didn't reach the bottom.

"They couldn't survive that fall," Rachel said, like she didn't dare believe it herself, quiet, listening for any sound that would prove her wrong.

"I killed them?" Carter said.

"No, Carter." Rachel turned back to her, bent low, pulling up her chin. "You saved my life."

"I killed them." Carter balled her fists, pressed them into her eyes. "I pushed them over. Dad's gone. But he's not my dad, is he? Charlie is. Was. Fuck."

Bel sat beside Carter, nudging her elbow, letting her know she was right here.

Rachel's eyes widened, glittering again. "Carter, you know?" she said. "That I'm your . . ."

"Yes," Carter sniffed, stars in her eyes too, from the flashlight.

Rachel's lips parted, dropped open. "How do you know, sweetie?"

"I guess I just sort of knew. Felt it. All the ways we were similar, even though we weren't blood-related, just my aunt by marriage. How nice you were to me, how much you wanted to get to know me. I thought it that first time you picked me up from school, when I helped you with your phone. Or really, I thought, 'Isn't Bel lucky, to have a mom like you.' And how I'm not at all like my mom, and how weird she is with me and needles, wouldn't let me get a blood test, even when the doctor said. I wanted it to be true, somehow, even though it was impossible. I ordered two kits from AncestryDNA the next day, told my dad it was dancing stuff. Fuck. Not my dad. U-uncle, I guess." Carter stared out, beyond Rachel, over the empty edge, where he had disappeared too. "I did one on me, one on Bel."

Bel blinked. "What? When?"

"I didn't want to tell you, in case I was wrong. And you were so wrapped up in Rachel, trying to prove she was lying, that she was bad. You wouldn't have believed me. You were asleep. I did the cheek swab."

Bel remembered now; the morning Carter woke her by poking her in the mouth. The same morning Bel woke up to find that her dad was missing. It seemed a lifetime ago now, that day, that version of her.

"Bel's results came through two days ago, didn't tell me anything," Carter said, looking up at Rachel. "But mine came this evening, just before Grandpa's dinner. It said that me and Bel were full genetic sisters, that we shared both the same parents." She blinked, a tear sliding down the ridge of her nose. "Which means you're my mom, and Uncle Charlie is . . . was . . ." She left it hanging there, his name disappearing with her breath.

Bel wiped the tear before it fell over the edge of Carter's nose. Looked into the eyes of her little sister. Carter knew before she had. The thing she needed to talk to Bel about on the stairs. It was important, she'd said. Bel should have listened. *Take care of your sister for me,* her mom said, when she thought she was going to die. *I know you always have.* Bel took Carter's hand, clammy and bony against her own. *My baby.* They'd always been sisters, Carter taking care of Bel just as much, even when she didn't want to see it.

Carter saved Rachel, and she'd saved Bel too.

"How did you find us?" Bel glanced over the lookout, at the tiny ant-town beyond.

"I saw what the note said at Grandpa's house, Rachel's message, before Dad—J-Jeff took it. He told me to stay, clean up the books. But I waited for him to leave, waited longer, then I left too. Your bike was out front, Bel. I got to the yard, couldn't remember where the gap in the fence was, went too far. But I saw you both, running to the car. Then I saw Dad and Charlie, coming after you, chasing you. What Charlie had in his hands. So I followed them, through the trees. I thought he was going to kill you. He was about to kill you. I'm sorry." She dropped her head.

Rachel picked it back up, finger under her chin. "You have nothing to be sorry for. You saved me from him, Carter. It doesn't matter that he was your father, he wasn't your family. That man was not worth saving."

"What about Da—J-Jeff?" she cried, more tears than Bel could catch.

"You didn't push Jeff." Rachel's eyes were both hard and soft. "Charlie pulled him over. You did not kill Jeff."

"But he wouldn't be dead, if I—"

"Jeff made his choice," Bel said. "He set Charlie free. He made his choice."

And that was true, but he'd made another choice too, and maybe that undid the first. *Protect my daughter, Jeff,* Rachel had told him. *You owe me.* It was Bel she meant, but when it came down to it, it was her other daughter he'd saved. Gave his life for it.

Rachel looked over the edge and when she turned back, there was something new in her eyes.

"Carter, listen to me." Voice hard, the mother and the survivor. "The DNA tests, could police access those results, if they went looking? See that you and Bel are sisters?"

"Don't think so. I unchecked the box about sharing information with law enforcement, just in case I was right."

"Good," Rachel exhaled. "No one can ever know the truth."

"What do you mean?" Bel straightened up. "The world should know what they did to you—"

"They are dead." Rachel pointed where they'd disappeared. "That's punishment enough. The world cannot know. You two are involved now and there is nothing I wouldn't do to protect you, keep you safe. My girls. Which means no one can know the truth, about what Pat did, what Charlie did, that Carter's my daughter. That you two were here when Jeff and Charlie—"

"They're only dead because he tried to kill you," Bel said.

"Because I kidnapped him and chained him up."

"He did that to you first! He asked Grandpa to kill you."

"There's no evidence he was involved, Bel. One of them gone, the other has no memory of what he ever did. Don't you think I would have gone to the police, if that was ever an option? But there *is* evidence here. This." She pointed harder. "A crime scene at the bottom of this drop that leads back to us. Carter saved us, but that's not what it looks like."

Rachel's eyes flicked down to Carter, sitting there on the rough ground, head in her hands, and Bel understood. Carter had killed Charlie, pushed him to his death. Justice to some, murder to others. It was Bel's job to protect her little sister, take care of her. Family first. Bel blinked and Rachel blinked back, a language of their own.

"What do we do?" Bel asked.

"We need to get rid of everything. Anything that could lead to the truth, that ties us to being here, right now."

"Like the note?" Carter raised her head. "*Help. My name is Rachel Price.* It was in Dad's pocket. It's in Jeff's pocket." Her pale eyes widened with horror, rubbed red-raw.

Rachel looked down, into all that nothing.

She swallowed, a clicking sound, like her throat was too narrow, crushed by Charlie's weight. "I have to go down there. I'll get the note. Jeff's car keys too. His phone: we can't leave that, they'll be able to trace him. I have to move the bodies."

"What?" Carter gasped.

"Can't leave them out in the open. They'll be found. No one's going to think they jumped, two brothers, together. A medical examiner will know Charlie fell backward, that he was pushed. Carter, didn't you say the gate into the mine was broken open? They're right by the entrance, down there. I'll drag them inside, and dr-drop them down the old mine shaft."

A second fall, to hide the first.

Bel chewed her tongue. "How far does it go down?"

"Far," Rachel answered. "The mine is supposed to be sealed off, it's dangerous, and you can't get down there, not without special equipment. It could be months, years, decades, but we can't guarantee they'll never be found. Which is why none of us three can ever be suspects, you understand? A stranger took me. He kept me in his basement for sixteen years. And none of this ever happened."

Carter nodded. Bel too. She reached into her pocket, pulled out Charlie's wedding ring. It wasn't warm anymore, or cold, stinging at her skin, just an old bit of metal that meant nothing to her.

"You should probably put this back on him." Bel handed the metal band to her mom. "No evidence, right?"

Rachel nodded, sliding it into her own pocket.

"You sure you're OK to go down there?" Bel asked. "Your ankle?"

"I've survived worse," Rachel said, a small smile to show she had, that no one had taken that from her. "I can do this, have to do this, for my family. But . . . I can't do it all on my own. I thought I could do everything on my own, my plan, my reappearance. I was wrong, I know that now, I'm sorry. I need your help."

"Anything," Bel said.

Carter stood up beside her. "What do you need?"

Rachel's eyes glittered, staring at her daughters, the moonlight picking out the same silver in all of their skin.

She cleared her throat. "We have to do everything tonight, before anyone knows Jeff is missing. I'll get down to the mine entrance. You two walk back to the yard. Take my car, Bel. Keys are inside, engine's on."

"But it's trapped, Jeff's car is—"

"Take this." Rachel picked up the axe, the thing that almost killed her, would have, if Carter hadn't appeared from nowhere. She passed it to Bel, their fingers crossing on the handle. "Break the chain on the gates. Once they're open, you can pull forward, turn around. Wipe your prints when you're done, the handle and the blade. Throw it back with the rest of the junk. Don't worry about the red truck. I'll get to that when I'm done here, get rid of everything."

Unmaking her own prison cell, so no one would ever know about the fifteen years, five months and twenty-five days she'd spent locked inside. The man who put her there. The baby she'd given birth to. The other man she'd locked up as revenge for starting it all. All of it would be gone by morning.

"Take Bel's bike with you," Rachel continued. "Then head to your grandpa's house. The key is under the—"

"—ceramic toad," Bel said, just as Carter said "Barry."

Rachel smiled. "My message in all of those books, you need to get rid of them. That's what I was trying to do before you found them, Bel. It's too dangerous to leave, says what happened, exactly where it all happened. You need to get rid of it, erase the pencil marks in all of those books. Always on the first fifty pages, never beyond. Can you do that? There must be an eraser in the house somewhere."

"We'll find one," Carter said.

"Yordan will be asleep upstairs, you have to be quiet. If he catches you—"

"We'll think of an excuse. *My dad told me to tidy these, I'll be in trouble if I don't,*" Carter offered.

Rachel's smile pulled wider. "I think that's it. No other loose ends that could lead police to the truth, to what happened here."

Bel's heart dropped into her stomach, more space, now the knot was gone forever.

"Ash," she hissed. "Fuck." She kicked out at a stone, sending it over the edge.

Rachel narrowed her eyes. "From the film crew? What about him?"

Bel ran her hands through her hair, pulling her face tight. "He's been helping me. I was . . . investigating you. I was sure you were lying about your disappearance and how you came back. Thought if I could prove it, life would go back to normal. Ash helped me. He has footage of . . ."

Rachel limped toward her. "What does he have footage of?"

"A lot." Bel shook her head, thinking back. "Mr. Tripp saying he gave you three thousand dollars before you disappeared. The sighting of you in January, we spoke to the store owner, saw a still from the camera. We have you looking for something in Grandpa's house, before you found the hidden camera. Fuck." She pulled her hair tighter. "We have tonight. The message in the book, in all of the books, me writing it down. Ash was recording."

"Fuck." Rachel covered her face.

"There's more." Bel dropped her arms, swinging useless at her sides. "He came with me, to the red truck. He stopped recording before we got there but . . ."

"Bel?"

"I'm sorry," Bel whispered. "Ash saw Charlie chained up in the truck, before I sent him away. I'm sorry, Mom."

Rachel bit down on her lip. She came even closer, face to face, Bel's eyes reflected in her own. "Don't you say sorry either. None of this is your fault. I'm not angry at you. You were right; I was lying to you from the start, I can't be mad that you were smart enough to see through it. Proud, actually. *I'm* sorry, sorry I lied to you. Maybe I should have just told you the truth, both of you. I just . . . wasn't sure you were ready to hear it."

"I wasn't." Bel hadn't been ready, not until there was no other choice. But she was ready now, and she knew how to fix this. "I can get to the footage, Mom. I know where Ash keeps it. He saw Charlie in the red truck. I don't think he'd tell anyone, but it won't matter, will it? Not if there's no proof. I can destroy the footage tonight, Mom."

Undo everything she'd worked for, all those moments with Ash, big and small, getting closer until it was far too late to pretend she didn't care. She would still care, she knew that now, but she had to destroy every trace of it, to protect her sister and her mom.

"You sure?"

"I can do it," Bel said.

Rachel glanced over at Carter.

"I can do the books at Grandpa's on my own," she said. "I can do that."

Rachel pulled her in and hugged them both, three heads pressed together, under the same stars.

"We can do this." Rachel wiped her eyes.

"Family first," Bel said. Not a threat, but a promise.

Rachel stumbled away from them, to where her phone had dropped, a yellow halo around it from the flashlight, trapped against the rock. She picked it up, stared at the screen. "We need to turn our phones off, so we can't be traced here. Turn yours off, girls. Now. Don't turn them on again until you get out of here."

Bel switched hers off.

Rachel was tapping her screen. "Not working. How do I turn this thing off?"

"Let me do it," Carter said, taking the phone out of Rachel's hand. "You hold this one, see." She showed her. "And then you swipe. Like that."

"Ah."

Bel smiled, watching them together, this small mother-daughter moment in this dark and wild place that broke a family and saved another. And the moon had seen it all.

Bel handed Rachel the flashlight. "You take it. You need it more. We'll stick to the trail. We'll be fine." She glanced at Carter, a small punch to her arm, because that was what sisters did. "I'll take care of her."

Rachel accepted it, the silver beam lighting up both her daughters. "It's going to be OK, girls. I love you. I'll see you later, when we all get home."

Bel picked up the axe, started to turn, but Carter hesitated, a croak in the back of her throat.

"Which home?" she asked.

"Ours, Carter," their mom said. "Our home."

FORTY-EIGHT

*Ash, I need you. I'm at the McDonald's. Don't bring the
camera, leave it behind. Have to tell you something.*

Bel waited in the darkness, became the darkness, pressed up against
the side of Scoggins General Store, where the streetlight couldn't
reach her. Back in the ant-town, just one of those specks she'd seen
from Point Lookout. Rachel would still be up there somewhere, dragging two dead bodies into Mascot Mine. But the night wasn't over,
and surviving wasn't the same as having to live with it. Which Bel
would, because a life had already been stolen from her and her mom
and her sister once before, and she wouldn't let anyone take it again.
Not Charlie, not the police, not the documentary.

Protect the truth, protect Carter.

She watched the entrance of Royalty Inn, waiting. She knew Ash
would come, because he cared.

McDonald's was the only choice; nothing else was open past
two a.m. Didn't matter anyway, Bel wasn't going. All she needed was
five minutes alone in his room.

The hotel door opened outward, glass reflecting the lamps either
side, hiding whoever it was.

Ash walked out.

Bel knew he'd come.

He walked toward the parking lot, moving fast, away from her, a black puffer jacket over cartoon-patterned pants. Probably pajamas, but it was hard to tell with him. Bel would miss that. Her heart kicked up, watching the wind throw his curly, unbrushed hair behind him as he passed under the next streetlight. She hoped he'd forgive her, that he'd understand, even if he never really would.

Bel unpeeled herself from the darkness, crossed the quiet street into the hotel.

The lobby was empty, only Kosa behind the front desk, sorting papers. She looked up, long black braid slipping off her shoulder.

"Good evening," she said.

"Late, isn't it?" Bel replied. "You know how film crews are. Night shoots."

Kosa nodded, because she didn't know how film crews were, and neither did Bel.

Bel's voice was gravelly, raw, from crying, from screaming, from talking to Carter all the way back to the yard, explaining how their mom disappeared twice, two plans intersecting on that day sixteen years ago, and a baby who appeared from nowhere. Why Carter should never feel bad about what she did to Charlie. It had all sounded so unreal, repeated in her own voice.

"There's dirt on your sleeve." Kosa pointed.

Bel picked at it. "We're filming in the woods, this reenactment thing. Speaking of, Ash just left here, the camera assistant?"

"Yeah?"

"He messaged saying he'd left the lens in his room. Asked me to pick it up. Is that OK? I need a key, sorry. Room thirty-nine."

Kosa blinked at her.

"Look, I can show you the text." Bel reached for her pocket. This was the easier way, but if Kosa didn't give her the key, Bel was going to break the door down and do it anyway.

"That's OK," Kosa said, a sigh, like she just wanted to get rid of Bel, get back to her papers. "I know you've been up there before. Here."

She opened a drawer, searched through, tongue tucked in her teeth.

"Thirty-nine." She handed over the spare key.

"Thanks." Bel saluted her, something Ash might have done.

She raced up the stairs, muscles still burning. Ash had probably reached the McDonald's already, but Bel still had time. He'd wait for her, because he cared.

Down the corridor, counting doors, up to number thirty-nine.

She slotted in the key and opened the door, flicking on the light.

Boxers on the pillow, again.

She walked inside, the familiar smell of him, her heart grabbing hold of it. Past a pile of his hideous sweaters, strawberries and dinosaurs, tracing her finger across. More memories here than just the ones stored on SD cards.

But those were what she came for.

Bel moved to the table at the far end, the desk chair and the armchair pushed together in front of it. His and hers. A stack of clear plastic cases on the surface, the memory cards stored inside.

She pulled them all out, opened the cases, the ones marked with a red X and those that weren't. One by one, she tipped the SD cards out onto the table. Rachel's secrets, buried in those tiny metal strips. Bel had connected them, found her way to the truth, but no one else ever could.

She ran her hand over the scattered pile, picked one at random.

Snapped it in half. And again, destroying the metal chip.

And the next one.

Making a new pile out of the broken pieces.

Bend with her thumbs, snap it with force.

Until the last one.

Except that wasn't the last one. Bel's eyes fell to the handheld camera, resting in Ash's chair. Just as much a part of him as his silly hair, or his ridiculous clothes, or the way he said *Oh* too much, or how he could keep up with her like no one else, exchanging unpleasantries. Bel didn't have to destroy it, she couldn't do that, but she needed to remove its memories.

She slid her fingers across the back panel of the camera until it clicked, came free. There it was, slotted in, the red edge of an SD card, same as all the rest.

She pressed it and it pinged out, giving itself up without a fight.

The card Ash used tonight: finding Rachel's message in all of the books, their trek to the red truck on Price & Sons Logging Yard, even though there were no *Sons* left anymore. This card held the biggest piece of the truth, the most dangerous one. She'd wanted him to record it all, for evidence. But now it was evidence against them.

Bel pinched it between her thumbs, then twisted them apart in one quick motion. It snapped into uneven halves, metal entrails stringing across.

Breaking them wasn't enough. She had to know they were truly gone.

Bel scooped up the broken memory cards, lying dead and dismembered in her cupped hands.

She walked them toward the bathroom, hands over the toilet bowl, and let go.

The pieces scattered down, floating on top, sinking below.

She pushed the flush.

The black-and-red shards swirled up, one last dance, then disappeared together, down the drain.

But she wasn't finished. Some of those cards might have been empty. Ash told her himself; he backed up the footage onto an external hard drive, then wiped the cards to reuse. Now Bel had to use that against him.

She found the small black box plugged into the laptop. *This bad boy here,* Ash had called it, tapping it with two fingers.

Bel tapped it with two fingers too, then unplugged it.

Dropped it to the floor.

Waited for it to land, to lie still.

Then she brought her heel down on it.

The plastic casing snapped.

She stamped again.

Right foot, left foot. Both feet together, jumping on it.

Bel didn't stop, not until it was in more pieces than she could count, picking them up, putting them in her pocket.

She straightened up.

Gasped.

There were eyes watching her, but they were only her own, mirrored in the dark screen of Ash's sleeping laptop. Bel moved closer to her reflection.

She didn't know if any of the footage was saved on here, and she didn't know the password to check. But she couldn't risk leaving it.

The laptop was already open, but she opened it more, bending the screen back, pushing against its spine until it snapped clean off. Ripped out the wires that tried to hang on, pulling the base free.

She knew the hard drive was in this part somewhere, under the keyboard, that was why it was coming with her too, tucked under one arm. The only way to know it was all gone was to watch it disappear. Throw it in the river on her way home.

Now she needed to go. Someone must have heard all that. The room below could be complaining to Kosa right now: *Some kind of party going on upstairs.*

But Bel couldn't leave it like this.

She turned over the dead, splintered laptop screen, the half she was leaving behind. Picked up Ash's red pen, pressed the tip to the pre-bitten silver apple.

Sorry, she wrote, in tiny red letters, not quite the color of blood.

Bel was the first one back.

She watched the clock on the wall. Past three now. Her mom and her sister were still out there, doing their parts, and all Bel could do was wait for them to come home. Flinching at the sounds an empty house made; the howl of the wind against the upper windows, the hum of the refrigerator she'd never noticed before, the patter of her own heart.

She counted the dark minutes and she waited.

A scrabbling sound at the front door, a shape hovering in the window. Bel pulled it open before they could.

Carter.

"You OK?" Bel pulled her inside.

"Yeah," Carter said, breathless. "Left your bike by the garage."

Bel took her into the kitchen, filled her a glass of water.

"How did it go?"

"Fine." Carter took a long sip, coughing it down. "Took a while, but I got them all."

She pulled something out from the waistline of her jeans. A book. *The Green Mile* by Stephen King.

"I kept this one." She looked down at it. "It says *we are being kept.* That was me, wasn't it? Me and Rachel."

Bel reached out, unstuck Carter's hair from her face. "Yes. You should keep it. It's a special book."

Carter's smile was weak.

"Did Yordan wake up?"

"No."

"Good. You did a good job." Big sisters were supposed to say things like that.

"Is Rachel—M-Mom . . . ," Carter stuttered, stopped herself.

"That's OK," Bel said. "I've only just started being able to say it. And I've had a lot longer to get used to it than you."

Carter nodded. "Is she back yet?"

"Not yet. But she had a lot more to do than us. She'll come home. She always does."

Carter's fingers danced around the edge of the book, never still, like Rachel.

"What do we do now?" she asked.

"We wait."

"OK."

"Do you need anything?" Bel said. "Hungry? I could make you a sandwich or something."

"Stop being friendly," Carter said. "It's weird."

Bel laughed, and it took her by surprise too, the sound. "Sorry. Just trying to be like a sister."

"You always were."

A crashing sound filled the house, a fist against the front door.

Carter dropped the book.

"Is that her?" she whispered.

It couldn't be. "Rachel has a key," Bel said.

It came again, three loud knocks, knuckles on wood.

"Police?" Terror filled the whites of Carter's eyes.

"Stay here," Bel told her, moving into the unlit living room, to the windows at the front. She pressed her eyes to the glass.

A lone dark figure at the door, fist raised. She recognized the shape of him; shoulder-length curly hair and a puffer jacket, splitting his arms into segments.

She turned; Carter had followed her.

"It's Ash," she hissed. "I'll deal with this. You go up to my room, get into bed."

Carter nodded, but it didn't shake the terror from her eyes, disappearing up the stairs.

Bel took a breath, opened the front door.

"Hi," she said, before he could speak. "Kinda late for a house call, isn't it? Is this an English thing?"

His eyes were wide and swimming, teeth glowing in the dark.

"I would have deleted it all, if you'd asked me." His voice shook. "You only needed to ask."

Bel stepped outside and Ash dropped to the step below. They were the same height now, eyes straightforward, unblinking.

"I don't know what you mean," she said quietly.

"Bel." He held on to her name, kept it on his tongue. "What happened?"

"We had a birthday dinner for my grandpa, then everyone went home."

He tried again. "What happened in that red truck?"

"What red truck?"

The breath hitched in his throat.

"Where Rachel was. Where we found your dad chained up."

Bel shook her head. "Rachel was taken by a stranger. Kept in a basement for sixteen years."

"Bel!" Her name, pushed as loud as a whisper could. "I don't care about the footage. I don't care about the documentary, that I've fucked it all up. I care about you."

She almost said it too, but "Thank you" came out instead. She'd never let someone close enough to care before. Ash had showed her that she could, she didn't always have to pick the way that hurt less. Some hurts were good: friends grew apart, people moved away, they left. It didn't have to last forever to count. Things ended, *this* was ending, but that didn't mean it never mattered.

"Bel." He lowered his voice. "Are you in danger?"

She gave him half an answer.

"Not anymore."

"Where's your dad now?"

"The police say he ran away to Canada."

Ash breathed out, eyes heavy. "What are you doing?"

"Protecting my family."

He nodded. "So this is it?" he asked, a sad lilt, dragging his words down.

Bel nodded too. "This is it."

"OK."

Ash turned away.

He walked down the stairs, his steps a hollow echo in the dead of night, reaching into her chest, skipping around her heart.

He crossed from their path to the street. It was ending, and he was walking away, like he was supposed to.

But Bel knew, suddenly, that that wasn't quite it.

"Wait!" She ran after him.

Ash turned and Bel crashed into him, a grunt of surprise.

Her eyes found his, his lips found hers.

Hand through his scruffy hair, pulling him in deeper, making it count.

His fingers brushed her neck, moving up, but the glow moved down.

It was goodbye, but it was something else too.

Bel pulled away, just an inch.

"It wasn't pointless," she whispered, lips brushing his. "And it did matter."

"I know." His nose pressed against her forehead.

She unwound herself, stepped back. "Could have told me sooner."

Ash laughed, and Bel did too, both of them standing there, under the moon.

"I should go now?" he said, almost a question.

"Yeah," Bel replied, pushing his shoulder with two fingers.

He gave her a salute, hand crooked, matching his smile, and he walked away.

Bel watched him go, all the way down the road, until he was little more than an outline, misshapen darkness.

He left, and that was OK.

Ash was always leaving.

And leaving wasn't the same as leaving behind.

FORTY-NINE

Carter was shivering when Bel climbed into bed.

Eyes staring, like she couldn't remember how to blink, like she'd never been taught.

Bel pulled the blanket up over her shoulders. "It's OK. I'm here."

"What if someone finds out what I did?"

Bel rested her feet against Carter's. "You didn't do anything. And no one will find out. We won't let that happen."

Carter's breathing was too shallow, too fast.

"Close your eyes," Bel said.

"They are."

"No, they're not. Just take a few deep breaths."

"I'm trying."

Carted shifted onto her back, eyelids fluttering, struggling to stay shut.

"Is she back yet?"

"No." Bel glanced toward the window, the gaps around the curtains. The darkness was softening outside, brightening, the first touch of twilight. "But she will be soon."

She had to, before the world woke up and realized Jeff Price was now missing too. That Price family; had a thing for disappearing, they did.

Carter's breaths slowed, rattling through her half-closed mouth.

"It's OK," Bel said. "You can go to sleep. I'll wait. Won't let anything happen to you."

Carter breathed in and out, almost in the shape of a word.

She slept, and Bel waited.

Eyes shut because they were too scratchy, and she didn't want to watch as dawn slowly crept up on them, filling the shadows of her room, creating new ones.

She waited. The hum of the refrigerator just a noise inside her head now, imagined, remembered. Carter sleeping too close to her ear.

Bel was listening, but she didn't hear. Not until her bedroom door nudged open, shushing against the carpet, silent feet behind it.

She opened her eyes, a blurry half blink before they closed again.

Rachel was standing there, in the darkened doorway, watching them.

She didn't leave. She stayed.

Bel could feel her there, a calmness that reached her in this in-between place: asleep-awake, today-tomorrow, sister-daughter.

She could finally sleep, now that Mom was home. Now she was here to watch over them both.

Bel breathed out and let go.

Rachel didn't let them sleep for long.

She came in with coffee at seven-thirty, sat at the end of the bed, crushed both their feet.

"Sorry." She shifted, handing one cup to Bel. Her favorite mug. Waited for Carter to rub the sleep from her eyes, then passed hers over.

Bel yawned.

"You can sleep again later." Rachel patted her leg through the comforter. "How did everything go?"

"All done my end," Bel said. "The footage is gone."

"And mine," Carter added. "All the books."

"Good." Rachel smiled, strained at the edges.

Bel sat up. "Yours?"

Rachel nodded, a faraway look in her eyes, a deep drop behind them, all the way down the mine. "All done," she said, quietly.

It didn't look like she'd slept at all. And there was a dark bruise forming on her throat, the blues and reds of a dying universe.

"Actually, not all done." Rachel sighed. "There's something else we have to do, together. Carter . . ." She looked at her younger daughter. "We have to decide what to do about Sherry."

"Fuck," Bel whispered into her coffee. "I didn't think . . . How will we explain Jeff going missing? What about Carter, Sherry's not just going to let you go."

"She'll probably be here soon, looking for Jeff and Carter, wondering why they never came home," Rachel said. "I have an idea. But, Carter, I want to know what you want to do. This is the woman you thought was your mom your entire life. I want you to know that it's OK if you care about her, of course it is. You should be the one to decide."

Carter took a sip to give herself time, even though it was too hot; Bel could tell by the tightening of her eyes.

"OK," she said, tapping the mug, fingers always moving.

Rachel told them her idea, talked it through, and Carter decided.

"Are you sure?" Rachel checked. "Once we do this, we can never go back."

Carter cleared her throat. "I'm sure."

The doorbell rang at twenty past eight. One long held note.

They knew who it was, and they were ready.

Bel got up to answer the door.

"Aunt Sherry," she said, blinking against the morning sun, her eyes craving the darkness again. "How are you?"

"Not good." Sherry shuffled past her. "Is Carter here? She didn't tell me she was staying over." She made her way into the living room, uninvited. "There you are. Come on, let's get going. Not sure where your father is. Did he stay at Grandpa's?"

Bel shut the front door and followed Sherry.

Rachel and Carter were sitting on the sofa, Sherry standing in front, purse swinging from her elbow.

"Carter." She clicked her fingers, impatient.

"Take a seat, Sherry." Rachel gestured toward the armchair. She was wearing one of Bel's sweaters, a blue roll-neck, to hide the bruise on her throat.

"That's OK, Rachel," Sherry said her name hard, biting down on it. "We have things to do today. Carter has dancing at twelve, then we—"

"Sit down, Sherry."

"No, really, Rachel, that's very kind, but we need to get going. Don't we, Carter?" Giving her no choice at all. But Carter had already chosen.

Bel passed Sherry, sat on the end of the sofa, Carter in the middle. The three of them against one of her. Sherry was outmatched.

"Sit down," Carter said this time, through gritted teeth.

Sherry looked at Rachel instead, narrowing her eyes.

"What's going on?" She sat but not really, perching at the very end. "Is there news, about Charlie?"

"This is about you, Sherry. What you did."

She frowned. "Rachel, I didn't know you were getting a cake too yesterday. I was trying to be helpful."

"Not about cake, Sherry." Rachel leaned forward, steepled her fingers. "This is about you stealing my daughter."

Sherry's eyes snapped open, fighting a gasp. Her gaze flicked to Carter.

"What are you talking about?" she said with a hoarse laugh, pulling her purse onto her lap, using it as a shield. "Bel only stayed with us for seven months, after Charlie was arrested."

"Not that daughter," Rachel said, darkly. "The baby you stole, almost sixteen years ago."

Eyes wider still, too much white above and below. Sherry shook her head. "I don't—"

"Yes, you do. Wearing fake bumps so you could pretend she was yours. She was just two weeks old when Pat took her from me, gave her to you."

Sherry's mouth moved, but no words came out.

"We know everything, Sherry. Jeff told us. But you've known a lot longer. Tell me, did you always know Carter was mine? You must have, how else did she look like a Price? Did you know, all this time, that Pat and Charlie had me locked up? That makes you complicit, you know."

Sherry pulled her purse into her chest. She was trapped; to deny some of it was to accept the rest. "I don't know what you're talking about," she said, choosing another option altogether. "Is this some kind of prank . . . for the documentary?"

"No," Carter said.

"Well, it's not funny, whatever you're doing," Sherry snapped, rising to her feet. "Come on, Carter. Stop messing around. You have dancing." She grabbed Carter's arm, tried to pull her up from the sofa.

Carter snatched her hand back.

"No, *Aunt Sherry*," she said, taking aim.

A shift; from shock to anger. It happened quickly.

"Don't call me that!" Sherry shouted, a globule of spit falling to her chin. "I'm your mom!"

"No, you're not. Rachel is."

"Don't be ridiculous."

"Sherry," Rachel said, a low warning growl. "It's over, stop fighting it. Jeff told us everything last night. Carter is my daughter. You stole her from me."

"No, no, no," Sherry said, her denials weakening. "I gave birth to that girl. She's my daughter, Rachel. Mine!"

Rachel cracked her neck, set her jaw, the same way Bel did before a fight. "You won't mind if we ask the police to do a DNA test, then, will you? But of course, you'll be going to prison for the rest of your life, because Carter is evidence of what you and Jeff did to me. Maybe you didn't know Pat was keeping me, that Carter was my daughter, not until I returned, but that's not what it looks like, Sherry. It looks like you and Jeff were involved in my abduction and captivity, then you kidnapped my child. The whole family in on it." Rachel clicked her tongue. "I'm not sure you're the kind of person who does well in prison."

Sherry spluttered, and the anger became something else. She smacked her hands to her face, sobbed into them. Bel couldn't see any tears.

"Stop that," Rachel said, "there's no time. You have a choice to make, Sherry. The same choice I presented to Charlie, and to Jeff last night."

Sherry wiped at her empty eyes. "Where is Jeff? Where's my husband?"

"He's gone. He admitted everything to us last night and he left. I gave him two options. Either I tell the police everything, get Carter tested, and you, Jeff, Charlie and Pat all go to prison. Or I give you another choice, because you're family." Rachel paused. "You leave and never come back, never contact us again. Start a new life, somewhere else. Charlie took that option a couple of weeks ago. So did Jeff, last night. He's gone."

"Gone where?" Sherry wailed.

"He followed Charlie," Rachel said, "to Canada. Probably there by now. He wants you to go with him, asked me to explain everything, so you could both start a new life together. Neither of you wants to go to prison, do you?"

Sherry swallowed, a shudder as she forced it down, eyes straying over to Carter. "No."

"You sure, Sherry?"

She nodded.

"Good. Jeff will be happy. You can't contact him but he's waiting for you. You have to listen closely, Sherry, things you have to do to make this work. First, you need to pack, just a small bag, can't take everything. Then you'll go to an ATM. Jeff said to use all the cards, max them out. Get as much cash as you can, you'll need it, and you won't be able to access your accounts after this."

Sherry stared down at her hands.

"Are you listening, Sherry?"

"Yes," she croaked.

Rachel pulled two items out of her back pocket. "He asked me to give you these. His phone, and his car keys." Rachel dropped them into Sherry's hands. "His car is parked down the street, outside the cemetery. He left it for you, said it's less conspicuous than yours. Once you've packed and you have the money, he wants you to drive to Barton in Vermont. His friend Bob—Robert Meyer—lives there. You remember Bob?"

Sherry's hands closed around Jeff's phone and keys.

"Bob will help you, OK, Sherry? Tell him you and Jeff are in trouble and you need his help. His phone number and address are in Jeff's phone. You can turn it on when you get closer. I've written them down for you, in case the battery dies." The details still memorized from her time in the red truck. "Bob will get a new passport for you and Jeff. New names, new identities. You'll have the cash to pay him, need to wait with him until they're done. Jeff didn't have time, so you need to do it for him. He was going to stow away on a plane this morning because he wasn't sure what choice you'd make, wanted to leave the country in case I got the police involved. But you'll both need new identities if this is going to work, so now you have to help him."

"OK," Sherry sniffed, like it all made perfect sense.

"When your IDs are ready, you drive to a John Mayne airfield, just outside Newport. The same place Charlie and Jeff went to. The address is on that same piece of paper. When you get there, you need to dump all your bank cards and old IDs. Any trash can, no one will find them." Rachel was a good liar, when she wasn't lying to Bel, when she needed to, to protect her daughters. "You won't need them anymore, and you don't want any trace of your old life following you there. Then you need to get on a small aircraft that's crossing the border. They'll ask to see your passport for the flight plan, for the authorities, but that's fine, because you'll show them your new ID. It'll pass all their checks and no one will know it was really you. OK, Sherry?"

"Yes." A muscle twitched in her chin.

"Once you land, wherever you land, you make your way to New Brunswick. You're looking for a small town in the north, called

Dalhousie. Jeff's waiting for you there, Charlie too. It's a tiny town, you'll be able to find them. It's a nice place. Beautiful, mountains, quiet. You'll be happy there, Sherry. A new life." The life the three of them were supposed to have—Rachel, Bel, Carter—and now she was giving it to Sherry. "But once you're gone, Sherry, you don't get to come back. Whatever happens. If we hear from you at all, I'll have no choice but to go straight to the police. I'm giving you this chance. Don't waste it."

Sherry dropped Jeff's phone, keys and the small slip of paper into her purse.

"Any questions?" Rachel stood and Bel helped her, weight on her good ankle.

Carter rose too, and Sherry's attention drifted up to her.

Her lips twisted, a downward curve. "None of this is my fault, you know. I love you, Carter. Only ever tried to do the best for you."

"That's not a question," Carter said, fiddling, making mountains into valleys in the fabric of her sweatpants.

Sherry's eyes weren't empty anymore. She'd forced one tear to the surface, a slow crawl down her cheek. "Do you really want me to go? I raised you."

"No, you didn't," Carter said, voice small, keeping it almost to herself. "Bel raised me. You *can* choose your family. And I choose them. I'm sorry."

Sherry wiped the tear away, let it trail down her finger.

"It's time to go, Sherry." Rachel nodded her head, just once. Not unkind, even though she had every right.

Sherry didn't say another word; she knew she was beaten, that she'd lost. Bel thought she might have put up more of a fight, like a mom was supposed to: bared teeth and glittering eyes.

Sherry hugged her purse to her chest and turned toward the hallway.

They followed, Rachel leaning on Bel, staggering beside her.

Sherry pulled open the front door, paused on the first step. She turned back, eyes only for Carter. "Bye, then," she said, her lip threatening to go, taking her eyes with it, and her feet.

"Bye," Carter said, the first crack in her voice. Her eyes told the truth; this goodbye was harder than she thought. Maybe she'd cry later, maybe they all would.

They stood in the doorway, their family of three, all that was left now, and they watched Sherry leave. Down the steps, down the street.

Carter broke free, leaning out for that last look, holding on for just a little longer, waiting until she was really gone.

"What about Grandpa?" she asked, to hide it. "I know Charlie started this, but Grandpa played a big part. He made his choices."

Rachel wrapped her arm around her younger daughter's shoulders, other hand reaching for Bel.

"He did make his choices, and I hate him for what he did to us. But . . . it seems almost cruel, to punish an old man who can't remember any of the horrific things he's done." Rachel bit down on her lip, ghost imprints of her teeth when she let go. "He doesn't have long left. We won't visit. But I'll keep paying for Yordan to take care of him, some comfort in the end. Saving him, but not really saving him. He'll die alone and confused. I think that's enough. Do you?"

Bel nodded.

Carter looked at her sister and nodded too.

They had to decide these things, together, as a family. Make their choices, to undo all the ones made for them.

Across the street, the door to number 32 opened, Ms. Nelson standing in her doorway, like they stood in theirs, watching them. A mother and her two daughters, though no one would ever know that, not even her, no matter how much she watched.

Bel raised a hand, waved, and Ms. Nelson waved back.

"Stop being nice," Carter hissed. "We're supposed to act normal."

"I'm sometimes nice."

They turned to her, her mom, her sister, the same look in their eyes. Bel smiled. "You're right, that was physically painful."

Rachel laughed, twirled her finger in the ends of Bel's hair. "You'll live, Bel."

And Mom was right; she would.

FIFTY

"What do you think happened to Charlie, and Jeff, and Sherry?"

Ramsey waited for the answer, sitting in the Royalty Inn conference room, haloed by the bright softbox light behind.

Bel was on the couch, cushions arranged neatly around her.

She wasn't alone this time. Mom was on one side, Carter the other.

Her knees pressed against the coffee table. A full bottle of water they weren't allowed to drink, three glasses this time. And the marble chessboard, still missing its queen. Bel had it in her pocket, was going to put it back when they were finished. She didn't need it anymore.

"I don't know," Mom said, taking this one.

It was their *Exit Interview.* At least, that was what the clapper board said. The last scene of *The Reappearance of Rachel Price,* with what was left of the Prices.

Ash was here somewhere, hiding behind the glare of the lights, wearing that ugly purple sweater again, the one with the dinosaurs. James was behind the big camera, Saba with the microphone tripod, its gray fluffy head hanging over them.

"It's been two weeks since Jeff and Sherry were last seen." Ramsey steepled his fingers. "Almost a month since your husband, Charlie, went missing. Do you have any idea where they are, why they left?"

"I don't know where they are," Mom said, holding his gaze,

blinking just enough to make it believable. "The police are convinced Charlie left the country, ran away to Canada. That Jeff and Sherry did too, they found evidence to support that, like it was planned somehow, the three of them. As to *why* . . . I can only guess."

"And what is your guess, Rachel?" Ramsey pushed.

She took a breath, like she needed time to think. "My reappearance put a lot of strain on the family. A lot of stress, a lot of adjusting, and it also came with a lot of scrutiny, a lot of questions, and a lot of attention from the media." She paused, holding it for effect, like Bel had told her to. "I think me coming back stirred something up. I don't know if they were involved in something illegal, but I think my return was the catalyst, part of their decision to leave, why they felt they needed to. Bel, you heard your dad and your uncle Jeff arguing a lot, even before I returned, didn't you?"

"Yeah," Bel said, picking up the thread. "A lot of fights. Always about money. That's why Dad actually agreed to this documentary in the first place; he was desperate for the money. I don't know if that had anything to do with it."

Her mom nodded, taking the floor again. "We don't have the answers. I've tried, wondering what secret they shared, what made them want to leave. Maybe they thought I knew something, from back before I disappeared, maybe that would explain it, but . . . I don't. I guess we just have to hope they'll all come home someday and we can work through it."

"What about you, Carter?" Ramsey turned to her. "Have you heard from your parents at all, since they took off?"

Carter sat up straighter. "Not since the night of Grandpa's eighty-fifth birthday."

"And how does it make you feel, that they've gone? That they left you behind?"

"It's sad," Carter sniffed. "Whatever the reason is, must be pretty bad for them to leave their fifteen-year-old daughter behind, no contact. I miss them, and I hope they're OK. But they chose to leave, and I like to think they left me behind to protect me somehow. I'm still dealing with all this. Only been two weeks."

"You've been staying with your aunt and your cousin?"

"Yes," Mom said, answering this one. "Carter is family too, and she will always be welcome to stay with us, for as long as she needs. We're happy to have her, aren't we, Bel?"

"Ask me in front of the camera, why don't you, so I have to be nice." Bel smirked.

Carter punched her in the arm.

Ramsey smiled, watching the two of them, giving the moment space.

"So it's another mystery, what happened to Charlie, and Jeff and Sherry?" he followed up.

Mom nodded. "Another mystery."

"Circling back." Ramsey leaned forward, which meant a difficult question was coming. "We still don't have answers to the main mystery of your disappearance, the man who took you, Rachel. You identified Phillip Alves after the incident at your home a couple weeks ago, when he broke in. But police have since discovered that Phillip Alves was in Mexico the day you were released, when you reappeared, so it can't be him. Any comments on that?"

"Yes," Mom said, like she'd expected it, because she had. They'd prepared answers for any question Ramsey might ask. "In that moment, I was sure it was him. It was dark, and I only ever saw my captor in the dark, he never got close. Maybe it was just the fear, when I saw him attacking Bel, and instinct took over. I was wrong. It wasn't Phillip Alves. The man is still out there, somewhere, and now I'm not sure I'd even recognize him, if I do see him."

Ramsey nodded, fingers cupping his chin. "Are you concerned, at all, that you'll never have the answer? That the police will never find him?"

They hadn't prepared for this one. Bel slid her hand along the couch, nudging her little finger against her mom's leg, letting her know she was right here. It didn't matter if the camera saw.

Mom looked at her, half a second, and that was enough. "If you'd asked me a few weeks ago, I might have said yes. I thought I needed that answer, that I couldn't live without it. But now, I think I'm OK with the not-knowing. I've been a mystery myself for a very long time, the past sixteen years, so I think I'm OK, living in mystery." Her voice cracked and it was real, Bel could tell the difference. "But I won't live in fear anymore. I did that for a long time, and I fought my way home, back to my family. It's time to move on, answers or not. And I have these two here, to help me find my way."

Ramsey sat back, a smile that was all eyes and no teeth, holding the three of them in his gaze.

"And that's a wrap!" he said, bringing his hands together, clapping, holding it out to them.

James joined in, behind the camera. Saba too.

And Ash, emerging in front of one of the lights, glowing, winking when he caught Bel's eye.

Bel clapped too, sent it his way. Then Carter. Then her mom.

The room came alive with the sound of their scattered applause, and no one wanted to be the first to stop.

They clapped, not just because it was ending, but because it mattered.

Because it had changed them, all of them.

"You're leaving today?" Mom asked Ramsey, out in the parking lot.

James and Saba were loading their equipment into the van behind. Ash was struggling to carry one of those large metal trunks, knocking into the hotel door with a crash.

"Yeah," Ramsey said. "Our flight is this evening."

Bel and Carter hung back, leaning against their mom's car.

"Well." Mom held out her hand. "Goodbye. Thank you, for everything, Ramsey."

Ramsey took her hand, but he didn't shake it, held it between both of his.

"No. Thank you, Rachel. We'll be in touch. About the film."

Ash dropped something else.

"Do you need a hand?" Carter asked him. "Yours clearly don't work very well."

422

Ash smirked. "Starting to sound like your cousin."

Ramsey's eyes flicked over to Bel. "I know you don't think you're slinking off without saying goodbye to me, Bel Price."

"Caught me, *mate*." She sidled over, replacing her mom, who went to help Carter. "So . . . the documentary is done."

"It is. Not going to be the plotty, twisty story I thought I had a few weeks ago," he said pointedly.

Bel dropped her eyes.

Ramsey knew. Of course he knew. He didn't know everything, the whole truth, but he knew as much as Ash. He'd seen their footage, before she destroyed it. He knew Rachel was lying, that a stranger hadn't kept her in a basement for sixteen years, that the answer was closer to home and the Price family had secrets, he just didn't know what.

The film that could have been.

Ramsey was watching her. "No," he continued, "it won't be the plotty, twisty story I thought I wanted. It will be something better, something with a *human element*. A quieter story, about a mother and daughter finding each other again, overcoming their differences and doubts. A journey that changes both of them. Not as shocking as the film I once had, no, it probably won't make as much money—it definitely won't—but it's a story worth telling."

Bel nodded, unsure what to say.

"Got something for you." He lowered his voice, pulling something out of his pocket, a memory stick. "I've been a filmmaker a long time," he said, almost a whisper. "I always make sure the footage is backed up to the cloud."

Bel's heart staled in her chest, dropping to her gut.

Lips open around a phantom word.

Oh no, oh fuck, the footage.

But Ramsey's eyes were kind. Not a threat, but a gift. He held the memory stick out toward her. "It's gone now. I deleted it all, permanently, everything you and Ash shot together. This is the last remaining copy. Thought you might want it."

He handed it over.

Bel took it, her fingers brushing his. Ramsey had the footage; he could have had that film he wanted, the one that exposed Rachel, the one that pitted her and Bel against each other, plotty, twisty, shocking. But he'd chosen not to. He'd made his choice.

"Thank you," she said, pushing the memory stick into her pocket.

Ramsey smiled. "It's your story, not mine."

He held out his hand. "Well, I guess this is goodbye, then."

"Don't think so, *mate*." Bel batted his hand away. She leaned up with both arms and hugged him.

Ramsey returned the hug, holding tight but not as tight as her. "If you ever need anything, sweetheart, just call me, yeah?" he said. "I know I'm halfway around the world, but I'm always here, OK?"

"OK," Bel said, muffled against his jacket.

Ramsey pressed a kiss to the top of her head, buried in her hair.

"Right, go on." He pulled away, eyes glistening. "Get out of here, before I start bawling." He wiped his eyes and waved his hand. "Go on, I'm serious, get out of here, mate. Can't be crying out on the street."

Bel laughed, stepping away from him, but she couldn't get out of here, not quite yet.

"Ash!"

He was standing right there, not helping, like he'd been waiting for his turn.

"What?" He walked over, flares swishing against the concrete. "I'm very busy."

"Too busy for this?" Bel dropped her backpack to the crook of her elbow, reached inside for the yellow fabric. She handed it over. "I went back to get this for you."

Ash unfolded the cropped T-shirt and his face lit up. *"Pugs Not Drugs,"* he said, turning it around to show her the sad, chubby pug. "I love this little guy. Gonna wear it all the time."

"Of course you will," she said. "You know, you're ridiculous, and strange, and pretty annoying, actually." She took a breath, unlocked her jaw. "But I'm glad I met you."

Ash pointed the pug at her. "Flattery will get you nowhere, Bel."

"That was the last one."

"Yeah." Ash balled up the T-shirt, holding it to his chest, in front of his heart. "I'll miss you," he said quietly.

"Really?" She sneered. "But I'm unpleasant?"

Ash laughed, pressed the T-shirt to his mouth. "Thoroughly unpleasant."

Bel stepped forward. She prodded him in the shoulder with two fingers. "I guess I'll see you," she said.

"I mean, we probably won't. I live in a different country, but . . ." He stopped himself, eyes shining as they found hers, glazing over. They would both cry about it, tears that felt happy but tasted sad, just not here, not now. He reached out, pushed two fingers against her shoulder. "I guess I'll see you too."

"Bel!" Carter called. "You ready to go?"

"I'm ready," she said, keeping it to herself.

Mom blipped the car, opening the driver's-side door.

Carter hesitated. "Where do you want to sit?" she asked Bel.

Bel paused, eyes floating from the front passenger door to the back.

"I'll take the backseat."

She climbed in, sitting here because she could. The backseat wasn't the thing that hurt her, it was the men who had chosen to. Her mom never abandoned her, so it couldn't hold that over her anymore. And really, it was just a seat, same as the front.

Mom started the engine, pulling out onto Main Street. Bel turned to watch the film crew standing there, waving, shrinking behind them, until they were just specks and stick people, then nothing.

Ramsey said it was her story, but it was his too. And that made her think of something, a memory that turned over, became something new.

"Ramsey filmed a documentary last year, it didn't get picked up, they said it lacked a *human element*. He shot it in Millinocket, Maine. But that's the same place you . . ."

Mom blinked; Bel watched her in the rearview mirror.

"It was you!" she said. "You were Lucas Ayer on Twitter. Left a comment telling Ramsey to look into the Rachel Price case. You're the reason this documentary happened."

Mom shrugged. "I saw the film crew around town, got scared that someone might spot me, recognize me in the background. So I laid low. But it got me thinking, that a documentary could be useful. I wanted to see Charlie have to lie on camera, pretend he had no idea what happened to me. But also, you know, money. That if I came back, they'd offer me more for my side of the story, that it would keep us going for a few years. So I tweeted him. Didn't think it would work. I guess I was too good of a mystery to miss."

"You told me you don't understand Twitter," Carter said, feet up on the dashboard, legs too long.

"No, that's still true. TikTok is the most confusing, though. Why is everyone so loud?"

Carter laughed. "You just need to turn your volume down. I showed you already, the buttons at the side."

"Too many buttons," Mom muttered.

"There's literally just three."

A squad car was parked ahead, Police Chief Dave Winter outside, writing up a ticket for someone. Dave spotted them as the traffic slowed. He waved, badge glinting. Mom nodded and Bel pressed her lips into a smile. She'd let Dave out of his promise. He had been right, he owed Bel nothing, and Charlie even less. As long as he stayed far away from the truth.

Carter stiffened as they drove past.

Mom noticed. "Anyway," she said, "I thought that interview went really well."

Carter shrugged. "I don't know. I think I took too long with my answers, that my face gave it away whenever Ramsey said Jeff or Charlie's names. What if they can tell I'm lying? What if people watch it and figure out that I killed them both?"

"Carter." Mom stopped at a red light, turned to her. "I don't want to hear you say that, even think that. You didn't kill anybody, trust me."

Carter pulled her legs back, tucked her hands between her knees. "I did, though."

"Listen to me, you did not kill anyone. Charlie pulled Jeff over the edge. He killed him."

"But I pushed Charlie. I killed Charlie."

Mom breathed in, held on to it for a long moment, the turn signal ticking, counting it down before she let it go. "No, Carter. You didn't kill Charlie. I did."

"What?" Bel said, mind reeling, doubling back, going for her heart. "What are you saying?"

Mom's eyes were on the road, not on them. "Jeff was dead. I thought Charlie was too, but he survived the fall, woke up when I was dragging him through the mine. He was in a bad way, couldn't move, couldn't really speak, but his eyes were open. He begged me not to do it." She coughed, sliding her hands down the steering wheel. "He didn't survive the second fall."

"What?" Carter's hands went to her mouth.

"You said you wouldn't lie to us anymore." Bel stared through the back of her mom's head. If she was telling the truth, why was she only saying this now, two weeks later?

"I'm not lying," Mom said, keeping her eyes to herself. "That's what happened. Carter didn't kill anybody. Charlie killed Jeff, and I killed Charlie."

There was a shift in Carter as she said it, almost instant; Bel watched it happen from the backseat. A lightening in her shoulders, a brightening in her eyes, a new ease in the way she held her mouth, the way the air passed through, not quite so heavy anymore.

And Bel understood.

Maybe Mom was lying to them, one final lie, but if she was, then that was why she did it. To keep Carter safe, not from the police, but from her guilt. And if that was what she was doing, then it was a lie Bel could live with, could forgive. A truth she didn't have to know, one last mystery of the great, disappearing Rachel Price. The kind of thing a good mom would do.

Mom pulled into the parking lot, backing into a spot. "So don't say that again, Carter, because it's not true. You didn't do anything wrong." She turned off the engine and reached across, losing her fingers in Carter's copper hair. "OK?" she said, tugging at a strand.

"OK." Carter pressed the word into a smile, wrestling her hair back. Maybe she'd even be able to sleep in her own room tonight. Not that Bel minded, except her little sister did kick in her sleep. Legs way too fucking long.

The spare room was now Carter's, and Mom had moved back into her old bedroom, new bed, new mattress, throwing out anything Charlie had touched.

"Right, come on." Mom unclipped her seat belt. "We have paint to buy."

"Not more paint," Bel growled, climbing out. "*Do you like eggshell, or oatmeal, or dove?* It's all white, Mom, just pick one."

"Have you seen the swatches she's put up on my wall?" Carter emerged from the car. "Says I can choose, but at least three of them are the color of vomit."

"Girls, stop bullying me or you're both grounded." She grinned.

"If you ground one of us for anything," Bel said, "it should be the number of times Carter says *fuck*."

"Fuck off." Carter tried to trip her, standing on her heels.

They laughed. Carter's laugh sounded like Bel's, and Bel's sounded like Mom's, fitting together, like they belonged.

"Carter!" a voice yelled across the parking lot.

They all turned to see where it had come from, Bel stiffening, her bones locking. But it was just Carter's friends from school, standing outside Rosa's Pizza, next to the hardware store.

Carter waved.

"Can I go?" she asked Mom, but her eyes flicked to Bel, waited there instead.

Bel dipped her head, tilted her chin. "Of course you can," she said, saying more than that with her eyes. "Go on."

"Thanks," Carter hissed. "I'll see you in there, Mo—Aunt Rachel," she corrected herself, people passing on the way to their cars.

Carter ran away from them, disappearing as her friends re-formed around her.

She left. And that was OK, because Bel knew she would come back. Carter would always come back, whether she was just going over there to say hello to her friends, or if she went all the way to New York for dancing school. The people who loved you, the ones who really cared, they would always come back.

Sometimes, they even came back from the dead.

"Guess it's just you and me, kid." Mom hooked her arm through Bel's, heading toward the entrance. "You OK? What are you thinking?"

"Nothing, sorry," Bel said. Actually, it was something. "I was thinking I would message this girl. Sam. The one who gave me the bracelet with the skulls. She used to be my friend."

The last friend Bel ever had, before she pushed everyone away. But she was ready to be somebody's friend again, now she knew how it worked. That it didn't matter if they drifted, or someone got hurt, or it didn't last forever. It still mattered.

"Yeah." Mom looked at her with a knowing smile. "You should. Maybe invite her over sometime?"

Bel nodded. She just might do that.

Mom picked out a shopping cart, wheeled it toward the doors. "We should get some bookshelves too. For the living room."

"I'd like that."

"Anything else you want?" Mom said, glancing down at the list in her hand.

There wasn't.

Bel just wanted to be here, with her mom, looking at a thousand shades of white and pretending to see a difference, because it wasn't about the paint at all. It was about them, a daughter and a mom, learning all the ways they could find each other again, fit back together, trying, until it was like it never happened, like no time had been taken from them at all.

They'd get there. They were already well on their way.

The automatic doors sprang open for them, and Bel helped her mom push the cart through, righting one of the wheels.

They crossed the threshold, walked inside.

The doors slid shut behind them, taking them away with a midnight shush.

They disappeared.

But this time, they did it together.

Acknowledgments

As ever, my first thank-you must go to my agent, Sam Copeland, for being my constant champion. I've made no secret that this was the hardest book I've ever written, in the hardest year for me both professionally and personally. Staring at the three full notebooks and a thirty-thousand-word document of plotting and planning, I almost lost my way at the start of this one. Sam's confidence in me never wavered, even when mine did. He knew I could do it, and I needed the reminder this time. Thank you.

To my film/TV agent, Emily Hayward-Whitlock, for being my stalwart supporter as we navigated my first book being adapted into a TV show, alongside writing *Rachel Price.* Thank you for celebrating the highs with me and holding my hand through the lows. And thank you so much for your thoughtfulness and excitement in looking after Rachel Price. I wouldn't trust anyone else with her.

Thank you so much to my editor, Kelsey Horton, for your unwavering faith in me. I think this time all you had to go on was the title *The Reappearance of Rachel Price,* and not much else. Thank you for trusting me to disappear for a few months and reappear, having turned that title into a full, living, breathing book (admittedly a little long this time—thank you also for your patience as I trimmed it down to a reasonable size). I am so grateful for all your hard work, and I understand that publishing one of my books isn't an easy ride, but there's no one else I'd want alongside me in the passenger seat.

To the absolute dream team at Delacorte Press, who work literal magic by turning a (very long) Word document into the real-life book that you're holding in your hands. Enormous thanks to Beverly Horowitz for so enthusiastically overseeing everything and for being so supportive back when I was a baby-author. Thank you, as always, to Casey Moses, for being such a genius designer, and for giving *Rachel Price* the cover she was always meant to have. And thank you to amazing photographer Christine Blackburne for capturing it all so perfectly. I'm so happy that readers get to judge my books by your covers. Thank you to Colleen Fellingham for all of your eagle-eyed hard work, and for having to go over this book almost as many times as I do, and thank you to Tim Terhune for everything you do turning everyone's hard work into an actual book. Thank you to Shannon Pender, Stephania Villar, Katie Halata, and Lili Feinberg, for your endless enthusiasm and cheerleading, and to everyone in Sales, who all do one of the most important jobs: making sure this book finds its way into readers' hands.

Thank you to Sarah Levison and the whole team at my UK publisher, Farshore.

Thank you to my family—Collis and Jackson—for always being my very first readers, and especially this time, when I was a husk of a person after writing this book. Those first reactions brought me back to life and made me realize all the pain and hard work had been worth it after all, that I'd created something that mattered.

Thank you to Joe Evans, for being brave enough to join the family, and for letting me steal your name and fictionally make you puke red Gatorade.

Thank you to the Horton family for giving me the setting for this book, and to Lily especially for getting such an early start on the local marketing. Somehow, this book and Gorham, New Hampshire, feel like home, even though I've never been there (apart from on Google Maps street view—A LOT!).

And thank you, yes *you*, reader. Thank you for trusting me to take you on this journey. I hope Bel means as much to you as she does to me. To those who have been with me since book one, I don't have words for the gratitude I feel. I will keep working harder every book to deserve you. So look away, because you know I can't end a book without a tearjerker:

Now for the two greatest thank-yous.

To my little sister, Olivia, who this book is dedicated to. Thank you. You knew I was struggling without having to be told: a language of our own, just like Bel and Carter. Thank you for taking so much of it off my shoulders when I wasn't strong enough. This is the best book I've ever written, and it wouldn't have been possible without you, so it's all yours. *Take care of your sister,* Rachel says. And we do.

Last, but never least, to Ben. We weren't married when I wrote this book, but we are as I write these acknowledgments. Thank you for always giving so much of yourself so that I get to live my dream, and for everything you take on to make sure I survive living it. It's my name on the cover, but you're with me for every word.

About the Author

Holly Jackson is the author of the #1 *New York Times* bestselling series A Good Girl's Guide to Murder, an international sensation with millions of copies sold worldwide, as well as the #1 *New York Times* bestseller and instant classic *Five Survive*. She enjoys playing video games and watching true-crime documentaries so she can pretend to be a detective. She lives in London.

♪ HoJax92   ⬚ HoJay92